BLACK CITY SAINT

BLACK CITY SAINT

RICHARD A. KNAAK

an imprint of Prometheus Books
Amherst, NY

Cover design and illustration by Jacqueline Nasso Cooke
Cover image © Crocodile Images / Media Bakery

Inquiries should be addressed to
Pyr
59 John Glenn Drive
Amherst, New York 14228
VOICE: 716-691-0133
FAX: 716-691-0137
WWW.PYRSF.COM

20 19 18 17 16   5 4 3 2 1

Library of Congress Cataloging-in-Publication Data

Names: Knaak, Richard A, author.
Title: Black City saint / by Richard A. Knaak.
Description: Amherst, NY : Pyr, an imprint of Prometheus Books, 2016.
Identifiers: LCCN 2015037541| ISBN 9781633881365 (paperback) |
    ISBN 9781633881372 (e-book)
Subjects: | BISAC: FICTION / Fantasy / Urban Life. | FICTION / Fantasy / Historical. |
    GSAFD: Fantasy fiction.
Classification: LCC PS3561.N25 B58 2016 | DDC 813/.54—dc23 LC record available
    at http://lccn.loc.gov/2015037541

Printed in the United States of America

For my mother, who long championed this particular project

CHAPTER 1

The old, black Model T touring car rumbling past the lone street lamp across from her house had seen better days, but it served the needs of the two young, gaily dressed couples heading toward the sounds of jazz in the distance. My client grumbled under her breath in German as a girl with dark, bobbed hair, obviously seeking her best to look like the actress Colleen Moore, leaned well out the back and waved our—or rather *my*—direction. With a glare at me, her beau snatched her back inside, and the jalopy continued on into the darkness.

"Noisy heap," muttered a voice that fortunately the woman before me didn't hear over the fading rattle of the Model T's engine.

Instead, her mood already sour, my client peered down at the beast beside me, her dubious expression one that greeted Fetch often. "What is that?"

"Part greyhound, part wolf," I answered. Not true, but with Fetch the best possible description for an impossible creature. Tongue lolling, Fetch sat. He wagged his tail, but none of his attempts set the woman at ease.

It was not exactly his fault, either. We—*I*—would not be here if her life had been as that of most people in Chicago. Difficult enough to deal with the trials and tribulations of dwelling in a city where the bootleggers of the North and South Sides were actively at war over territory, but to have one's sanity questioned by neighbors . . .

Full of build, her sixty years marked by deep lines all over her face, it was easy to read in her eyes her frustration, not at the flapper and her friends, but rather at this latest intrusion into her home, which I represented. By this time, she had had at least two, likely three visitations by those claiming to be able to rid her of her "problem." Psychics. Fortune tellers. Mediums. Charlatans who were all the rage these days. I understood full well that most, if not all, had left cheerfully, believing that they had made a good dollar off her paranoia.

But I knew better. Her distress could not have been a symptom of her imagination if she had finally seen the advertisement. No one saw the advertisement if they had not been touched by something from the shadow folk.

The woman frowned. It was clear that I did not look like her idea of the sort to solve her particular problem. My appearance was that of a clean-shaven man perhaps forty, no more and maybe something less, with short flaxen hair and a face with hints of a Mediterranean background that had initially likely raised a bit of concern I might have blood ties to Big Al's mob. If she paid close attention to my eyes, she might see them as sea blue . . . or perhaps frost green. I chose not to let her stare at them for too long.

I was clad in a presentable suit and wore a long brown coat that well-matched the sudden turn in the late September weather. I had purposely left the coat open so that she would see I carried no weapon—or, rather, that I carried no *visible* weapon.

Evidently finding nothing in me that made her too uneasy, she said, "All right, Mr. Medea. You can come in, but *that* stays outside. My little ones won't tolerate him."

Fetch wagged his tail harder. He loved cats. They were his favorite meals when I did not keep him under a tight rein.

"He won't come in with me, Mrs. Hauptmann."

She squinted past us to the street. She was looking for a vehicle, especially one not suitable to be in front of *her* home, despite the fact that the neighborhood itself was clearly not what it had once been. Now the area, including Hudson Street, was becoming popular with a more flamboyant and raucous crowd, of which flappers were only the latest and in many ways *least* shocking members. However, there were still those like my client who held on tightly to their ways and their memories.

"As promised, discretion," I said. It was one thing for wild young-sters to go barreling past, another for a stranger's car to be in front of a widow's house, even if only for business.

She pointed at the small black case in my right hand. "That all?"

"That's all."

"The last bunch, they toted in enough machinery to double my electric bill. Made quite a scene, too. I almost didn't call you because of them."

"They didn't know what they were doing."

Mrs. Hauptmann cocked her head to the side, the first sign that I had gained some approval. "True enough." She stepped aside. "Please come in."

Her tone gave some hint that I should hurry. I indicated to Fetch that he should lie down. Tongue still lolling, he obeyed like any well-trained dog, which he wasn't.

The house looked to be well over sixty years old but renovated maybe twenty years ago, just after the turn of the century. There were a few hints of where the old gas lamps had hung, but whoever had installed the electric lines had done a good job overall. In addition, the crisp, clean interior—despite the three cats already coming to investi-gate the newcomer—spoke of the old German work ethic that the first settlers in this area had brought with them and that Mrs. Hauptmann vigorously maintained.

"Not allergic are you?" she asked, as two of the cats rubbed against my leg.

"No. I've had cats before myself."

I went up in her estimation again. "They like you. They didn't like the last men."

There was a sitting room downstairs that looked as if it had not changed since the house was built. The furniture was old but well-crafted and well-kept. The only recent addition was a wide, illumi-nated radio quietly set to WGN. The news announcer was reading about a bust at a speakeasy on the South Side. Someone had obviously not paid off enough local officials or else that wouldn't have happened. Liquor flowed well in Chicago despite Prohibition, maybe even more so because of it.

"My Opa—my grandfather—came to this area with his family back in the Migration," Mrs. Hauptmann informed me, as if everyone should know about the German Catholics who settled in the region in the decade or so before the Civil War. As it happened, I *did* know. "My father—he was Opa's youngest—he moved us out about forty-five years ago to a place more north, but I always wanted to come back."

"Was this your family's home?"

"No, that's gone. But this one's close enough. When things got better here for a while, I wanted to come back to the neighborhood. My husband and I bought it, then he died shortly after."

"I'm sorry."

She gave a slight nod. "Basement's through that door there on the right. Kitchen's in back. Three bedrooms on the second floor." She paused. "Attic entrance is in the hall between them."

Of course, the attic was the focal point. Shadows and deep corners. Places to hide from the sun, from the mortal world. The basement might have been another choice, but I'd expected the attic in this case.

"I saw one window up front. Are there others?"

"One in the back. They've been sealed tight for years. Since before my husband passed—and don't go telling me it's him haunting this place. Some verrückt woman carrying around a glass ball kept insisting it was him, but what she described wasn't my Klaus!"

I simply nodded agreement. "Will you be leaving?"

"Certainly not." She crossed her arms tight to emphasize the fact that she would not let any stranger wander about her home without her being nearby.

I had assumed her answer already. "I must ask you to remain

in one room on the first floor, then. Either the sitting room, or the kitchen, perhaps."

"I'll be in the sitting room, reading." Mrs. Hauptmann gave me one last survey. "And I'll be listening."

She guided me upstairs, which consisted of three bedrooms and a bath. The ceiling door to the attic came into sight even before we reached the second floor. A metal cord hung from the door.

Before pulling the ladder down, I looked around my feet. The cats had stayed on the first floor.

"They won't come up here at all lately," Mrs. Hauptmann murmured, for the first time her stolid appearance crumbling. "I've come to sleeping in the sitting room more and more."

"Tell me again what you've noticed." I already knew what I now felt, and that gave me a much better understanding. Still, there might be another detail the woman had missed in our earlier conversation.

"It's just a sensation . . . a feeling that something is creeping around, waiting, getting stronger." Her gaze drifted off to the left and her tone grew softer. "This house was just out of the path of the Great Fire and so survived, Mr. Medea, but a lot of other things—and people—didn't. Maybe it's some of those lost souls. . . ."

I did not dispute her romantic notion of ghosts. It was not entirely wrong, but hardly right. Besides, what she sensed was no simple spirit. It had all the signs of something from the realm of the shadow folk . . . and that in itself was not a good sign.

That the woman could feel its presence marked her and explained why whatever it was had chosen her residence. The shadow folk were drawn to the things in this world that still had a touch of their old one. It was also the reason why she had not yet been taken by it. Through Mrs. Hauptmann, it was actually drawing strength from the other side.

Of course, before long, it would be strong enough to desire a more powerful conduit . . . and then it would deal with her.

"You lost two cats?"

Again, her facade cracked. "I even went up there and looked for them, but there was nothing." She steeled herself. "I know those men and that woman before them thought I was some dithering old woman with too much of an imagination, but they took my money regardless! Psychics, my—" Mrs. Hauptmann caught herself, instead finishing with, "I expect better from you, Mr. Medea."

I did not need a watch to know that it was near midnight. That had no significance for this situation save that night in general was best for what I hunted, but, like many people, Mrs. Hauptmann believed well in the witching hour, and that was to my benefit. "Then, I'd best go up there."

"It'll be done with tonight?" Her voice quivered suddenly.

"Either there is nothing up there or there will not be when I'm through." A simplistic reply, but it satisfied her.

"I'll be waiting."

I hesitated until she had descended, then pulled down the door and the ladder. A deep darkness greeted me from above. I looked around, found the switch for the attic that someone had installed in the hallway during some more recent renovation, then flicked it. To my surprise, the room above lit up.

Case in hand, I climbed up. A musty scent greeted me, as did another, more subtle odor. The cats would have noted it and been repelled. It was the distinctive smell of death caused by the shadow folk, a mix of decay, fear, and old magic.

Eye would see . . .

The voice came as a hiss in my head, a low, insistent echo. *Not yet.*

A sense of resentment flowed next, but I had dealt with it so long that it barely touched my thoughts. I turned my attention back to more immediate matters. The dweller was near, even though nothing yet was visible.

I glanced behind me at the window at the front of the house, then the one at the back. I could see only the top half of the second window, dusty boxes stacked up against the wall obscuring the lower part. The single bulb high above created small shadows here and there, but nothing that gave a hint as to my quarry.

I put down the case, then pulled the ladder up. The attached door slammed shut.

The light flickered out.

My hand was already within my coat. My heart pounded faster and a sweat spread across my forehead. I could see nothing, but I sensed something . . . everywhere. It closed in around me, seeking to emotionally crush my mind and rip apart my soul.

Now at last I understood what was hiding in the attic, feeding slowly, building up its strength. But to fight it, I had to see it.

Eye can show us . . .

He was aware that I would have turned to him for this, anyway, but it was a reminder to me that while I held sway over him, I could not do without him. Having a far more imminent situation with which to deal, I simply replied *Show us . . .*

The world erupted into a glittering scene of emerald green.

In what had been a tiny shadow to the right of the backyard window, a thing the size of a man but more like an arachnid, with too many limbs that ended in almost human hands, perched several feet above the floor. It glared at me with three orbs pale as bone and clacked a sharp beak together in both astonishment and rage that it could be seen despite its cover of darkness.

And perhaps what set the creature off a bit more was that it in turn could see the transformation of my own eyes from those of a recognized prey to something more narrow, more reptilian, more ancient.

More the predator than even it.

The sensation of fear and despair struck me harder, but faded immediately. I knew the emotions for what they were—false emanations.

My hand slipped free of my coat, bearing in it a small blade.

Blessed in Constantinople well over a thousand years ago, the silver-tipped dagger had never failed me.

The shadow creature paid scant attention to the dagger, more inclined toward the case. From its mouth, strands of blackness shot forth and seized the black bag. Having no doubt observed my predecessors—and laughing at their inability to notice it in the least—the dweller assumed that anything of true value against it would be contained within.

That was as I had intended.

I dove in toward the shadow as the tendrils pulled in the case. The dagger cut into the darkness, severing it as if it were truly of the mortal world.

The arachnid hissed. Words in a tongue older than man spilled through my thoughts, a curse cast upon me. It had as much effect as the fear but for a different reason. I was already cursed in a far more terrible way.

I swung for the pale orbs, the least protected part of this shadow folk. It was not one of the *Wyld*, but it was still a powerful enough being, especially after having built up its energies for so long. I suspected that the cats Mrs. Hauptmann could not find had only been a part of its diet and that there was a lack of birds, mice, and other small creatures in the vicinity of the house. The dweller did not have to leave its lair to draw to it those most susceptible to its magic.

The "hands" reached for me as I neared. The dweller intended to take advantage of my drawing toward it to engulf me. It sensed that the purity of the dagger, while anathema to it, would require me to bury the weapon deep more than once if I was to kill it before it tore me apart. I knew that it also could sense no other such dangerous weapons on my person. The case had been forgotten, too, the contents radiating no blessing or magic that might harm it.

I retreated from the grasping appendages. The tendrils of darkness shot forth, but again the dagger severed them before they could touch me. The shadow dweller scuttled forward, both of us aware that not only was the ladder door too cumbersome a thing to lower before the creature could reach me, but that the one window I could reach was too narrow for me to fit through.

Neither of us awaited Mrs. Hauptmann's frantic rush to see what all the noise was above her. No sound escaped the attic, an early precaution set in place by the dweller when it had chosen this lair. I had assumed such a spell even before arriving at the house. In the deadly world of Her Lady's Court, even a fiend so lowly as this would have to have skill at hiding its presence if it hoped to survive and thrive there. And in the comparably magic-depleted mortal world, that was doubly true.

The dweller had noted my difference from the start and had calculated that remaining obscured would not be sufficient. The more I felt of its power, the more I was aware that it had already nearly grown strong enough, anyway. Mrs. Hauptmann probably would have "vanished" within a few more days had she not become aware of the advertisement.

And if I did not stop the shadow creature now, she still might be its final meal before it departed for a better lair. Of course, that would also be after it finished me.

I switched my grip and threw the blade. It soared past four grasping appendages and struck the middle orb exactly. As the dweller hissed in pain, a foul, greenish substance spilled from the ruined orb.

Enraged, the fiend threw itself at me.

Eye can help! the voice ever in my head bellowed. *Set me free!*

I ignored his demand, aware that I might never be able to regain control if I did as he bade. I had planned exactly for these circumstances, and only one thing thus far—a significant one thing—threatened to unravel all my intentions and leave me—*us*—to suffer a grisly fate.

From behind my foe there came the crashing of glass.

The last piece fell into place . . . and Fetch landed atop the shadow dweller.

Fetch opened his mouth and from it dropped a silver medallion. I had had it with me since Silene, since the beginning of my curse, and although it could not cut, its very creation and blessing made it burn into the fiend as a hot coal tossed upon a patch of ice.

The hiss grew shrill. The shadow dweller reared back, tossing Fetch into the stack of boxes and sending the medallion tumbling to the side. The fiend sizzled wherever the relic touched.

"Be damned!" Fetch growled, as he vanished among Mrs. Hauptmann's forgotten possessions. The curse was followed by a whine as the boxes fell upon him.

As the creature rose above me, I drew a second weapon from beneath my coat. It glowed a sinister crimson and, as I pulled it free, it became a sword with jagged edges and stones in the gold hilt that looked as if pieces of the moon had been taken to make them.

That the sword had escaped the monster's notice was not due to any mishap on its part. It would have taken one of the greater Wyld to sense the gift of Her Lady.

The shadow dweller's underside was open to me. With the dagger, only the orbs presented a viable target. With the Lady's sword, however . . . I merely had to swing.

The crimson blade sliced through the fiend without pause, stretching farther than its mere physical presence warranted.

With one last shrill hiss, the monster fell in two pieces. I immediately thrust, not for the portion where the orbs still gleamed, but rather deeper into the base end, where the mind of the shadow dweller truly existed and still survived.

The blade sank into the wiggling abyss. As it did, the blackness adhered to the edge. I turned the sword over and the blackness sank into the blade.

In barely a breath, the sword devoured the latter half of the fiend, swallowing it and briefly leaving the blade's finish muted. Yet, even as I raised the weapon, the foul brilliance of Her Lady's gift returned.

A growl brought my attention back to the remnants of the creature. The front end continued to grab for whatever might be before it. The orbs no longer saw and the movements were reflex only, but Fetch, who had at some point extracted himself from the boxes, now snapped at them as he tried to decide which to bite off first.

"Stop playing," I ordered him, at the same time raising Her Lady's gift. Fetch growled one last time, then retreated from the vicinity of the sword.

"Mind ye not swing that shiv too wide, Master Nicholas," he rumbled, well aware that his undoing would be much akin to that of our quarry should the blade so much as scrape him.

I ignored both his warning and his growing use of current slang, the latter seeming to affect Fetch the more he lived on the streets. The sword removed the remaining evidence. I then returned it to my coat, where it vanished into that place outside of both realms until I needed it again.

Fetch circled the area where the shadow dweller had fallen, as if still seeking some sign of the fiend. I retrieved the dagger and the medallion. "Did anyone notice you out there?"

"Ye think if someone'd seen me leapin' up the back of the house that we'd not be hearin' sirens by now?"

I expected such an answer, but with Fetch it still paid to ask the question. He was trustworthy for what he was, but that still did not make him entirely truthful at times.

"That turned out to be duck soup," Fetch remarked, his words readily understandable, even despite his canine maw not designed for speech. This close to me, he was slightly more than a pale reflection of his once-proud self. "Thought it'd put up more a fight . . ."

Duck soup. I fought back a frustrated glare. Fetch had done his part, but I'd been facing the front. The struggle had been short, but hardly duck soup, as he'd put it. "The dweller was not the point of our coming, though its destruction was necessary. Do you smell anything out of the ordinary?"

His nose wrinkled as he tasted the air—and other things. "No trace. Nothin' to mark who opened the way, Master Nicholas."

He did not have to call me as he did, but thus was Fetch's way, even despite his recently found love for the colloquialisms of this decade. I desired mastery over no one, though fate had decreed otherwise.

The bulb abruptly flickered to life. I glanced at the window through which Fetch had arrived. It had not been by chance that he had chosen it for his entrance. Mrs. Hauptmann had been unaware that we had scouted the house before announcing our arrival—ever a necessary precaution. "Best leave now. I'll meet you out front."

Without preamble, he wended his way to the broken pane, then leaped outside. I waited a moment, heard nothing, and then retrieved the case I used as a decoy. At the same time, I blinked, returning my eyes to their normal appearance.

You are welcome . . . came the bitter voice within. *As ever . . .*

I ignored him as best as I always could. Descending from the attic, I was greeted by one of the cats, who energetically rubbed against my leg in what I suspected was gratitude for ridding its home of the menace.

True to her word, Mrs. Hauptmann was in the sitting room, reading. She'd shut off the radio at some point, probably to listen for me. I cleared my throat as I entered. "I'm finished here."

My client jolted, then quickly recovered her composure. Her gaze narrowed. "You've given up?"

"No. I've gone over the place thoroughly. There's nothing up there."

She frowned. "I promise you, there is!"

"I found nothing. You owe me nothing. If you decide that you want me to try again, we'll take it from there."

I had often seen the expression that spread across her face at those words. "I shouldn't be complaining, but that's a peculiar way to run a business, Mr. Medea. Very *charitable*. I'm tired of being thought— what do they call it—a 'patsy'? Just what are you up to?"

I forced a chuckle at her suspicion, even though she was right to be distrustful. "I mean what I say. However, if after a day or two you feel anything is still wrong, call me and I'll search again."

"You sound more like you dealt with something, not just did like the others and tried to prove I was only verrückt—crazy."

"You're not crazy, Mrs. Hauptmann." As if an afterthought, I added, "Oh, some bird must have collided with the back window. I found it broken."

Mrs. Hauptmann had naturally not heard the crash any more than she had the struggle, so had no reason not to believe my explanation. "I'll call someone in the morning. Thank you for letting me know."

The repairman would see that most of the glass was inside the attic. It would look very unlikely that I had anything to do with the damage.

She finally led me out front. Fetch, seeming not to have moved at all since she had last seen him, wagged his tail and looked back and forth from Mrs. Hauptmann and myself.

"Good night," she muttered, as she closed the door. Her disappointment was obvious, but she would soon realize that her home was clear of the darkness she had felt. By then, if she sought to contact me through the advertisement to let me know, she would find neither any trace of the notice in her home nor any listing in any paper. The magic was thorough in that regard.

Fetch made a noise as if wanting to speak, but I ignored him until we were out of sight, even though the street was deserted. Mrs. Hauptmann would have been surprised to find out that no car awaited us around the corner. Not only did I not own a vehicle, but this visitation had actually taken place not far from where I both lived and worked. Not that she would be able to discover that, either.

Despite my best attempts, Fetch finally had to speak again. "Master Nicholas, I smelled nothin' of Her Lady's Court, but ye still act wary . . ."

"I appreciate your help tonight," I answered instead, my mind already deep into the very subject of which he had spoken. However, for now, Fetch's part was done. I had no desire to draw him into something far worse than a lone shadow dweller, though that creature was the very mark of how great the danger was. "You can be off now . . ."

Fetch started to move, turned back, turned away again, then turned to me once more. His desires and instincts fought with his loyalty to me, something I'd never asked from him. I was the closest thing to a friend that he had had since being cast out by Her Lady. He was now a shapeshifter who could not shift shape because he was too far removed from the realm of Feirie and could only talk here in the mortal world because of the curse on me that inadvertently returned that ability to him when he was within roughly twenty feet of me. That at least enabled him to keep remembering that he was not simply some horrendous mixed breed prowling the streets of Chicago at night for whatever warm meal—rats and other vermin, at my insistence— that he could hunt down. I'd tried to give him shelter one time, but the alleys were his preference, as was the bringing down of prey.

I feared Fetch would lose what remained of himself one day, unless somehow he earned Her Lady's favor again.

Of course, if that happened, I might have to slay him.

"It's bad, isn't it?" he asked. His lupine features contorted as he sought a more modern term. "Not . . . *copacetic* at all?"

This time I didn't hold back a grunt of annoyance at his insistence on constantly trying out the latest word he'd heard. "It's bad." I saw no reason to pretend otherwise. "That kind of shadow dweller could not have entered on its own through some spell."

Fetch growled low. "The Gate's been breached, Master Nicholas?"

"The Gate's been breached."

He nodded. "I will be standin' with ye when ye need me. Just—"
To his credit, the shapeshifter bit back another new expression, simply
finishing with, "I will be standin' with ye."

He rushed off into the darkness, heading for wherever he chose to
call home for the night. I should also have headed home, but I had one
more visit to make. This time for my own sake.

CHAPTER 2

"**S**till praying for redemption, Georgius?"

I had come to St. Michael's, an old brick church that had survived the Great Fire, just to do that, but I would not say so to *him*. I looked up from where I knelt in one of the last pews and eyed the gray-haired figure clad in what at first glance might have seemed a monk's robes. His rough-hewn features spoke of an eastern European birth and, like me, he had the appearance of someone who had once served in the military. In fact, I had once served *him* well and faithfully.

And yet, despite that loyalty and faith, I had been betrayed.

"I thank God for every blessing he gives me, Diocles."

"Has he given you so many that you spend so much time here?" Diocles surveyed the interior, something he had done countless times before, and yet he always seemed to be seeing it for the first time. "A rustic and yet enchanting place, I admit, and I would be the last to prevent your prayers—" He grimaced as my brow rose at this remark. "You know that I speak the truth . . . now. Still, it amazes me how strongly you believe, especially in this day and age and under the heavy yoke you bear."

"Spoken oddly for a late convert."

Diocles looked uncomfortable again. "Spoken because I do not know if I could have suffered as you and remained so true."

Compared to my unwanted companion's formal manner of speech, I sounded at times nearly as casual as Fetch sought to be. I wished Diocles away, but naturally he remained where he was. Aware that he would speak regardless of my obvious desire to continue praying, I sat back in the pew. For Diocles, I would no longer stand at attention, and he understood why, even if he had paid for his betrayal and I was supposed to forgive. I knew that I was in the wrong, at least where the forgiveness was concerned, but it was something that I could not, even after all this time, change in me.

"You had an incident tonight," he went on, in an obvious attempt to change to a safer subject. "You rarely come this late unless you have been in contact with one of them. One of the shadow folk."

The prayers and the calmness of the church itself had just begun to ease my tensions when he had interrupted. I struggled to maintain my composure. Diocles knew that he ever stirred old angers in me and yet it was *his* curse to come to me again and again until something—perhaps true forgiveness on my part—enabled him to move on.

"It was one of the lesser folk. A shadow dweller. Fetch and I dealt easily with it. It hadn't even started to prey on the locals save for a couple of cats."

A grim smile spread across Diocles's marble face. "You permit Fetch forgiveness . . ."

"The incidents do not compare," I replied, finally rising as frustration made it impossible to remain in the pew. I glanced past him to a statue of the church's patron. St. Michael and I had our own differences, but I understood why he had done what he had. It had been his duty to come to me at that time.

"When you were on the other side of the Gate, that mongrel of a werewolf tried to kill you at the command of his damned queen!"

I stared into his eyes, forcing him, despite his condition, to look away first. "*He* failed."

Diocles's hands tightened into fists and now he turned his eyes to one of the statues of St. Michael. "I'm sorry, Georgius—"

"*Nicholas*," I angrily corrected him. "Especially to you. Nicholas or Nick Medea. Never anything else."

He tried to look at me again. Tried and failed. Instead, his gaze fell to the well-trodden floor. "Nick Medea," Diocles muttered unhappily. "Nicomedia. So long as you choose to keep some variation of that name, I can never be free, lad. It'll always be there to remind you, even if you could forget on your own."

"And that's the way I prefer it, Diocles. I have fallen from grace, and though I pray, as you said, for redemption, I cannot release either of us from this particular curse . . ."

From near the altar, there came the creak of a door opening. Diocles and I immediately turned our attention there.

A young priest with large, round glasses and thinning blond hair stepped out. He looked toward us and managed a relieved smile. "Nick! I should've known it'd be you. For a moment, I feared robbers."

"Evening, Father Jonathan." Next to me, Diocles grimaced.

"I know that Father Peter considered you a special member of the congregation, with the unique privilege of having your own key—which, between you and I, the archbishop would frown upon—but this is late even for you."

"I was in the area. I felt the need to pray."

He looked concerned. "Anything I can help you with?"

"No, thank you, Father."

Father Jonathan looked slightly exasperated. I could not blame him. "I don't know what you do, though you've more than once promised me that it doesn't involve this current gang war or any other sinful activity going on. I wish we had the trust that you and Father Peter had. Perhaps someday . . ."

"Perhaps." Father Peter had learned the hard way about my existence and the dangers of it. I was hoping to keep his young successor safely ignorant. Father Jonathan was a good man, but he did not know about Feirie. Bootlegger wars paled in comparison to even the slightest aspect of the shadow realm.

"Well, I hope that you find comfort in the Lord. May his blessing be upon you."

"Thank you, Father."

He started to leave, then stopped. "Were you talking to someone else just before I came?"

"No one."

"I thought I heard you speaking. That's in part why I came to see—"

"My prayers got a bit loud," I lied, aware that in this house I had added another sin to my long list.

"Damn you, Georgius," Diocles muttered.

"Nothing wrong with that, I suppose," the priest replied with another smile. "Good night."

"Good night."

The moment that Father Jonathan left, I turned to depart. St. Michael's would provide me no respite this late evening.

"Georg—Nick—" Diocles tried to grab my shoulder, but his hand went through. Sometimes, even a ghost forgot that he had no substance.

"Sleep well," I responded bitterly, not looking back at the specter. There was no warmth in my words, and both of us were quite aware that sleep was a release beyond his grasp. Diocles could only haunt the vicinity of St. Michael's and other churches day and night, seeking some end to his eternal wandering, especially from the archangel who gathered up souls at death for judgement. He had about as much chance of that happening as *I* did.

"Nick . . . we must talk . . . There is something gathering. I feel—"

I looked back. "You feel nothing. You're dead."

He faltered. At the moment before his passing, Diocles had silently turned to Heaven, the same Heaven whose followers he had viciously persecuted. Death often changed one's perspective, but I could not see past his crimes, not yet . . . Not ever, perhaps.

The ghost regained control of himself. "Nick . . . I only want to warn you! I was hoping to see you here sooner. There is most definitely something—"

I saved us both further need for conversation. "The Gate's been breached."

I stalked from the church. Behind me, I knew that Gaius Aurelius Valerius Diocletianus Augustus—the late Emperor Diocletian of Rome—stood gaping in horror. I was not proud of how I left him . . . but neither was I sorry.

The walk, more than an hour long, did not help clear my head. I entered the gray Queen Anne house that functioned as my home and my business. On a rare occasion, I had to bring people in need or trouble somewhere, and so I had long ago established this location. It was one more old, reasonably well-kept house among others. My neighbors saw little of me and did not care. When we did meet, I greeted them and they greeted me. After that, the magic made them forget.

They were far better off that way.

Once, I had only believed in magic as a thing of evil, but over time I saw that by itself it was neutral. The evil came from those who wielded it for vile purpose, such as the shadow dweller. Such thoughts coming from me would have shocked many who had known me before my execution.

The back of my neck throbbed, ever a reminder of that time. I felt *his* presence within me, silently laughing at the memories the throbbing resurrected.

"You should think what that moment meant for you," I said out loud.

The humor vanished. *Eye am tired. We must sleep.*

On that, I concurred. It had been three days since last I rested. There were aspects of sleep I did not like, but the need could not be escaped. I entered the living room, a place with furniture that would have impressed Mrs. Hauptmann for its age and condition, though perhaps not its style. Most of what the house contained was of a Mediterranean bent, and not all of it was from the same region. Much came from the east—Greece, Turkey, Lebanon, and more—and to the ignorant eye would have seemed to have been collected at random. Yet, in truth, each marked a place in my past, a moment of life gone so very long ago.

I retired to a low, long couch with a curling, wooden frame upon which stylized birds had been carved. Falling onto the ivoried cushions, I let exhaustion take me away. I did not sleep on the upper floor and rarely even used it. The house was merely a rest stop, albeit one I had inhabited since the last was destroyed more than fifty years before.

As I settled down, I readied myself for what sleep would bring. The dream had variations, but it was always the dream.

I slipped into it within seconds, almost as if it and I were eager to embrace one another, when, from my end at least, the mere thought of it always almost set me to screaming.

I rode a great charger across a field of wailing women clad in black tunics. The spear I held stretched to the horizon. The horse raced along and along, his sweat splattering the silver breastplate and kilt I wore. Even though I knew what was going to happen, still I rode with the greatest urgency. I had no choice.

The sweat suddenly became blood. Blood everywhere. The women vanished, but their wails grew louder, more horrified.

Diocles suddenly appeared, Diocles with his arms stretched in greeting to me. Now the blood splattering over me came from him and a figure in shadow behind. I knew who it was even though the face remained blank. Galerius. Always whispering in Diocles's ear, warning him that his friends were his enemies.

I tried to veer the horse toward the half-seen figure, eager to impale Galerius at the end of the spear. Yet the spear started bending to the side, and, no matter how I adjusted, it always turned another direction.

And then . . . a single feminine voice screamed. At the end of the spear hung the limp, crimson form of a young woman clad in a regal white tunic. No longer on horseback, I ran to her, trying all the while to pull the incredibly long spear from her chest.

The spear abruptly twisted in my hands as if alive. Now it was a long, brown-and-green-scaled tail, with a ridge running across the top. The strength of it flung me in the air. I flew up, then plummeted toward an abyss encircled by mountains with sharp peaks.

But as I neared, the sharp peaks became teeth, the abyss a gullet. A hissing voice laughed at my feeble attempts to keep from falling within.

Then, out of nowhere, Diocles swung a mighty sword that became Her Lady's gift and cut off the head of the behemoth into whose maw I dropped. I tumbled onto a gray plain as the head rolled toward me. However, although once as huge as the steed I had ridden, the head shrank more and more as it neared.

And when it came to a stop only a few feet from me, it was now not only as small as my own . . . it *was* my own.

I did then as I always did—awoke in a cold sweat. Every sensation in the dream had touched me a thousand times harder than in the waking world. I sat up on the couch and waited for my heart and my breath to calm. I was not consoled by the fact that my constant companion had also become distressed by the dream. I felt his quiet brooding, and on this rare occasion understood him well.

My heartbeat began to slow. I finally noticed that it was just about dawn.

I also noticed that someone was knocking on the door.

I lived hidden among the other inhabitants of Chicago because I must be near the Gate and yet have sworn to prevent threat to others as much as is in my power. In order for me to be better able to perform my duty, what could best be called a spell of *shunning* had been set around my abode. It discouraged visitors or intruders of any sort. I received no mail, no packages. If I needed something shipped to me, it was sent to a local post office box.

No one came to me willingly.

Set me free . . .

"Be silent," I murmured, already rising. The knocking ceased. I strode toward the door and, risking much, immediately swung it open.

There was no one outside. A black Lafayette coupe, far more stylish than the slightly older Maxwell Twenty-Five parked across from my house, drove by, but a quick glimpse revealed the occupant as the portly doctor living two blocks further. I knew he'd done work for Deanie O'Banion before—as Fetch delighted in putting it whenever the Irishman's name came up—the "harp's bloody bump off" at his flower shop. The good doctor now performed the same "off-duty" emergency care for the North Siders' new trio of bosses, especially Hymie Weiss—a Catholic Pole despite his moniker and coleadership of the mostly "harp"—or Irish—gang. It was obvious immediately that the doctor had nothing to do with this odd visitation, but I still made a note to keep an eye on him. He was flaunting his extra wealth more and more and, if the police didn't finally arrest him, one of the South Siders might decide he was fair game.

It would not pay to have the war spread to my neighborhood.

I had slept with my coat on—a necessary precaution—and so Her Lady's gift was there for me if I needed it. I peered further outside, still seeing no figure. Just in case something saw past the shunning, the minimal landscape in front of the house had been designed to prevent most threats from hiding nearby.

Glancing down, I saw what looked like a business card turned face down. Plucking it up, I read off the name.

Claryce Simone. The name stirred something within, but I marked it as coincidence. The card indicated that she was an executive at something called Delke Industries. I had no idea what Delke was and did not care. However, Claryce Simone was another matter and not merely because it was still rare, though less so these days, to find a woman in an executive position. I noticed that the card was filthy on both sides, as if it had lain by the door for some time, maybe even been stepped on by me when I returned during the night.

I did not believe in coincidence. This could very well be bait set by one of the Wyld, although I could think of none alive with such audacity. The only one who had tried to take me in my sanctum had learned to his regret that here was one place the Feiriefolk should especially fear.

I took one last look around the neighborhood but saw nothing out of the ordinary. An elderly man stepped out of the house behind the Maxwell to retrieve his morning paper. A young blond woman in a waitress's uniform, who worked at a diner three blocks down the street, passed my own dwelling without a glance my way. A perfectly normal neighborhood scene . . . if I hadn't been part of it.

Returning inside, I considered contacting Claryce Simone but decided a shower would do first. Setting the card aside, I dealt with washing away last night's memories. The cold water soothed me and cleared my thoughts. By the time I was dressed, a light coat now taking the place of the longer, darker one I'd worn previously, I was better focused. I would call Miss Simone and—

The candlestick telephone set on the small wooden table in the front hall rang.

The telephone *never* rang unless someone had seen the advertisement, and they could only see it if something from Feirie had found its way to the mortal realm through the Gate and into their lives.

I immediately snatched up the handset and brought the phone to my lips. "Hello?"

There was a brief crackle on the line, then . . .

"Mr. . . . Medea?" a woman asked.

"This is Nick Medea."

"My name is Claryce Simone."

It was fortunate that she could not see my expression. When she did not continue, I said, "Yes, Miss Simone?"

"I saw your—are you really what it claims?"

There was no need for me to ask what she meant. "I research the paranormal, if you're referring to the ad. I assist people in deciding whether they have a potential incident or merely something mundane that they didn't understand."

She exhaled. "Probably the last. I'm foolish for even calling you, Mr. Medea—"

The woman was not aware that this call would not even be taking place if her problem was of a mundane nature. "Call me Nick, please, and don't feel foolish. While I've yet to find a true incident of the paranormal, some of the actual reasons for what disturbs a client can be fascinating. This is an old building, I assume?"

"No, not really. It's not even mine. My employer, Mr. Delke— William Delke—actually owns it, but there was a fire involving my apartment and he was kind enough to let me use it until the repairs are finished. He's staying at his office penthouse in the meantime." She added the last quickly, as if thinking I might believe there was something untoward between them.

I hadn't even considered that. I was more interested in the place in question. A newer building. I found that odd. Those of Feirie were more drawn to older, darker abodes. "And Mr. Delke's noticed nothing?"

Another exhalation. "Not that I know. I haven't asked him . . . Nick. I would've ignored it, but last night . . ."

This drew more of my attention. Was there some connection with my confrontation with the shadow dweller? "What happened last night?"

"I'd rather—I think I'd rather explain it when we meet. Do I come to your office?"

"No. This is taking place where you live. With your permission, it'd be better to meet there."

She agreed and gave me the address. I knew the area, located on the Southwest Side. Five years had made a big difference in that part of the city. Since the race riots in Chicago right after the Great War and the fall of the Kaiser, the wealthy had begun to migrate farther from the city center, especially toward Claryce Simone's temporary home. William Delke was apparently no exception to that migration.

"We can meet today," I suggested.

"I won't be able to until tomorrow night," she said, in a voice that indicated today would have been very much her preference. "I have to take the train to Milwaukee for William's business and I'll be staying overnight there. I should be back by eight in the evening. Will that be all right? Do you charge extra for after hours?"

"Since the paranormal tends toward the night, my regular hours generally begin once the sun goes down."

This brought a light laugh from her. "That makes sense. Will that be okay, then?"

I assured her it was. We exchanged farewells. What I had not told her was that her short business trip worked better for me. Tonight, I would visit the address alone.

Only as I prepared to leave the house for a few errands related to the night's excursion did I realize that I had never asked Ms. Simone about exactly when she had stopped by my own house. The lapse bothered me as much as the fact that she had actually been here. I vowed to get a thorough answer when we met.

The early October sky was overcast and the temperature was cool, a change from the oddly warm September. I welcomed both as I headed to where I would find a passing taxi. From there, I visited three antiquity shops where my sources had indicated that there were relics supposedly tied to Her Lady's Court. I was always in search of those, both for possible clues to the whereabouts of any Wyld or as potential weapons against them. The first two shops turned out to have nothing but excellent reproductions, but the third held an item of interest, an oval clasp with the sign of the full moon inscribed in the middle. A series of runes bordered the clasp, and in some of them I could sense latent power.

The price was high, but not too high. Centuries had allowed me to gather and maintain the funds I needed to perform my duty. I wasted nothing on lavishness. I had no need for anything but necessities.

The last shop placed me near Claryce Simone's temporary residence. I purchased a coffee from a local diner and added to it a seasoned beef sandwich topped with a pickled vegetable salad called giardiniera, bought from an elderly, heavily mustached street vendor who found it pleasing to speak with someone who understood his native Italian tongue so well. The sandwich proved a rare, pleasant respite, and I ate it slowly as I headed toward the address, with the intention of studying the structure in the light.

I was almost there when a black Ford Runabout with the emblem of the Chicago Police Department pulled up just ahead. Even before the driver's door opened, I knew who would emerge. Thus, the fact that he was Mexican—if a fairly tall one—*and* a detective did not startle me as it would have most others. The young detective wore a well-tailored gray suit that I knew his family had scraped their savings to purchase. His oiled, black hair was short and neatly parted on the left side. I knew that his brooding, narrow face was popular with women—not just those of his people—but Inspector Alejandro Cortez had eyes only for his petite Maria.

"Nick Medea!" he cheerfully greeted me, as if we had not seen one another in years as opposed to only two weeks. "A small world, eh?" The Mexican pulled out a pack of Luckies, took one, and then offered the pack to me. "One from the deck?"

Alejandro Cortez—"Alex" to his white superiors when they were not calling him "greaser" or worse behind his back—had no discernible tie to Feirie that I could sense, but more than once he had become involved in incidents concerning the shadow folk. I had tried to divine exactly why he so often turned up and could only surmise that the inspector was too good at his job.

Someday, either it or his sense of justice in a department riddled with corruption would make Maria a widow.

"Cortez," I greeted him back, but with much less enthusiasm. "A little far from your precinct." To his still-proffered cigarettes, I shook my head. "Thank you very much, Inspector Cortez, but no."

"Ah, Nick Medea. Always so formal. I ever tell you that you sound like my *abuelo*—my grandfather? He was always the gentleman, always stood stiff and proper, like you do even when you're doing nothing at all . . ." When I only stood there in silence, Cortez blithely went on, "I'm on a special assignment for the mayor's task force on crime, you know?" Not looking the least slighted for my turning his offer down, he slipped the pack away. Cortez had a habit of ending many of his comments in the form of a question, which often made those he was investigating underestimate his cunning. I was under no such misapprehension.

I was also under no misapprehensions about his "assignment." Cortez had been taken on along with a few other colored and ethnic officers, to send into trouble spots where the chief of police did not want to waste those of a distinctly lighter skin tone. That made Cortez's appearance here a more curious one. "They have you protecting the upper crust from your own, or is the Outfit making a move and the department needs every man?"

He came around the back of the car to join me. Cortez did not know who or what I was, but in our last encounter he had come to suspect me to be more than a mere "ghost-breaker," as he put it. The inspector had no idea what had actually happened below the old water tower, but he knew that I had been there and that things had quieted after I left.

As he neared, the golden cross he always wore close to his throat glistened despite the overcast heavens. Unlike many who wore such decor these days, Cortez was deeply devout. It was the only reason I could divine for him recalling our meetings so vividly, rather than gradually forgetting them as happened with most. The shunning appeared not to work on the good detective.

"I got to protect the whole city," he responded, sounding a bit more serious and not at all put out by my comment about his possible reasons for being here. Cortez had no doubt developed an iron hide even before joining the cops, but I still found it astounding he had survived this long with so much against him. "The task force, they want me wherever I need to be, you know?"

I pretended to believe him. He was here because something had happened that had the potential of disturbing someone of great influence. If anything went bad, Cortez was there to blame. If all went well, his superiors would lay claim to the success. Cortez was possibly one of the best men on the force, but no one above him—and pretty much below him, too—was going to admit that.

I suddenly thought of Claryce Simone's quarters, only a couple of blocks out of sight of here. More than ever, I doubted the coincidence of running into the good inspector here.

"You usually wander more north, northeast of here, Nick Medea." He often called me by my first and last name. I could not help feeling that he was a bit suspicious of whether or not I had been christened so. "Run out of spooks there, or were you just tired of the Cubbies losing again and had to get away?"

There were few modern pastimes I paid any attention to, my ageless task demanding my focus day and night, but moving pictures, with their vivid if silent images, and the sport of baseball had both caught my attention. Fetch had dared once suggest that these two things—along with my own slipping into the occasional colloquial-isms or slang—were the first cracks in my armor, that I was finally becoming part of humanity again, but after the stare he'd received for that remark, he had never brought up such foolishness again.

That didn't mean that I hadn't found some truth in his words, despite the danger of letting down my guard in any way.

"Your Sox haven't fared much better," I answered casually, com-fortable with this part of the conversation at least. "Last year, Eddie Collins couldn't keep the slide to last from slowing any better than Evers and Walsh before him. Fifth this year isn't that much better. No, I simply decided to take the day off and see a different part of the city."

He let out a brief *hmmph*, the closest to a laugh he usually got where his work was concerned. "Wait'll next year for both of us, right? Never mind! Lucky chance, us finding each other today. Thought I was going to wear out my dogs looking for you!"

I tried to keep my demeanor calm. Despite the way I often acted, I liked Cortez. I just didn't want him poking around near me, for his sake as much as mine. "The police need a paranormal debunker?"

"No, I just had a question of my own about the break-in at the Art Institute."

I'd heard something about a break-in but had not had time to read up on it. Still, for some reason, the news made me stiffen. "What would I know?"

He held up his hands in mock defense. "Easy, Bo! You're not in dutch!" Cortez ignored my raised brow at his use of such slang. With others, he knew to at least to try to fit in and the slang was an easy way, but his previous encounters with me should have been enough to remind him that I couldn't have cared less what color or race he was. Worse, I didn't want to start thinking of him and Fetch in the same light. "I'm not asking if you were the culprit! They stole some interesting items but not the priciest ones, you know? Bits of ancient armor that hadn't been on display for years. Real old stuff, they say . . . third-century Roman or something. Donated by some European Jiggs who moved over here right before the turn of the century."

I knew nothing about some millionaire's museum donation nor its theft, but the date of the antiquities bothered me much. I revealed none of that to Cortez. "I've a fondness for antiques, but this is the first I've heard of all this."

"Don't you listen to the radio or read the *Trib* or the *Daily News*?" he asked, referring to two of the more prominent of the city's many papers.

My concentration had been on other matters, but I did vaguely wonder how that had escaped my notice. I continued to play ignorant, something only half an act at this point. "I've been busy."

He took my answer for what it was worth. "Understand that. Me, I'm always busy, too. Maria and the little ones keep me up when I do get home, but, hey, makes my life a good one." As he spoke, Cortez reached into his jacket again. "Actually, for you, I got one other question. Nothing concerning the break-in . . . I think. About a so-called 'cursed' statuette." The item he pulled out proved to be a photograph. "You know about curses and things. The piece in this was stolen the same night as the articles from the Institute. Reported by the woman in the picture, though she's not the owner. I don't know, the timing of the thefts could be coincidence . . ."

I still distrusted his supposed reason for wanting to speak with me, but I had no choice. I took the photograph.

Before I had a chance to even glance at it, Cortez added, "A very lovely, elegant lady." Cortez always took care to speak well of white women. One wrong word heard by his fellow cops could not only have him broken in rank but also broken in pieces. "Her name's Claryce Simone. You know her?"

Even despite so much practice keeping my expression from revealing my thoughts, it took great effort to hold back my surprise.

"Don't know her," I replied. "Let me take a look at the statuette—"

But I'd barely glanced at the picture when all sense abandoned me. I let the photo drop as if it were on fire. Only once since the Night the Dragon Breathed had I felt so stunned, so unable to even think straight.

Cortez grabbed hold of me. Not aware of the true reason I had reacted so, his voice was filled with real concern. "Hey! You all right? Having a heart attack? Say something, Bo!"

"No—I'm—it's all right . . ."

"Yeah." He sounded skeptical and with good reason. I had no doubt that I was as pale as one of Her Lady's courtiers, possibly more.

Gingerly releasing me, the inspector scooped up the photo, granting me one more glimpse of its subject. The statuette, a foot-high dryad draped sensually around her tree, was of some general interest to me for its possible origins, but it was not the cause of my overwhelming shock. That had to do with a woman in an elegant silk blouse and stylish long dark skirt and jacket posing next to the statu-ette, which sat upon a small stand. Her cloche hat fit snuggly around her brow but otherwise did not obscure her features.

The woman called Claryce Simone.

She was young, fair of hair, and with a hint of perhaps the Medi-terranean in her background. There was no denying that she was beau-tiful, with full lips and wide, expressive eyes I knew, despite only having the black-and-white photo before me, would be the color of dark chocolate.

Unfortunately, there was also no denying that she was a woman I had seen die horribly twice, the last time nearly a hundred years ago.

CHAPTER 3

My jolt proved to be the excuse needed to end my undesired encounter with Cortez. After reassuring himself that I would not need medical help, he returned to the car with the promise that we would speak again at a better time. I nodded noncommittally, unable to focus on anything else but the realization that I was again about to repeat a terrible cycle.

Refusing to simply give in to that destiny, I abandoned my intended study of the building. All but fleeing, I returned home. Only there, in the house, in the dark, was I able to begin to think again.

And what I thought of was a woman cursed to come into my life over and over with the hope of saving me, only herself to perish.

I thought of Cleolinda.

At that point, *he* laughed at my fear.

Eye was wondering when she would come again . . .

I kicked out at the wooden table in front of me, caring not a whit that any antique dealer would have shrieked at my careless use of the six-hundred-year-old piece. It tumbled onto its side, spilling notes I had made prior to my visit to Mrs. Hauptmann. The act was a foolish, futile one but all I could do when unable to strike a creature who existed only within me.

"She'll be left out of it this time!" I snapped at the air and him.

You and Eye know better . . . we three are bound . . . you and Eye by the blood shed between us . . . she by love and virtue . . .

He said the last with mockery, love and virtue alien to his reptilian nature. He blamed her for what had befallen him, as much as he blamed me, the one who had impaled him.

"Love has nothing to do with this," I finally managed to argue. In the beginning, I had only tried to keep her from harm and had never intended to pressed any suit. However, fate had played its own devious game, stirring love between us, only to have death apparently separate us forever.

He only laughed again at my poor denial, the harsh sound echoing through my head until it ached. *Eye know the truth . . . Eye know you best, oh pious saint!*

"Be quiet!"

He said nothing more, but I could still sense his amusement. There was very little he had. No corporeal form. No chance to wield his monumental power for nearly a hundred years. Death had even forbidden him release, instead forever trapping his essence in the weaker, mortal body of his slayer.

It was surely enough to drive even a dragon mad.

It meant nothing to him that I suffered, also. He had pointed out often in the past that *I* had control of the body. *I* decided our current fate. He did not wish to die again, but rather regain his grand and glorious might, even if it meant guarding the Gate by himself. I, on the other hand, simply wanted to make amends for my ignorance and foolhardiness, though if it meant standing watch until Judgment Day.

I thought again of Silene, of that place where I had not only faced a dragon and became a legend, a *saint*, but also where I had met Cleolinda.

Saint George is no saint . . . came the dragon's voice suddenly. Before I could argue with him, he receded into the background again.

Leaving the table where it was, I rose to stare at a small painting hanging over the unused marble fireplace. I had hung it there to always remind me of how it had all began, not that I really needed my memory stirred. My constant companion had once declared that I enjoyed my misery so much that there had been no choice but to set such a blatant reminder where it would always be seen. I could not argue with him.

Seeking anything that might keep me from concentrating too much on the revelation concerning Claryce Simone, I went to the room I used as a study and turned to the heavy, wooden file cabinets where I daily stored any and all articles cut from the half dozen or more newspapers available to me. Someday, I hoped that there would be a device—like the great computation machines that were currently being devised, only much smaller, more compact—that could make my tasks a little simpler. Until that happened, though, I'd continue adding to the files on a daily basis.

A radio more expensive and elaborate than Mrs. Hauptman's took up most of a small table to the side. I considered dialing up the news on WMAQ but held off. Silence was what I needed for my current research. Retrieving a file from one of the cabinets, I went through the most recent articles concerning the Art Institute. Although I had not paid them much mind when I'd cut them from the *Tribune*, the fact that they concerned that place had guaranteed they were saved in the first place. The Institute had a wealth of art . . . and more than one item with origins linked to Feirie. Most were inconsequential, but a few I kept an eye on, which made it all the more disturbing that I had not paid attention to the theft.

The three articles I discovered essentially contained the same information, save that one made mention of the fact that the pieces had been stored for so long that only those who kept the inventory even knew that they existed. There was no description of the actual items save what I knew from Cortez and the first article—some armor of ancient make and two weapons. They apparently represented an intriguing art style—which is why they had been donated in the first place—but I was more concerned with their functionality. Did they possess some power that made them of value to one of the Wyld living in the mortal world or perhaps one of those humans who were versed in the magical arts?

Feirie and this realm had existed side by side since the dawn of time. However, Feirie, the nexus of what was simplistically called "magic," had developed much earlier. The Court in all its mad majesty had spread throughout Feirie even before mankind discovered fire.

But it was when mankind began to grow into its own that the two worlds became more and more intertwined. There were those that said that the imagination of the mortal race fueled the power of Feirie and that the magic of Feirie in turn stirred the souls of men toward the arts and creativity. I was never certain if any of that was true. I only knew that it had been discovered that there needed to be a balance between both, that the two realms could never truly meld into one or even allow one to overwhelm the other. Both worlds had seen the folly of that when Her Lady's Lord had decreed, for the good of Feirie, that the mortal plane should be vassal to the Court.

He had almost succeeded in his desire more than once. For humans, that had each time meant a return to barbarism and unthinking fear of the dark. For Feirie, it had provided first a monumental, uncontrollable rise in wild magic, beyond the Court's command, and then a fading of that magic until even the Court itself had grown mortal. Oberon himself had failed to recognize what disaster his deeds caused his own subjects, so certain had he been of the righteousness of his cause.

The panic ensuing after one of the later incidents had been such that the Court had eventually turned in protest against His Lord himself. But Oberon had remained deaf to their entreaties . . . and so it had finally taken Her Lady's coup to cast out her king, realign the Court, and see that Feirie survived.

That the mortal world was also salvaged in the process was coincidental.

However, there were those among the Wyld who still pursued Oberon's foul legacy. They did so, fortunately, without a master. Exiled to this realm, Oberon had followed the Gate, which had—thanks to my tremendous foolhardiness and ignorance—moved across the world for centuries of its own accord and without warning, possibly following some intention no one understood. When it had come to rest near the rising city of Chicago, he had been there to seek to claim its power and make the mortal world and Feirie one again, regardless of the consequences.

But we had been there also, of course. The dragon and I. The guardians. The sentries. The cursed. We stopped Oberon. At my decision, for the first time since he and I had become one, the dragon breathed.

And while the Gate remained sealed, while Oberon perished in the pure flames that only a dragon can breathe . . . the city, too, burned.

But with His Lord, and with Chicago, had perished a woman whose face and form had been the same as that of Claryce Simone . . . and the Princess Cleolinda of Silene.

I saw all three women in my mind. I saw them as if the two previous savored life as Claryce Simone surely did. Behind them began to form the shadows of other figures, other tragic incarnations—lost lives reaching all the way back to that fatal event in the third century.

Though I could not yet see their faces, I knew that every one would be identical.

It was all I could do at that point to keep from shoving over the file cabinet in anger. Instead, I satisfied myself with merely crushing my fist against the wall. The wall gave way, but I could feel some of the bones in my hand crack.

In my head, he laughed.

Eye will take care of that . . .

No sooner did he make the promise than I felt the bones knit. In the process, the pieces scraped against one another, causing me to wince.

There was no benevolence in his act. I belatedly realized that he had been the one stirring the memories, that he had been the one resurrecting those tormenting moments.

It was the only avenue of vengeance left for a titan now bereft of even the slightest physical act. It was a savage game we played over the centuries, hating each other yet bound as none could imagine. *Saint* George and the dragon, forever one, forever guarding the Gate. It was a duty I, who had set in motion the initial chaos, had willingly accepted . . . but ever prayed to Heaven that I would be able to perform alone someday.

Eye will always be with you . . . and you will always be with me . . .

He did not torture me now, only stated a bald fact we could not escape. That he referred to himself as "Eye" was because he had known no name when alive, had not even understood the concept. There had been other dragons of legend with names, but he had never had one. Now, he called himself by the only part of him that had some existence, the only part I regularly summoned from darkness. I needed his unique vision, his ability to tear away many of the veils hiding those of the Feirie who crossed into the mortal world. Now and then, I had been forced to summon other aspects of him, but only in desperate straits.

I reached for the clippings again—and the second phone that I kept in the makeshift study rang. The dragon shared my distrust at this unexpected moment. I had expected no call and only one other knowingly had the number. *He* wasn't supposed to call yet, but . . .

I quickly answered. "Kravayik?"

But the voice on the other end was the last I expected to hear. "I'm sorry. Do I have the right number? I'm looking for Nick Medea. This is Claryce Simone."

"*Claryce?*" I blurted out her name before I could stop myself.

"Is this Nick?"

"Yes . . . I'm sorry. I thought it was another call," I quickly responded. A new feeling of dread draping over me, I asked, "You're still in Milwaukee?"

"No. Matters ended early and I came straight back. I'm just gathering a couple of things I need from the office. I was hoping that we could meet earlier, perhaps even in an hour, hour and a half?"

Her voice all but pled with me to agree. The hair on my neck stiffened. Something had changed since our last conversation. "Do you have a particular reason?"

"I-I'd rather not say. You'll think me crazy. Can we meet earlier?"

My constant companion gave every indication of wanting me to refuse. It was one thing to torment me with visions of the past, but another for both of us actually to reenter a cycle of damnation.

I wanted to side with him—a rarity—but I knew better. "I'll leave now. I should be there shortly."

The gratitude in her voice only filled me with more regret. "Thank you, Nick."

I bid her farewell, then, after hanging up, picked up the receiver and dialed another number. The phone rang several times before a low, tentative voice with a heavy, unidentifiable accent said, "Yes? Who is speaking?"

"Nick," I answered.

"Kravayik awaits your command, Nicholas."

I grimaced. Compared to Kravayik, Fetch treated me with utter disdain. "I don't command you, Kravayik. You do me a favor. I'm grateful. All's well?"

"It remains," he replied. "Peace is with us."

I breathed a sigh of relief, even though I had been certain that he would answer so. "Thank you, Kravayik."

"No . . . thank you for showing me the way."

I ended the second call before I could grow too uncomfortable with his gratitude. Like Fetch, he felt that I had saved him from certain doom, but, unlike the shapeshifter, Kravayik had embraced his new life in a way I had not expected and for which he credited me too much.

I already knew that someone was using my new client as a pawn to reach me. If that had not been obvious when I had seen her photo, it certainly had been when she had called me using a number unavailable to her. Logic dictated that it might be her employer, Mr. Delke. I remembered that there had been a couple of other photos in the *Tribune* articles and grabbed a magnifying glass.

In one grainy picture that spoke of Delke's contribution to the Institute, there proved to be a partial shot of the man himself. Delke appeared to be someone who did not like the limelight despite his philanthropy, but there was enough to enable me to identify him should we meet. Delke was a heavyset man clad in a suit likely as gray as the photo made it and who looked to have once been athletic before success made his life too easy. He had a squat face and only a ring of graying hair. His eyes were watery, and in the picture he wore a pleasant if uncertain smile.

He was no one or no thing I recognized. Delke—William Delke—was human, no elf or any other race of Feirie. It was possible that he was possessed, though. Questioning Claryce Simone might help answer that question.

As I departed, I did so knowing that my ultimate adversary expected me to meet with her. He also expected me to be suspicious. He also knew exactly who I was and where I could be found.

He could only be one of the Wyld . . . and, judging by his breaching of the Gate, a most powerful one, at that.

I saw her approach the house just minutes after my own arrival. I sat on a bench across the street from one of the most unlikely homes to be threatened by the "paranormal." William Delke's property was modern, clean, and no doubt filled with iron. It could not be more than twenty years old and had clearly recently been renovated to add symmetric Art Deco touches to the exterior, a popular European style just now touching Chicago.

It was no place that a "ghost"—and certainly not one of the Wyld—would invade.

She'd foregone her hat and the hair now free from it proved longer than I'd imagined. It swept down past her shoulders and, in doing so, made her more resemble Cleolinda than even the last incarnation.

"That her?"

"Quiet, Fetch." I had made one slight detour before arriving. Of those exiles I could even somewhat trust, only Kravayik was more staunch than Fetch, and Kravayik had perhaps the most significant of tasks already. That left me with Fetch. "It is."

He had not seen the previous incarnations. "Quite the cat's meow, Master Nicholas."

This time, I waved him to silence. He assumed his usual image, tongue lolling and tail wagging as he sat next to me. I judged the situation for a few seconds, then rose. Fetch followed at my side.

As we crossed, I called out, "Claryce Simone?"

She turned, her hair flying, her face at first looking puzzled and then hopeful as she realized who I must be.

I, in turn, stumbled to a halt in the street. She was Claryce Simone, but she was also Cleolinda. I had known that, had seen that, but still the moment caught me.

With an anxious growl, Fetch shoved me forward. At the same time, I saw Claryce suddenly growing fearful.

The truck horn blared in my ear as both Fetch and I just managed to make it to the curb. A deep voice shouted angrily in Sicilian. Claryce leapt forward, pulling me toward her. She had no idea that, while extremely painful, the truck would not have killed me. That would require much, much more. Still, I was very grateful to Fetch for keeping his presence of mind when I had acted like a fool.

But even knowing that, I was hard-pressed not to stand there only inches from her and simply stare. So many decades since the last time I had seen that face. I had hoped to never do so again and yet had yearned for one more chance.

I did not want either Claryce or Cleolinda dying again because of me.

"Are you all right?" she asked in great concern.

"Yes . . . I stumbled. Fortunately Fetch here is well-trained."

"'Fetch'?" She knelt down and without fear scratched his head. Fetch wagged harder and would have licked her hand if he had not known my opinion on that. "What a unique dog! He looks like something out of the Brothers Grimm!"

"He's part wolf, part greyhound."

"And part something else," Claryce remarked offhandedly as she straightened. "Well-trained, definitely. A regular Rin-Tin-Tin!" She turned her attention back to me. "Are you certain you're all right?"

"Other than feeling clumsy, yes. I arrived a little early, so I took up a place across the street and waited. I thought it was you, so I tried to catch you before you reached home."

"'Home.'" She looked at the house, my near accident all but forgotten now. "I should have mentioned something to William, but I felt so foolish—and still do." Claryce looked down. "I'm sorry, Nick. I think I've had you come here unnecessarily."

"Then why ask me to join you even sooner, Claryce?"

She frowned. It was all I could do to keep from calling her Cleolinda. Whatever ties she had to her former life, she was very much Claryce Simone, and I reminded myself I did her an injustice by even for a moment thinking her otherwise.

Suddenly wrapping her arms around herself as if freezing, she answered, "The night after I first called you . . . before I took off for Milwaukee . . . I felt as if something hung over me. Not stood over me or hovered, but *hung*. I felt as if it hungered for—for my soul." She blushed. "That sounds so silly at the moment."

Fetch growled before I could stop him. I understood his concern. This did not sound like something so "basic" as a shadow dweller. This bore the taint of something from the darker stretches of Feirie, even beyond Her Lady's Court.

"Show me where," I ordered.

My taking command of the situation comforted her, and she nodded. It was not any weakness on Claryce's part that she so readily accepted my control of the situation. She was faced with something beyond her ken, something of which I was supposed to be an expert.

I silently prayed she would not die because of my rash decision to forge ahead.

"Fetch will wait out here," I offered. With a house as modern as this, I expected that she would not want to risk offending William Delke by inviting in an animal that looked capable of ruining a room in more ways than one. Besides, he would enter through other methods.

Claryce surprised me. "No, bring him in. He makes me feel even more secure. William won't mind a dog in here. He had a mastiff he adored until it died suddenly last year."

She received a strong tail wag; Fetch was rarely invited inside any place but my own spartan abode. He cheerfully trotted into the house ahead of us, making certain to remain within a few feet. As he moved, he smelled the air. The shapeshifter gave no hint that he detected anything, but this was only the entrance.

The decor was as I anticipated. As modern as the house and as spotless as the exterior, with more Art Deco designs spread throughout. I noticed Fetch being very careful not to rub against a white couch as he trotted in the direction of what I assumed was the kitchen. Delke's home seemed to demand that there be no dirt, no disorder.

In contrast to the rest of the house, a number of elegant, stately paintings decorated the walls, but what interested me more was one of William Delke himself. Portraits were far less common these days, but some of the wealthy were willing to pay the time and price to feel as if they were part of the old aristocracy rather than modern businessmen. Delke looked much as he had in the photo, albeit with fewer lines and a touch more youth—more likely the artist's doing than because the painting was older. He was seated and holding what appeared to be a tiny book, although the hands obscured exact details.

"A tradition among the Delkes," Claryce replied helpfully. "You'll find the previous generations decorating the levels above."

The sun was nearly down. I decided that there was no time to waste. Creatures of Feirie inhabiting the mortal world preferred the night, though some who adapted, as Fetch and Kravayik had, were comfortable even in the sunlight.

"Can you show me where you feel most uneasy?" I asked her.

"This way."

I whistled to Fetch, who immediately joined us. A staircase rose through the middle of the house, various Delkes greeting us as we ascended. They all sat in the same pose, holding the same small, obscured book. The features ran true, although each previous generation appeared thinner than their progeny. Good living had evidently filled out the Delkes over time more than I had initially thought.

I expected Claryce to stop at the second floor—where there were obviously at least three bedrooms—but instead she continued on toward the third floor. "You don't sleep here?"

"The other rooms are reserved for visiting family," she explained. "But there's one suite on the left side when we reach the top."

Upon arrival on the third floor, I noted another door to the right. "What's that?"

"It's another suite, but it's under renovation. He was kind enough to have them halt until my own place was ready."

I immediately turned toward the unfinished suite. Before Claryce could stop me, I tried the knob. Finding it unlocked, I swung the door open. Fetch stood at my side, ready to fight.

Dust was all that met our unplanned entry. Whatever furniture was in here had been removed. Sheets covered most of the walls, but I could see here and there some repeated archlike pattern that did not seem to quite match the Art Deco style Delke now liked.

Fetch sat, a sign that he sensed no threat here. Likewise, my constant companion inside showed only boredom at our discovery here. Still, well aware that someone was toying with me, I took a moment longer to look around. Unfortunately, my search revealed nothing, which left me with one choice.

Eye will help . . . he replied indifferently.

The transformation to his reptilian gaze always began with a peculiar tingling. The room shifted, turned emerald.

And still there was nothing beyond the obvious.

Claryce joined me. "William wouldn't like you being in here."

"My apologies," I returned, immediately willing my own eyes back. Turning to her, I gave a shrug. "I didn't think it would do any harm to at least look." Feeling as if I had yet missed something, I shut the door behind us as we moved on to her suite. Another, older, painting of a Delke watched us as we passed, but I paid it scant mind, already too familiar with the reoccurring features of the bloodline.

The decor of Claryce's suite matched the sumptuousness and modern feel of the rest of the house and again radiated the notion that no Wyld or any other creature of Feirie would find comfort in this building.

Fetch trotted through the room, going from closet to en suite bathroom and on. I dared not summon the dragon's gaze, but I studied the corners and possible hiding places for any sign.

Something occurred to me. "Where is the entrance to the attic?"

"There is no attic. The house was designed without one."

I glanced up at the ceiling, which arched high. No attic. True, a basement would serve a shadow dweller as well, but they were generally too secretive to constantly make their way up three—four—flights of stairs merely to hang over a sleeping woman. My gaze continue to journey around the bedroom even though I was at a loss as to where there might be a hiding place for even the smallest, weakest denizen of Her Lady's Court—

My eyes froze on an etched border—yet again not fashioned in the latest style—running across the top of the wall opposite the entrance. The border did not repeat on the other walls, but that was not what stopped me. Slowly, I was beginning to understand what the pattern represented. The suits of a deck, but not the suits so well-known to anyone who had played cards in Chicago or anywhere else in the mortal world.

"The cards . . ." I muttered without thinking.

I felt he within me stir to anxiousness. Fetch, who had just emerged from peering under the bed, froze and stared at me.

"'Cards'?" Claryce said, evidently hearing me but misunderstanding what I had said. In contrast to my own growing consternation, she gave a light laugh. "I shouldn't tell you, but William's family fortune was made from playing cards. His great-great grandfather was said to be a real shark. He turned his winnings into the start of Delke Enterprises—"

I no longer paid any attention. Something I'd seen in the other suite now made terrible sense. I barged past her, Fetch at my heels. The dragon hissed urgently as we raced to the other set of rooms.

Throwing aside the door, I rushed to the opposing end of that suite and tore down one of the sheets covering the walls. For the first time, I had a good look at the repeating arch pattern set directly across from the card border in Claryce's room. I saw, much to my dismay, that it was not actually an arch, but rather a representation of a rounded, shimmering form more reminiscent of a rainbow turned inward at the bottom. Within the rainbow itself was a half-seen landscape. I knew that landscape as Feirie.

The border was one repetition after another of the *Gate*.

CHAPTER 4

Imagine the ability to shuffle time and reality and make of them what you will. That was the power of the *Clothos* Deck, so named for the arcane plateau in Feirie where it was first found. No one, not even those high in Her Lady's Court, knew its origins. All that could be guessed was that it was the work of one of the first and most powerful spellweavers to rise in the nether world. Somehow, he, she, or it had tapped into the very essence of reality and bound a bit of it into the deck. Why the spellweaver had chosen a deck was a matter of the oft-twisted minds of those of Feirie. Possibly because the deck gave the potential outcomes more variation, possibly just because the deck's creator had been mad even beyond the standards of the dark realm.

Some said that the cards had been in part responsible for aiding man by drawing back Feirie's dominance and thus letting man rise. I didn't know how much truth there was in that nor who had wisely decided to scatter the cards throughout both worlds, but I did know too well what the power of *one* card had been when wielded by Oberon that last encounter. Razing the city, and the deaths that had resulted from it, had been necessary to prevent further catastrophe, but the card had left its mark. No one now recalled where the Chicago River had actually flowed or the entire city block—inhabitants included—near Wabash that had simply ceased to exist.

No one recalled it but me . . . and the dragon.

Oberon might be dead, but William Delke, either willingly or as a puppet, somehow served his legacy. I dared not say anything to Claryce, but I knew that somehow I had to get her far away from here.

"Nick?" She put a hand on my shoulder, steadying me. Only then did I realize I'd been shaking. Inside, the dragon was faring little better.

Fetch suddenly growled at a marble fireplace on the wall to the right of us. Although I could perceive nothing in the darkness within, I still felt the hair on my neck stiffen.

I tried to keep my expression and tone even. "I'd like to look around here. You can wait downstairs for me."

She did not leave. "You shouldn't even be in here. I can't just—"

"I'll just look around. I won't touch anything. There's probably nothing, but this way we can be certain."

Fetch tried to help by nudging her toward the door. Claryce finally nodded. When she was at the entrance, she glanced back a last time. "You won't be long?"

"One look around. That's all. I promise."

Fetch casually bumped against the door, pushing her toward the hall. Claryce shut the door, finally leaving us alone.

"What do you smell?" I asked Fetch.

"Wyld."

I waited for more, but the shapeshifter had nothing else to add. Fetch was basic; he had smelled Wyld. That was enough. Had he noticed anything more, he would have said so.

The Wyld had to be well-shielded or else I would've sensed it myself. Trying not to be distracted by that or by further thoughts concerning the cards and the Gate, I moved toward the fireplace. The scrollwork on the edge of the white mantle had a touch of the woodlands in it that reminded me just a bit too much of Feirie. The interior remained a black pit, so black I wondered if it had purposely been painted that way.

I began to sense the same otherworldliness that Fetch had. My hand stayed near the inside of my coat. I still couldn't pierce the darkness, and that bothered me.

Eye will show you . . .

I blinked and the world turned emerald . . . except in the fireplace.

Fetch growled a warning.

My hand thrust deep into my coat.

A tremendous suction pulled me toward the fireplace. Had I not been prepared for some threat, I would've sunk right into the darkness . . . the very Wyld I'd been seeking. Instead, I managed to twist enough to get my feet first. They slammed into the sides of the fireplace, shaking every bone in my body but for the moment bracing me against the suction. The strain was awful, but I knew that the other choice would be far worse.

Fetch's growling warned me that he was trying to come to my aid. "Keep back!"

There was nothing he could do for me, and getting closer would only serve to endanger him as well. This was no mere shadow dweller. This was a primal force from the darkest recesses of Feirie. The Wyld, those that crossed from Feirie without Her Lady's permission with dark purpose in mind, came in many forms. Yet, in more than a millennium and a half, I'd never seen a thing like this before . . . and if I survived, I hoped I'd never see one again.

The sword came out. I could see nothing to strike at, only the gaping blackness. It was as if I fought a hole, a very deadly hole.

My knees were about to buckle and my grip on the sword grew shaky.

Eye can help! Let me out!

It was tempting to let him take over, but the transformation would take too long and force me to release what remained of my footing. Yet, I couldn't see a target, couldn't find something to bury the point into.

Probably just what William Delke or whoever might be controlling him had planned.

I gritted my teeth as the agony grew. As one foot began to slip, I grew very tempted to throw away the weapon so that both hands would be free to make one last desperate grab for the mantle. It was the only sensible course left to me—

And then I realized that doing so was just what my true enemy intended.

I gripped the blade with both hands and pointed it at the center of the darkness . . . then leaned forward.

The powerful suction tore the last of my footing away. Instead of my feet going in, though, I dove headfirst, or rather *point* first.

Her Lady's gift sank into the darkness.

A deep moan thundered in my head. Something shook me so hard I almost lost the sword. I knew that doing so would be my end.

The suction magnified. I was certain I'd miscalculated for the last time.

Before I knew what was happening, I dropped hard on the fireplace's stone base. The drop knocked the air out of my lungs. All I understood was that I couldn't let go of the sword.

But then it finally dawned on me that there was no more suction. To that was added Fetch's cold nose prodding my cheek.

I looked up to see the gray black interior of a perfectly normal fireplace. Peering up only revealed the long, dark interior of the chimney.

A quick glance at the sword enabled me to just barely catch the last bit of black fading into the bright blade. My exhalation of relief echoed in the fireplace.

"Master Nicholas? Be you all right?"

"Yeah." I pushed myself out. The trap had lasted only a few moments—not even as long as my fight with the shadow dweller—but I felt as if I hadn't slept in weeks. My heart pounded wildly, and even my unseen companion appeared shaken.

But none of that compared with what awaited me when I turned around.

Fetched whined and with good reason. He should have noticed her first.

Her mouth agape, Claryce stared, not at me but at the sword in my hand. She shook but didn't faint, a credit to her, but a problem to me. Had she fainted, I could've convinced her that she'd been mistaken about anything she thought she had seen.

"I saw—there was *something* in that fireplace! I saw—no, I sensed it!" She looked at me. "Your eyes! And that sword! And Fetch! I heard him talk—"

"Woof," Fetch said unhelpfully.

I thrust the sword back inside my coat, at the same time forcing my own eyes to return. Claryce shook even more upon seeing the latter normal again.

"You shouldn't be in here!" I abruptly shouted, rushing toward her. "The gas leak's already getting to you! We've got to get downstairs fast—"

She shook off my hand as I tried to lead her to the door. "I know what I saw! I—"

A sharp pain struck me in the chest. I stumbled back, reaching inside the coat. Claryce went from anger back to confusion.

Her Lady's gift dropped to the floor, falling out of that magical place it hid when I didn't need it.

The blade was as black as the fireplace interior had been.

Fetch whined.

I tried to grab the hilt, but the point swung toward me. I barely backed away in time to avoid being cut by it.

"Nick! What's happening?"

That was a question I wanted an answer to. "Get out of here, Claryce!"

Pain again jolted me. I opened the coat and saw more of the blackness spreading over my side and waist. At the same time, a horrifying chill began to spread through me.

I stumbled back, which inadvertently saved me from another slash by the animated sword. I had been tricked. I had been made to believe that I'd vanquished the Wyld as I had so many other creatures of Feirie before. Never had I had one that could not only resist the gift's sinister power but seize it.

Someone had searched long and hard for this particular fiend.

Eye can help! my companion roared as loud as he could in my head. *Eye can help!*

The cold crept over me at a faster and faster rate. I felt as if I were falling and falling and falling.

With no other choice, I allowed him to help me. He briefly railed at not being given more freedom but then struck at our common foe.

My left hand twisted, changed. I'd long ago gotten used to the pain that came with any change, but the added burden of the growing chill made me groan hard. I felt as if my fingers were being torn out one by one.

Through tearing eyes, I watched the scaled hand rake the sword with long, sharp claws. With each strike of the claws, the gleam of Her Lady's gift returned to those areas. The blade's animation slowed.

With the threat lessened there, he brought the hand to my side and slashed once more. I groaned louder, but although the claws dug deep, no blood or bits of flesh spilled from the spot. Instead, shreds of darkness fell away, leaving in their wake my whole flesh. As that happened, the chill started to recede.

He slashed a final time, inside taking some satisfaction at the physical discomfort he caused me in the process. More of the darkness dropped like silken ribbons to the floor. Once there, it melted away as if it had never existed.

Weak but cleansed of the taint, I let him return to the sword. With two quick slices, he rent the Wyld from the blade as if wiping grime off the unique metal.

I watched with relief as the last lingering foulness faded away. Someone had planned well for me but hadn't taken my companion into account.

The scaled hand suddenly grabbed the hilt. That had not been my choice but rather his. I tried to regain control. Unfortunately, my exhaustion was still too great.

I realized only then that *he* had expected just that.

From somewhere behind me, Fetch growled. I knew that he was growling at me—or rather, at the dragon.

"Nick?" Claryce couldn't know exactly what was wrong with me, only that something really bad *was*. She took hold of my left arm.

I—the dragon—turned to glare at her. Claryce gasped and took a step back but then steadied herself. She reached forward again.

My treacherous companion eyed her with suspicion. Knowing who she was, he could not immediately decide what best to do with her.

Before he could decide some possibly monstrous fate for her, I fought for mastery again. This time, I found the strength. He roared silently as he receded within me. My hand returned to normal, and I knew that my eyes had done the same.

But, meeting Claryce's gaze, I understood that everything else would be different.

"What are you?" she asked in a remarkably calm voice. "What happened here . . . and don't tell me I've inhaled gas!"

Inside, the dragon chuckled at my dismay. I let my anger at him be known with a number of silent expletives that would've shocked someone who had known me as long as Diocles.

Eye do not fear you, he retorted. *Eye am beyond your threats . . . beyond any of your weapons . . . even the accursed spear which slew me . . .*

It frustrated me to admit that in many ways he was right. I chose to do as I often did in such arguments and focused again on Claryce.

"It'd be best if you forgot all about this. Actually, it'd be best if you left Chicago forever."

She gave me a look that ended any further discussion about departures. That was a trait I knew too well from every incarnation of her. Again, the dragon snickered.

"I'll ask you one more time." Claryce glanced at Fetch. "Tell me everything . . . including why I heard him speaking."

This time, Fetch managed a more natural bark, but it was too little too late. He looked apologetically at me, but I shook my head. This wasn't his fault. It was mine. I'd been tricked. Yes, I might've died, but it was also clear to me that, failing that happening, someone had set forth a challenge. They were being blatant in their disregard for secrecy. Secrecy was a strong trait in the Wyld, in all creatures of Feirie. Even more than among man, the struggle for power over another was constant not only in Her Lady's court but throughout the realm.

Once again, I thought of William Delke.

I hid the sword. Claryce's eyes widened briefly, but she remained stolid otherwise. I admired that. "Obviously, you weren't imagining that something was watching you."

"But what was it? How did you know where it was?"

"Fetch noted it first. Collectively, they're called the Wyld."

"'Wild'?"

I spelled it for her. "All the legends, all the stories of fairies—the old ones, not the cute, fanciful ones in children's books—have a basis of truth. This thing was from that realm. Feirie. A place ruled by Her Lady."

She frowned. "Their queen? Is that what they call her?"

Exhaling, I tried to give her the short answer. "We call her Her Lady because to call her by her name is to gain her attention."

Fetch whined his agreement. A mistake. She looked at him again. "And is he one of the—the Wyld?"

"Yes and no."

"You speak," Claryce insisted to the shapeshifter. "Don't deny it."

She continued to display the steel with which I remembered Cleolinda and the more than half a dozen other incarnations. Fetch sought my approval, which I gave with a grudging nod.

"I do speak, mistress, when near enough to Master Nicholas. But I'm all Jake, all white. You can trust me . . ."

Claryce's brow deepened, and she looked at me.

"Yes," I answered her unspoken question. "He *does* talk like that."

"I'm eggs in the coffee," Fetch added eagerly, apparently trying to win her over with every expression he thought might work.

Evidently, it did the trick. This time, Claryce didn't even bat an eye. Instead, she smiled. That earned her a strong tail wag. Thankfully, for the moment she didn't ask more about his background.

Unfortunately, now that she was done with Fetch, that left her with one subject. "And who are you, Nick? Are you also from Feirie?"

She asked in a tone that indicated she doubted that. A number of stories—all false—rushed through my thoughts. Yet, somehow, I couldn't lie to her. I could omit some things, but I couldn't lie to her.

"I guard the Gate. The path between our world and Feirie."

Claryce wouldn't let it stop there. I'd hoped she would but had doubted I'd be that lucky. "You guard the way. What about that— what about that other part of you? Who are you really? How long have you been doing this?"

Tell her not! my companion insisted. I told him to stay quiet. His insistence only spurred my desire to open up more, even though this was exactly what I hadn't wanted earlier.

"I'm a soldier. I've been a soldier for well over sixteen hundred years. I served as a tribune in the Roman Empire, though my family was Christian. During that time, I encountered a beast. A dragon."

"A dragon? They exist, too?"

"They have always been few and they serve neither man nor Feirie. They are said to be older than both, though even they don't know."

We were first . . . and first to be enslaved! snarled the dragon.

I kept to the story. "I slew the dragon, not realizing that he'd been set to guard the gate. There needs to be a balance between the worlds. Without a guardian, without a way of keeping both sides from flowing too much into the other, everything risked destruction."

Claryce glanced at Fetch, who nodded at the truthfulness of my answers. Who exactly I was, I still didn't want her to know. That might be too much and might eventually lead to the truth about herself.

"The blood of the dragon had mixed with my own. It brought us together, so to speak. It enabled me to take up the mantle, which I've willingly done since then."

The dragon raged more, furious at so much detail given, even if so much remained hidden from her. With all the magic surrounding me, there was no way I could avoid telling her something. Whichever of Oberon's followers was behind this had discovered her first and had intended from the beginning to toss her into the situation. My best hope was to convince her of the partial truth and pray that it would serve to scare her away. I had no choice but to face my foe, but I still believed there might be a small chance of keeping this incarnation of the princess alive.

"I don't know why . . . but I believe you." Claryce took a step back to the door. As she did, she looked up at the border. "You mentioned something about cards. What was—"

I was saved from having to explain the Clothos Deck by a tapping at the window. The three of us looked there to see a large black bird pecking intently at the window.

"We need to leave," I quietly but firmly commanded. Fetch had already passed her to take point at the entranceway. I moved to take her hand—a necessity to make certain we didn't become separated, I told myself.

"What is that?" she demanded as we moved. "Is that bird after us? Is it something like what was in the fireplace?"

"No, it's another associate." Fetch was not the only exile who helped me on occasion. The bird—for lack of a better word to describe what it really was—had come through, along with several other refugees, during the chaos just before the Great Fire. Even after so many decades, I knew little about it, just as I knew little about most of the other exiles and escapees. Fetch was one of the few with a past I shared.

The black bird helped me when it was so inclined. I'd contacted it just before heading here and hinted that this might be the work of one of Oberon's followers. That had been enough.

We darted down the stairs, but not before I hesitated at the oldest of the Delke portraits. Something drew me to the painting, despite the black bird's warning. I peered at the tiny book held by the founder of the Delke dynasty.

But it wasn't a book. It was the back of a playing card.

I pushed us on to the next painting below, then hesitated once more. Sure enough, the son of the first Delke held a card of the same design.

"I hear someone," Claryce whispered.

Below us, Fetch let out a very low, almost inaudible growl. He needn't have bothered. I could hear the intruders as well. A moment later, the shadows of a trio of hoods moved toward the bottom of the staircase. I couldn't see the shadows' owners, but they had to be close. Fortunately, at this point that meant that neither could they see us.

Someone spoke. I couldn't make out the words, but what was even more important was the accents. Not the hint of Italian I'd thought would come from thugs hailing from the South Side, but the Irish brogue from the North.

It was too coincidental that a trio of North Siders—probably tied to Weiss and his partners—would risk entering so deep into Outfit territory—those sections of Chicago controlled until recently by Papa Johnny—to sneak into Delke's house just at this moment. Neither Wyld nor their human counterparts were above hiring muscle. Sometimes, there were things that magic could not do that simple force could.

One shadow halted, but the other two continued on toward where we hid. The silhouettes grew more distinct, if not also more distorted. I could see that the pair were armed, at least one with a barreled weapon I suspected was a tommy. As a former soldier, I could appreciate its power but not the fact that it gave beasts on two legs the ability to deal death indiscriminately.

"Keep back!" I whispered to Claryce. Fetch, now near the bottom of the steps, suddenly backed up. His ears flattened, and I could see his distress, though I was certain it had nothing to do with a pair of hoods.

But then the shadows moved even nearer to the steps and I saw why Fetch was so distressed.

The shadows were not attached to bodies.

CHAPTER 5

The shadows stretched along the far wall as they moved, their shapes further distorting. The second had what was probably a revolver, but the weapons didn't bother me as much as what the shadows themselves were capable of. I'd not seen this magic before, but I knew that it had to be bad.

"Is there another way out from the upper floors?"

"There's a fire escape."

I signaled Fetch to come up. I wasn't the type to sacrifice an ally of any sort. He rushed past us, doing so not out of fright but because again he took the point ahead. The fire escape might be a safe way out, but, then again, it might be exactly where our visitors wanted us to go.

As blatant as this trap was, it in no way risked whoever was behind it to public scrutiny. They knew that I didn't dare do anything to draw attention to myself from outsiders. I did eye a phone in the hall as we reached the third floor, but although it was one of the newer, pricier carriage types, quickly snatching up the combination handset and listening verified that the line was dead.

"Was this working before?"

"Yes."

I replaced the handset and rushed with Claryce toward where she'd indicated the fire escape. As we passed through her suite, I eyed the border there again. Everything about this situation struck me as a taunt. My foe knew me well, which meant that he had to have been part of Oberon's inner circle. I could count the possible number of survivors on one hand with fingers left, but none of them struck me as having this sort of mocking mentality. The Wyld preferred torture over taunting, the more monstrous the better. Yes, many of them enjoyed teasing their victims, just not in such a manner. This was more human . . . which brought me again to William Delke, who might be better able to deal with North Side gangsters like Weiss or his partners—"Schemer" Drucci and, more volatile and the only Irishman of the trio, "Bugs" Moran.

Fetch had already made it to the fire escape. However, he did not leap out onto it, which boded ill. I tried to surreptitiously peek below, only to have a single shot nearly give me a second part in my hair. Whether by magic or mundane means, our pursuers intended to take us.

"What do we do now?" Claryce asked.

Let me free! was my invisible companion's incessant suggestion. Doing so would only add fire to the fuel, so to speak, as he would likely try to bathe the entire area in flames. I didn't need that any more than this situation.

Fetch had backed away when I'd moved to the fire escape, and now he growled low behind us. I didn't need to be told what he was growling at.

The first shadow entered the suite.

For a moment, the silhouette of the tommy gun sharpened greatly. I knew something was going to happen. I doubted that the shadow gun would be firing anything as simple as bullets and threw both Claryce and myself behind the bed.

An unsettling *phut-phut-phut* noise repeated itself over and over. Fetch crouched down near us. I looked up and saw black splotches in the wall near where we'd been standing. They weren't bullet holes but inky dots that caused the areas they touched to decay. I didn't want to think what they would've done to flesh.

The noise ceased. It would've been nice to think that the shadows had left. I didn't hold my breath.

I tapped the floor once. Fetch, who had a better view of the room, peered at me. I gestured toward the door. He looked that way, then let his tail sweep once to the right.

With care, I drew the sword. Claryce shook her head. I ignored her. Fetch let out a low grunt, the signal I'd been waiting for.

I leaped up over the bed, slashing hard as I did. On the surface, my act appeared a suicidal one, the sword not possibly long enough to reach a target on the other side. Her Lady's gift was no ordinary blade, though. Its slash stretched far beyond its mundane length, the only reason I could attempt what still might mean my doom.

Fetch had pointed me true. The shadow of the gunman pressed against the wall nearest to the headboard, the outline of the tommy stretched forward.

The blade cut a swathe across the silhouette of the barrel. I'd hoped for better, but was happy to watch the bit of shadow fall away and fade to nothing.

The shadow figure peered down at the ruined weapon, then at me as I raised the sword for another cut. Ghostly fingers let the rest of the tommy fall, then brought both hands together. One hand moved as if removing something from the fingers of the other.

The silhouette vanished.

Fetch jumped past me. The second shadow stood by the door, the gun raised. The shapeshifter snapped at the second intruder, only to fall *past* the silhouette. Still, the shadow reacted like a living man, pulling back in surprise at the unexpected attack. The shadow turned to fire at Fetch.

This time, I struck true. The edge of the blade cut through the wrist of the hand holding the gun.

The outline of the hand and the weapon dropped away, fading as had the barrel of the tommy.

Somewhere outside, a man screamed.

I had barely cut off the hand when the rest of the shadow disappeared as well. I could only surmise that the severed hand wore whatever enabled the gunmen to cast their shadows separate from their bodies.

"Billy's mitt!" a raspy voice blurted from the downstairs hall. "Lookit Billy's mitt!"

"Pipe down and snatch that thing—"

A car horn blared. The goons shut up. Footsteps receded into the distance. With them went the moans of the one gunman.

Sirens rose in the distance. Someone had alerted the police. Before they could arrive, I raced down the steps to the front entrance. Just outside, I came to a halt. An oddly small pool of blood dripped down the front step, but there was no sign of any severed hand.

The black bird alighted on my shoulder. "Follow? Follow?"

"If you wish."

The avian took off after the car. I quickly returned to Claryce, who had just reached the bottom. Her expression made me halt; the fear in her face was all for me.

The sirens grew louder. I hid the sword in my coat and joined her as we both waited for the police.

But to our surprise, the sirens continued past. Their wail died shortly after, as if the emergency was over.

Fetch gazed up at me in bewilderment. I couldn't blame him.

"One of the neighbors must've told them where the shot came from!" Claryce insisted. "Why didn't the police stop here? They had to have known where to go!"

There was only one answer that made sense to me. I gritted my teeth. "Your employer has pull. Someone ordered the officers to leave it be."

"The police wouldn't listen to an order like that . . . would they?" She shut her mouth at my look. This was Chicago, after all, even with William "Decent Dever" Dever mayor for two years after the nod-and-wink reign of "Big Bill" Thompson. Corruption was rife, with both Capone and the North Siders greasing many uniformed pockets.

Chicago had many names, some good, some not good, some not repeatable in public. One of those, just roughly twenty years past the

Fire, had been meant as a sneering critique of a grand lily white display at the Columbian Exposition. The clever writers who had come up with the Black City had, at the time, no idea just how accurate that name actually was. Not just because of the likes of Capone or Moran in this generation, but especially because of the shadow folk. And, of course, because of men like William Delke, whose lives and ambitions affected both sides of the Gate.

We evidently weren't about to be interrupted by the police, but I didn't want to wait and see if my unknown foe had something else in mind here. "Is there anywhere safe you can go?"

"'Safe'?" A number of emotions crossed her face. Here was a woman who had lived a fairly secure life, had made a good career for herself, only to find everything turned upside down in an instant. She had just discovered that she could not even trust her own boss . . . or whoever controlled him, whatever the case might have been. "I don't know . . ."

I thought quickly. "There's somewhere I can take you. You should be secure there."

"Can't I just go to my own home?"

"You know better than that—"

The phone rang. The phone so conveniently dead minutes ago.

Fetch growled at the one nearest us. Claryce and I studied one another, then, before I could stop her, she took up the handset.

"Hello?" To her credit, she kept her tone even.

I watched as she listened for a few moments. With a nod, Claryce then answered, "Yes . . . yes, of course. I'll certainly be there."

She listened again. With a last nod, she added, "I'll see you then."

With some hesitation, she hung up. "That was *William*."

My brow arched. "What did he want?"

"He reminded me—he reminded me—" Claryce put a hand to her head in exhaustion. "Excuse me . . ."

I was at her side in a breath. "Let me help you."

She gratefully accepted my arm around her. I tried to hide how uncomfortable I felt doing it. This close, there were too many reminders of what I had lost the previous times I'd failed to protect Cleolinda's incarnations.

Steadying herself, Claryce went on. "William reminded me that there's a gathering tomorrow. He needs me to deliver some papers I've been working on to him there. That's all. He also apologized for not calling me sooner, but he's been—been under the weather."

Or setting all this up, I thought. "Where is this gathering?"

She swallowed. "The Tribune Tower. The company has a major office there."

A very public place. I couldn't see the danger in her being there, but neither did I trust that all would be as simple as it sounded. "You needn't go."

"No. I think I will. I have to—I have to make sense of all of this."

Claryce was strong, just as I always knew every incarnation to be, but there was something different. I couldn't put my finger on it, except to say there was a resiliency that seemed stronger. I wondered if I hadn't noticed it in the previous variations, but I doubted that.

It doesn't matter! I reprimanded myself. *Get her away from all this. That's all that's important at the moment . . .*

There was only one place I could think of for tonight, a place I trusted and that the Wyld could not enter.

I only hoped Father Jonathan wouldn't mind.

"I'm not certain I can do this, Nick," the priest replied.

"You've got those two extra rooms in the back where Father Peter's sister stayed for her convalescence during the Spanish Influenza epidemic. You're not using them, are you?"

He pondered. "No. Not at all. And it's not that I don't want to help a woman in need—"

"This isn't necessary," insisted Claryce. "Nick, William wouldn't—"

"William might be unaware of the North Side's kidnap plot," I interjected, before she could say too much. "Until we're sure they've given up on you, you need a place they'd never look."

"Illicit booze, illegal gambling, murder, and kidnapping!" Father Jonathan looked aghast. "What a terrible and bloody century this has been so far! I pray that peace prevails over the rest of it! At least we shall never see anything as monstrous as the Great War . . ."

I cleared my throat. "Father . . . can you house her here or not?"

"It's not that I don't want to, but there's only myself here at the moment. It might not look proper, you see."

"What about Mrs. Gelb? Could you ask her to stay for a few extra days?" The widow acted as Father Jonathan's housekeeper, staying a few days at a time every couple weeks. No one would ever think anything improper between the young priest and the gray-haired matron. Mrs. Gelb carried a candle for her late husband, a major lost in the Great War.

Giving Claryce another glance, the priest pondered more. With reluctance, Father Jonathan finally acquiesced. "I'll give her a call." To Claryce, he added, "In the meantime, let me make sure the eastern room can be used tonight. That would be the best for you."

The eastern room was also the farthest of the two from the good father's own chambers. Father Jonathan was a very devout man—perhaps even more so than his predecessor—but there were always those who might gossip nonetheless.

I was grateful for his help. There are places that the Wyld cannot touch or enter, churches among them. All creatures of Feirie have the Old Magic flowing through their veins—even if technically some didn't have veins—and as such they were affected by blessed places. They were also affected to a lesser degree by any structure with sufficient iron in it, but the only place with enough iron would've been a jail cell.

That made me think of Cortez. Considering the sudden disinterest by the police in the happenings at Delke's house, I think I understood the inspector's special assignment. Mayor Dever had sworn to clean up a lot of the corruption ignored by the previous administration, and with so many untrustworthy officers he would've been desperate enough to even turn to an outsider like Cortez. If the inspector was looking into corruption on the South Side and neighboring regions, he might just hear about the questionable decision by someone to avoid the Delke situation.

I pushed aside the potential trouble with Cortez for the moment. Claryce would be safe, providing she stayed here as I asked. She'd agreed reluctantly earlier and that reluctance was growing before my eyes.

With the priest momentarily gone, Claryce sat down in the front pew while I peered past her, supposedly watching the front entrance. Instead, I glared at Diocles, who was staring at her back with a brooding expression. I could imagine some of the things he was thinking.

Claryce abruptly looked back. Even though he was invisible to ordinary people, Diocles instinctively vanished.

"Who was that?"

Ordinary people. "Who was who?"

She looked up at me. "I thought I saw—never mind. I guess this has been just too mad a day for me."

"You'll be able to rest here. I'll come for you tomorrow. We'll get the papers Delke asked for and take it from there."

"I just can't believe that William would be involved in something so—so impossible!"

There was nothing I could say.

Father Jonathan came back. "The room is usable. I also gave Mrs.

Gelb a call. The dear lady says that she can stay as long as needed. She'll be over shortly. She can help the young lady better arrange the room, and maybe clean it up a bit."

"Thank you, father." Claryce rose and turned back to me. "Thank you, too, Nick. I—I'll see you in the morning, I guess."

Before I could stop her, she leaned forward and kissed me on the cheek. I stood there wordlessly as Claryce followed the good father away.

"Once more caught in the web, Georgius?" murmured Diocles from behind me.

"Nick," I reminded him almost absently. For a moment, I relived the kiss on the cheek. A simple act, more grateful than passionate, but it remained with me.

"She will perish again, and you may do so, too, while futilely trying to prevent her end."

I turned on the ghost. "Be quiet, Diocles."

"Nick—"

This time, I walked right through him. He said nothing more as I left the church.

Fetch awaited me outside. "She'll be all right, Master Nicholas?"

"She should be."

"What if it sends more muscle? Mortals, I mean."

He chose to use the word "it" since we weren't yet sure exactly who or what was ultimately responsible, but I had been contemplating the same question. I hadn't dared mention the obvious to Claryce or else she might have refused even staying on the church grounds and followed me instead. While the Wyld could not enter a blessed area, their mortal servants generally could.

"They don't know where she's staying. We'll settle this before they find out."

"Tomorrow?"

"Maybe. If all goes well."

The dragon chuckled at my desperate optimism. I said nothing to him.

We were halfway to the house when fluttering above warned me of the black bird's return. The avian materialized out of the night sky, alighting on my arm.

"Did you trail them?"

"Yes, yes."

"Can you lead me there?" I lost all interest in rest. Perhaps I could end this tonight.

"No, no. The way is lost, the way is lost."

Fetch snorted. "Lost them, did ye?" He sniffed both in disdain and to show off his muzzle. "Next time, best leave tracking to those of us with a beezer, not a beak!"

The black bird snapped at him. "Shunned, fool! Shunned!"

Shunned. I understood better now. The gunmen had carried some sort of talisman to keep anyone from following them. The artifact would've eventually made any pursuer inadvertently turn the wrong way and thus lose the trail.

"Thank you for trying. Will you help me tomorrow?" I quickly told it what I needed.

"Yes, yes," it answered confidently.

"Appreciate that."

The avian cawed once, then took to the black sky. Fetch and I continued on. I hadn't expected much from the bird's attempt, but I was still disappointed.

The neighborhood was quiet when we arrived there, most good folk long asleep. I was glad for the silence, my mind on what tomorrow might entail. The question still remained as to Delke's part in this. Claryce saw him as a victim; I had seen too many greedy mortals to believe him to be innocent. There was still that chance that she was right, though, and tomorrow would tell.

I hoped.

Fetch growled.

An engine revved. I summoned the dragon's eyes in the hopes of seeing better in the dark, but only caught sight of a dark auto vanishing in the distance ahead. Fetch started after it, but I whistled the shapeshifter back.

"It was parked in front of your place, Master Nicholas," he muttered.

That was something I *had* seen. I picked up my pace. Through the dragon's eyes, I surveyed the area.

And there it was, on the front step.

A hand.

A hand, on closer inspection, that had been neatly cauterized at the end.

The hand, I knew, of the hood whose shadow I'd severed.

CHAPTER 6

I burned the hand in the old furnace in the cellar, not to hide any evidence but because there was always the chance that the severed appendage might have some spell attached to it. Neither the dragon nor I could sense anything, but it was better not to take a chance.

It was possible that the hand had simply been left as a message. Certainly, it was proof again that whoever was behind this knew me so well he could even penetrate the protections surrounding the house. I was glad that I hadn't fallen victim to my first impulse, which would've been to hide Claryce here.

When the last ashes had cooled, I went upstairs and took a brief nap. The next thing I knew, the phone rang. The sun hadn't come up yet. Fetch, who had stayed for once, looked up alertly, but I waved a calming hand. This was a phone call I'd been expecting.

"Kravayik?"

"As you have asked, I make my weekly call. I know we spoke this week already, but—"

"But you did the right thing." When first he'd taken his post, I'd asked Kravayik to contact me once a week and report anything, however minute, that seemed out of the ordinary.

"I thank you for saying so. I must report, though, that nothing is amiss."

"You're absolutely certain?" With all going on, I was warier than ever.

"I have kept my eyes watching all, Master Nicholas. I will swear on my lowly life, if that is enough."

"There's no need for that." Kravayik took his task with deathly seriousness.

"You are so very kind, so very kind."

I grimaced. "You're doing *me* a great favor. You're the one being kind." Before he could argue that, I added, "Best to keep a really good eye on it until I tell you otherwise. Something's up. Understand?"

"Yes, very much, I do, Master Nicholas! I will double—no, *triple*—my most best efforts! I swear upon my—"

"I believe you. That's good enough. Thank you again, Kravayik."

He thanked me in turn three more times before I was able to get off the phone. I turned on the radio and let the news blare as I readied myself. However, other than a brief comment on John Scopes's appeal against his guilty verdict for teaching evolution in Tennessee despite the Butler Act, nothing attracted my attention. Even the so-called "Monkey Trial" wouldn't have been of interest to me save for one of Scopes's attorneys, Clarence Darrow. I had no doubt that he in turn still recalled me from our run-in during the Leopold and Loeb case last year, a dark case with touches of Feirie to it. Darrow knew some of the truth, enough to despise me even though he *had* managed to get his clients off with life plus ninety-nine years.

I left the house with Fetch, who immediately ran off. Most cabbies were not happy carting a beast like him around, even if the "owner" was there to handle him, so Fetch would run along and meet us at the address given to Claryce by Delke. Fetch did not tire as fast as a true dog or wolf. He was also stealthy, meaning no one would likely notice him scurrying through town.

I saw no sign of the black bird, but I assumed I would at some point by the time we reached the Tribune Tower.

I returned to St. Michael's to find Claryce anxious but ready. We had gathered some clothes for her before leaving Delke's house. She smiled in relief upon seeing me, a smile that sent my blood surging despite my efforts to remain detached. That, naturally, brought a mocking chuckle in my head.

Claryce and I took another cab to Delke's main offices, a non-descript building located near the American Furniture Mart on Lake

Shore Drive. I remained with her as she retrieved the files without incident, then we headed southwest to the Tribune Tower on North Michigan. Three years back the tower's design had been part of a huge international contest, with the winner a Finnish architect by the name Saarinen who'd come up with a radical, simplified tower without all the neo-Gothic decor of so many other buildings. The tower rose up sleekly into the sky, each succeeding layer smaller but still pushing toward the clouds. There'd been arguments for another design favoring the neo-Gothic, but Saarinen's design, almost like something out of a science fiction story, had prevailed.

And, somewhere in there, I would at last meet—or actually just observe—William Delke.

At my suggestion we got out a block before the building. I caught sight of a dark gray-brown form slipping among the unseeing throngs filling the sidewalks. That Fetch could be more or less invisible around so many people showed that a touch of his true Feirie nature remained even in the mortal world.

Sleek Duesenbergs, gleaming Rolls-Royces, and stately Lincolns lined the front of the tower as other businessmen arrived. I was surprised to see that this was a more formal affair than I'd calculated, and, while Claryce could easily mingle among such, I stuck out a bit with my coat and worn clothing. I was used to not standing out as a matter of safety and, after so long, habit.

Even the two surly harps watching the doors as Delke's associates entered were better dressed. They had the look of North Side goons and in fact I recognized one as a particular associate of Moran. I didn't doubt that Bugs in particular had a big hand in all this—his ambition to extend the North Side territory was even greater than that of his cohorts. I noticed no weapons, but the fine jackets they wore probably concealed at least a gun and knife apiece.

"I think you should go in alone, Claryce. I'll find another, less busy entrance."

She nodded reluctantly, then moved on. As she reached the entrance, the "doormen" initially gave her a cursory glance, then shared a pair of admiring grins as they more closely watched her enter.

Once she was well inside, I headed to the far side of the building. I was confident in Claryce's safety for now, which gave me the opportunity to locate Fetch. I found him around a corner, in the shadow of the tower, munching on something. He immediately swallowed the entire meal, then looked sheepish.

"Fetch . . ." I reproved.

"A rodent, Master Nicholas!" the shapeshifter promised, his ears flattened. "Only a dirty rat! No feline or hound, I swear!"

I wasn't angry about that, although I was glad to hear him swear it was nothing more than a rat. "I don't need you distracted. Understand?"

"Yes. I do. I am so sorry."

"Never mind." I heard a caw from high above. The black bird perched near one of the windows high above. I didn't have to tell it anything more; once I was inside, it would head up until it found a window giving it the best view of whatever was going on inside.

Delke had made no comment to Claryce about her needing to remain once she brought the papers. Of course, he hadn't mentioned these other arrivals, either. I hoped I would be able to evade Delke's muscle for as long as we had to stay here.

For the lock on the nearby door, I had to rely on the dragon's power. It was only a minute of use, but I could still feel him seeking some way to get a further hold over me. We were, and would always be, reluctant allies and possibly always enemies.

Even more than fifteen hundred years hadn't changed the last.

With Fetch trailing close behind me, I entered the building. Once in the main corridor, it wasn't difficult to mingle with the general population, as the tower was a beehive of activity. With so many news people about, many of the conversations had to do with what was happening not only in the Windy City but in the world beyond. While much of the talk had to do with some grand national monument planned for the desolate Black Hills of South Dakota, the name Capone was bandied about more than once. "Papa Johnny" Torrio's retirement after his near assassination had left his top man and heir apparent, Capone, completely in charge of the South Siders. However, there were rumblings that the North Side—especially Weiss and Moran—didn't plan on letting him live long enough to enjoy the throne.

Thinking of the North Side boys already so cozy with Delke made me wonder if those rumbling might be right soon. I hadn't picked up any word of Capone's side having dealings with the Wyld, so if Delke was truly connected with the Feirie, the South Side was going to be seeing a lot of blood. I considered the fact of Delke's new house being down there. Maybe that had been the first step into enemy territory.

Yet, somehow I knew this had to be more than just a magic-fueled bootlegger war.

Ignoring the elevators, I headed to the utility stairway. Fetch, once more all but invisible to the crowds despite his immense size, quickly entered with me. As a creature of Feirie, he had the ability to almost always be at the peripheral of a human's vision, one of those things in the corner of the eye one generally pays little mind to. Still, I was grateful when the two of us were away from the crowds again.

Eye could have brought us here easier, my eternal companion haughtily reminded me.

No major magic this near. Remember? I chided him. On the off-chance I hadn't been noticed yet, I wanted to keep any magic to a minimum. The brief and minor spell to open the locked door had been necessary, but that was the extent to which I wanted to push matters.

The dragon said nothing more, but I knew that he thought me a fool. He would have gone in with all his great physical and magical might at the forefront, tearing apart his enemies with teeth, claws, and spells.

And, as he had back in long-lost Silene, he would've perished against a more prepared foe.

Two floors below our destination, I had Fetch move ahead. He slunk up out of sight, returning a few moments later.

"One goon," the shapeshifter reported quietly. "Carries a piece in his jacket." He bared his sharp, sharp teeth. "Shall I take him?"

I ignored his eagerness for a kill. "No magic surrounding him?"

"I smelled nothing but his scent. The rat smelled better."

"Lure him down here."

With a slight glance of disappointment, Fetch trotted up out of sight again. A moment later, I heard his whine of surprise, followed by his stumbling down the steps again.

The goon's heavy steps followed. He probably just wondered why a huge dog was loose in the stairwell and had no fear of leaving his post just to go down a short distance.

Fetch ran past me. I spun around to face the startled guard, who reached into his jacket as I lunged.

But what he pulled out was no gun. It gleamed like dark steel and was shaped like a wolf's claw.

I knew black silver when I saw it. A precious and deadly metal found only in Feirie. I also knew what it would do to me if it tasted my blood.

He took a step back up as he drew the claw. I shoved my shoulder into his legs. The goon toppled over me, hitting the steps below hard. Somehow, though, he managed to keep hold of the claw. Half-stunned, he swung the artifact wildly in my direction as he tried to rise.

Fetch clamped his jaws around the wrist and pulled the arm back. I used the moment to kick the goon in the chin. He fell back, the claw flying beyond Fetch and clattering on the steps below.

Fetch released the unconscious guard's wrist. To his credit, the shapeshifter hadn't drawn more than a few drops of blood.

"What do we do with him, Master Nicholas?"

"Leave him." I went down to where the claw lay. Or should've lain. It was nowhere to be found, even when I surveyed it through the dragon's eyes. It was possible that there had been a spell on the piece so that it would fade away if lost, but there was also the chance that it had returned to whoever was in command.

I hurried back up the steps. Fetch followed me to the door, then hung back. He knew that here was where he had to wait.

As a precaution, I said, "No snack."

He glanced back at the unconscious guard. "Not even if he begins to wake?"

"He won't . . . and I've warned you on this."

The shapeshifter cowered. "Yes, Master Nicholas! Yes. I will be white . . . good."

"You *are* good. You just need to keep reminding yourself."

He wagged his tail at this. Despite his insidious background, Fetch had a code of honor not nearly as tricky and convoluted as most from Feirie. If he said he would follow instructions, he would follow instructions. He wouldn't constantly try to find loopholes like most of the others.

Finally satisfied, I slipped through the door and into the corridor. My original intention had been to locate a vantage point overseeing the office doors and hope to spy William Delke as Claryce maneuvered him into view. Instead, I found myself in a hallway filled with people whose suits and cigars indicated that they were all part of the same gathering. By their numbers, I could see that Delke's office would be so crowded that he would have to stand outside for me to even get a glimpse.

I strode past a pair of businessmen exiting one of the elevators. Their small talk concerned how best to profit off the rash of tornadoes that'd ripped through the Midwest a few months earlier. They didn't say a word about the hundreds killed, just the potential to move in and find new business opportunities. I gathered Delke Industries would have a strong hand in whatever enterprise they chose. At this point, I also wondered if it had had a strong hand in the tornadoes themselves.

Two more goons stood near the elevators, but their attention was on new arrivals there, and the slight glamour I finally reluctantly used made the one that glanced my direction miss me entirely. That I even had to borrow this much of the dragon's power was a risk. My unseen companion silently chided me for needing him, but I ignored him as another elevator opened and out walked a most unexpected guest.

Big Bill Thompson might not've been mayor anymore, but he didn't act as if he knew that. A full-figured man in stripes, with a strong double-chin and a face like a determined hound, he did not seem like the kind of man who'd controlled Chicago. Surrounded by half a dozen fawning cronies and wearing his famous cowboy hat, he walked with chin high toward the Delke offices. The parting of the crowd ahead of him only served to add to his appearance of a king among his subjects . . . a king, though, who had clearly come to see an emperor. I doubted that Big Bill had anything to do with my investigation, but it did tell me that Dever was going to be facing a rematch come next election.

Moran's goons seemed uninterested in Big Bill's appearance—a curious thing since there were rumors he was tight with Capone. Of course, should Thompson get reelected next time around, that would aid both the North and South Siders. Delke obviously had some sway over both major gangs, which boded even more ill.

The attending businessmen greeted Thompson even as they gave way. Thompson shook hands as if already running again, but he kept on the move toward the offices.

Just before he reached the doorway, Claryce exited. She hesitated when she saw Big Bill and, even though he was married, the ex-mayor tipped his hat, then paused to take her hand—though she hadn't offered it—and kiss the fingers.

I gritted my teeth, earning a mocking laugh from the dragon. *Eye thought you weren't going to fall prey to her this time . . .*

I had no chance for a reprimand, Big Bill at that moment saying to Claryce, "You make for a charming greeting, little lady! Are you to guide me to the good Mr. Delke?"

"No, I—"

"Never a guide, however lovely, for such a prestigious guest," came a deep voice from behind Claryce that made me stand alert. I cautiously strengthened the glamour, to prevent any chance of Delke noticing me.

Claryce's boss appeared at the door. He thrust a hand at Thompson, who took it eagerly. I couldn't see Delke completely, but what little was visible matched the photo and so far gave no hint of anything out of the ordinary.

The half-seen businessman guided Big Bill in before him, then paused to signal a guard near the door. Again, Delke remained only partially visible among those crowding toward the door after Thompson. I was only mildly irritated. I hadn't sensed anything unusual. Thus far, Delke looked to be either a willing pawn or a dupe of some Wyld who had remained far from this gathering. I began to wonder if I'd been played a fool again. There seemed no reason for me to be here.

But as Big Bill entered, Delke paused to speak with Claryce. With the growing rumble of voices, I couldn't make out what he said, but it seemed a courteous dismissal. Claryce nodded and started moving against the flow of silk suits and spats.

And it was then that a brief break in the crowd finally left William Delke fully exposed. I studied him intently.

He suddenly stared back . . . and smiled darkly.

The crowd obscured him again. I took a quick glance at Claryce just in time to see her enter an elevator, then looked back at the office entrance. The door was closed now and there was no more sign of Delke, but I'd seen enough . . . more than enough.

Fetch reared back as I entered the stairwell. The guard looked untouched, so I ignored him.

"Master Nicholas—"

"Downstairs, Fetch!"

He did not question me. We rushed down. I wanted to join Claryce as soon as possible. I prayed that I hadn't let her walk into disaster, that she *would* step out of that elevator safe and sound.

I knew the truth about William Delke. There was more to it than him having seen *me* despite the glamour I'd cast. There was more to it than the fact that I, in turn, had sensed *no* Feirie magic even though I had the evidence of it. That spoke of tremendous power.

No, the truth had to do with the briefly revealed *actual* eyes of William Delke, eyes that had in that one instant revealed so very much to me. Only to me. They were the silver eyes of one of the High Feirie, one of the Wyld. The thing that had stood in the doorway, stood there and mocked me, might have looked exactly like business tycoon William Delke, but that was only because my adversary was wearing Delke's *skin* just like one of the many silk suits worn by the witless pawns gathering.

But what was worse, what was unbelievable . . . was that I knew those eyes well.

They were Oberon's.

CHAPTER 7

He should've been dead, consumed by the dragon's flames. I'd seen it happen.

But it hadn't. Clearly it hadn't. I'd known those eyes too well, had them burned into my memory too strongly, not to recognize them after a few scant decades. Yet, even as I descended, I kept reliving that last moment over and over. I saw through the dragon's own accursed orbs as the flames enveloped the area where he stood. I saw Oberon, his fist raised tight, glaring at me.

And then . . . nothing. The intensity of the dragon's flames wouldn't have even left ash. That should've been the end of it. It *should've.*

But it hadn't.

I was uneasy but not panicked. Close to the latter, but not quite there. I'd expected one of Oberon's circle, a bad enough thing. Had I not, I probably would've been more dismayed. Of course, Oberon was a danger far exceeding any other Wyld.

I wondered if Her Lady knew, but that was something for another moment. My greatest concern proved not to be for me or even the Gate but instead for Claryce. I bolted through side door and only slowed when I reached the busy street.

There was no sign of her at first and my heart pounded harder. I imagined that now that Oberon had revealed himself, he had only one interest in her. I could see him killing her simply to further shatter my resolve.

Most of the cars were gone, their drivers evidently told to return after business was concluded. I waited anxiously for Claryce to appear.

When she did, my heart only pounded harder. He'd let her go. I could think of a hundred reasons, all of them bad. Still, I gratefully rushed out to her, grabbing her wrist as I neared. We headed down the street as quickly but casually as we could manage. I paid no mind to Fetch, aware that he would follow in his own fashion.

Claryce kept her demeanor calm, but I could feel her pulse pounding as we walked. I knew she was wary, maybe scared, but she handled herself as well as anyone I'd known in several hundred years.

Several blocks from the Trib, we finally entered a coffee shop. Hal Totten's voice rose from the radio behind the counter, the sports writer turned broadcaster finishing up a summary of the Cubs' dismal season. Not an auspicious third year on radio for the team. I chose a table next to the window. Claryce gratefully sat down, while I signaled the waitress, then rubbed her feet as we silently waited to be served. Once our coffee arrived, she stopped and stared deep into my eyes.

"What happened back there?" she asked, quietly but firmly. "I saw your face when you came for me. You tried to hide it, but I saw it! What happened upstairs after I left?"

Tell her at your own peril . . .

I ignored him. "How well do you know your boss?"

"I've worked for him for five years."

"Has he changed in any way?"

Her expression showed that she didn't like the direction of the questioning. "No . . . not that I can think of."

Either Oberon had made the change subtly, or he had been disguised as William Delke for a lot longer. I thought of the paintings in Delke's new house and began to wonder if there had ever *been* a William Delke.

The black bird alighted on the sill outside, startling Claryce, who knew nothing of this associate of mine. I hadn't expected the avian here, never having had a chance to alert it to my sudden departure. I could only assume that it'd realized something was wrong and left in time to see me leave with Claryce.

The black bird tapped on the window once, then looked over its shoulder before flying off. I followed its gaze just in time to see a black Chevrolet Superior go by. The driver had his cap low over his eyes and seemed focused completely on the street ahead. Another hood slouched in the back, but I knew his gaze had been on the coffee shop.

Again, Oberon had planned ahead. He'd probably ordered them to keep watch for Claryce when she left, and they had followed us. I cursed myself for being so shocked by Oberon's survival that I'd let this happen. Still, we were safe here, and I was already planning how to evade them, even as I talked with Claryce.

She, meanwhile, had been putting together the clues from my questions. Brow raised, she finally asked, "Are you saying he's *not* William?"

She already knew too much for me to simply brush off the question. "It could be he's been William for longer than you've known him . . . but he was never born William Delke or any other human."

A visible shiver ran through her. I started to reach for her hand, but she grabbed for the coffee first. Taking a large gulp, she murmured, "He's one of these . . . these *Wyld*."

"Not just one of them. The worst."

The brow rose again, but she didn't look shocked. "The worst . . . What happens to us now, then?"

"First, we return you to Father Jonathan. Second—"

"I'm not leaving you alone!"

A couple of other customers glanced our way at her outburst. Claryce took to her coffee again, while I peered out the window once more. A punk with a matchstick in his mouth leaned against a wall across the street. He was too obvious, which meant that there was another observer—some servant of Oberon and not a human—nearby. I'd already figured that would be the case.

I tried to deal with Claryce's safety again. "I only want you to stay there while I go back to the house you were staying at—"

She shoved aside the coffee and stood. "Let's go."

"Claryce—"

"I'm going with you. I can't just sit in the church waiting! Either you take me with you, or I'll follow on my own."

The look in her face told me that she would do exactly as she said. Other than tying her up, I had no way of stopping her—

Eye can do that.

Never that! I countered. I would not—*could not*—use the dragon's magic on *Claryce*.

"All right." I left money for the coffee, but, instead of leading Claryce to the front door, I headed toward the kitchen.

"Somethin' you want?" the waitress asked.

I said nothing, simply gesturing toward the back. The waitress turned away as if no longer noticing us . . . which she didn't.

We walked into the kitchen, where I gestured toward a door in the back as soon as the two men there looked my way. Like the waitress, they turned back to their work as if we were no longer there.

It was the mildest of the dragon's magic, but I felt guilty at turning the minds of innocents. This wasn't a spell of shunning, which simply made others look aside, but one that made these people *forget*.

At the back door, I paused to look at Claryce. "Be prepared to run. Even if I fall behind, keep running."

"Nick—"

"Just do as I say. I'll catch up." The last was an assumption, not a promise.

Before she could say another word, I flung open the door. Taking her by the hand, I leaped outside.

The dragon's eyes came into play again. In that emerald world, I saw the two large black spots against the right side alley wall. Seeing nothing to the left, I all but threw Claryce that direction.

"Go!"

Even as she ran, the spots detached from the wall. They weren't monstrosities like the thing in the fireplace but rather a pair of spindly figures who, in the shadows of the alley, could just barely pass for human.

One started for Claryce, while the other lunged at me. As both moved, they each drew a pair of curved swords such as I'd only seen on the other side of the Gate. The black silver blades glittered in the darkness.

Release me! the dragon roared.

I ignored him. He was just as likely to tear apart the city block as deal with this pair.

Pulling free the dagger, I threw it at the one closing on Claryce. Haste made my throw poorer than hoped, but the blade did scrape the assassin's leg.

A streak of golden fire burst where the blessed blade touched the Wyld. From the murk that was its face there came a short, shrill sound. The assassin lost one blade and dropped to its knees. Claryce looked back but continued into the safety of the open.

I barely had time after tossing the dagger to draw the sword and parry one of my own foe's weapons. When the blades touched, ebony sparks flew. There was no time to take a breath; the second sword sought my stomach. I turned Her Lady's gift downward and managed to deflect the second blow.

Both black silver blades slashed at me again and again, creating dark sickle moons of ebony light visible only in the shadows. Her Lady's gift defended me well against the pair, but I saw the other assassin recovering enough to seize the lost weapon and turn back to me.

The dragon raged at his impotency, use of his penetrating vision not enough for him in this dire situation. I shoved his demanding voice to the farthest corner of my mind as I lunged at a meager opening.

Her Lady's gift cut through the forearm. The spindly limb went flying, but no blood—nothing whatsoever—splattered me. The nature of Feirie was that nothing was natural by mortal standards; a thousand and one types of life existed in Her Lady's realm, each more bizarre than the previous.

Unhindered by the loss of limb, the first assassin slashed for my throat. The second attacker closed on our struggle.

Just before it could reach us, a growling, feral form brought it down from behind. Fetch opened a mouth full of far more sharp and deadly teeth than he usually displayed for me and ripped into the murk that was his prey. An aborted squeal escaped the creature as Fetch did his savage work with far more glee than I preferred.

My own foe now tried to retreat. I saw no use in taking it alive; Oberon would never let it know anything of value.

Against one sword, Her Lady's gift had no peer. I battered away at the black silver blade, then twisted the other weapon downward. I then plunged Her Lady's gift deep into what passed for a chest on the stick figure.

Like the other, it squealed as it died. I watched as fragments of the creature scattered in all directions before fading away. Denizens of Feirie did not last long in the mortal world after death.

The swords were gone, too, though not for the same reason. They had vanished, just like the weapon used by the goon in the stairwell. Oberon continued to cover his trail, even as he mocked my every move.

Retrieving my dagger, I suddenly thought about the fact that Fetch was here and not with Claryce. "You should've stayed with her!"

"She commanded me here, Master Nicholas! I didn't want to go, but she said she would run back to you if I didn't help! I could say nothing, being so far from you, and so I finally acquiesced!"

Giving Fetch another scowl, I dismissed the dragon's eyes and rushed out of the alley. To my tremendous relief, Claryce stood near a lamppost that gave her a safe view of the entrance. Smiling, she walked casually to me. I could see she strained not to run.

Claryce kept her voice low. "Nick! Are you all right?"

"I am." I looked around, but there was no sign of any hoods. "This way."

Fetch trailed us. He would stay near until we chose to use a taxi. I thought about the attack behind the coffee shop. It couldn't have been set up for very long; even Oberon couldn't have predicted where I'd stop.

And there was another thing that bothered me. Why set it up at all? Even aware of me all the time, he'd let Claryce and I go. There'd been chances to take us in and near the Tribune Tower.

A drug store caught my attention. "I need to get to the phone."

We crossed to the store and headed to one of the three telephone booths in the back, Fetch waiting outside the establishment like the good hound he pretended to be. Unlike the elderly woman in the booth to the left, I did not put in a dime nor ask for an operator. I simply waited, and, as I waited, I peered around the store for anyone suspicious. I wished I could use the dragon's eyes, but I couldn't risk someone seeing them.

"Who is this?" came Kravayik's tense voice over the receiver.

"It's me. Have you noticed anything?"

"Should I have, Master Nicholas?" he asked in turn, his tone growing more concerned.

I took his own question as meaning that he hadn't noticed any intruder thus far. Kravayik had acute senses; even Oberon himself would've had difficulty sneaking past his guard.

Of course, it was still possible.

"I'm sending Fetch your way. He'll keep watch from the outside."

"Yes, Master Nicholas."

I hung up the receiver. Claryce wore a look of exasperation; in the short time she'd known me, I'd left her in the dark about too much.

"What was that about?" she asked. "Who was that you talked to? You're not telling me everything, Nick! It sounded as if you know who's behind this! It sounds as if you know what *all* this concerns!"

"I think I do." I prayed I was wrong, but everything pointed in the same direction. "He wants the card."

Her exasperation increased. I wanted to explain there and then—avoiding who I was—but not now and not here. I no longer wanted to go directly back to Delke's—Oberon's—house, not until I made a couple of preparations and tried again to keep Claryce safe.

"I'll explain, I promise," I finally told her. "First, let's get back to Fetch so that I can send him where he needs to go. Then, we'll return to Father Jonathan—"

"I'm going nowhere but with you! My entire world's turned upside down in barely a day or two, and you think I can have patience while gunmen and—and *things*—"

A clerk at the soda fountain counter near the front of the store glanced our way. Claryce clamped her mouth shut at that point, but her eyes continued to burn into mine with a fury worthy of the dragon. I considered what more I could tell her that might make her see reason . . . except that reason sounded like nothing remotely connected to the present circumstances.

I finally surrendered, at least for the moment. "All right, you stay with me for the time being." Another plan ensuring her safety had already begun to brew, but first I had to make sure certain things hadn't been compromised. "I'm going to give Fetch some orders. Stay here, at least, until I finish. They won't be able to do anything in so public a place."

She didn't look at all happy to separate from me for even that long, but she finally nodded. I left her by the phone booth and headed outside.

Fetch wagged his tail, then trailed after me as I stepped to the side of the building. His demeanor shifted the second we were out of sight.

"I need you to go to Kravayik and check things out. See if someone or something's been snooping near him."

The shapeshifter's ears flattened. "Ye think they be after that orchid ye've got hidden there?"

Fetch did not know exactly what I'd left Kravayik to protect, only that it was something of tremendous value and power. "Yes. The orchid."

He saw that, even despite me needing him to help out Kravayik, I still wasn't going to tell him just what his fellow exile had for so long been guarding. Fetch's ears rose again and he wagged his tail, but I knew that he was annoyed by my lack of trust in this regard.

"Ye want I should scram now, Master Nicholas?"

"I'd appreciate it."

Fetch twisted around and raced down the narrow alley next to the drugstore, once more running at a speed no hound could match. I felt a sudden regret that I couldn't have finally trusted him with the knowledge of the card's hiding place, then refocused my attention on Claryce.

I'd been confident that she'd be fine where she was, but I still found myself exhaling in relief when I saw her. Claryce also looked relieved, which set my heart pounding in a way I didn't like.

And in my head, my omnipresent companion chuckled.

"It's done," I murmured as I joined her. "Now. Is there anywhere you can think of where you might be safe? Family?"

"No. I was an only child and my parents died in a crash six years ago."

I hid my dismay at hearing about her parents. The crash might've been an accident, but I knew Oberon well enough to know that he would be willing to set plans into motion years ahead if he thought it'd achieve his goals.

Why not take her home?

It was as much his tone as his question that made me nearly swear out loud at the dragon. He knew that there were a score of reasons I didn't want to bring Claryce there, even though it made the most sense.

She put a hand on my arm. "Are you all right?"

"I'm fine. If you won't go back to the church, there's one other place. Mine."

"Yours?" Claryce instinctively hesitated, for which I couldn't blame her. Claryce was hardly like the flapper I'd seen while in front of Mrs. Hauptmann's. The church no doubt sounded a lot better now.

Voices rose from near the soda fountain. I looked over my shoulder.

Two hoods faced the anxious clerk. I couldn't hear what the one asked, but his thick Irish brogue was giveaway enough, even if I didn't also recognize his voice from Delke's home.

"Keep back . . ." I whispered to Claryce. I was astounded that Oberon intended to press the hunt so much that he would risk a scene in a public establishment. True, these thugs were only human muscle, but Wyld generally did not like any sort of attention turned their way.

I considered the exits. The front was out of the question. That left the back, which suggested a repeat of the earlier trap. I'd never known Oberon to be the unimaginative sort, but perhaps it was another sign of his impatience. He desperately wanted the card . . . but why?

And then, to my surprise, the two hoods turned and *left* the drugstore.

I waited until they were completely out of sight, then made my way to the clerk. As I approached, I heard him humming an old ragtime tune by Joplin. Pieces like that weren't so popular anymore, what with jazz taking over the scene around the end of the Great War, but the tune wasn't what bothered me. Instead, I wondered why he was acting so "copacetic"—as Fetch would have remarked—after just being harassed by the pair.

I leaned on the counter. "Excuse me?"

The clerk, in his early twenties but already with thinning blond hair, smiled companionably at me. "Sarsaparilla? Root beer float?"

Shaking my head, I bluntly asked, "What did those two want?"

Instead of answering, he first glanced at a couple of young women sitting on stools and enjoying their orders. "Root beer floats, both of 'em. You want—"

"I don't mean them. The two men. The two Micks."

Despite my bluntness this time, all I received from the clerk was a look of puzzlement. "What two men?"

I straightened. "Never mind. My mistake."

Claryce frowned as I returned. "What happened there? I couldn't make out what you two were saying, but you didn't look happy."

"Did you see the two thugs?"

"How could I miss them?"

"Well, apparently you and I were the only ones. The soda jerk acted as if they'd never been here."

"*William . . .*"

I gave her credit for making the connection immediately. "Exactly. The question is, why just barge in and harass the clerk, then make him forget?"

"To play with us? To keep us on edge?"

A clever one she is, Eye say . . .

It was a trait all Cleolinda's incarnations had shared, and one that bothered me. That cleverness, that adaptability to accept the elements of Feirie as real, had only served to lead each variation that much quicker to her doom.

When I didn't answer, Claryce then asked, "Do we leave through the front door?"

We had no choice but to do so. I still couldn't believe Oberon would be desperate or impatient enough to try a snatch out in broad daylight. Even still, I undid my coat a little more. If it came to it, I'd use Her Lady's gift in the open and damn the centuries of secrecy.

And *again* the dragon chuckled. *This is the human thing called love . . .*

I led Claryce to the door. As we passed the soda jerk, he looked up, smiled, and called, "Come back again soon . . . and I hope you like the tour!"

We hesitated. Claryce took the lead. "Tour?"

Still with a grin on his face, the clerk replied, "You know! The show at the Art Institute!" The balding young man indicated me with a thrust of his chin. "The one he asked me if I knew was any good . . . not that I did. A little too ritzy a place for me to go!"

The clerk returned to his work, leaving Claryce and I to stand silently by the door.

"You didn't ask him, did you?" she finally muttered.

"No." I thought for a moment more. "He used his hoods to send a message. He wants me to go to the Institute."

Claryce caught her breath. "Well, you won't, obviously." When I didn't reply, she leaned closer. "Nick . . ."

"I'll be going, yes."

Ignoring any possible reaction by the other people in the drugstore, she forcibly turned me to face her. "You *know* it's a trap. You know that."

"I do."

I couldn't blame her for the expression crossing her face when I said that. We'd just barely finished being chased after my discovering who it was who toyed with me. Now, despite all that, she saw that I still intended to walk right back into the jaws of danger. Of course Oberon planned a trap at our next meeting.

And what Claryce couldn't understand was that my knowing it was a trap was in itself one reason why I *had* to go.

CHAPTER 8

There were only two exhibits of consequence going on at the Art Institute. The first revolved around dolls. The second was the Thirty-Eighth Annual Exhibition of American Paintings and Sculpture. As I could not see Oberon playing with dolls—unless they contained the trapped and screaming spirits of his enemies—I decided that the latter was the choice.

It'd been too late in the day to go to the Institute, and Oberon would've known better than to expect me to meet him there at night. He offered a public place so that I'd feel safe enough to come even if I knew that he had something up his sleeve.

Not for a minute did I think that Oberon had wanted such a meeting in the Trib Tower. That encounter had been designed to do just exactly what it had done; Oberon had wanted to take my measure, both during the actual event and the pursuit after. He had never expected that his assassins would be able to slay me. They'd been expendable, just like the hoods using the shadow magic to attack us in the Delke home.

With no choice left to me yesterday, I'd finally surrendered and brought Claryce to my home. She had given no sign that she'd ever been there, which had answered the question as to who had left her business card there. I'd said nothing about that to her.

Her exhaustion had also given me the opportunity to guide her directly to the bedroom she'd be using and prevent her from seeing what hung in the living room. Once I'd had Claryce situated, I'd hurried downstairs and removed the painting.

The dragon had laughed at my antics the whole time.

After more than an hour of sharp discussion, I'd managed to convince her not to come with me today. The house was the only place she would be safe. Whatever agent of Oberon's who'd left the card had *not* been able to cross the threshold. Oberon would've never let such an opportunity pass if it had been possible.

The cabbie dropped me off a block farther south on Michigan Ave. Fetch wasn't available to me, but the black bird perched on a street-light near the corner across from the Institute. I gave it only a brief look, then strode up to a shoeshine stand that gave me a view of my destination.

The elderly negro greeted me with a wide smile. "Shine, suh?"

I nodded. He gestured for me to have a seat. His worn clothes were a contrast to the fine suits and fancy dresses passing by. He bent by my feet and got to work while I studied the Institute for some hint of threat.

"Goin' to see the art, suh?"

I could've done like many probably did and simply ignored him, but I still remembered the Nubian warriors I'd met during my original lifetime. "Thought I'd do that. Ever been in there?"

He briefly looked up at me. "Me? Yessuh! I try to go at least once a year. Just been there not too long ago. Go to some other places, too, though not so fancy as this one. At one of those I saw a fine painting by a man called Motley—man just like me. *The Octoroon Girl*, it's called. Real good painter, that Motley. He studied here at the Institute's school, you know, just like my boy's doing now."

Impressed as I was at this unexpected side to the old man, the black bird chose that moment to caw from its position. I stared closer at the entrance to the Institute.

"William Delke" stepped out of a black Duesenberg, whose door was held by the same Irish thug who'd harassed the soda jerk. Oberon said something to the goon, then paused to survey the area.

I made no attempt to hide and wasn't at all surprised that his sharp eyes quickly caught me. Oberon smiled and although he wore a human face I recognized that smile. Fortunately for me, Oberon could not see the shiver I felt.

The Duesenberg drove off. Another hood joined the first. The pair flanked Oberon and walked with him up the steps and inside.

"All done!" the shoeshine man declared. "Not a painting, but pretty good art if I do say so muhself!"

It *was* the best shine my shoes had ever seen. As I rose, I tossed him twice his price, which earned me another wide smile. The contrast between his grin and Oberon's was night and day.

"Thank you, suh! If'n you ever need another shine, you just come and see ol' Michael!"

The name made me hesitate. "Michael?"

But the shoeshine man was already turning toward another potential client and didn't hear me. I grimaced at my overwrought imagination and started toward the Art Institute. One saint wandering the mortal plane was enough of a stretch; two was an impossibility, even if I could've used the help of the archangel right now.

The Institute was filled with art lovers of all types. The banners for the exhibition dominated. I headed toward the entrance of the exhibit.

The Mick with whom I'd become familiar stepped in front of me. Tall as I was, he was taller . . . and much wider. He had a broad, flat, and ruddy face that reminded me of some of Galerius's favored guards.

"Hall to the right!" he growled under his breath. "Next to the third painting. Git goin'!"

I went without a word, not caring whether or not he followed me or stayed where he was. Oberon was the only real danger here, and at that moment it occurred to me that his Feirie nature didn't preclude the death of every human in this building should it further his purpose.

I was so distracted that I didn't see the dapper young man in spats coming around the corner. He accented our collision with a curse, then tried to shove me back. I shifted, letting his momentum take him stumbling into an oil of a ship on a churning sea.

And as the young swell fell past me, I saw an amused Oberon watching the incident.

I saw nothing else but the former lord of Feirie. While at our last encounter I'd retreated, this time I all but ran toward him. Each moment, I expected Oberon to slip away, but he stayed where he was, a glass of wine—a drink that should've had him cuffed and dragged off to jail—in one hand.

Just before he would've been in arm's reach, the *same* goon who'd sent me here blocked my way to him. No human moved that fast, but I saw nothing about him that said he was anything otherwise.

"Close enough, buster."

"That's quite all right, Doolin. He can come as near as he likes."

"Okay, Mister Delke." Doolin slipped to the side, still not revealing the incredible speed with which he would've had to use to reach Oberon before me.

Now there were only the two of us. Oberon took a sip of his wine, then offered me a glass of my own. No one around us noticed that the glass had not been in his hand a moment before.

"Don't bother worrying about breaking a quaint law. No one will notice our glasses," "William Delke" commented as I took the glass. "A fine bouquet, for a mortal vintage. From one of my own vineyards."

I didn't care to think just how vast an empire Oberon had created in the decades since his supposed death. For that matter, none of that empire mattered much; it was all part of the masquerade. Oberon had no care for mortal things, save that they furthered his goal of bringing Feirie—under his hand, naturally—back into dominance.

The crowds continued to mill. Vague conversations concerning this painting or that sculpture continually wafted to my ears. I tried to convince myself again that Oberon wouldn't try anything with so many people around us and failed once more. My hand stayed near enough to the inside of my jacket, just in case.

"And how is she?" he asked without a touch of malice, even

though speaking of the one creature he hated more than me. "How is my precious and treacherous Titania?"

It wasn't as if I'd never known Her Lady's name nor heard it used before, but there were few who did not fear using it. Her Lady had strong hearing and a wicked mind. Only Oberon, even as an exiled Wyld, dared speak of her in such a manner.

"You should ask her yourself. I'm sure she'd be happy to have you at court."

"Soon enough. Soon enough." Oberon continued to play his Delke persona perfectly, hiding the malevolent spirit that was his true self behind the businessman's congenial face. "You know what I want. We can play this game a little longer or you can see sense and give it to me."

"I've no idea what you're talking about."

He smiled wider . . . and for a moment, a bit of Oberon shone through. The smile sent a shudder through me. "Come now. I'm only asking you to be fair. I gave you something of tremendous and rare value; I only ask that you reciprocate."

"There's nothing you could've—" I stopped dead when what he meant finally hit me.

Oberon took a step closer, the inhuman smile remaining in place. "You and I do share one thing in common. The feminine aspect of our lives has always been of a complicated complexion. Mine would see me dead . . . and yours continues to die . . ."

I almost crushed the glass. "Leave her be, Oberon."

"So many times lost, so many times found, so many times lost again. I've come to know her this time better than in any previous. I can see what you admire. I doubt that she'd try to slit your throat like my darling Titania."

"She's played her part for you," I countered, trying to keep my blood from boiling. It didn't help that my invisible companion had also been stirred up by Oberon's close presence. I could feel him fighting to come out, but I kept him in check. "Leave her be now."

"But Claryce is so much more than merely a 'part.'" Oberon turned from me, but not before indicating that I should follow. He walked toward a painting of a landscape. Pausing before it, the ousted lord of Feirie chuckled. "A bit of talent here, more than the artist knows, don't you agree?"

At first, I only cared about Claryce, not some picture. Only when Oberon continued to stare at it did I finally give the painting a second glance.

And only then did I notice its hint of compression, its claustrophobic feel despite the wide, lush landscape it represented. This was not so much a simple forest but rather a place hinting of nightmare in each dark shadow hidden between the trees.

It was *Feirie*, or at least a glimpse of it.

"The Gate cannot keep the essence of both realms from touching one another," my infernal enemy said. "You may be able to stem the tide, but that is all . . ."

"We were talking about Claryce—"

"We were. And here she is now."

I stiffened. He had to be jesting. I'd made it very clear that she had to stay at the house. I knew that Oberon *had* to be trying put me even more off guard.

But still I looked in the direction he indicated . . . and saw her.

Worse, I saw Doolin and the other thug coming up behind her. My hand immediately went into my jacket.

"Now, now, my tainted saint . . . you should not have done that."

It was more of a warning than I would've expected from Oberon, and I could never be certain whether he was giving me a fighting chance or simply seeking to draw my attention from Claryce's danger.

Either way, when I turned to face him, Her Lady's gift already half-drawn, it was to find the painting once more before my eyes. The moment the landscape caught my attention, I discovered that I couldn't pull away. Worse, the mortal world began to recede from me, and the scene from the painting took on a reality that reminded me too much of my previous visits to Her Lady's Court.

And as the painting became my reality, I heard Oberon whispering behind me. I couldn't make out what he was saying, but I knew that it couldn't be good. I struggled to pull my gaze away from the forest—

From the shadows between the trees emerged a pair of black-armored figures, with swords that reminded me too much of Her Lady's gift. I had no doubt as to what their intent was, even before the first figure raised his blade.

I brought up Her Lady's gift in time to deflect his blow. The clang of metal against metal echoed so loud that I wanted to drop my sword and cover my ears. Yet I knew that I'd be skewered the moment that happened. Instead, I ignored the pain in my ears and lunged.

As I expected, my foe backed away. That gave me the respite I needed to take a swing at his twin. I had no idea what sort of face I might find behind the visored helms. They might be human pawns, they might be Wyld. It didn't matter in the end.

The whispering continued unabated, growing so insistent that it threatened to take enough of my attention away that I'd soon enough leave myself open to one of the armored figures.

Eye can help! Let Eye out!

I had blades coming at me from opposite sides, the forest snaring me more and more in its false world, and Oberon's mocking whisper in my head. My heart pounded and my body felt like lead. Even though I managed to parry both swords, I felt doubt filling me that I could last more than a breath longer.

Just a little! my unseen companion roared. *Let Eye out just a little!*

Just a little . . . I took the risk.

His primal power rushed through me, filling my soul and burning it. I let that pain overtake that caused by Oberon's whisper.

The world of the painting took on the familiar emerald hue. I felt stronger, much stronger, while at the same time I also felt myself receding.

I was suddenly wrenched from the painting. Bits of the Art Institute's interior flashed across my gaze, but there was something wrong with them that I had no time to put my finger on. For that matter, I no longer even *had* any fingers—a strong pair of taloned claws were now held out before me. Where Her Lady's gift had gone, I couldn't say. All I knew was that more and more, the dragon held sway over our body.

Claws raked across an armored breastplate, tearing through the metal like butter. A flash of black light burst through from the interior, but before I could see what that meant, the dragon had already turned on our second attacker.

Our emerald world exploded into fiery crimson.

I could just imagine what was left of whoever had donned that armor for Oberon's cause. I felt no remorse . . . in fact, I savored the destruction. With the dragon, I eagerly looked around to see if Oberon or any of his other pawns had been foolish enough to remain near. Eye yearned for more destruction, more death. Eye thought about how nicely this mortal building would *burn* . . .

And then *she* stepped in front of Eye. Eye's first instinct was to melt her flesh, cinder her bones . . . but something held Eye back.

"Nick? Nick! Look at me! Can you hear me?"

Eye could hear her from a far distance . . . and so could I. Suddenly, the dragon and I were two distinct spirits again. I stared in fear at Claryce, so close to a force she was unaware was more than eager to brutally slay her.

There was no sign of Oberon, Doolin, or the other thug. I didn't really care. The dragon was the imminent threat and the awareness now of just what he'd almost done to Claryce was enough to make me fight harder to regain control.

"Nick! What's the matter with you? Speak to me!"

The growing strength of her voice was evidence I was winning. I felt the dragon reluctantly slipping back into the abyss in the far recesses of my mind. He gave up the struggle with an abruptness that was both curious and of great relief.

Gasping, I fell to my knees.

Hands gently took hold of my left arm. I peered up at Claryce, whose expression only held concern for me.

And then I noticed two other things. One was the smell of sulphur that always brought back memories of the night Chicago—and Cleolinda's last incarnation—burned. The second was a silence around us.

The Institute was empty.

Well . . . not entirely empty. There *were* two still forms on the floor not all that far from me, armored forms with some vague resemblance to those I remembered emerging out of the Feirie forest in the painting.

The painting . . .

The second armored body wasn't the only thing scorched by the dragon's breath. The painting Oberon had directed me to was nothing but charred wood and paper. Not a glimpse of the landscape remained. Oddly, the dragon had focused his flame so tightly on the painting that there were only faint black marks on the panel behind it.

I tore my eyes from the ruined painting, drinking in the much more pleasant sight of Claryce. Unfortunately, I couldn't let it stay at that. "Where is he? Where'd he go?"

"William—I mean that thing that looks like him? There was no one but you here, Nick! No one!"

"No . . . you were here. I saw you."

She shook her head. "I only arrived here a few minutes ago. You *never* came back. I know you said to stay at your house, but I didn't know what else to do and I kept worrying about you—"

She suddenly flung herself into my arms. Before I knew what I was doing, I was holding her tight. Claryce didn't say a word; she simply leaned against my shoulder.

Over her shoulder, I caught a new glimpse of the armored bodies. They began to disturb me. I finally and reluctantly separated from

Claryce so that I could look them over. They didn't lay on the floor like the usual stiffs—to use another word Fetch loved—did.

I kicked the leg of the one with the scarred breastplate.

"Nick! What are—" She cut off as the lower half of the leg rolled away.

Not actually the leg, of course. Just the bits of armor that made it up.

The suit was empty.

I didn't need to get close to the second to know that it was the same. I also had no doubt that somewhere else in the Institute two sets of armor were now missing.

"But when I came in . . . Nick . . . I saw them move!"

I grimaced at a thought that I'd been trying to ignore all this time. "What else did you see?" When she didn't answer, I stared hard at her. "What *else?*"

To her credit, Claryce didn't pull her gaze from mine. "You—there was some—I couldn't quite focus on you, even when I finally ran up to you. I only knew that you were struggling with something . . . something inside."

She hadn't seen the transformation. I couldn't remember retaining any control at all over my treacherous companion, but apparently some part of me *had* or else this entire building would've been in ruins.

Still, she'd seen enough and yet she hadn't run away. In fact, even if Claryce wasn't aware of it, she'd not only saved *me*, she'd very likely saved much of the city.

Eye wouldn't have done that . . .

We both pretended that he was telling the truth. It was one of the ways we kept the necessary truce between us going. It didn't serve the dragon to have anything happen to me if he had no control over the body. He valued what little existence he had as much as I did, and I knew that he always hoped that someday *he* would finally and forever be master of his fate.

For the sake of *both* realms, I hoped that never happened.

Once again, Claryce put a comforting hand on me. Only then did I notice that my pulse had resumed pounding harshly. Her touch quieted it and allowed my thoughts to clear more.

I glanced toward a window. It was night. The only lights on in the Institute were those focused on the area around which I stood. More questions popped up.

"How'd you get inside?"

"The doors were open. I pulled at one. That's all."

"And there was no guard anywhere?"

She pursed her lips. "No . . . I was too worried to think about that. I just knew I had to find you. I saw the signs for the exhibition, then heard noise coming from here." Claryce gestured at the suits of armor. "I came in just when you—when you—"

"Took them out." I heard a noise outside that sounded too much like a distant police siren getting closer. Somehow, I doubted it was going to pass the Institute. "We're about to have company. Let's get out of here before that happens."

We encountered no one on the way out. I wondered about the guards, aware that Oberon wouldn't blink an eye at killing them just to arrange *whatever* this was supposed to be.

And that was a question burning within me as harshly as the flames the dragon had let loose on the animated suits and the painting. I was missing something again. I knew one reason that Oberon might've not actually tried to kill me himself; if he wanted the card, he had to guarantee that he'd have access to it. Oberon knew that I'd have put it where only I could get it and no amount of torture on his part would've drawn that knowledge or support from me. He'd *tried* torture on me the last time, if for different reasons. He knew better than to try again.

So what *had* he been up to? What didn't I remember from the moment he arranged the scene with the false Claryce and the malevolent painting to the time when the real one came to *my* rescue?

The sirens blared louder as we exited the Art Institute, which meant they were much nearer, too. I steered Claryce in the opposite direction.

We had barely gotten around the corner when I heard the flutter of wings. A familiar sight alighted on a lamp.

I was very interested in what the black bird had to say, but now was not the time. Without alerting Claryce, I tipped my head to the side, indicating it should move on. The exile fluttered off without so much as a caw.

A block away, I hailed a taxi for us. We kept silent while the cabbie drove, but I could see that Claryce had several questions of her own. I knew that more than a few of them had to do with the vague glimpses she'd had and what that had to do with my earlier hints of my blood mixing with that of the dragon when I'd slain him. This night, she'd seen a bit of what that meant . . . and I had no doubt that it frightened her more than she let on.

Good . . . my undesired comrade hissed. *Let her be frightened . . . let her run far, far away from us . . .*

Be quiet! Still, I found myself in part agreeing with him. If Claryce ran . . . and ran far, far away, as he'd said . . . then maybe at least that curse would be avoided for once.

But at that moment, Claryce set her hand on mine, set it there and briefly squeezed. I looked deeper into her eyes and knew that there was no chance whatsoever that she would leave.

And I also knew right then that there was no chance that the curse would let us be this once . . . which meant that the woman next to me was still destined to die.

CHAPTER 9

Claryce lay asleep on the couch, so exhausted by her worry for me and the events that followed that she barely had time to sit down before drifting off. She wasn't a weak person, but she'd had to accept a lot that would've been too much for most normal folk.

That gave me the chance to respond to the tapping at my back door. I peered outside, then opened it. However, rather than step back and let the new arrival inside, I walked out.

In the dim light of the moon, the black bird perched atop the branch of a twisted oak in the backyard. It fluttered off the branch and alighted on my arm.

"Well?"

"Saw him! Saw him!"

"Oberon. I know. What else?"

"Two manlings."

I sighed. Sometimes, it took patience to glean the information I needed from Feirie exiles. It wasn't that the black bird didn't want to tell me everything it had witnessed; it was just that, like so many of its ilk, it had its own unique manner of speech.

I tried a different tack. "When did he leave? How long after I entered?"

"Fourth hour down. Fourth hour down."

Down. That meant four hours after the noon sun. To a creature of Feirie, that was the closest thing to keeping track of time.

Four hours . . . Oberon had spent a lot of time in the Art Institute. Just exactly what he'd been doing all that time while I'd been trapped by the painting, I didn't know . . . and *that* worried me more.

"Did you follow them?"

"Followed them, yes! Followed them long!"

"Which way?"

The black bird stretched a wing. I was both relieved and bothered by which way the creature pointed the feathered appendage. Oberon had headed in nearly the opposite direction of where Fetch and Kravayik were located. I respected Feirie's former lord enough to believe that he had at least some inkling where the card was, even if he couldn't directly take it. I'd sent Fetch to Kravayik more as a precaution than because I'd believed that Oberon had discovered some special means by which to get past the safeguards. Still, I'd expected more from him than this.

And again I asked myself, *What is he up to?*

Questioning the black bird further gained me only one more useful piece of information. Oberon had not headed back to whatever he used for his lair but had instead continued on well into the North Side. There, his car had parked in a dark lot next to another car, from which had stepped out a human better dressed than Oberon's guards but to the black bird clearly of the same ilk. The exile was maddeningly vague in its description—all humans looked more or less alike to it—but had noticed with its exceptional nocturnal vision the long scar along the right side of his neck.

That alone was enough to identify Oberon's new companion to me as George C. "Bugs" Moran . . . and it was also enough to cement my suspicions that perhaps Hymie Weiss and the Schemer were on their way out as bosses. Oberon didn't deal with lieutenants. It was very likely he was even maneuvering things so that Moran would take over the North Side soon. Moran's violent and erratic manner well-matched the dark insanity of Feirie; it was possible that the Irishman had a touch of that world in him.

I thanked the black bird and let it fly off to wherever it called home in this world. Stepping back inside, I saw that Claryce still slept. Leaving her be, I went into the other room and called Kravayik.

"Who speaks?" he asked on the second ring.

"Me. All quiet there?"

There was a slight pause that gave me the heebie-jeebies—another expression I'd apparently picked up from Fetch—before Kravayik eased my tensions by replying, "Yes . . . on the rare occasion when he stops talking."

I exhaled. "Tell him he can leave. Also that I need him tomorrow at first light."

"I will gladly tell him both, Master Nicholas . . . and with gratitude to you in mind for the first part . . ."

"The gratitude is mine, Kravayik."

He said nothing. The connection broke, Kravayik no doubt eager to inform Fetch that his duties we're at an end for this evening. Kravayik was the only other being around whom Fetch had a voice. For the shapeshifter, it was a rare chance to speak to someone who also knew Feirie well. For Kravayik, it was simply a long headache.

Returning to Claryce again, I considered waking her in order to enable her to go to her bed. One look at the peace in her face put a kibosh on that. Instead, I sat down in a chair facing her and, while searching in vain for any even subtle differences in her features, fell asleep.

I woke to the smell of eggs, bacon, and coffee. The coffee scent was particularly strong. Claryce greeted me a moment later with a plate full of food and a mug of dark brown nectar. Coffee was something I'd developed a taste for since the fifteenth century, when I'd followed the Gate in the Kingdom of Kaffa, in what was now Ethiopia.

"How can you drink that—that tar?" Claryce asked with slight amusement and clear distaste as I sipped the coffee. "I've never tasted something so thick and strong. I thought at first I'd ruined it. I would have watered it down for you, but I wasn't sure if you would like that."

"It keeps me awake." There was truth to that. My senses were already sharper than they'd been before the first swallow. "Thank you for the breakfast."

"I've done little enough so far. Glad I could at least handle this." Her humor faded. "I still can't get over yesterday, and I *know* a lot more happened than I saw."

I used another long sip as an excuse to keep from replying.

She did not take the hint. "Nick, there's a lot you haven't told me, have you? You said that this Feirie was ruled by something—someone—you call Her Lady. If William—that *Wyld*—is so dangerous, don't you think it might be worth the risk to ask for her help? I gather he's not loyal to her, and, if he's also a threat to her rule, then perhaps she'd—"

"She won't be a part of this. The sword is her only offering in this or any other effort, especially if *he's* involved. It's not that she doesn't have her own ambitions in our world, but where he's concerned, as long as he can be kept out of Feirie, she's satisfied."

Claryce nodded, but she clearly had more questions. However, the one she asked next was not what I expected.

"There was a picture over that fireplace. You can see hints on the wall that it was just taken away recently. What happened to it?"

I was saved trying to make an excuse by a knock on the door. Claryce all but leapt at the sound and even I managed to let some of the coffee dribble on the floor.

Setting the mug down, I rose. "Stay here."

"Nick . . ."

Waving her to silence, I exited the room and headed to door. The knock came again, a little harder, this time.

I peered through the narrow window next to it.

An impatient Detective Cortez raised his fist to knock a third time. He let out a grunt as I swung the door open.

"Detective. What brings you all the way out here?"

He peered around the doorway. "Nice place you got here, Nick Medea! I think I was here once, wasn't I?"

I didn't answer that question, reminded once again that Cortez had the odd ability to recall more about me than most people did. He'd actually been here three times. There was some hint that the shunning worked on him, but not to the extent it should've.

"What can I do for you, detective?" I asked.

He chuckled, but there was something serious hidden behind the sound. "Mind letting me in?"

"Any reason?"

"I don't know. Maybe not wanting folks to see a greaser on your doorstep? Had worse reasons thrown at me than that."

I shook my head. "You know me enough to understand I don't think that way."

"So does that mean I can come in?"

Peering past him, I saw only his auto. No other cop. "I'd think this part of the city was well beyond your beat, Cortez."

The detective no longer smiled. "If you won't let me in, how about joining me at my car? Probably best, anyway. Wouldn't want to bother your lady friend, you know?"

I frowned at him, which was just the reaction he was looking for, I realized too late.

"Quite a doll, she is," he whispered conspiratorially. "Good gams, you know?"

"Listen, Cortez—"

He didn't back down. "No. Listen to me, Nick Medea. We've gotta talk. You don't want to do it in there, then we can do it by my car. Be better if it was inside, but we need to talk either way, you understand?"

Whatever misgivings I had about Cortez, I knew him to be an honest cop, an honest *man*. He had something he needed to tell me, and I decided that it was probably something I needed to hear.

"Your auto."

"Suits me, Bo."

I shut the door behind me and followed him, hoping all the while that Claryce would stay out of sight even if the detective did have a pretty good notion as to her being with me. That he had a misconception about the extent of our relationship was still something I was sore at him about . . . but that had to wait.

"Hate this jalopy," Cortez groused when we reached the vehicle. "A real hayburner, too. All I'm worth to those higher up, you know? Need someone for a dirty job? Don't even let George do it, let the greaser! He's expendable . . ."

It surprised me a little to hear that bluntness. If Cortez had mouthed like this near a lot of people, his head would've ended up on a pole.

The detective pointed at the passenger side. "Hop in."

I considered the fact that he might just drive off to the station with me in tow if I did as he said, but that didn't strike me as something Cortez would really do. I got inside and waited for him to seat himself.

He shut the door, then pulled out a pack of cigarettes. "Gasper?"

I shook my head. He took a cigarette for himself. After taking a puff, the detective eyed the view beyond the windshield. "Nice neighborhood. Really white."

"You got something to tell me other than that?"

"I do, I do." Still looking away, Cortez said, "I hear about this funny incident the other day. Gunshots at the ritzy house of a bigwig by the name of Delke. You ever hear of him?"

"Some businessman."

"Some businessman, yeah. A real big cheese. Far as I hear, Delke wasn't there. Someone else was, though, you know? Heard it from a good source, a real stool pigeon."

"What of it?"

Cortez took another puff. "Funny thing is, there's no report on it. Nothing. Checked it out carefully. Incident at a house like that and no one knows anything about it?"

"Maybe this Delke doesn't want the publicity. Maybe your superiors don't, either."

"You're not speaking bushwa there, Nick Medea. Been told to dry up more than once already, how about that? But you know, I can't let it go . . . and I think you wouldn't."

I still had no idea where this was going except that it was circling around me too much. "Probably not, if I was involved at all."

He grinned. "Now, I ain't saying that . . . but there *was* another case that made me think about giving you a visit. Just to get your opinion, you know?"

"What's that?"

"They fished a stiff out of the Chicago River. Penny-ante thug with possible ties to the North Side. Muscle mostly, but also good with a typewriter."

Cortez wasn't referring to office work. The corpse he was referring to had been a hired gunman known for using a Tommy gun. Suddenly, I had a bad idea where the good detective was heading. "What would I know about a dead hoodlum?"

"Well, not him personally, but you're always into the spooky and strange stuff." Cortez suddenly made the sign of the cross. "Real strange stuff at times."

I couldn't argue with the last since we'd both there at the end of that older case. Still, I didn't want him constantly linking me with bloody situations like that. "That was different. When I help people who claim they've got ghosts, I don't expect murder to be involved."

The detective flicked his cigarette out the window. He muttered something under his breath, which I realized was a short prayer to Our Lady of Guadalupe, the patron saint of the new church planned for his neighborhood and one his parents had apparently followed back in Mexico.

"Call that *murder*? I seen bootleggers shot to pieces by rivals that looked less messy. Still get chills thinking about it, you know?"

"So what is it about this one that made you think of me? Was it that bad?"

"Not so bad, but strange, you know? First, the guy, he's missing a mitt."

I shrugged. "Only one? Don't they sometimes cut off both and even the head, too, to keep the identity hidden?"

Cortez reached for his pack again. "Yeah, and if they'd done that, I wouldn't have bothered. Funny thing, though, only the one hand was gone and the stump . . . looked like someone tried to—what did the doc call it?—*cauterized*. That's it. You know what that means?"

"I do." I also knew exactly what my connection was to all this, even if Cortez didn't. This was the thug who'd lost his hand when I'd severed the one on the shadow. I knew the wound had been bad, but I also had expected it to be one he could survive, especially now that Cortez had mentioned that it looked cauterized.

"Now, of course, that's not what killed him," the good detective went on, as if reading my thoughts. "Had a second grin from ear to ear, you know?" He ran a finger across his throat for emphasis.

I tried to fathom the reason for the goon's execution. Originally, I'd thought Oberon had been trying to kill me, but everything pointed to him merely showing how helpless I was. In retrospect, it was a typically Feirie style of thinking; reduce your enemies to help-less, quivering prey, in part for your sadistic pleasure, then squeeze them of any value they have before finally putting them out of their misery. I doubted that he actually thought that he could bring me to the point that he had so many of his victims when he'd still been His Lord of the Court, but he'd already proven that he knew too many of my weaknesses. Enough so that I was definitely concerned about the Clothos card . . . and even more so, I discovered at that moment, for Claryce.

I realized that I'd been silent too long. "I still don't know how I can help you."

Leaning closer, Cortez whispered, "My chief, he asked me some funny questions about Miss Simone, almost like someone else was really wanting to know. Now she seems a nice, innocent skirt to me, and I'm sure she does to you, too, Bo. I ain't certain where this is all going, but something's rotten."

"I appreciate the concern for her."

He sat back. "Another thing. That little statue that vanished? The stiff had it tucked in his jacket nice and plain for anyone to find. Almost seemed like a message."

Cortez was proving a fount of info, most of it ominous. I waited for more about the statuette, but all the detective did was scratch his chin and stare down the street ahead.

"Funny. Thought I saw a *coyote* or something. Awful big one if it was." He shrugged. "That's all I got for you, Nick Medea. That's all I got for myself. Those're the real goods. Don't really know why I came to you, but it seemed the right thing to do, you know?"

I didn't. There was something going on with Cortez that I had no explanation for. He acted too much like he knew more about me than even he should've.

Slay him now! Bite off his head and burn his body!

A grunt was all I gave the dragon in reply to his drastic suggestion. Cortez took that grunt for an affirmative reply to his last comment and nodded in turn.

Some distance ahead, a dark form slipped around a fence. I'd already had suspicions about what the detective had glimpsed and now I knew.

"If I hear or see anything out of the ordinary, I'll let you know," I informed Cortez, half-telling the truth. How much I dared involve him, I couldn't yet say, but even though Cortez was by his appearance forced to be something of a loner, he still had access to information I didn't.

He gave me another nod as I exited the auto. "You're a swell one, Nick Medea. More ways than one."

The detective didn't have to tap his cheek to show he was referring to his skin. Without waiting for a response, he started up the auto. Only then did I happen to glimpse what Cortez had set near the wheel, so that he could always see or touch it. Actually, there were *two* items, the first being the only one I'd expected—a symbol of the Lady of Guadalupe, the Virgin Mary as she'd been seen there.

And because of her, I'd failed to notice the second, even though it should've stood out more for me in particular. The weighing scales dangling from the hilt of the sword. There were a hundred or more variations of this symbol, and I knew them all.

St. Michael.

Cortez drove off, which saved me from maybe asking a question I'd regret. For that matter, the detective's "coyote" chose that time to make his appearance.

"Something not copacetic, Master Nicholas?"

"Keep quiet until we get inside," I reminded him.

For once, Fetch had the good sense not to tell me that he would do just that. He just quieted and followed.

Claryce stood near the door, her eyes wide with concern. She patted Fetch as he entered, which earned her a tail wag.

I shut the door behind us. "Claryce, how well do you know Detective Cortez?"

"That *was* him I saw, then. What was he doing all the way out here?"

"His bosses have given him a pretty long leash," I replied, waving Fetch to silence before he could bring up an old argument of his about the cruelty of leashes. "If he gets strangled by it, it won't be any loss to them, but so long as he's useful they seem to let him have the run of every precinct."

"Could he work for—" Claryce had still not settled on just what to call her employer.

"The name you want is *Oberon* . . . and, no, Cortez is straight. Troublesome, but straight."

She eyed Fetch, then me again. "Oberon . . . as in Shakespeare's Oberon?"

"As in dangerous knowledge something from Feirie once whispered in the Bard's ear and that he was foolish enough to put to quill and paper." I declined to mention to her that I'd also *met* the playwright himself because of that very situation, the Gate having shifted near London at that time.

Claryce absorbed this new info. "So does Detective Cortez know about Wil—Oberon?"

"I don't think so." I could answer no better. "He suspects a lot. Enough to get himself rubbed out. Oberon's used his Delke identity to build ties with the North Side. Even if they're as much in the dark as Cortez is about who they've made a deal with, they won't care for a bull poking around their business."

"You asked how well I knew the detective. What did he say about me?"

I told her everything, only leaving out Cortez's comments about her appearance.

"Should I go to him, Nick?"

"He didn't seem interested in that. I'm sorry . . . he made a pretty good guess that you were inside . . . and probably made some assumptions from that, too."

I expected her to be upset about her reputation, but she just frowned more. "You and I both know the truth. With everything else going on, I could care less what he might think."

"Still, it'd be good if you returned to the church. You'd be safer there."

Claryce gestured at our humble surroundings. "How could I be safer anywhere than *here*? This is *your* home, after all."

"Master Nicholas—"

I waved him silent again. "The church has its factors that outweigh—"

"*Please*, Master Nicholas."

I looked down at him. "What is it?"

"There was some muscle keeping watch on you and the detective. I would've rubbed them out, but you gave orders never to do that around your sanctum." His ears flattened as I glared at him. "They probably scrammed when the detective hit the road—"

"Wait!" I headed back to the door. "You didn't *see* them leave?"

"No. I thought nothing of it, Master Nicholas, except that you'd want to know—"

There came a crash from the back of the house, followed by a horrific *whoosh*.

The crackle of fire filled our ears.

I ran to the kitchen. The entire room was engulfed, and the flames were already advancing. In the midst of the inferno, I saw the fragments of a bottle. Bootleg liquor burned well.

Returning to the others, I calmly ordered, "The front door."

Another bottle shattered a nearby window. The lit rag in it started the shades on fire even before the bottle came crashing onto the floor.

A third crash warned us that the upstairs was now on fire as well.

Fetch was the first to the front door, but not due to any cowardice. Closer to the ground, he was less of a target for the hoods no doubt waiting outside. With ease, he twisted the knob with his mouth, then pulled the door open.

"Keep to the side! Fetch knows what to do." This was not the first time he risked himself for me in this manner. I vowed to learn to appreciate him better.

To her credit, Claryce remained calm. So calm, in fact, that she was able to ask the question that had already been coursing through my thoughts.

"What happened to the protections around your house? I thought this couldn't happen!"

It *shouldn't* have been able to happen. At worst, Moran's goons should have been able to set the grass on fire . . . not exactly a useful stunt, since the fire would've died the moment that it tried to pass the protections shielding the house.

The same protections that had now failed. Even Oberon should have had an almost impossible time penetrating the defenses, but he'd had fifty years to figure out how to bypass them. I should've understood the hints he'd already left, toying with me by first revealing he knew where I lived, then by leaving sinister gifts on my doorstep.

I recalled the hand. In my overconfidence and lack of understanding just who it was I faced, I'd thought burning the severed appendage had been enough. The only trouble was, the moment I touched it, I'd guaranteed some trace would be brought in with me.

And now, the entire building was an inferno.

I didn't expect the firemen to arrive in time. They'd be warned off by the gang. Nor did I think any police would be coming. Cortez was probably the only one who might've, but they'd waited until he'd gone. He probably wouldn't hear about it until tomorrow.

"The coast is clear!" Fetch growled from the doorway. Without waiting, he lunged outside.

"Stay behind me," I ordered Claryce.

We charged after Fetch. Some of my neighbors—a few of whom were probably shocked just to see someone living in the house—stood gathered safely across the street.

The three of us veered away from the small gathering and headed a few yards down the street. Fetch continued to take the point.

When I deemed us safe, I called to Fetch. Taking on his hound persona, he turned around and wagged his tail as he sidled up next to me.

"Master Nicholas—"

He kept his voice low, but the fact that it was still a *voice* frustrated me. "Quiet!"

"Master Nicholas! The painting! It's still in there!"

"Forget it!"

"What painting?" Claryce asked.

"An old one. Nothing important." Thankfully, the sound of a siren interrupted the discussion and admittedly surprised me. I'd been certain that no one would come until there was nothing left of the house but ash.

As we'd talked, I'd continued to look around. I was looking for something.

And there it was. Behind my fearful neighbors stood an extra shadow. It broke away and faded into the background. I didn't even bother trying to chase after the thing. Whatever thug had cast it was blocks away.

The fire continued to burn. The truck came, but there wouldn't be much remaining. A pang struck me, and I remembered the Night the Dragon Breathed.

A little bonfire this, he said with his usual mocking. *I did so much better . . .*

You failed to kill him, I reminded my constant companion with both bitterness and regret. *You failed to kill Oberon when you had him . . .*

That was enough to silence him.

"What do we do now?" Claryce asked, as the firemen started unloading.

"We start walking." I turned us from what I'd so casually thought of as just the latest in my endless series of temporary outposts but now realized had housed my entire cursed existence.

She did not question me. I knew that what remained of the shunning would still achieve one goal—everyone nearby would eventually forget who had lived there. Once more, my trail would be swiftly and utterly erased.

And once more, I knew that Oberon had shown me that no matter how much I thought that I was prepared for him, I wasn't.

CHAPTER 10

I hailed a taxi and had the cabbie take us directly to St. Michael's. We found Father Jonathan by the great organ the church had obtained last year. He rose from his inspection of the over two thousand pipes and greeted us.

"I wondered what had happened to the two of you," the priest said with some anxiety. "I shouldn't speak like this, but there was a rather disreputable gentleman here yesterday who asked about you. A large man with a rather thick Irish brogue."

That sounded like Doolin. I'd known that even the church was probably no longer safe, but it was the only place I had for Claryce right now. I did not want her with me where I had to go, just in case matters were compromised even worse than I imagined.

Unfortunately, Claryce did not see things my way. "Meaning no offense to Father Jonathan, but I don't like being left behind, Nick! After what happened to your house—"

"I'm only going to be gone a short while. Make sure you stay in the room. Fetch will be outside St. Michael's. He'll keep you safe until I return."

She finally gave in. "All right . . . but you better keep that promise this time."

"I will."

I left her in the room that Father Jonathan had let her use the last time, then went and thanked the priest for his exceptional patience. He didn't know me like his predecessor, and yet he'd taken Father Peter's word that I should be trusted.

"I've already called Mrs. Gelb," he immediately informed me, as if I needed to be assured about that. "I know that there's something bad going on, Nick. You know you can confide in me as you did Father Peter."

I wasn't ready for that yet. "How much did Father Peter tell you?"

"He said the good Lord had set you on a troubled path, but that there was no better man to be found who could stand up to those troubles. He got rather poetic and started quoting from the story of St. George when speaking of you." The young priest smiled. "Quite an admirable comparison, Nick. He thought very highly of you."

Father Peter'd just been reciting what did exist of my life story, but yeah, he *had* thought highly of me. Probably too much. I'd abused his admiration too many times, which had ended up with him being permanently injured and forced to retire. Father Jonathan had been told that the injuries were the result of an auto accident. It was better that he never found out the truth about them.

I'd stood silent after his comment. The priest finally cleared his throat. "And Father Peter also said you'd act just like you are doing right now. I'll respect your privacy until you've decided you can trust in me enough, Nick."

"It's not that, Father. One day, unfortunately, you'll know why."

"How thoughtful you are of others, Georgius," another voice, tinged with sarcasm, said from behind me. "Well . . . most others."

I waited until Father Jonathan had left before turning to face Diocles. Out of a moment of frustration with everything, I purposely walked right through him.

He swore in Latin—impressively, I had to admit—then reformed in front of me. I nearly charged through him a second time, but held off.

"You are not looking well, Georgius. I heard some of what you talked about with *her*. I know the Gate has been breached, but not by what."

"What do you care? You're dead."

"And left in purgatory, thanks to you. I do not want you dying before I win my forgiveness."

"Very considerate of you to worry so much about yourself."

The late emperor sighed, even though he didn't have any breathe with which to do it. "You know I pray for you every day and night. The priest often prays for you, too, by the way. A good man . . . and it's good of you to keep him ignorant. The less he knows, the less the darker powers might touch him."

"'The darker powers'? That sounds more in line with your old beliefs. Been praying to Jupiter as well?"

"If I thought it would keep the two of you safe, at this point I would."

He'd succeeded in making me feel uncomfortable. I almost began to have regrets . . . but then the memory of my execution stirred and those regrets vanished. "I've got to go."

This time, Diocles had the good sense to vanish before I walked through him. I held my own breath until I was out of the church.

Fetch was waiting for me. "Where do we go, Master Nicholas?"

"'We' go nowhere. I need you to patrol St. Michaels. Make certain that Claryce stays safe."

His tail drooped and his ears flattened. "I should go with you, Master Nicholas!"

"Father Jonathan told me that one of Oberon's thugs was here. While I'm gone, make certain that doesn't happen again. I'll be back shortly to bring her to a safer place." *I hope.*

"Yes, Master Nicholas. I'll not let you down!"

"I know that." But I still planned to do my best to get back quickly.

Even though I'd lived in the house for several years, I'd also made sure to have at least one other place to go in case of emergencies. The secondary hideout wasn't as glamorous as the Delke home, or probably even as classy as Claryce's own, but it was situated exactly between St. Michael's and Holy Name Cathedral and so had some protective influences from both spread over it that I hoped would keep Claryce safe while I worked to turn this entire situation around. Oberon had had me on the run since the beginning; that was going to end.

While the Gold Coast near Lake Michigan was seeing new apartment buildings rising higher and higher, my emergency quarters consisted of a number of rooms over a millinery store that'd shut its doors during the short but harsh depression about four years ago. After buying the building with good, solid gold from the previous owner, I'd kept the shop windows boarded over but had rebuilt the upstairs for my needs.

One look at the state of the building when I got there was enough to prove that the shunning spell on it was still strong. I felt some shame at bringing Claryce here, but I swore that it'd be very temporary. Besides, while the outside was overgrown with weeds, the inside was probably cleaner than many more ritzy establishments . . . not to mention entirely vermin free thanks to the same spell.

I entered through the back with my key and investigated the inside. Other than dust, the shop looked exactly as it had when they'd gone out of business. There were even still tables and stands and one or two hats that hadn't been worth the trouble to pack up.

Upstairs was different. While I purposely left the shop looking long-vacant, the living quarters I'd kept tidy. I'd never had to bring anyone here—the house having sufficed until now—and I wasn't all that fond of dust myself. The dragon's laughter often echoed in my head whenever I cleaned up.

The saint of the hearth, he mocked even now. *Will you take up your trusty lance there?*

The "lance" in question was the broom I'd left from last time. "With a sharpened point, it'd do you in just as good as the original."

He quickly receded from my notice. Satisfied, I went on with looking over the rooms. It didn't take long to see that everything was in order and that, despite there having been no tenants in years, the plumbing and everything else still worked. I plugged in the Kelvinator I'd bought last year and began making a mental list of what food to stock in it.

The hair on the back of my neck stiffened.

I looked around but saw nothing that would've set off my senses. After a moment, I realized that whatever had disturbed me was more distant.

A glance out the lone front window revealed nothing. The sun was still high enough in the sky that it seemed unlikely that any Wyld or shadow folk would be lurking about. Most of the Wyld did not have Oberon's stamina; the daylight burned them almost as badly as it did the proverbial vampire. As for the shadow folk such as had haunted Mrs. Hauptmann's attic, they were just like their name implied. If the sun caught them right, they often melted away immediately. The only problem was actually getting them into that light, especially as they could sometimes project their own dark protection.

With one hand near the inside of my coat, I descended into the millinery shop again. Down here, the sensation was more evident, but whatever I'd noticed was clearly not in here, either. That eased some of my anxiety, but I knew I couldn't just leave the matter.

Outside, I felt the wrongness even more, so much so that I could even pinpoint the direction.

That led me to another building that had seen better days. However, unlike the one I'd purchased, this one still had a business on the bottom floor. I reached for the door handle—and the presence receded from the vicinity.

Quickly stepping around to the back, I saw nothing out of the ordinary. I summoned the dragon's eyes . . . or at least tried to. I sent a mental curse at my invisible companion, which finally stirred him from wherever he'd been hiding in my thoughts.

Eye will show you . . . he promised belatedly.

The world turned emerald. I immediately surveyed the area, searching the tiniest bits of shadow between various buildings.

But all I discovered was that the sensation that some creature of Feirie was near had faded even more.

"What you doin' here?" rumbled a deeply accented voice.

I fought down the dragon's gaze just before a heavy hand turned me about. A swarthy mountain nearly comparable to the hulking Doolin sneered at me. A heavy wave of garlic washed over my face.

I answered, but I did so in fluent Italian, a language I'd picked up easily, having known Latin already for so many centuries. "Just goin' to grab a smoke! Didn't know anyone here'd mind!"

My accent might've been a little odd to the thickly mustached bootlegger—there was no denying just what he was—but the ease with which I spoke it and my somewhat dark complexion made it easy for him to assume the wrong thing.

Though in English, his own words dripped heavy with a Neapolitan touch . . . not coincidentally, I knew, the same region from which Papa Johnny Torrio and Capone had roots. "You sent here for a pickup? Nothin' before dark, you dope!"

I switched to English myself, but kept the accent. "My boss, he just said go pick up the hooch at this place. Needs it for a party tonight."

"Yeah . . . tell him nothin's goin' out tonight or tomorrow. Da Micks are pokin' their noses around."

I acted worried. "No hooch? He'll bat me silly!"

"Tough. Dat's Snorky's order and no one changes it 'cept him."

I threw up my hands and muttered three or four of the best epithets I'd learned in my years as a tribune. They might've sounded a bit archaic, but they earned the approval of the guard.

"Ha! My nònno, he used say somethin' like that last one! You from Naples?"

The last time I'd been to Naples, his grandfather's grandfather's grandfather probably hadn't been born yet. I gave a noncommittal shrug, which I knew would make him believe that I did have some blood from his region, even if it was probably not due to any holy or legal union.

"Get goin'," the guard said in a friendlier voice. "Once we start up again, you come by. I'll see you get some of the better stuff. That'll make your boss okay, right?"

I thanked him in the mother tongue again, then hurried off. The unexpected encounter had given me more than I'd bargained for. The quarters above the shuttered shop were still safe, but how long they'd remain so was a good question. I'd been worried about the war spreading too close to the main house, but I'd never assumed it would come to this neighborhood. Papa Johnny had been a cautious businessman when he'd run the South Side. This had all the earmarks of the impetuous and aforementioned "Snorky," also known as "Scarface," aka Alphonse Capone, Torrio's successor. If Capone thought he could push his way into the North Side through this area, then he wasn't afraid of what Moran and his partners would throw at him.

The only thing was, I doubted that Capone knew that the North Side had ties with the power of Feirie. Worse, I now understood the curious sensation that some creature of the other realm had been nearby. My mistake had been to think that it was here because of interest in me. Instead, it was spying on the South Side gang, no doubt so that Oberon could keep his pawns on the North Side placated for as long as he needed them.

But for one of the shadow folk to dare the daylight like this meant that Oberon had spent a fair amount of power to shield it. The creature had to have some importance to the former lord of Feirie, which meant that it might serve me to return here again and see if I could better track it back to its master.

First, though, I had to make certain that Claryce would be safe, and then finally see to Kravayik myself.

Claryce leapt to her feet when I entered. I decided not to mention either bootleggers or shadow folk for the moment.

"The place is secure," I assured her, "but you'll have to stay inside and away from the windows once you're there."

"I still don't like this, Nick. I think I'd be safer with you and Fetch. Just look what happened to your house!"

I declined to admit the truth in what she said. "You'll be safer where I'm bringing you."

She reluctantly followed me out. Father Jonathan bid us farewell. Diocles watched Claryce and I leave, the emperor's ghost staying clear of her range of vision. I wondered if she had noticed him again, but I figured I could ask my former executioner that when I had the chance. It wasn't like Diocles was going anywhere.

Fetch joined us the moment we exited St. Michael's. Unfortunately, he seemed none too happy, a worrisome change from my arrival a few minutes earlier.

He was not alone in joining us, either. The black bird was with him, and the fact that the pair weren't snapping at each other only increased my concern.

"Saw one! Saw one!" the black bird cawed.

Fetch's ears *and* tail hung, not a good sign. "I smelled it, too, Master Nicholas! I did!"

I quieted both while I looked to see if anyone else—the priest included—was nearby. Satisfied that we couldn't be overheard, I gritted my teeth and asked, "Saw *who?*"

The avian was beside itself. "Hers! Hers!"

I'm certain that my face drained of blood. Claryce's concerned eyes when I looked her way gave every indication of how terrible I must've looked.

Peering at Fetch and the black bird once more, I snapped, "It's just an observer! Nothing more than a pair of eyes!"

To his credit, the shapeshifter took up my suggestion. "Yes,

Master Nicholas, surely you are as right as rain. Just a pair of peepers! That's all."

"What are all of you talking about?" Claryce demanded, rightfully annoyed that she was constantly in the dark. "'Hers'? What do you mean—" She cut off, as some of the truth dawned on her. "Nick, you talked about—"

It probably didn't matter at this point, but I still kept Claryce from even saying the title. If the focus had to be on any of us, I would let it be on me. "Yeah. You've got it right. *Her Lady*. That's who we're talking about."

"Is she *here*?"

"There wouldn't be much left of Chicago if she was. No, she's only sent one of her spies, one of her sentinels. By this time, she at least has a hint that Oberon's not only alive but very active. He hasn't exactly been surreptitious in his actions." I mulled over that fact myself for a moment. "In fact, he's taunting her. She'd still be powerful on this side of the Gate, enough for all of us to worry, but he's been here a long, long time. Our side has things that Feirie fears as much as we should fear Feirie's power."

"Is that true, Fetch?"

He gave a limp wag of his tail. "You have a world of iron. We sicken around so much iron unless we surrender a part of ourselves and become more . . . of this place."

"True, true!" echoed the black bird.

"What does that mean? Nick, is that why Fetch can only talk around you?"

"And Kravayik!" the lycanthrope offered too readily.

"In part," I immediately interjected, hoping she wouldn't pay attention to the name. "It's also in part why, even around me, Fetch can't become his true self." And for that, we should've all been grateful. As loyal as he was, I knew that Fetch hungered for the power he'd once wielded. After all, he hadn't been sent to kill me because he'd been expected to fail.

Claryce considered what I'd said. "Then, wouldn't she be less of a threat, too?"

"The only thing you can compare Her Lady with is His Lord. Oberon's power *was* Feirie. Even exiled, he wielded a lot. If she decides to come here, it'll be because she intends to kill him as quickly and assuredly as she can before he does the same to her. That the city might be destroyed and hundreds dead would mean nothing to either."

"But Oberon must be a deal weaker than he once was. Surely she might be able to take him without much trouble and without any damage to Chicago—"

I shook my head. "You're thinking in terms of our realm. The great powers of Feirie think in terms of theirs."

Claryce had a lot of questions, but there was no more time for them. I had just one I needed answered and that from the black bird. "Where did you see it?"

"The house, the house, the house, the house!" Its constant repetitiveness showed just how distraught even this exile was at the thought of Her Lady's servant so near.

I was intrigued by the answer. The servant had spent some time near the burnt remnants of my former sanctum. I wondered if it knew what could still be salvaged from the seemingly ravaged grounds. At the very least, Her Lady's servant appeared to be headed on the wrong trail if it was investigating the fire.

"Was it still there when you took off to find me?"

"Yes, yes!"

"We should be safe from it," I told Claryce. "From what I've heard, it's merely looking matters over. Her Lady understands what it would mean to breach the Gate. Even she's got to consider those consequences."

Claryce gave me a slight smile. "If you say so, then I trust you, Nick." But just as I was beginning to calm down a bit, she asked, "And what about Kravayik?"

"Oh, all's copacetic with him," Fetch blurted. "He's on our side—" He snapped his muzzle shut when he realized how hard I was staring at him.

Claryce also noticed, though. "Tell me who Kravayik is, Nick. I'm tired of secrets, especially when I'm caught in the center of them."

"Kravayik is watching something for me," I finally admitted. "Like Fetch and the bird here, he's an exile from Feirie. Unlike them, he's taken a different course in trying to survive in this world."

"And what's that?"

Before I could answer, Fetch decided to jump in again. "He's found religion, Mistress Claryce," the shapeshifter cheerfully offered. "Kravayik's joined the Church!"

CHAPTER 11

Holy Name Cathedral had been built on the ashes of Chicago after what most people called the Great Fire, rising to become a symbol of the city's rebirth. I'd been a silent part of it since its inception and even before the cornerstone was laid almost three years after the Night the Dragon Breathed, I'd set matters in motion to protect the Clothos card from being stolen by any Wyld. When the church had sought out donations for the cathedral's construction, I'd been among the contributors.

It was the least I could do considering the sacrilegious act I'd committed by placing such a dangerous thing inside its hallowed halls.

The imposing Gothic structure loomed above me, the last fading glimpses of the day giving it a condemning appearance. I knew that the notion the cathedral was judging me for my terrible sin arose from my own sense of guilt, but I still made the sign of the cross despite that.

I would've preferred to enter during the day, but for what I needed to do it had to be past sunset, at a time when Kravayik could gain us privacy. The clergy barely even noticed his presence anymore, so adept had he become in fading into the background. It served my purpose well, and the fact that he considered his task an honor made me feel slightly less bothered by my tremendous abuse of his gratitude.

True to her nature as I knew it from so many lives, Claryce had refused my entreaties to stay behind after we'd visited the quarters over the shop. I'd been tempted to use the dragon's abilities to set her to sleeping, but, as before, couldn't bring myself to do it. It wasn't just that she was Cleolinda reborn; it was also because she was *Claryce*.

More and more, it was because she was *Claryce*.

I finally relented and left her in a public place, another diner not far from Holy Name and still on State Street. The black bird I'd sent off to keep an eye out for any other sign of Her Lady's spy. Fetch, though, was to remain at Claryce's side at all times. She'd wanted to come with me, but that would've meant revealing the card's existence to her as well, and the less she knew, the better.

When night had finally claimed the city, I walked up the steps and tested one of the cathedral doors. I'd no idea whether they were generally locked at this time or whether Kravayik had made certain the way would be open.

I'd seen some of the most elaborate, most ornate churches and cathedrals in my long term of service and, while there were certainly those that outshone Holy Name, I still couldn't help be awed by what had been wrought here. I made the sign again and continued on as if I was supposed to be there.

I headed straight for the altar, the focus of the chamber and the safest hiding place I could imagine for the card.

The cathedral remained silent save for my breathing, but I knew when Kravayik neared. The shadows in the corners deepened a little and a cool breeze with no discernible origin wafted through the chamber.

"Master Nicholas," he murmured, much too reverently for my taste. "I am honored by this blessed visit."

Despite the legends, despite Kravayik's words, I'd never much felt like a saint. Certainly not like Michael or any of the archangels, nor like someone like Paul or Francis. I had been and always would consider myself a soldier. Hopefully an honest one, but still a soldier.

Much like Kravayik had once been, even in the Court of Feirie.

He stood taller than me but almost half as wide at the shoulder. If someone could manage to focus on his face long enough, they might see the black eyes were too big, the nose too small, and the head as a whole elongated like no normal human skull. They'd have noticed that the ears were sharp and that the receding hair—cropped short and patterned in what was almost a monk's cut—had a hint of dark green in it.

But not even the clergy that'd hired Kravayik, on the letter of recommendation from a European archbishop none of them would ever speak with, ever realized that they never focused on the caretaker long enough to actually see those peculiarities. That was due to influence on Kravayik's part, for which the exile prayed for forgiveness—along with the many other things he prayed for—for hours each day and night.

As Fetch had told Claryce, Kravayik had indeed found religion.

"Immediately after your sudden but welcome call, I did my best to make certain that we would not be interrupted. I felt that your need to be here was strong enough reason to cast the very slight glamour on the blessed archbishop and the rest." His Feirie features distorted into a reasonably human expression of remorse and fear. "Did I do all right?"

"Yes, you did very well." I prayed for my own forgiveness just in case I was wrong. Whatever my mounting sins, there was no reason that Kravayik should also suffer because of them.

He drifted—yes, *drifted*—toward me. Outwardly, his garments appeared to be a black shirt and black pair of pants. Truthfully, they were illusion, Kravayik's actual form not quite built to wear such garments. However, the robes and silver-thread armor he did wear would never have been accepted by his employers and, while Kravayik had the highest respect for them, he also knew the importance of the task—or curse, as I often felt—that I'd set for him after saving his life.

"I am heartened to hear that," he replied with true relief. "Each time I abuse my gift and my rebirth, I feel as if I am becoming one of the dark ones again."

By "gift," he referred to the fact that, despite having been born of Feirie, he still retained power in such a holy place. Not only were shadow folk not able to enter churches, mosques, and other similar sites, but they could not even affect the sites with their power. Feirie magic failed at the very edge of holy ground.

But somehow—and I couldn't argue with Kravayik's own interpretation in this case—a miracle had been granted to the former servant of both His Lord and Her Lady. Not only had he been able to freely enter holy ground, but a form of his magic abilities had remained.

And that had only made him more invaluable to me.

"You know why I'm here, don't you?"

He hesitated, then, "Someone of the Court has taken interest in the card. Is it Her Lady? Has she extended her foul reach here?"

She'd done just that, but I chose not to mention her. Even more so than Fetch, Kravayik disliked both Her Lady and her former mate. As a member of the Court, he knew more than most what the two were like and saw Her Lady as no better. I could only scarcely disagree with him on that. At least Her Lady respected the balance between the two realms better than Oberon.

"No. *He* survived that night."

I didn't have to say his name. Kravayik recoiled in recognition, his features distorting more and losing some of the false humanity he wore so that he could exist among mortals.

"*His Lord*? His foulness still stains this precious world?"

"His *name* is Oberon," I interjected, trying to sound more confident about matters than I did. "*Oberon*. He's no longer lord of Feirie. He is not the Court personified, not the essence of its power!"

The last was virtually a quote from Kravayik himself, uttered to me when first he'd come here as an exile. He nodded slowly, aware that what I said was true, but also aware that even as a refugee himself Oberon was a very, very dangerous force.

"So . . ." His somewhat more human face reshaped. He pursed his lips in thought. "So . . . you need to *see* the card."

"It's not that I don't trust your abilities—"

He waved off my apologetic tone. "This is about *Oberon*. There is no precaution too great to take with him, Master Nicholas. If I have proven insufficient in my duties, I would know that as well!"

I gave him an appreciative nod. Had I been born a creature of Feirie, I'd probably have been a lot like him. I respected Kravayik as I did few others.

I took a deep breath. Kravayik blinked twice, the first time he'd blinked at all and a sure sign of just how anxious he was. The pair of us took up positions directly before the altar. We reached toward it with our right hands, his much longer and more tapering than mine. I whispered a prayer.

A seemingly solid part of the mensa slid open.

From within, a faint emerald glow arose. Kravayik gasped and muttered the Lord's Prayer.

With as little eagerness for this deed as he'd just shown, I stepped up and removed the Clothos card from its resting place.

To the uneducated it most resembled a tarot card and with good reason. It was the basis for the *first* such decks, all of them pale attempts by the powers of Feirie to recreate what apparently could not be recreated even by His Lord. Those attempts had gradually spilled over into the mortal realm.

The card was small, fitting in the palm of my hand. It had rounded edges trimmed in gold. I'd placed it face down—for good reason—which thus displayed for me an intricate pattern of leaves and branches, with the black silhouette of a snarling wolf in the center. The leaves were emerald in color and the source of the glow. The branches were silver.

"It is . . . so frail-looking," Kravayik muttered.

"Yeah, it looks like it, anyway." Neither of us had seen the card in twenty-five years, when I'd decided to reassure myself that no one had managed to move it since it'd first been placed in this small tomb. That last visit I'd not even turned it over, preferring not to risk keeping the card out in the open any more than I had to.

This time, though, I all but felt compelled to look.

"Master Nicholas! I'd not advise—"

His warning went unheeded. Not since the last time I'd confronted Oberon had anyone gazed upon the face.

Three cups greeted my anxious gaze. Three silver goblets. Each was held by a hand similar to Kravayik's. A black liquid filled the three goblets. A constellation never seen in this world hovered over the cups.

I knew from a thousand decks I'd seen over the centuries what the Three of Cups meant to most. Groups coming together for a common goal. Support and counseling. A score of other similar meanings and a few not so akin.

But none of those meanings had anything to do with this card or any part of the Clothos Deck. What tarot cards attempted to do, the Clothos Deck *did*.

Imagine if one could change the entire world—and *everything* else, for that matter—by simply shuffling a tarot deck and adjusting the cards drawn as needed. That only began to explain what the Clothos Deck was capable of.

And with this single card—this card that was hardly the most powerful of the pack—Oberon had nearly obliterated an entire city and every living soul in it.

As I held the card, I began to think of the good it could've done if wielded by someone not only expert enough but also of strong moral values. I wasn't the best choice in that respect, but I couldn't help thinking at that moment that at least I would've done better than many. With a little careful practice, maybe I could even—

A hand gently took hold of my wrist.

"You do not want it, Master Nicholas. It will only cause misery and grief for you, those you love, and everyone else . . ."

I turned the card over, for once welcoming the sinister lupine shape on the back. Kravayik removed his hand. I took a deep breath, then set the card back into its resting place.

The granite lid slid over the card, sealing it in. The solidity of the mensa reformed. There was no hint that the stone was not one piece.

We stepped back together. I finally looked at Kravayik.

"Thanks for that."

"I had the utmost faith in you, Master Nicholas, but felt a little encouragement would not be rejected."

I grunted. "Your faith in me was stronger than mine was."

"You are a humble man, part of the reason you are a saint."

"That's not quite how it works," I muttered. I eyed the altar, both admiring the handiwork I'd paid dearly for but also giving thanks that providence—or perhaps God above, as Kravayik believed—had given me such a guardian for it.

"Is all as you expected, Master Nicholas?"

"It is." But it didn't help me as I'd hoped it would. Still, at least I knew that the cathedral hadn't been breached . . . so far. "There may be some visitors to the cathedral soon. Are you ready for them?"

Kravayik straightened. "Though I may sin deeply for it, I will stand against any who enter."

"Don't assume that since they'll probably be human that they'll be easy to take."

For the first time, Kravayik looked a bit offended. "I did not survive so long in the Court underestimating even the least of my rivals. I will take care. I promise."

He paused, considering something. I didn't like when he considered something. It was never good.

"I am reminded of a few incidents of late, Master Nicholas. I thought nothing of them. There have been such in the past . . . but now, with the knowledge that *he* is alive, they are perhaps of significance."

"Like what?"

"Small accidents. Little things. Even the fire in the rectory. All with explanations . . . just as *he* would desire."

Kravayik still couldn't bring himself to say Oberon's name *too* often. "They might be something. Keep an eye out."

"There is one more bit of news. I feel I have failed you for not mentioning this, too—"

"Forget that. What's this news?"

Still looking as if he'd betrayed me into the very arms of Oberon, he said, "Someone offered to *buy* the cathedral."

He had my full attention. *"Holy Name?"*

Clearly sharing my astonishment, Kravayik continued. "They have made the offer twice. A very princely sum, I must say. The offer even includes an excellent alternative site, plus assistance with all building permits and necessities."

"Are you usually privy to church business?"

"In my attempt to remain a humble servant, I am sometimes overlooked by my employers when even in the room. I fear I may have sinned in this regard, though."

"Do you happen to remember who the offer was from?" I asked, ignoring his constant concern. Though born of Feirie, it was likely he'd be accepted into Heaven long before me.

"I did by sheer luck happen to see the first letter. It was from a lawyer named O'Rourke. It did not name the actual source of the offer."

The Irish moniker was enough for me to tie it to the North Side, which in turn tied it to Oberon.

He *did* know where the card was . . . and apparently had for some time.

"It is him, is it not, Master Nicholas?"

"I think so. I don't know how he found out. I didn't think he knew, but he does. Still, he can't directly take it . . . and that must drive him crazy."

It was another shock, another example of Oberon having spent the past fifty years building to this point. Yet I felt some relief in knowing that, despite everything, he hadn't been able to get the card yet. "Let me know if the offer comes up again."

"If you ask it, I shall do it."

I started to turn, only to spot another vague figure near the image of Saint Peter. Kravayik said nothing, which meant that he didn't see him. Few did other than me.

"Such power in such a tiny thing," Diocles quietly declared as I neared.

Ignoring him, I looked to Kravayik one last time. "Be careful. Please."

He smiled as if I'd literally blessed him. "I shall be. I am grateful for your concern and all that you've done for me. Never in all my existence in the Court could I have imagined a world such as you gave me! A path that does not subsist on constant and eternal treachery, with only oblivion as the final reward!"

It was a shortened version of the speech of gratitude he'd given me more than once since I'd saved him. "Get some rest, Kravayik. You'll need it."

"I shall pray, yes." For the exile, prayer *was* rest. Kravayik had gone from drawing his strength from the machinations of the Feirie Court to drawing it from his faith. Even after fifty years, he spoke with the zealousness of a new convert. "Good eve to you, Master Nicholas."

Kravayik drifted away from me, disappearing into the shadowy area from which he had emerged. As a caretaker, he had quarters in the cathedral, very spartan ones consisting of a bed, a table, and an icebox. Not needing to eat much—a few sips of broth and a cup of water every couple days—he saved most of his pay so that he could donate it to the church again. He, who had once reaped rich benefits from having the favor of the most powerful forces of Feirie was now more than satisfied with his current, simple life.

Simple until Oberon's return, anyway.

I went from my admiration for Kravayik to my disdain for Diocles. I'd hoped he'd not show up here, but our infernal bond meant that whenever I entered a house of worship, so could he. He remained for the most part within St. Michael's for the simple reason that it was the church with which I was most tied.

"You can forgive that creature his sins despite knowing how he served the Feirie Court . . ."

Despite having determined that I was going to ignore him, I

stopped and answered, "There's no comparison between Kravayik and you. Kravayik took on a transformation from what he'd been bred to be to something his realm couldn't even comprehend."

He gritted his teeth, the let out a cry of frustration. "By God, Georgius! What must I do to earn your forgiveness? If I could reverse the centuries and prevent your execution, I would! You know that!"

"I do," I admitted, "but it's not so simple."

"Then, tell me! What will it take?"

"More than you can *do*," I snapped.

The late emperor swung at me. I'd never seen him so furious and wasn't prepared to defend myself. Of course, I remembered how foolish we were both acting just before his fist went through me.

Diocles glared. "If I am condemned to follow you until the end of days, I pray that Heaven grants me one time I can strike you solid!"

"Not so penitent after all, eh, Your Imperial Majesty?"

"More than *you*, Georgius!"

"Nicholas," I flatly reminded him.

"*Nicholas*," Diocles the phantom repeated with still-smoldering bitterness. "*Nicholas*. Well, *Nicholas*, I wish you nothing but the best in this endeavor. I know who you face. I know what he wants. I know you fear that *she* will be slain as the others were. I pray for your victory, knowing the magnitude of its importance . . ."

"Thanks," I managed as I stepped around him. "Go home now, Your Imperial Majesty."

He actually had no choice. Once I exited the cathedral, he'd immediately return to St. Michael's.

"Wait."

Although certain that I'd regret it, I looked back. "Well?"

"Father Jonathan preaches a fine sermon, don't you think?"

In truth—a truth Diocles also knew—I'd hardly ever attended the good priest's actual sermons. I preferred quiet reflection late at night, when I could be alone with my thoughts.

"He gave an especially good one this last Sunday, *Georgius*. It certainly affected the Hispanian sitting in the last pew."

I hated games, whether they were the deadly, sadistic kind like the Feiriefolk played or the little jibes that were all that were left to the late, unlamented Emperor Diocletian. "What's the point?"

"He talked to Father Jonathan briefly after—"

"Listening in to confessions? That's a sin, I think."

"No confession. He walked up to the priest after the sermon. Thanked him for it, then asked questions. You know how cunning the Hispanians can be—"

Hispanians. I'd paid little attention to the word, Diocles often describing modern groups by the regions of his former empire. The Irish were Hibernians. Hispanians were anyone of a Spanish tone, including even Mexi—

I cut him off. "What did he look like?"

Diocles gave a very detailed description. With so much time to kill and having already memorized every detail of St. Michael's long ago, the dead emperor looked forward to the sermons not only for their value, but also because they brought new lives into his limited existence. Diocles could tell me much about the majority of Father Jonathan's congregation, to the point that he sometimes sounded like a gossip. Whenever there was a new member, he was certain to tell me. If he'd said that the man had been anything other than Hispanian, I'd have ended the conversation there and then.

But a Hispanian who asked questions . . .

Even before Diocles finished, I recognized Father's Jonathan's latest addition as Inspector Alejandro Cortez. Even if I'd somehow managed to accept that Cortez had gone to St. Michael's for the usual reasons, the question of why his Maria and the children hadn't been along for the ride was one I doubted had a good answer. Cortez had found me in my sanctum; now it seemed he was looking into my interest in the church.

Eye think he should burn . . .

I let that suggestion remain uncommented on, instead saying to Diocles, "Was that the only time he's been there?"

"The only time."

"Let me know if he shows up again, whatever the day."

"As you wish, G—Nicholas."

His use of my current name was as much an attempt to get on my good side and hopefully someday gain his desired redemption as it was to help me, but it *had* been news I was interested in so I gave him a grateful nod. We'd be at each other's throat's soon enough again. "I've got to go."

"Cleolinda awaits you."

"*Her* name is Claryce."

He looked apologetic again. "I pray you save her this time."

I should've thanked him for that, but we'd talked more than enough for my comfort. I couldn't allow my bitterness against him to fade. I might then actually give him what he wanted.

I wasn't ready for that. Not now. Not even with the shadow of Oberon over me.

Claryce and Fetch awaited me just outside the entrance to the diner. I'd told her to stay inside and suspected she'd stepped out for Fetch's sake. After my conversation with Diocles, I couldn't help stare at her anew. Yes, she was *Cleolinda*, but again I couldn't help noticing the differences both in appearance and character that made her very much Claryce.

And by the light coming from within the diner, I could suddenly see something else. I could see the shadow cast by Claryce, the lesser one cast by Fetch . . . and the third one just behind Claryce with no visible body to which it could be attached.

CHAPTER 12

Fetch must've noticed the subtle change in my posture. He snapped at Claryce's skirt, grabbing up a good mouthful. Before she could protest, he jerked her to her left.

It was probably the only thing that prevented the widening shadow hand from managing to grab hold of her waist.

There were too many eyes around for me to readily draw Her Lady's gift, but that didn't prevent me from charging at the shadow. It withdrew the oversized hand and melted into the darkness.

Eye will show you . . .

Without interruption, the view changed. Darkness gave way to the emerald world. Now I saw the shadow and the direction it headed. Being what it was, it glided from the side of one building to the next. Unimpeded by a human body, it ran at a pace I was having trouble matching. Fetch might've done better, but if he knew what was good for him, he would still be watching Claryce no matter what she might order this time.

The shadow man twisted around a corner. I kept praying that he wouldn't simply disappear like the ones in the Delke house. All the thug to whom the shadow belonged had to do was pull off whatever Feirie artifact Oberon had given him and the trail would end right there.

And then I wondered just *why* the hood didn't do just that.

I whirled around—and had what felt like Ed Healey crash into me. But even the Bears' tackle wasn't as heavily muscled as the giant that fell on me. As we crashed to the street, I heard a low curse in what I knew was Gaelic. A gloved hand tried to crush my throat.

Fighting for breath, I twisted onto my back and reached up.

Through the dragon's gaze, I saw the grinning face of Doolin. I'd figured that he was strong, but not *this* strong.

Let Eye free! Eye will bite his head off and swallow it whole!

The temptation to let him take over was great, but I couldn't help thinking that giving in would result in something far worse happening.

Doolin squeezed tighter. That was when I finally felt the metal digging deep into my throat and realized he wasn't wearing a glove but a *gauntlet*.

I didn't know what its use was, but it made me even more certain that I'd chosen right by not giving in to the dragon. However, that wasn't preventing Doolin from crushing my windpipe. It was possible that the gauntlet was augmenting his already great strength, but either way, I only had seconds left before I suffocated or else he made a pulp out of my throat.

Doolin was no simple bruiser when it came to fighting. He had his knee on my left arm and held the right one with his other hand. For many in my position, that would've been enough to determine the outcome of the struggle.

But those many hadn't spent lifetime after lifetime already fighting to survive against even more vicious opponents than Doolin. He'd pinned my arms but not my legs. I twisted sharply and managed to use the left one to shove him off me, in the process freeing a hand.

Even then, though, I only bought a reprieve. Doolin's grip on my throat loosened but no more.

"Damned wop!" he growled, as he tried to squeeze again.

I wasn't sure if Oberon had told him I was a Roman or if Doolin just thought I was Italian since my skin was swarthier than his pasty flesh. It was possible he even believed I was part of the South Side gang. Whatever the case, his assumption seemed to fuel his attack, making me wonder about his past history with Capone's boys.

In his growing eagerness to throttle me, he failed to remember that one hand was free. I wanted to punch him in the throat, but the angle only permitted me to hit him in the side of the neck.

It was enough to make him hack and cough and nothing else. He tried to shift to his original position.

A hound's savage growl filled my ears. I swore, not because I thought another creature was about to attack me, but because I knew that it was coming to my rescue despite my earlier admonishments.

However, rather than falling upon Doolin, Fetch's growl faded further down the street. I tried to see what was happening with him but couldn't turn my head.

Then, Doolin grunted and crumpled to my left. He wasn't unconscious, but he was stunned. I marveled more that he could move at all when I saw the size of the broken brick Claryce still wielded.

"Nick! Are you all—"

I'd barely started recovering myself when Doolin shook off Claryce's blow and grabbed for her. It was enough to stir me on. I grabbed for the gauntleted hand, hoping to tear the enchanted artifact free.

The deadly short burst of a tommy gun echoed ominously from the direction Fetch had gone. Doolin swore in Gaelic again and threw himself off me. His heavy body bowled into Claryce.

Her Lady's gift was meant against the creatures of Feirie, but with Doolin wearing Oberon's artifact, I saw no reason to hesitate in using the blade against the thug. It still wasn't clear exactly what the glove did, and I couldn't take the chance that it might be deadlier than he'd revealed so far.

I reached into my coat.

Doolin pushed himself to his knees, murder very much in his expression. He thrust a hand into his own dark coat for what I assumed was a gun—

And immediately vanished.

If he'd simply tried to shield himself from my sight, the dragon's eyes would've still ferreted him out. My companion's magic was an older, deeper thing than that of Feirie, which was why it'd proved so invaluable to me, despite its source. If Doolin had still been between Claryce and me, I would've had no trouble discerning that. Yet all I saw was the welcome sight of Claryce quickly bending down to help me.

"Are you all right?" she asked, as she looked me over for injury.

"I'm okay."

"Where'd that beast go?"

Assuming that she meant Doolin and not Fetch, I answered, "Doolin's gone. In addition to the gauntlet, he had some sort of other artifact in his coat."

"Gauntlet? Doolin? Who's that?"

"Our friend with the eagerness to rip apart my windpipe. From the North Side gang. Did you get a look at him?"

"I didn't see anything at first except you slowly choking to death and clutching at the air above you. I thought there was something on top of you, but I couldn't make it out clearly. I found this piece and made a guess where there might be a head. He grew clearer after I hit him, but I never got a good view of his face."

"Name Doolin mean anything? Someone around William Delke?"

"No."

I hadn't forgotten Fetch and the possible danger he might be in, but until now I hadn't had the strength to go after him. Leaping to my feet, I ordered, "The diner's still open. Go there—"

"No! I'm not listening—"

The screech of car tires resounded on the empty street. I grabbed Claryce and threw both of us toward the curb as a black Lincoln sedan barreled toward where we'd just been. However, those inside appeared not at all interested in us but rather the huge, four-legged shape racing behind them. No normal hound could've caught up with the swerving Lincoln, but there was nothing normal about Fetch.

From the front passenger side emerged a gritty thug armed with a tommy. He fired at Fetch, but the lycanthrope dodged aside.

"Keep back!" I warned Claryce. I reached into my coat, but not for Her Lady's gift. Instead, from the other side I drew the silver-tipped dagger. I'd kept it with me since meeting Claryce for the simple fact I could throw it.

And I did, aiming not for the shifting gunner but rather the front passenger tire. My aim was perfect. The blade sank into the rubber. I felt a little guilt using the blessed weapon so, but decided the guilt was worth protecting our lives.

The tire exploded. The Lincoln spun in the direction of the ruined tire. The hood with the tommy retreated inside.

The auto drove over a curb, onto a sidewalk, and against the brick wall of the building beyond. The force of the collision had to have stirred up everybody for the next ten blocks, but I didn't care.

Fetch leapt atop the wrecked vehicle. I came around on the passenger side, ready to draw Her Lady's gift if I had to. I doubted Doolin was in the auto, but I couldn't risk not finding out.

Neither the driver, the gunner, nor anyone possibly in the back had emerged. They'd hit hard, but not so hard that someone shouldn't have at least made a sound.

"Nice work with the shiv, Master Nicholas."

"Quiet!" No one had as yet stepped out to see what'd happened, but that'd change soon. I needed to see the passengers, then get Claryce out of here.

Grabbing the dagger from the tire, I peered into the passenger front. Two dim shapes lay still. There was no one in the back, which meant that, since I'd caught a glimpse of the gunner, I had to hope that Doolin had been driving.

It'd been a faint hope at best, but naturally the other figure was too lanky to be Oberon's hulking killer. I reached in, hoping to shake the thug awake and find out more . . . and then saw that the driver wasn't *breathing*. Not only that, but up close I could also make out that his eyes were half-open, as if he were asleep.

I immediately leaned in to take a second look at the gunner. He was the same. I touched the throat of the driver and felt a flesh so cold even I recoiled. The cold was something I'd come across only a couple of times and both of those had involved the events before I had to set Chicago aflame. Those men had also been serving Oberon, though they hadn't known it probably any more than this pair had. All they'd known is they were paid well by a man who knew what humans called magic and what was merely the nature of the high born of the Feirie Court.

A siren sounded. No one had come out to investigate yet, and I had to assume it was because they thought a turf war had broken out between bootleggers. However, someone *had* been brave enough to call the police.

"Take off, Fetch."

"Yes, Master Nicholas!"

He bounded off the Lincoln and raced down the street in the direction of the safe house. I quickly rejoined Claryce, then hurried with her from the scene.

We were three blocks from the scene by the time the sirens sounded as if the police had arrived. In this part of the neighborhood, people were far enough away from the danger to be emboldened to walk out onto the street and take a few steps toward the sounds. We mixed into the crowd, then turned toward where we could hail a taxi.

I had the cabbie drop us off two blocks from the safe house. Careful to avoid anything that put us in view of the bootleggers, I finally got Claryce to the temporary quarters.

"How long do we stay here?" she asked, rubbing her arms from tension.

"As long as need be. For tonight, I'll sleep downstairs in the old shop—"

Her brow wrinkled. "Why would you do that? There's room here, and I certainly *don't* want to be alone. This isn't any different than your house was."

"Claryce, I shouldn't have ever even allowed us to meet. Oberon used you as bait; if I'd let you be, he would've lost interest in you and tried a different tack. You would've been safe—"

"Safe . . ." She stepped in front of me, so close that I could hear her breathing. Too close. "There's more to this, isn't there? There's a reason *I* was picked by Wil—Oberon! What is it, Nick? What?"

There was a fairly good chance she'd believe me, no matter how wild the story might sound. But if I told her about Cleolinda, if I told her about the other lives, the other hers, she might only see it as a reason to stand beside me even against Oberon. *That* would only guarantee her death.

I couldn't bear to watch Cleolinda die again, and I discovered at that moment that it bothered me even more that *Claryce Simone* in particular would perish.

Arms now crossed, Claryce continued to await my answer. Instead, I strode over to the one bedroom and opened the door. "Better get some rest now. We may have to leave here before sunrise."

"Nick . . ."

Still not looking her in the eye, I went to the Kelvinator. "There's eggs, bacon, coffee, some fruit, and a few other things available. The stove works fine."

"I know all that already—"

Now I looked at her, but not directly into her gaze. From my coat, I pulled the dagger. After placing it on the table in the kitchen area, I added, "You won't need this, but I've left it just in case. Its presence alone should keep anything from entering, but this entire place is also surrounded by a shunning . . . A spell that turns away everything I don't want here. I know it failed with the house, but this one's been strengthened."

She reached for me. "Nick . . ."

"With all that said," I continued, fighting not to reach back. "I'll still sleep ready below in case you call me." I went to the door, ignoring her entreaties. "Sleep well."

"Nick!" Claryce called.

I shut the door behind me and descended to the shop's office, which, like the shop itself, had been abandoned with pretty much everything still intact. I'd left a blanket and some other essentials there. The dust wasn't too bad, not for someone who'd slept in deserts much of his original life. I heard Claryce stomping back and forth—much harder than she needed to, even considering her heels—and felt renewed guilt at not having told her the truth. I was certain that I'd done the right thing, but I was also certain that Claryce *did* deserve the truth.

I prepared my makeshift bed and settled in. My thoughts briefly turned to Fetch. I could've had him stay here as well, but I needed him to see what he could learn in the alleyways and other parts of the city. Fetch, Kravayik, and the black bird were hardly the only refugees from Feirie. To call the reigns of His Lord and, after that, of Her Lady *harsh* would be to make the understatement of all time. Feirie was a realm of power, and those with power worked to crush everyone they could under their heel. Chicago seemed to be following Feirie's lead and not because of any taint spreading through the Gate from Her Lady's realm. After so many centuries among my fellow men, I'd seen the evil that they could do, evil that the darkest of Feirie would've admired. That men could still find redemption and the path to Heaven was something that I readily believed in despite those bloody centuries.

I leaned back, my head propped up by a second, smaller blanket. Claryce moved about for a few minutes more, then evidently settled down. I prayed that at least she would have a good night's sleep; my last one had been the night before Diocles's executioner had done his handiwork.

The *telephone* rang.

Along with the plumbing and other necessities, I'd left the telephone line live. Live, but with no outside connection.

Naturally, I answered it. "Hello?"

An elderly male voice with a heavy Mexican accent said, "I am looking for Mr. Medea."

"This is Nick Medea."

"I am Juan Alonso Perez. I work with an organization that is seeing to the building of a church in South Chicago."

I frowned. The call sounded as if it concerned my "occupation." If it'd come at the house, I'd have thought nothing of it. Here . . .

"How can I help you?"

"For now, we have a small wooden church serving our needs. It was finished only last year." Despite his accent, Juan Alonso Perez spoke excellent English. "A good place. Much respected by the parishioners."

I could hear hesitation when he spoke about the church, which meant only one thing. "You have unexpected things going on at the church?"

"Yes!" he immediately blurted, grasping at my way of describing the situation rather than admit the truth. "Unexpected things . . . such as you mention in your ad."

Everything about this call sounded as it should. The ad found those who needed it. Mr. Alonso Perez appeared to be one of those.

But with the exception of Diocles, I'd never known anything to actually haunt a church . . . unless the ground was no longer consecrated.

My duty to the Gate demanded I check it out, but I didn't want to bring Claryce there with me just in case. "I'm rather busy right now. How urgent is this matter?"

"Very urgent! I would ask you to come this night still, Mr. Medea, if I thought you would accept."

It wasn't out of the ordinary for me to meet "clients" at hours even later than that at which I'd met Mrs. Hauptmann. Still, I wasn't certain about taking on this particular case. Maybe one of the shadow folk had managed to infiltrate the church and make its lair there. I couldn't be sure, though.

I made a decision. "I'll tell you what. I'll—"

There was a click on the phone.

"Mr. Alonso Perez?"

"I am here."

"As I was saying, I can come by tomorrow night. We can discuss this in more detail, then. Will that do?"

There was a pause, then, "Thank you, that will do, Mr. Medea."

He didn't seem inclined to continue, so I asked the obvious. "Where's the church?"

"9024 South Mackinaw Avenue. Our Lady of Guadalupe. Do you know it?"

I had to credit myself for not sounding odd when I answered. "Yes, I've heard of it. Will you meet me there?"

"I will."

"Sounds good, then."

"Thank you very, very much, Mr. Medea. Good night."

This time the click I heard was my new client hanging up. I dropped the receiver and thought. There was no telephone upstairs, so I knew that Claryce hadn't somehow been listening. More importantly, the line should've only rung on its own if it was someone in true need. Everything indicated that Juan Alonso Perez was who he claimed to be.

But I thought it very interesting that he represented the same church where Detective Cortez normally took his family . . . except when he was spying on St. Michael's, of course.

I slowly drifted off with that thought still playing around in my mind. Naturally, the dream started anew the moment sleep took over, and once again I fought in vain to keep Claryce alive from the dragon—

Some sense of danger woke me just as my unconscious mind noticed the fact that the dream had altered exactly who I tried to defend. I knew that prickly feeling immediately.

Oberon's sentinel was back in the vicinity.

I was fairly confident that it didn't know we were here and that it was again investigating the bootlegging operation nearby. I was tempted to simply try to ignore it, but I suddenly felt concerned that despite the shunning it might yet notice something about this building.

Slipping out of the back, I came around so that I could observe the area ahead. Without a word to me, my unseen companion shifted our gaze. In the emerald world, I got my first glimpse of what might be Oberon's spy.

All I could tell was that it had wings or something like them. It was perched atop a roof next to the building, apparently watching for any outside activity by Capone's goons.

I kept my hand near the inside of my coat but didn't draw Her Lady's gift just yet. Doing so might actually alert the shadow creature, which I didn't want to do unless necessary.

Something caught the observer's attention. It fluttered to the ground in a strange way, almost more like a kite than a bird. I rethought the possible choices based on my previous encounters, but nothing similar came to mind.

I should've gone back inside, but it was then that I caught a glimpse of a *second* and very different watcher.

This one was nothing more than a black shadow, darker than the night in which it traveled. I wondered why Oberon needed a second watcher . . . then understood that this wasn't one of his.

It was *Her Lady's* sentinel.

I silently swore in a manner that would've made the bootleggers inside blush. The dragon chuckled.

Eye can deal with both vermin . . . let me out and I'll burn them . . .

And the neighborhood along with them, I pointed out. I pushed on, concerned about two shadow folk from opposing sides confronting each other among mortals.

Her Lady's pet vanished behind another nearby building. I caught another glimpse of Oberon's watcher and knew that it was just a matter of moments before the pair came face to face—assuming that, being part of Feirie, they even *had* faces.

As I was considering what to do when that unwanted confrontation happened, the back door of the hidden barrelhouse opened, and the same huge bootlegger who'd discovered me last time stepped out to take a smoke.

Unfortunately, he did it right in front of Oberon's observer. The light from his match illuminated the front of the creature.

It had a face, but one that made the hood's mug as handsome as Douglas Fairbanks's in *The Thief of Bagdad* or his newest sword epic *Don Q, Son of Zorro*. In fact, what the Wyld had was a face for which Lon Chaney probably would've given his entire makeup collection to be able to reproduce. I'd seen the posters for next week's release of *The Phantom of the Opera* and suspected that what Chaney came up with this time *still* wouldn't be half as frightening and grotesque.

There was no chance I could've saved the man. From within what I now saw was some kind of cloak, both long, sinewy hands of the Wyld thrust out.

The long nails at the ends of each four-fingered hand thrust through coat, shirt, flesh, and bone and into the lungs of the bootlegger. They withdrew before the thug even had time to understand that he was already dead.

I don't know if I made some sound, or if the creature just decided to look my way as the body fell, but suddenly Oberon's pet saw me. And even though I couldn't make out its ugly mug any more, I could imagine its glee at having the chance to kill another innocent.

I grabbed for Her Lady's gift—and my hand went numb.

The Wyld lunged at me. Even though I could see him closing on me at a fantastic rate, my hand refused to move.

And I realized it was the *dragon* doing it.

Before I could understand why or how, something came between us. The shadow passed across Oberon's watcher.

I heard it squeal in fright, then in pain. The squeal didn't carry far, which was probably a good thing for the sanity of anyone who would've heard the bloodcurdling noise.

Just like that, it ended. The shadow moved away. Right there, I wished I could've dismissed the dragon's gaze, because it gave me a good view of the putrid mess that briefly pooled on the ground before sinking out of sight.

I started to back away. My hand still wouldn't budge. In my head, I screamed at the dragon, but he kept oddly quiet.

And then . . . Her Lady's sentinel swooped down before me.

CHAPTER 13

It started as a blot of utter black in my emerald world, a blot that stretched and stretched until it stood at least two feet taller than me. The outline reminded me of nothing less than the proverbial Grim Reaper, though even thinner and with no discernible arms or legs visible in the shrouded shape.

My hand suddenly became movable again, but I knew better than to draw Her Lady's gift. It'd probably work against her servant, but then again, it might not.

Gatekeepers . . .

The word came to me like the low groan of an ancient sarcophagus being shoved open. I knew that sound well, having been forced to free myself from my own after discovering I was alive again—not still— and buried.

I also noticed that the shadow creature'd used the plural. Of course it knew about the dragon. Anything closely serving Her Lady would be well-informed.

"She knows . . ." I finally said.

She knows . . .

"That still doesn't give her cause to breach the Gate!" I growled, as quietly as I could. "She's only making the situation worse!"

The shadow creature rippled, something I would've missed without the dragon's eyes. I wondered about the movement.

When it didn't reply, I pushed on. "What do you know about Oberon's presence here?"

Again came the rippling. This time, I thought I understood. However fearsome this sentinel was, it still feared two things—Her Lady and His Lord. It might've been sent to observe or even hunt

Oberon, but that didn't mean it didn't fear Oberon. Any sensible creature would've.

"Do you know what he's up to?"

She commands . . . this obeys . . .

"Not much for conversation, are you?" I was beginning to miss Fetch, for more reasons than one. Without the ability to draw the blade, I was in very precarious circumstances.

Remove him . . . or she will send the Court . . .

I had just enough idea what that meant to be very ill at ease. "*Nothing* else comes through! If I find it has, you know what will happen."

I reached up as if to pull the coat open in advance of drawing Her Lady's gift.

And once more, I saw the sentinel ripple. However, before our confrontation could go any farther, excited voices rose from inside the illegal distillery. Without even looking back, the sentinel stretched higher and higher as if a piece of taffy pulled upward by some giant hand. At the same time, it grew thinner . . . until finally it became so thin that the shadow creature simply vanished.

Its unsettling departure had taken all of a single breath to complete. I didn't have such luck. Aware what it'd look like if they found their pal with two huge holes in his chest and me standing just a short distance away, I retreated into the darkness as fast as possible.

My eyes once more normal, I returned to the safe house and found Claryce waiting for me in the shop. She was still dressed and looked as if she hadn't been sleeping. In her hand she held an Eveready flashlight I'd left upstairs just in case. With one palm she'd smothered most of the light, so as not to take any chance of it showing beyond where she stood.

"What happened?" she demanded. "Where did you go?"

"I was just checking on our bootlegger friends—"

Before I could say more, we heard an uproar. I rushed to the window, Claryce right behind me. She had the presence of mind to keep the light covered.

Through the crack, I saw two autos go screeching around the corner and past our building. From their speed, I wasn't worried that they planned on searching the neighborhood. They already had something definitive in mind.

"What's going on out there, Nick? Is it a turf war?"

"That's what they think." Even as I said that, I knew it was the wrong thing.

She turned me to face her. "Are you involved in that? What *did* happen?"

"One of their men got killed. I didn't do it. They think it was the North Siders."

"And what do you think?" Claryce asked pointedly.

"I think the North Side's involved." It was a truthful statement. Oberon's spy *had* been keeping an eye on Big Al's boys in part for Moran and Weiss.

Claryce didn't look entirely convinced, but she finally gave in. The racket outside faded, probably because most of the hoods had taken off after the rival thugs they thought had made the monstrous hit. I realized that both autos had headed in the quickest direction leading to the North Side stronghold. It was doubtful that they'd dare go all the way there. Once they figured that the killers had successfully taken it on the lam, they'd circle back, with someone making sure to let Capone know what'd happened.

"Who was that on the telephone?"

I hadn't thought that she'd heard. "No one. Wrong number."

"A wrong number? To you?" She leaned against one of the counters. Her expression was one I'd seen before, and not just on the face of Claryce Simone. I'd been confronted by it more than once by her earlier incarnations. "Was it *Oberon*?"

"No . . . but you're right. I'm sorry. I should've told you the truth. It was another client—"

"Someone worried about the supernatural? Calling this late?"

"Do you remember the ad?" When she'd nodded, I continued, "It says to call any time, especially at night. He did."

"He—are you sure it's real?"

I nodded. "He couldn't have reached me if he wasn't the real thing. It doesn't work like that."

Claryce slumped. "I'm sorry, Nick. I don't think I really know how *anything* works anymore."

Against my better judgment, I walked over and put a comforting arm over her shoulder. She leaned against my chest. After the last time she'd done that, I'd sworn to myself it wouldn't happen again. Too late, I felt the rush of emotions.

Kiss her . . . my malevolent partner mocked. *Or would you prefer Eye did?*

I jolted, then pulled my arm away.

"Nick?" Claryce looked up. I knew what those eyes were saying.

"We'd better get you back upstairs," I said in as casual a manner as I could.

To both my relief and my regret, she sighed, then went to the back door without another word. Claryce took one last look at me. "Good night, Nick . . ."

I only nodded. I listened to her footsteps, especially once she was above me. Claryce spent little time moving about, which I prayed meant that she'd finally gone to bed.

Returning to my own makeshift quarters, I tried not to think of what would've happened if I'd let things proceed as they'd been about to. If it hadn't been for the dragon's snide remark . . .

You are welcome . . . The words oozed mockery.

I shut my eyes, for once welcoming the coming nightmare over my more and more troubled personal thoughts.

I'd arranged for a radio in the quarters above and so, once Claryce let me know it was safe to enter, I tuned in WGN and listened for any news out of the ordinary. I didn't have to wait long. Eddie Zion, a former bodyguard for Genna Brothers associate Samuzzo Amatuna—himself gunned down just days ago outside a West Side barber shop—had been drilled shortly after Amatuna's funeral. There was no doubt in my mind that it had the fingerprints of Moran on it, even if he hadn't actually been one of the triggermen. I also knew that he'd done it with the okay of "William Delke." Gunning for the Genna Brothers was a step toward facing Capone head on again, even though the Gennas and the Outfit weren't exactly on the best of terms themselves.

There was no mention of any incident near the safe house and, to my further interest, not a word about the torching of my original sanctum. I'd been combing the papers and radio for some word of the fire but found nothing. I wondered why that was. Without a building to shield, the shunning would've faded away almost immediately.

Claryce'd been listening with me while we ate. She picked up on my slight reactions right away. "Are these tied into everything else?"

"If Moran and his friends are involved, then Oberon's involved."

"But why the senseless killing?"

"A turf war keeps the cops occupied and, even though they're only *human* in his eyes, Oberon leaves nothing to chance." That made me think of Detective Cortez and the call concerning Our Lady of Guadalupe Church. Rather than wait until tonight to see what my client wanted to talk about, I decided to take matters in my own hands. "I need to make a call to the good detective."

"Cortez? Nick, he seems like a decent man, but I can't shake the thought that he knows more than he lets on."

"Maybe . . . or maybe he's just good at his work. Either way, I'd like to see if he can clarify anything for me."

She followed me downstairs to the telephone. I plucked up the receiver and dialed the operator. She would see the line as being from one of several locations around Chicago, none of them near where we actually were. I asked for Cortez's home precinct.

The sergeant who answered had an Irish brogue that momentarily put me on greater guard. For every crook with roots from the Emerald Isle, there were also more brave souls with similar blood working to keep the streets safe. Unfortunately, some of the former wore the same uniforms as the latter.

"Detective Cortez," I said, assuming that there'd be little chance the sergeant wouldn't know the one Cortez in the entire precinct. "He knows me. Nick Medea."

"Cortez?" The sergeant didn't work hard to hide his lack of respect. "The squirt's out. Seein' to the latest mess."

I took a guess. "Eddie Zion?"

"Yeah. If you want Cortez, you'll have to wait awhile."

I thanked the sergeant and hung up. Cortez was methodical and therefore took much more time at the crime scenes than some of his comrades, especially the ones on the take. Unlike some, Cortez wasn't likely to write off the murder as just one more unsolvable case.

"Cortez is on the murder case." I doubted that he was the chief detective, just the one given the dirty tasks. Even knowing how his bosses used him, Cortez would see about getting as much pertinent information as he could, even if the odds were against anyone being brought to trial.

"Are we going to go see him?"

"Claryce—"

"If you start off about leaving me behind again, you're just wasting your time. I'll find a taxi and follow you if I have to."

I knew there was no room for an argument and tried to convince myself that, with so many police around the area, nothing would endanger her. Tried . . . and again failed.

We slipped out the back and made our way a few blocks to a brighter, busier street. When our whiskered cabbie heard the address I wanted, he beamed. "You're in fer an excitin' time there, you two are! They just had a dago gunned down there. Probably one o' the Micks did it. Looks like we're gettin' ready for another break out for turf!"

Out of the cabbie's view, Claryce jabbed a finger at the license, which marked our driver by name as another "Mick." He'd spoken about both sides with the same contempt for their background. It wasn't too surprising. The Irish mob had only one Irishman among the three bosses, while the Outfit had its share of thugs who probably spoke much better Gaelic than the man in the front seat likely did.

I had us dropped off a block from the scene of the gunning. We'd hardly gone a few yards before I noticed something long and gray moving just at the edge of my right eye.

"Wait," I told Claryce. I bent to tie a shoe and glanced in the nearest alley.

His tail wagging, Fetch stared back at me.

Straightening, I casually turned Claryce around and toward the alley. Once out of sight, I eyed Fetch.

"What're you doing down here? This isn't your usual haunts."

"Heard about the hit through the grapevine, Master Nicholas! Wanted to see it—"

"You wanted to see the blood and the body."

His ears flattened, and he looked sheepishly at Claryce before answering, "Just checking in case it was important to ye, Master Nicholas! I swear!"

"Hmmph." I let it pass. I was actually glad to have Fetch nearby. His keen nose and eyes might be of help while I talked with Cortez.

There was no doubt in my mind I'd get a chance to speak with Cortez. He had enough interest in my doings to wonder why I'd come here. I didn't see myself risking anything; the detective wouldn't think I'd actually been involved in the shooting.

I finally had Fetch follow behind us. With his ability to slip unnoticed through crowds, he'd be far less conspicuous on his own rather than pretending to be our pet. That would only draw attention to his unique looks, something I didn't want right now.

There were fewer cops than I'd thought would be here. The body'd already been removed. The two uniformed figures I saw looked bored and ready to leave as soon as they could. They weren't interested in the splotch of red nearby nor paying much attention to their duties guarding the vicinity. Both seemed more interested in what was going on in a nearby building.

I knew that I'd find Cortez there.

"Claryce, will you at least stay here?"

She'd come this far, but to my relief grudgingly agreed. "Fetch, stay with her."

He wasn't so willing. "But Master Nicholas—"

"Fetch . . ."

"Yes, Master Nicholas."

Acting as if I belonged there, I crossed into the scene and headed toward where I assumed Cortez was. I was mildly surprised that neither cop looked my way, but I finally gathered that the only reason they were still here was because Cortez had ordered them to be. I was sure that would go far to adding to his popularity with his fellow policemen.

Before I could reach the building, the good detective stepped out. He didn't bat an eye when he saw me. I watched as he put a small notebook in his jacket and then signaled the two officers. Taking a look, I saw the pair hurrying off.

"They love me, you know?" Cortez mocked. "Didn't want to leave me here alone, but I had to finally insist . . ."

"Yeah, it looked like that's what it was."

He shrugged, his expression growing more honest. "Hey, me, I'm used to the icy mitt." He smiled grimly. "And why do I find you here, Nick Medea? Not your beat."

"I'd say it wasn't yours, either, but you seem to be everywhere doing everything."

He gestured at the blood stain in mock surprise. "What this? Oh, this fits into my investigation. A lot of things and people fit into my investigation, you know?"

And I'm one of them. I made use of that. "I was nearby with a client. Something came up, and I needed to ask you a question. I called the precinct, and they said you'd be here of all places."

Cortez made a *tsking* sound. "They ain't supposed to do that. You must have a way with you . . . or it might be they didn't care who was looking for me." He pulled out a pack of cigarettes. "Gasper?"

"No thanks."

He lit one. "My Maria, she doesn't like me to smoke by the kids, and I don't *ever* do that, you know? She don't like the smell and she says it makes her cough." Suddenly, Cortez lost interest in the cigarette. He dropped it by his feet, then crushed it under one shoe. "I should quit for her. What do you want, Nick Medea?"

"Caught a glimpse of you at St. Michael's last Sunday. It surprised me."

"You were there? Didn't see you."

Before he could press on that, I countered. "Didn't see your Maria and kids with you. Did they go to Our Lady of Guadalupe instead?"

"You know it?"

"I saw the Lady in your auto."

He chuckled. "Good peepers! You should be a cop . . . no . . . maybe not. Yeah, they went there. I was in the area so tried St. Michael's. Very nice place. Too nice for me."

What Cortez meant was that he stuck out as much like a sore thumb at St. Michael's as he did at the precinct. Still, he'd given me just the opening I needed for my main point. "But they're building a new church by you, aren't they? Or at least planning one?"

"Yeah, they're gonna build a nice one."

"I heard that something happened there, though. Something odd."

For some reason, that made Cortez immediately reach for his pack again. He didn't answer until he had the cigarette lit again. "Yeah. The statuette. Made by a man from Guadalupe. Blessed, too, they say. You might've seen it in the papers . . . if you looked way in the back. Not big enough news for the *Trib* or the *Daily News*, you know?"

I cocked my head in agreement. "Stolen?"

"Yeah. Don't know why. Only valuable to us. Me, I think it was someone who doesn't like greasers. Mr. Alonso Perez mention it to you?"

Now he caught *me* by surprise. "You know about him?"

"Hey, Nick Medea! Who told him to call you? Well, actually, he said he kept seeing strange shadows after the statuette disappeared, ghost things. I remembered you and said he should try to find your number. Guess he did."

What he said made sense, but it still bothered me. Cortez's suggestion could've easily set my new client to seeking someone who could help him with the supernatural, and the mention of shadows fit in with creatures from Feirie, but I'd never had someone come to me by such a path.

"Well, I appreciate the business, detective," I replied without missing a step. "I'm supposed to meet with him tonight."

"Hope you can help him . . . *if* you can help him."

I gave him a look of pretended outrage. "Don't you believe in the supernatural?"

"Oh, I believe in God, the Virgin Mary, Jesus, and the church! I also believe there're some things I don't know that might be floating around." He took a long puff. "Just don't know if *you* can help him."

"I'll do what I can," I responded with the same false indignation. I'd heard what I needed. Everything pointed to this being part of Oberon's overall plan. There had to be some touch of Feirie involved in either the statuette or the making of it. I just had absolutely no idea *what*.

"I know that. You're straight, Nick Medea. One of the straightest."

He tossed the half-smoked cigarette to the ground. "How's Miss Simone? Thought I saw her back behind you somewhere."

"She's all right. Didn't want her getting too close to this, in case they hadn't cleaned up everything." It wasn't true—Claryce was showing herself more than able to handle things like this—but it was a good excuse to keep her from Cortez.

"You ask her about the Delke house?"

"She doesn't know a thing."

The good detective crushed the second cigarette. "Maybe. I should really talk with her . . . unofficial, of course, you know? For her sake." He started to grab for a third cigarette, then apparently thought better of it. "Maybe when she's back at the house, she and I and you can do some more talking about Mr. Delke."

I was surprised to find out that Cortez hadn't heard about the fire. In fact, considering the cause, I would've thought he would've contacted me about it. "Have you—"

Cortez was still trying to shove the pack back into his jacket. Eyes and attention on that task, he cut me off. "Tried to stop by to ask you about a funny death I heard about, mug with two funny holes in his chest. Right through the lungs, you know? Known to be a two-bit embalmer—bootlegger—for the South Side."

"What would I know about that?"

Looking at me again, he grinned. "Probably nothing. It was just strange, so I thought of you."

"Thanks."

The detective started to extend his hand to my shoulder, as if to give it a friendly pat, but suddenly withdrew it. Cortez probably wondered if I'd let our "friendship" go that far. After all, to many, he was still not much better than a negro. "Anyway, I better get back to the station and file this. Probably it'll be lost after that, but I try."

I was happy to put an end to the conversation. We nodded at one another, and I turned to where I'd left Claryce.

"Oh, hey," Cortez called back to me from near his auto. "Meant to say. I stayed discreet when I went back. Don't want your neighbors getting the wrong idea about me coming by again."

I hesitated, not certain I'd heard right. "'Again'?"

He opened the door. "Yeah. Last night. Came after dark so as not to be seen." He tapped the brim of his hat. "I think about these things. I know how I look outside of my neighborhood, Nick Medea."

He hopped in without another word. I didn't wait for him to drive off. It was all I could do to keep from running back to Claryce.

"Did you find out what you wanted?" she asked when I reached her.

"Too much." At this point, I needed more than a taxi. Fortunately, I'd seen a Hertz Drive-Ur-Self nearby—still known by many as Rent-a-Car, even after the sale two years ago. The Model T was in fair shape and did well enough with speed, but each minute that passed as I drove seemed like one of the many centuries through which I'd already marched.

As we neared where the house used to be, I slowed. Fetch, whom I'd told to come with us, pulled his head back in. "Shouldn't we keep going fast, Master Nicholas?"

"Not here and not for the sake of your enjoyment. Just keep in the back and keep quiet."

Claryce sat next to me, showing tremendous patience with the fact that, once again, I hadn't explained myself. I'd had thirteen hundred years of only the dragon as my constant companion, with even those tragic reunions when Claryce's earlier incarnations had been drawn back into my curse only brief interludes where I'd always kept my counsel from the one person to whom I could've spoken.

Just before we turned onto the street where the house had stood, she dared grab my wrist. "Nick, can you finally tell us why we're back here? What did Detective Cortez say? Did the police find something in the ruins?"

Before I could answer, we came in sight. I immediately stopped the auto. Claryce, seeing what I did, gripped my wrist tighter. Behind us, Fetch whined.

The firebombs had been tossed with expert aim. I'd known that even with the efforts of the firemen there'd be nothing left but ash. Oberon had wanted to make certain that I'd have no sanctum left to go to, that there was nowhere he couldn't find me.

Which made it all the more jarring to find that Cortez hadn't misspoken. He'd been back here, all right.

Seemingly untouched, the house stood before us.

CHAPTER 14

"**H**ow can it be standing there, Nick? How?"

I didn't drive closer. I could already sense something different about the house. There was no shunning on it. It was just one more house on the street.

No . . . it still wasn't.

Show me, I ordered him.

Claryce gasped and let go of my wrist. I should've warned her, but I couldn't wait. I needed to verify my suspicions.

Through the dragon's eyes, I saw the truth. Outwardly, the house was the same, as if the fire had never happened. Only through the dragon, only through his emerald world, did I see the shadows saturating the house.

Feirie. Whatever had resurrected my sanctum had done so with deep power from the shadow realm.

So very kind of them . . .

There were few of the Feiriefolk who could possibly wield such might in the mortal realm. I'd thought it beyond Oberon even with what I'd seen of him already, but maybe I'd been wrong. The only other choice was no choice at all.

As if reading my mind, Claryce asked, "Did Wil—Oberon do this?"

"I don't think so." Try as I might, I kept returning to the one other force that could stretch its power so far into the mortal realm and do this.

And behind me, Fetch let out another whine. "Master Nicholas . . . I smell *her* touch."

"She can't be here, Fetch. You know that. If she tried to pass through the Gate, there'd be hell to pay."

"Isn't there?"

Claryce looked back at the shapeshifter, then to me. "Who are the two of you talking about?"

"She who rules Feirie now," Fetch answered before I could stop him.

"Nick, is that possible?"

"Her touch is here, but that doesn't mean she is. She can't be." I kept repeating that in my head.

"But why would she do this?"

Let us go inside and see . . . the dragon persisted.

As much as I loathed it, I was starting to see his side. I finally drove up, stopping just before the property line. As I started to get out, I answered Claryce's question as best I could. "There's only one thing Her Lady fears . . . and that's Oberon. This may be her way of helping me work toward the ends she desires."

It may also have been for a variety of other reasons, some of them incomprehensible by mortal standards. Her Lady *was* Feirie, and so all its dark and unimaginable nature was part of her as well.

Claryce shivered, but then said, "I suppose we'd better go inside."

Of the three of us, she was the one most vulnerable, which made it more impressive that she managed to take the lead for as far as halfway to the door. I succeeded in getting ahead of her at that point, with a perhaps wiser Fetch taking up the rear.

"This gives me the shakes, Master Nicholas," he muttered.

"Hush." Taking a deep breath, I opened the door. That it wasn't locked didn't shock me. While in general I held a door open for a lady, this one time I immediately entered.

With no one about the vicinity, I'd kept the dragon's eyes. Through them, I saw absolutely nothing out of the ordinary. There was even a tiny crack in the wall near the front door that I remembered from before the fire. If I hadn't seen the house going up, I'd have sworn that somehow the firemen had salvaged it.

That was the power of Feirie . . . something that shouldn't have been possible on this side of the Gate.

"Fetch, how do you feel?"

"Well enough . . . shouldn't I?"

"You feel different at all?"

His ears twitched. "No, Master Nicholas, everything's jake."

He still didn't understand what I was talking about, and I decided to keep it that way. Better that he not start trying to experiment. If he showed any signs of transformation, I'd probably have to kill him before he tried to kill me.

Other than the faint shadows in places where there should've been none, the house appeared to be exactly what it looked like. Nevertheless, my hand kept near the side where I hid the sword. Before this reconstructed sanctum, I'd only ever received one gift from Her Lady, and that'd been to replace the blade I'd had blessed alongside the dagger. It'd been worth the weapon's destruction to end that part of Oberon's plot, but I'd needed something more to confront some of the worst of the Wyld he'd gathered with him. Still, I'd accepted the new sword aware that it was a tainted thing. At the time, it hadn't seemed to matter. Claryce's last incarnation had already died, although I could never actually prove that it was directly due to Oberon.

"Nick . . . what *is* that?"

I looked up at where she pointed. One of the shadows lurked there, shifting slightly with each passing moment. I saw nothing about it different from the others—and then realized that Claryce shouldn't have been able to see it.

I decided to test her. "What do you think it is?"

"It's—I don't see it any more. I thought there was a darkened area that . . . that seemed to be moving now and then."

She didn't see it now. That was the second time I'd noticed her *almost* seeing something . . . or in the case of Diocles, someone. "Hints of *her* power," I answered. "You may see them here and there."

They were more than that, just as her viewing them for even a few moments was more than it should be. I couldn't recall any of her past lives sharing this ability.

"Fetch, check the kitchen."

"As ye wish." He slunk toward the back. It was probably the slowest and most reluctantly I'd ever seen him head toward a kitchen.

By the time Fetch returned, we'd checked the rest of the first floor. He said nothing, merely shaking his head and looking relieved to be back with us.

I eyed the staircase. "You two stay here." Claryce opened her mouth, but I waved her to silence. "Stay here."

With each step up, I waited for Her Lady to spring her surprise. More and more, this felt like her touch. How she'd succeeded in bypassing the restrictions of the Gate, I still didn't understand. It was opening a new and troubling path for me. One thing I'd always been certain of was that the power of Feirie had its limits here. In fact, that had been in part what Oberon had sought to accomplish in order to achieve his ultimate goal; he could only truly bring the two realms under his sway if he could strengthen Feirie's magic here before that.

I reached the second floor untouched. The small hints of shadow continued to haunt the house, but I couldn't find anything malevolent about them other than their very origins. I began to have some notions as to their purpose, a purpose that had little to do with me and more to do with that one thing Her Lady truly feared.

My bedroom was just as I'd left it, even to the incidentals. I couldn't help a smile, thinking of Feirie magic used to recreate such mundane items. So much trouble. I'd known that I—or rather, the *dragon* and I—were of interest to her, but not to this extent.

As I entered the room I'd set aside for Claryce, I felt I had a good hunch about why Her Lady had gone to all this trouble for something that should've been so beneath her deadly presence. It didn't stun me to see that there were more shadows in the upper corners of the second bedroom, either, nor that—

"Nick?"

Claryce's voice didn't come from downstairs, as it should've. Instead, it sounded very near the landing. *Too* near, considering I'd just come across the one actual alteration in the house and something I didn't want her to see.

The two-and-a-half foot by almost two foot painting hung prominently, so that anyone entering would see it immediately. It was hardly where I'd left it before the fire. Then, I'd stuck it down in the cellar, deep in a corner. By no stretch of the imagination would I have wanted Claryce to see it.

Leonardo'd been known for his genius, but even more because of one particular painting he'd done. Her smile was recognized the world over.

But what wasn't so recognized the world over was the piece he'd done when he'd discovered just who I was. St. George and the dragon. He'd painted it in secret around the same time as Raphael had started his, and, while Raphael's was hailed even now as a masterpiece, Leonardo's wasn't known to anyone because he'd given it to me the moment he'd finished it. With that eye for detail, he'd done my face perfectly, leaving no doubt who I was.

And to make matters even more prickly for me at this moment, he'd also met Claryce's incarnation of that time. Met her and knew her for the part the original had played.

The moment I heard Claryce call my name, I ran to the painting and tugged at it. Fortunately, Her Lady or Her Lady's servant hadn't let their perverse Feirie humor hold sway, and the painting came away with ease. There was no choice left to me but to toss it facedown under the bed.

"Nick! Are you all right? Did you find something?"

I'd already managed to straighten up and turn her way. Standing in the doorway, she looked, without realizing it, almost exactly as Leonardo had depicted her. When he'd given me the painting—after her death again, it turned out—I'd been torn between keeping it and burning it. I'd finally found I'd settled on the latter when my hands refused to let go of the painting over the fire I'd set. Leonardo had also made the piece small enough that I could carry it with me wherever I went, although he probably wouldn't have liked the way I'd removed it from the gilded frame and rolled it up to make it even more compact. Even despite the size, though, no one would've mistaken St. George or Princess Cleolinda as anyone other than myself and Claryce.

And for more than four hundred years, I'd managed to keep it to myself, whether as a reminder or to just torture myself, I still hadn't figured out.

"I thought there was something," I finally answered, "but I think it was nothing."

She peered up at the nearest corner, squinting as if not sure what she saw. "You're sure?"

That gave me an opening. "Just to be certain, let's head back downstairs."

Claryce nodded quickly, her eyes still drifting to where the patches of shadow remained just out of her mortal view. I was still curious as to why she'd shown hints of noticing things she shouldn't have been able to, but most of all, I was relieved to get her away from the painting. I still held out some hope that keeping her ignorant of her truth would help save her this time.

It was a hope that was rapidly fading, though.

Fetch wagged eagerly when we arrived downstairs. "She insisted on going up, Master Nicholas!"

"It's not his fault, Nick," Claryce added.

"For a watch dog, he's not watching too well." When he looked more upset, I shrugged. "It's all right, Fetch."

Claryce continued to study the house. "So, do we stay here? Is that what's intended?"

"It's what's intended by someone, which is why we won't just yet. Come on." It wasn't just the fact that Her Lady had recreated the house that made me want to leave quickly, but that she'd also toyed with my secret. I didn't need Her Lady's attention focused on Claryce; there were already too many factors threatening yet another terrible repeat of the fate of every previous incarnation.

We returned to the auto and drove off without another word. I thought about my agreement to meet Mr. Alonso Perez and considered calling him to cancel. If I called from the safe house, I wouldn't need his number to reach him. The telephone would just find him. However, I held off. From what I'd learned from Cortez, the problem at Our Lady of Guadalupe might offer some clues I desperately needed.

Of course, that'd mean trying once again to convince Claryce to stay behind.

I pulled the Model T around the back of the safe house. Fetch, new to the vicinity, ran around familiarizing himself. I finally had to call him to make him join Claryce upstairs while I took a peek at the secret barrelhouse.

The place was quiet. I had no doubt that there were guards inside, but that most of the activity would take place once the sun went down. I circled around, trying to see if there was any way to take a look inside, but, before I could get very far, I noticed someone *else* watching.

It wasn't Doolin, but I'd seen this thug at the Art Institute nearby, before my meeting with Oberon. He'd chosen a good spot to avoid being seen by anyone in the distillery while still able to watch *them*. After all that had happened, I was tempted to take him. There were important questions he might've been able to answer, such as where I might just catch Oberon unaware.

More and more intrigued by that possibility, I decided to come around behind him. I didn't worry about using Her Lady's gift against this lone hood. My fist would do.

But as I neared him, something atop the building moved. The watching thug immediately shifted his stance. From his jacket, he drew a good-sized gat and peered up.

Her Lady's sentinel dropped down on him, falling so fast that the hood didn't even have time fire. I fought back the instinct to leap forward to defend a human being from something of Feirie. Even if I'd wanted to help, it was already too late.

But where Oberon's creature had suffered an awful demise, the hood seemed to merely freeze. Her Lady's servant completely enveloped him . . . and then sank into the body.

Understanding at last what was happening, I moved forward.

The hood turned to face me . . . but I knew those eyes were no longer human.

"Gatekeeper . . ." he acknowledged.

It was interesting to hear that the strong brogue remained, even if this wasn't really Moran's man, anymore. "Just what do you think you're doing?"

His gaze flickered to my hand, which hovered near but not too near my coat. He knew it wasn't a gun I had there.

"What she commands. He will not be permitted back into the Court."

Oberon gaining access to the Feirie Court would mean the end of Her Lady's reign. More important to those who'd allied themselves with Her Lady, it'd mean the most intricate of tortures would follow, as Oberon taught each and every one of the traitors what it meant to defy him. Those tortures would go on far beyond a human lifetime.

"I don't want war breaking out here."

The sentinel managed a crude version of a smile. On one of Moran's men, it actually looked appropriate. "War is already here, Gatekeeper."

I couldn't exactly argue with that, but I didn't want it to become a full-fledged conflict that would engulf Chicago the way even the fire hadn't. A conflict that would spread to everywhere beyond the city afterward.

"Listen. You and your mistress just can't—"

The sound of an auto pulling up near the barrelhouse made me instinctively look that direction. Even as I did, I cursed myself for doing so. When I looked back to the sentinel, he and his temporary shell had already vanished.

Gritting my teeth, I decided that he'd had the best idea. I snuck back to the safe house, where Claryce gave me yet another reproving look.

"And what happened to you this time?"

"I was checking on the bootleggers. There was a slight commotion, and I had to take the long way back." I wasn't about to mention the sentinel, although I did notice Fetch eyeing me warily.

She grimaced. "Is this place actually any better than the house now?"

Her tone indicated that she wanted me to say yes. The best I could do was, "For now. Tomorrow, I'll decide if we head back to the house."

While it wasn't the answer she desired, it was clear it was the one she'd expected. "All right, but if you travel anyplace else, I'm definitely going with you."

"You don't need to—"

"No, Nick. I *do*."

"Me, too, Master Nicholas! Me, too!"

I openly glared at the shapeshifter for supporting her. I still thought she'd be safer here, especially since the sentinel had chosen to move on in his hunt for Oberon. I wasn't sure how smart the shadow creature's decision had been, but at least it turned the focus of the troubles from the vicinity of the safe house. At least for tonight, I was confident that Claryce was safer here, not with me.

"I'm only seeing a client," I told her.

"A client? You're just seeing a client? Where?"

I purposely told her just the address, not that it was Our Lady of Guadalupe.

My luck remained consistent. "I know that area," Claryce murmured. "Will—I've *got* to stop calling him that—Oberon had some business matters going on near there. Something to do with a church . . ." She frowned. "Are you going there?"

"Yes. It's probably nothing."

"I'm still going with you." Her tone brooked no defiance.

Fetch wagged his tail in her support.

I surrendered. "All right. We leave just before dark."

After we ate, I stepped out the back and concentrated. A short time later, the black bird alighted near me.

"Follow us, all right?"

"Yes, yes."

"Keep high in the sky."

The avian cawed, then took to the sky again. I watched it vanish into the sky, wishing that I could be as free.

Eye can give you wings . . .

Aware of what that offered entailed, I said nothing. There were worse things than endless servitude to the Gate, and believing the dragon was at all a thing I could trust with my life and my soul was one of them.

Our Lady of Guadalupe was a simple wooden structure probably much too tiny already for all the Mexicans working the nearby steel mills. Even in the dim street lights, I could see that even though it'd just been built last year it was already showing wear. The new one that they hoped to build would be far larger and far better designed, with brick and everything.

The church was dark. I'd expected at least my client to be here. I didn't think the parish priest would be around, of course. With the exception of a few priests like Father Peter, most of the clergy were uncomfortable with the thought of the supernatural.

I turned to Claryce.

"Don't you dare tell me to stay behind, Nick."

With a sigh, I stepped out. Claryce joined me, as Fetch trotted off as if a mere hound interested in the landscape. What he was actually doing was making his way around to the back of the church, where he would find entrance should I need him.

"Are you certain we've arrived at the right time, Nick?"

I said nothing, my hand already near my jacket. *Show me.*

Eye will, naturally . . .

Our Lady of Guadalupe took on an emerald aura. At first glance, I saw nothing sinister. The only questionable thing remained the fact that there was no sign of Mr. Alonso Perez.

The flutter of wings alerted me to the black bird's presence. With everyone in place, I finally knocked on the church door.

It slid open a crack at my touch.

I needn't have watched as many mysteries as I had to recognize the ominous sign. The only sound from Claryce was a faint intake of breath that told me she knew what this meant, too.

There was a chance we were both just imagining too much. I didn't believe that for a minute.

"Now you definitely stay behind me," I whispered.

Claryce didn't argue. I'd given the dagger to her, just in case. If I needed a weapon, I'd cheerfully draw Her Lady's gift.

Asking for yet more forgiveness, I kicked the church door open and jumped inside.

The darkened chamber greeted me. I used the dragon's eyes to look for those shadows that didn't belong but saw no danger. With the greatest caution, I moved on.

The floor creaked slightly as I passed the first pews in back. I kept reminding myself that this was hallowed ground, untouchable by those of Feirie save for believers like Kravayik. There was no possibility that the church contained some—

There was no mistaking the limp shape sprawled before the front pews. I slid my fingers into the coat, felt the hilt of Her Lady's gift shape into my grip. I didn't draw it yet, but kept it ready.

Kneeling beside the body, I used my free hand to turn it over. Not for a moment was I surprised to see it was Mr. Juan Alonso Perez. He'd been killed the old-fashioned way, a shiv across the throat.

And, as I expected then, something spilled forth from the narrow cracks between the floorboards. It flooded up on every side of me, flowing over the late Mr. Alonso Perez and the nearest pews. As it did, it began to coalesce into one large shape.

I'd seen more than enough. I drew Her Lady's Gift—or rather, I *tried* to.

Free my hand! I silently shouted at the dragon. *Free my hand!* I couldn't understand why he'd do something so mad. Oberon's creature wouldn't provide us with a quick, clean death. It'd do things that'd make even a dragon shriek in agony.

This is not Eye's doing! he suddenly replied, his anxiety matching mine. *Not Eye's at all!*

The shadow creature took on partial form. There were hints of something like a bat or an octopus or something with bits of both. It never completely fixed on one shape, not that I cared. All that mattered was that I couldn't draw the sword.

The shadow creature lunged at me.

CHAPTER 15

Forget the blade! Set me free! Set me free!

At any other time, I would've laughed at such an insane suggestion. Set free the dragon, who lived for carnage? It would've been like unleashing the plague to put an end to the bootlegger wars. Capone's and Moran's boys would all be dead, but so would everyone else.

And yet now I barely hesitated. I allowed him to come out as I hadn't since the Great Fire.

The world receded. I was and was not me. I grew taller, stronger. My hand came loose—a hand quickly becoming a claw.

That claw seized the shadow creature by what passed for its throat. Although our attacker was not entirely incorporeal, had it been anything but the dragon—the essence of power and old magic—attempting to seize the thing, their hands would've gone through.

The Wyld hissed and spat. A hundred hands stretched to rake the dragon's—our—flesh.

The dragon *breathed* ever so slightly.

Flames spilled over the shadow creature, spilled over it and yet over nothing else.

The struggling Wyld twisted and wriggled and scratched, but the dragon held on while the flames rapidly did their work. The fire didn't harm us in the least, for it was as much a part of us as the scales covering our body.

We watched with eagerness and satisfaction as our puny foe burned away. We savored its pain, its cries. When there was nothing left, we brought the flames to us—

And at that point, *I* managed to remember that I was not a part of him. *He* was a part of me. *Dismiss the fire,* I demanded. *Your part is done . . .*

Yes . . . yes, it is . . .

With that, the dragon doused the flames and quietly withdrew into the recesses of my mind.

I was left gasping for air and gripping one of the pews for support. A faint scent of sulphur permeated the area, but otherwise there was no hint of any fire, not even some singed wood. The dragon could control his flames if they were contained enough, something beyond his control years ago, once the blaze had spread far enough through Chicago. Of course, at that time, he'd had no desire to keep anything under control.

"Nick!" Claryce came up behind me. Her touch on my shoulder soothed me and helped my heart beat normally again.

"You—shouldn't have come up here," I finally succeeded in telling her.

"I don't—" For the first time, she saw the body. Her only reaction was to look more concerned. No gasps, no screams. She'd become accustomed to my world much too fast for her sake.

"My client," I pointed out needlessly.

"What was that thing? Was it like that monster in the fireplace?"

I straightened. "Only in that it's also of Feirie. The shadow folk come in many shapes and sizes, not to mention countless disguises. But one thing they all still need when in this world is darkness—even of their own making—to shield them."

Claryce looked me in the eye. "Nick . . . I saw it—him. A part of him, I guess. Is he—is he always within you?"

"Always . . . unless I let him out."

"But how do you force him back in?"

Generally, it was a struggle. This time, though, *he'd* made the choice to return to my thoughts. *Why did you do that?* I couldn't help asking him. *Why?*

It was what was wanted.

I couldn't deny I'd wanted it, but that he'd obeyed so willingly startled me. He'd have had a strong chance of retaining dominance for quite some time afterward. I probably would've regained control, but not before he'd have wreaked chaos on the world.

It was what was wanted, he repeated.

I couldn't believe what I was hearing. The dragon had given up his chance because he'd known it was what I hoped.

Thank you, I finally replied.

Even as I said that to him, I teetered. Claryce grabbed me tighter, then helped guide me to the nearest pew.

"We can't—we can't stay here very long," I told her. "Oberon probably also reported the murder to the police. He'd know there was a chance his trap didn't work and so at least set up something to keep me tangled up afterward."

"I thought he wanted something from you, Nick. That's why he's played all these games, isn't it?"

There'd been no doubt in my mind that if I hadn't let the dragon seize control, my much prayed for death would've been preceded by enough torture to make me give Oberon the information he needed to regain the Clothos card. Time was evidently no longer an ally of the former lord of Feirie.

I tried to rise again, but failed. In the short time that he'd controlled us, the dragon had drained me more than I could recall from previous incidents.

Rest . . . we need rest . . .

I had no disagreements with that, especially since it also meant vacating the church before we were discovered with the body of my unfortunate client. "Claryce, I want you and Fetch to return to the car. Before you do that, though, look up to the top of the church and whisper—definitely whisper—'you're needed inside.'"

Claryce had seen the black bird, so she understood what I meant by that. Still, that didn't make her any more pleased about following the instructions. "I should stay with you—"

I shook my head. "I won't be long. I've got to deal with a couple of matters here, but I'll be out in a minute or two, I swear."

She hesitated, then finally surrendered. I was glad that Fetch at least had stayed outside or else I knew I'd have to have argued with both of them about leaving me alone.

As she walked out, I stooped and said a prayer for my unfortunate client. I was already also trying to think of what I'd have to say when Detective Cortez hunted me down to ask when I'd last seen Juan Alonso Perez alive.

The black bird alighted on the pew next to me. Head cocked, it stared with much too much interest at the corpse.

"Don't even think about it," I growled. "I want you to make a quick flight around the church ceiling. Find anything out of the ordinary, but steer clear." It was possible that there was some clue remaining up there.

As I stood up again, I wondered what'd happened to me when I'd reached for the blade. This'd been the first time I'd tried to draw it since the Art Institute. There'd been no hint then that Oberon had done anything to freeze the link between Her Lady's gift and me.

Then I thought of my encounter with Doolin and some things fell into place. Oberon knew that the sword was my best edge against his kind. It wasn't my *only* edge, but in this case there'd been no time left to try anything else. If it hadn't been for the dragon, there would've been no hope.

You are . . . welcome . . . he suddenly said hesitantly.

He continued to startle me. I began to wonder if Oberon's unexpected return had made my constant companion feel his mortality again. The dragon was certainly aware that if death claimed us, there'd be no coming back—

Fetch let out a ferocious growl that was punctuated by a painful yelp.

Forgetting my own situation, I ran for the entrance. I still hadn't had a chance to deal with whatever trick Oberon had used on me, but that didn't matter.

"Claryce!" I shouted as I rushed outside. "Claryce!"

I ducked as a tommy raked the ground and the car. In the darkness, a Packard roadster tore off down Mackinaw. I hurried to the car, only to find all four tires flat.

At that point, I think I shouted Claryce's name and then Oberon's. Maybe Fetch's, too.

Let Eye give you wings . . .

As grateful as I was for what he'd done inside, even the threat to Claryce wasn't enough for me to give in a second time. I cursed myself for my distrust, but I still couldn't come around to letting him loose again so soon.

She will die . . .

"All right!"

Somewhere in the back of my mind, a part of me screamed not to do this, but all that mattered to the rest of me was that there was nothing else I could do to prevent Claryce from becoming the latest incarnation to die.

I was and wasn't the dragon this time. Unlike in the church, he didn't dominate so much as mingle. Even then, the next minutes passed as a blur. I remember seeing the lights of the city *below* me, but nothing else of the actual flight until a roadster appeared in the emerald world of the dragon's gaze.

And just as abruptly, the speeding auto filled my view as we dived toward it.

I landed atop the roadster. Me. No dragon. No hint of dragon. I barely had time to acknowledge what he'd done for me again before someone perforated a good portion of the Packard's soft roof and nearly me with it.

The gunner leaned out of passenger side. He wasn't Doolin, but he could've been his cousin, so huge and ugly was he. The tommy's barrel pointed right at me.

I let the Packard's jarring swing me around. My foot caught the barrel and shoved it high. The tommy slipped from his grip, dropping into the street.

He tried to seize my foot but missed. I didn't. Foot met face. The roadster's door swung open, and the thug fell out backward. He hit the pavement so hard there was no doubt he'd be joining Deanie O'Banion either at the *other* Gate or in Dante's Inferno.

Clutching tight, I swung down into the roadster, just in time to meet an automatic pistol pointed directly at my head. I'd already expected the worst and ducked before the driver fired. Two rapid shots temporarily deafened me in one ear, but otherwise left me untouched.

Grabbing the hood's wrist, I pointed the gun skyward. At that point, I already knew I'd been had. There was no sign of either Claryce or Fetch in the roadster. I'd already been concerned when I'd been close enough to see how small it was.

"Where is she?" I demanded, twisting his wrist almost enough to crack it.

He let out a yelp, but otherwise didn't answer. The Packard swerved onto the wrong side of the street.

I tried again, squeezing as I twisted. The automatic fell between us. "Last time!"

He jerked the wheel . . . then went stiff.

I felt his skin grow icy. It didn't take him slumping over the wheel for me to know that not only was he dead, but he'd died through Feirie means.

And that left me in a speeding car veering toward an oncoming truck.

I pulled at the wheel as best I could. The truck's horn blared loudly as the two vehicles just missed each other.

The Packard spun in a circle. I dove for the brakes. The auto came to a screeching halt. Now, all I had to do was pray that no one would hit us.

But when I got up, the street was mercifully clear. I leapt out of the auto, came around the other side, and shoved the body to the passenger seat. A moment more, and we were on the way back to Our Lady of Guadalupe.

I was afraid that Oberon had already had someone tip the cops as to the murder in the church. Even when I saw that things were still quiet there, I didn't waste time. I headed inside and searched for the black bird. It wasn't around. My hope was that it'd followed the actual kidnappers. The pair I'd followed had been more of Oberon's expendable pawns. Goons that Moran had probably dredged up just for "William Delke's" needs and not a major part of the North Side gang. Just like the ones in the other auto. I could guarantee that there'd be no evidence tying them to Moran and Weiss, but I still had a need for both the body and the Packard.

Returning to them, I pushed the body back to the driver's seat, then halfway out the door. I left the automatic next to the stiff. The police would find poor Juan Alonso Perez dead and one of his likely killers cooling outside. I decided to let *them* puzzle out just how the thug had died. It'd give them something to occupy themselves with while I hunted for Claryce and Fetch.

The tires on the Model T were another problem. I'd been tempted to switch autos, but there was a chance that somehow I'd still be linked to the T despite the shunning. Oberon had shown me that everything I'd trusted in could be easily overcome on his end.

With silent apologies to Heaven and Our Lady of Guadalupe, I used the rectory phone. All the while, I wondered where the local priest was but had to hope that his body wasn't one I'd just missed.

"Yes, who is speaking?" a rough-hewn voice asked.

"Nick here. Your friends. A Model T. The tires." I gave him the church address. "Have them leave it near you."

"They will attend to it as they always do, Nick. Thank you for this opportunity."

I grimaced as I set down the receiver. Like Kravayik and Fetch, there were others who felt they owed me a lot. Not all of them were exiles like that pair. Some were people who'd gotten in too deep in matters they should've known to leave alone. Barnaby was one of those. He *did* owe me big, especially for keeping his son from becoming another victim—intentionally—in the Winged Foot Express crash six years ago, but I still didn't like using him any more than I did Kravayik.

"There must be at least a dozen sins surrounding your work this evening," Diocles declared from behind my back.

"If you've nothing useful to say, just vanish. I've seen enough of you of late, anyway."

He appeared in front of me, dour as ever. "Is it my fault you've chosen to visit every church in the city?"

I glared at him. "Do you have to make your presence known *each* time?"

His gaze widened and he looked even more dour, if that was possible. "There is a mirror behind you. Please take a look."

I did and saw nothing out of the ordinary save that I still had the dragon's eyes. "What do you want me to see?"

"You *never* kept them like that for so long . . . except that night."

He meant when the Dragon Breathed. The great fire. I'd had no choice then, not with Oberon involved. "You know why."

He is correct . . .

I'd scarcely believed that the dragon would not only join the conversation—one-sided as it was since Diocles couldn't hear him—but that he *agreed* with the late emperor. "I might still need them."

My former lord and master was swift in recognizing that I wasn't talking to him. His brow wrinkled deeply, but he said nothing.

Eye will be there . . . when needed . . .

I took a deep breath. Already aware of my willingness, the dragon withdrew. As he did, the room darkened. Only Diocles remained perfectly visible.

"You were speaking to that devil." To the reformed emperor, the dragon was nothing less than an offspring of fallen Lucifer. I'd stopped trying to correct him centuries ago. "Speaking in a familiar manner."

"We had to come to a few agreements today."

The ghost sneered. "Never trust the devil."

"As opposed to my good friend and master who removed my head?" I cut off his incessant apologies as something occurred to me. "Were you here the first time I entered?"

"In spirit."

Not certain as to whether he was answering straight or making some poor attempt at humor, I continued, "Did you happen to see outside?"

"I barely know what the outside looks like anymore, Georgius. You know that."

I was disappointed, but not surprised. There'd been a small hope that he could tell me more about the kidnapping—

The telephone rang.

I didn't believe much in coincidences. I picked up the receiver. "Yes?"

"Nick! Oh, thank God! At last! I've called every other place I knew to! I tried this number on the off-chance you went back to look for a clue!"

"*Claryce?*"

"Nick! I barely got away! He sacrificed himself to help me escape!"

I could only imagine she was talking about Fetch and, while I wanted to know more about that, I needed to make sure I reached Claryce before Oberon's goons did. "Where are you now?"

She gave me the address. It was several blocks north. "It's all right, Nick! This isn't near where I was held! I found a taxi after I got free and had him take me somewhere familiar! There are people all around me!"

Claryce sounded fairly safe but not enough for my tastes. "I'll be there as quickly as I can. Stay as visible as possible."

As she hung up, I considered my choices. One became very obvious.

"Do not do it, Georgius."

"I can get to her in no time. I've done it before."

The ghost formed by my side. "And it gets easier and easier to accept it. There are other ways, though. Safer, sufficient ways."

"Such as?"

"The chariot outside."

He meant the one I'd already set up to make this look like a rubout by some overzealous bootleggers. "It won't be fast enough—"

It will be . . . and if it is not, Eye will be there for you . . .

I no longer knew what to expect from the thing inside me. He could've kept silent. I would've given him another chance at partial freedom.

"He agrees with you," I commented to Diocles.

"Does he?" The late emperor looked as if he'd just eaten something that'd disagreed with him.

"Excuse me." I barged through Diocles without a pause. As I exited the church, I heard faint sirens. I didn't know if they were headed here or somewhere else, but it didn't really matter. I dragged the thug's body from the Packard and made sure to leave the automatic near his side . . . and without my fingerprints on it. That done, I shoved the top down, so that no one would get a good glimpse of the shot-up roof, and drove off to where Claryce said she was.

I assumed that I'd have to go searching for Claryce, but to both my relief and concern, she was on the corner near the address she'd given, already watching for me. Behind her, some good jazz that Armstrong himself might have been leading danced out of the club from where she'd apparently called.

I pulled up the Packard. She wasted no time in climbing in.

"Nick, this isn't—"

"No, it's the one I followed. They cut up the tires on the rental."

She looked frightened . . . for me. "Won't they trace it back to you?"

"I've got someone taking care of it." I had faith that the rental would be gone before the police arrived. Barnaby hadn't let me down yet. "Before we go anywhere, though, I need you to look me directly in the eye and not flinch."

Claryce didn't understand, but she did as asked.

Show me . . .

Just for the briefest of glances, *his* eyes returned. I not only saw Claryce through his emerald world, but anything about her that *wasn't* a part of hers.

Nothing. I'd been half-certain that Claryce's quick escape hadn't been what it seemed, but there was no hint of Oberon's influence about her. It wasn't a hundred percent guarantee, but it was near that. I looked away, blinked my eyes back to normal, then faced Claryce again.

"I wanted to see if Oberon had magicked you in any way. I didn't want to tell you that until after I was certain things were well, just in case."

"Did—did you notice any problem?"

"No." Ironically, that made me feel worse about what I intended. "Do you know where they took you? Can you describe it?"

Naturally, Claryce had taken the time to remember *that* address as well. It was an area with plenty of empty buildings and just perfect for nefarious activities. I made a calculation. I hoped Fetch wouldn't hold it against me, although I would've.

"First, you're not going with me. I've got a friend with whom you'll be safe . . . I swear." My record thus far hadn't been very good, but I had more confidence this time, even if in some ways I was also bringing her to the very last place I should've.

I was bringing her to Holy Name. To Kravayik.

And, unfortunately, to the card.

CHAPTER 16

Kravayik, of course, was happy to be of service to me, even though I was bringing a woman—an unmarried one at that—into his personal quarters. Neither of us were worried about the clergy, since most of them barely even recalled that he lived there. However, I still didn't like bringing her to the vicinity of the card, even though it was as secure as ever.

"All will be well, Master Nicholas," the exile quietly assured me. "I long ago made up the attic just in case some poor wayfarer needed a roof over his or her head." He shrugged. "Perhaps another sin on my shoulders, but even though I also had to make certain that my dear employers wouldn't think of going up there, I thought at the time the benefits would perhaps balance the scales out."

"You thought right." I was pleased by his planning ahead. It made me feel a little better about what I was doing. "I don't think St. Michael's is secure enough. It'd take Oberon much more effort to do anything here, even with his thugs."

Kravayik put his impossibly long hands together as if in prayer. "The poor benighted souls. This war cannot go on. The news said another one was bumped off last night, the stiff left on the street—" He frowned, but not at the death. "Dear Lord, I begin to sound like that noisome Fetch, if you and Heaven can forgive me for saying so."

He already knew what I planned and despite his words had already said a prayer for the lycanthrope's safety. I wasn't sure if one prayer was enough for Fetch, but I wasn't about to turn away any type of help, including divine intervention. Not that I'd ever received any of the last before. I seemed to be a saint in exile in more ways than one.

Claryce had been warned somewhat about Kravayik and so she

accepted him with a grace he honestly appreciated. I was so used to being alone most of the time that I'd forgotten that someone like Kravayik had once been of such stature that he'd constantly been surrounded by those seeking his favor. Now, he had only his new beliefs and his prayers. I knew that they were more than enough to satisfy him, but Claryce's company was certainly an added pleasure for the exile.

"Have you eaten yet?" he asked her, as he led her to her hiding place. "I have been dabbling with local dishes. I am especially fond of Italian food. I would be delighted if you joined me in a meal. Today, I cooked an eggplant dish . . ."

I marveled for a moment how talkative Oberon's former hunter suddenly was. He knew better than to speak about the card, fortunately.

I looked around for Diocles and was gratified to find that for once he wasn't waiting in some corner for me. Why he'd decided to leave me be for this once, I didn't know or care. I had enough to deal with.

The drive to Holy Name had given me time to question Claryce about what had happened to her until Fetch's surprising intervention. She hadn't been a prisoner too long, but even a few minutes in the company of Oberon or his stooge Doolin was more than enough. I'd seen Oberon destroy the mind of a man in only a handful of seconds, leaving a babbling, drooling shell in the wake.

And Oberon himself *had* been there, accompanied by Doolin and four other hoods. When I'd asked Claryce about anything odd concerning Doolin, she'd mentioned his thick gloves, too large and too heavy for the weather we were having. I guessed that now Doolin wore a match to the gauntlet he'd had on when he fought with me, and that the only reason he'd not had both in the first place had been to secrete Oberon's toy on me, the one that'd kept me from being able to draw Her Lady's gift.

I still hadn't found it, but I couldn't let that stop me from trying to do something for Fetch, if belatedly. I did have the dagger and a few other items. I hoped they'd be enough.

Still looking like William Delke—probably to keep everyone other than Doolin from being spooked—Oberon had questioned Claryce about one thing . . . well, two things that were very similar. The statuettes. There was the one I'd assumed he already had, the dryad. Why he'd asked her about that one at all, I couldn't figure. What I found more intriguing was his interest in the one stolen from Our Lady of Guadalupe. I'd assumed again that he'd it taken, but he seemed to be in the dark concerning its whereabouts.

When Claryce hadn't given good enough answers, Oberon had turned her over to Doolin, which said much about the goon's talents for torture, if Oberon was willing to sit back and watch rather than enjoy the task himself. Thankfully, Doolin had never had the chance, for that's when Fetch had given himself for Claryce.

I'd thought Fetch injured and taken along with Claryce, but all that'd happened to him initially had been the equivalent of the butt of a gat against his skull. Unfortunately for Oberon's puppets, they didn't know the truth about Fetch and had probably assumed him some tough but very mortal hound. The true kidnappers had barely taken off when he'd recovered enough to give pursuit. There'd been no time to warn me, of course, but Fetch had done his best to follow their trail all the way.

He'd fallen behind a little, but thankfully not enough to let Doolin get to work. Fetch had crashed through window, landed behind Claryce, and used one paw to rip through the ropes. I'd seen him use those paws before and could picture just how easily the thick bonds had given way.

The only positive aspect of Oberon being in the room had been that, like with me, Fetch could speak in his presence. He'd told Claryce to scram and then hit like the Bears' defensive line into Doolin.

That was all Claryce could tell me. She'd been smart enough to figure out that she couldn't help Fetch in any manner except to make good on her escape and then find me. That hadn't taken her as long as she'd feared, but long enough.

And I'd only made it longer and more certain that Oberon had had plenty of time to entertain himself with Fetch's screams.

I fought back my growing guilt as I pulled the Packard up on a darkened street just a block from where Claryce said she'd been held. By that time, I'd also been able to think about what Oberon had done with the sword. A simple thing by Feirie standards, so simple I should've caught on.

The tiny strand looked so weak, so thin, that it shouldn't have bound Her Lady's gift where it was, but being of black silver inside it'd been more than enough. All Doolin had had to do was find the hilt, then wrap the strand around it. He hadn't even had to do it well. Touched by Oberon's power, it'd completed the work itself for Doolin.

Removing it was as easy as unwinding it. That was the curious nature of Feirie, even those elements able to act on this side of the Gate. Some could be incredibly complex, others child's play.

But what mattered now was that I could draw the blade.

I moved carefully toward the building. There were two autos outside, one a roadster like the one I'd taken from the dead thug, the other a Model T. I doubted that Oberon would've ridden in either one of them, even if he'd evidently worked all these years to keep the heavy amounts of iron from burning him. As either himself or Delke, Oberon would've traveled in better style.

That didn't mean that Fetch wasn't inside. Of course, it also didn't mean that Fetch was alive, either.

Show me, I ordered grimly.

The emerald world took over. I saw not only the two goons left to guard the front door, but also the webbed shadow over that door. The guards were decoys; the webbed shadow was the danger. I'd seen a shadow like that eat the top half a soldier's body away so quickly that it'd left the bottom still walking a few steps before the gruesome truth set in.

Without the sword, I couldn't have entered. With it, the web didn't concern me.

Neither of the two bored thugs heard me as I moved in on them. I'd fought in a hundred wars over many centuries, all my battles to preserve the sanctity of the Gate as it continually shifted from location to location. This pair was nothing more than street trash picked up by Moran to give Oberon the muscle he asked for. Expendable.

I put one hand over the first's mouth, then slammed the back of his head against the wall. As he dropped, the second started to reach for the gun he should've kept out, rather than put away so he could light a smoke. I was already on him before he could do that or yell for help.

Covering his mouth while pressing the hand in his jacket against his chest, I muttered, "Make this easy on yourself—"

He tried to yell despite the hand. At the same time, I sensed something amiss. I didn't have to look up to know that the shadow was dropping on both of us.

I had no choice but to push away. Thinking I'd for some reason given him a second chance to draw his piece, the guard grinned. As the automatic came out, he tried for a third time to yell.

That was when the shadow covered him.

His scream went as unheard as his yells. I already had Her Lady's gift drawn, but it was too late for the thug. There was a soft, *squishing* noise as he vanished into the living web.

A thing like this could feast for hours on a meal still struggling. I did the guard a favor by skewering both at the same time.

The shadow fragmented, but didn't die. Oberon had probably found it in the same place he'd uncovered the one I'd fought in the fireplace. They weren't so much life as the essence of Feirie, which made them no less hungry and no less evil. The web reformed, creating a thing with one huge moon-colored eye and a mouth that stretched big enough to consume two or three of me. I could still see bits of guard in its crimson teeth.

I did the only thing I could do. I let it lunge at me.

It impaled itself on Her Lady's gift. There were those creatures of Feirie, like the Court, that had clever, insidious minds. There were other, more primal things like this, incapable of thinking of anything but devouring flesh and soul.

I took particular pleasure in watching the sword devour it in turn.

Oberon didn't want too much outside attention to his activities, so he'd once more picked a beast that hunted in silence. That suited me. I could still feel its agony as Her Lady's gift took pleasure in ripping it to pieces and absorbing it. The blade burned black for a moment, and then its shining brilliance returned. This time, there'd be no repeat of the unexpected incident at the fireplace. The sword had adapted to that trick.

Taking one last glance at the weathered wooden door, I kicked it open.

Dead silence greeted me. I'd already assumed one of two scenes. The first was Oberon facing me with pretty much everything he had. The second was this. An almost empty building.

"Hello, Fetch."

He managed to pick up his head. I was struck by how emaciated he was, even though I'd just seen him otherwise only hours before. Now, he looked as if someone had starved him for a month.

"Master—Master Nicholas . . . is everything d-ducky with her?"

Even as ruined as he was, Fetch still had to be Fetch. I took that as a promising sign. "She's fine."

"I seem—seem to be snared."

Through the dragon's eyes, I could see that. Fibers of darkness crisscrossed where he lay. I could see that each of them pulsated. I could also see that they were *feeding* from him.

And as I followed some of the fibers to their origin, I also saw that "they" were actually a "she."

I'd just found the other shadow's "mother."

She filled the ceiling, filled it with one huge eye and a mouth that stretched from one end of the huge room to the other. I'd seen some horrors from Feirie, but she was by far one of the worst. I tried to figure out just how Oberon had managed to sneak this through the Gate. I also tried to figure out if even Her Lady's gift would be enough.

"Mother" decided not to give me the time to do either.

The air filled with black strands, all of them streaming toward me. If I'd not worn the dragon's eyes, they would've been invisible to me. I wasn't sure whether seeing them made me any happier, but at least I had a better target.

I spun around, and Her Lady's gift cut through them as if they were nothing. I severed a hundred or more, and still they kept coming.

One finally got past my defenses. Then another. Each one went through my clothes, my flesh, and somehow into my soul. I felt an emptiness, a hollowness, growing.

Her Lady's gift made short work of those strands, but others replaced them. I managed to keep the numbers from growing, but I knew that I couldn't just stand there.

"Master—Master Nicholas . . ."

I looked at Fetch, still being eaten away inside. Still a creature of Feirie, he was feeding her something other than a soul . . .

I knew what I had to do.

Spinning again, I used Her Lady's gift to create a momentary respite. Rather than just stand there, though, I charged toward Fetch.

Strands darted at me from all sides, as "mother" began to understand just what I was doing. Small wonder that she'd been able to grow so large in this realm. How many exiles had Oberon fed her over the years to get her this way?

Two strands caught my leg. I stumbled, giving several more the chance to perforate my back. I wanted to curl up and pray for the emptiness to either go away or consume me, but I knew better than to do that.

Half a dozen more strands dug into me before I reached Fetch. I tried to focus only on his situation. Anything else threatened to take what remained of my resolve.

I slashed over Fetch, severing nearly every strand attached to him. "Mother" tried to restore her vampiric link, but I kept them at bay. I also succeeded in cutting the last few.

The effect on Fetch was almost instantaneous. He began to fill out and, while his eyes remained a bit sunken in, he soon looked like his old self.

That was good, because I wasn't feeling very well anymore. "Fetch! Light!"

He darted for the chain dangling near the door. At the same time, I made an even more concerted effort to slash at every thread in range. I didn't know how much pain cutting them caused "her," but apparently more than I thought, because suddenly the entire ceiling seemed to be raining on me. It was as if "mother" had turned entirely to strands. I slashed and cut, but I knew that I couldn't stop them all—

The light *finally* came on.

"Mother" squealed, a sound that cut through my soul as harshly as the strands. If I'd tried the light before I'd freed Fetch, I doubted it would've hurt her much, but the moment I'd severed her link to a fellow creature of Feirie—the greatest reservoir of primal energy from which she could dine—she'd started to lose strength. I'd counted on that, aware that such power couldn't be maintained without constant replenishment.

But even if Oberon's beast was losing strength rapidly, she was hardly defeated. The downpour buffeted me to one knee, more strands than ever eating into my soul. My grip started to slip.

Eye will help! Let me help!

I was just about to give in to him when something else—*someone else*—took precedence in my thoughts. Claryce. I suddenly feared for her if I lost now. Oberon wouldn't leave any loose ends that Her Lady might use against him.

I squeezed the hilt, then, with a scream fueled by both my pain and my fear, I shoved to my feet and cut a swathe over my head. The strain on my soul lessened, enough to enable me to focus on "mother" herself. Even as she poured over me, I once again aimed not for the eye but for the bottomless maw.

She swallowed me. I felt the chill on my soul grow again, but not as much as it might've. I heard the voices of her victims, their essence forever trapped as part of her, their endless torture part of her very being.

Even though most of them had probably been as dark of spirit as my opponent was, I said a prayer for all of them, then thrust Her Lady's gift where the voices most seemed to come from.

The blade burned *dark blue*. I'd never seen it do that before. I might've worried about it if I didn't also immediately notice the blackness that was the shadow creature melt away. The voices faded at the same time.

And suddenly I stood in the middle of the building, sword raised, facing nothing.

Lowering Her Lady's gift, I turned to Fetch. He sat under the light chain, his breathing still rapid.

"You okay?" I asked, as I returned the Feirie blade to my coat.

"I have a great urge to pull a Daniel Boone," he rasped. "I still have the screaming meemies from that thing, Master Nicholas."

"Try to hold it in," I recommended. As he nodded and swallowed, I surveyed the interior. Without "mother," it was completely empty.

"He left me for ye," the scraggly lycanthrope muttered, as he joined me. "He said, 'Let's see how good a friend ye've got, mutt. Will he come after ye, or is the girl the only thing he ever cares about?'" Fetch looked disdainful. "Can ye believe he called me a 'mutt'?"

I could see that Fetch was recovering fast, but not completely. I noticed he still had a bad arch to his back. "Did he do anything else to you before he left?"

As I'd spoken, I'd begun to reach a hand for his back. Fetch, though, shied away as if I were about to beat him.

"Little things, Master Nicholas. Little things. I'll be right as rain soon enough."

I doubted I'd find anything else around here, but I did a swift search, regardless. As usual with Oberon, I was certain I was missing something, but what it was I couldn't say.

With Fetch at my heels, I finally left the building. The one guard was still out. I decided to leave him where he was. Either someone would find him with half of his partner nearby, or he'd wake up, see what was left of his buddy, and run. Oberon wouldn't have left him with any important info, and so he was nothing to me.

I'd barely made that decision and walked past the slumped thug before I heard a savage growl from Fetch. Her Lady's gift already drawn, I spun back and discovered Fetch atop the guard.

Fetch, his jaws full of blood.

He done a tidy and mercifully quick job of tearing out the hood's throat. I glared at him, remembering the Fetch I'd first met, the one who'd come close to killing me when Her Lady had thought it better served her purpose to rid the Gate of its guardian. When I'd spared him then, and saved his life from Her Lady's wrath, I'd made the shapeshifter swear by his own existence that he'd never wantonly kill again.

"It's all jake, Master Nicholas! It's all jake! He opened his peepers right after ye went past him, then went for his heater! I had to stop him!"

One of the automatics did lie near the hood's limp hand. It wouldn't have been the first time I'd had an enemy play possum on me. I probably would've noticed it myself if I hadn't still been so drained from the strands.

"Good job," I finally said. "There's a puddle on the other side of the street."

He didn't need any more suggestions. Trotting over to the puddle, Fetch sloppily lapped up the foul water, rinsing most of the blood off in the process. I didn't have to worry about him getting sick from the puddle; his guts were a lot stronger than that. I just didn't want anyone, especially Claryce, wondering where the blood had come from.

"Nice iron," he commented a few minutes later, as we climbed into the Packard. "Better than that jalopy you rented, Master Nicholas. A little airy on top, but I like that."

"Pleased to know." My mind was already focused on Claryce. Not just how she was doing but how merely thinking about her had given me the wherewithal to keep battling. I knew that my fears of how deep she might get into my heart had all come to pass. In fact, if anything, they'd proven to be worse than I'd expected. If Claryce died like her earlier incarnations . . .

"Where's the mistress?"

I didn't think Fetch had read my mind, only that he'd seen my expression and made the logical assumption as to what or who it concerned. "With Kravayik. We're going right there."

He beamed. "I like Kravayik. He listens well."

It was late enough that I paid no mind to speed, driving as fast as could. I got no arguments from Fetch, who thrust his head out the passenger side, the roof, and, before I shoved him back so that I could see, *my* window. I was secretly glad to see that he was doing so well, even if his back still had that stiffness to it. Oberon had done something awful to him, but Fetch still wouldn't say what. It was just one more thing on the lengthy list of things His Lord had to pay for.

Deciding that the Packard didn't exactly look like the kind of auto the clergy at Holy Name would desire to have parked in front, I located a spot around the corner and left it there. I reminded myself to check with Barnaby when I had the chance, to see how the rental was doing. With the Packard having no owners that'd claim it, I figured I'd continue to make use of it for a while.

Fetch paused at the edge of the cathedral grounds. "Can Kravayik come out?"

"We'll see." When I'd had Fetch keep an eye on Holy Name before, by necessity Kravayik had had to check with him now and then. I already knew from Kravayik what those confrontations had been like, and so I doubted he'd be that happy to rejoin Fetch too quickly.

The lycanthrope sat, his tail wagging in anticipation. I noticed his back still had trouble bending, but I refrained from saying anything more.

As ever, I had no trouble gaining entrance. I prayed for God's forgiveness for constantly trespassing but doubted I'd get it. I eyed the other saints as I walked through the empty interior, wondering if they'd felt as I always did when it came to my growing mountain of sins.

"Georgius . . ."

I looked into the shadows near the altar. "Here I was thinking maybe you'd moved on when you weren't here last time."

He gritted his teeth. "Georgius! Let us put aside enmities for the moment! I have to tell you—"

After everything that'd happened tonight, I had absolutely no patience for him. "It's *Nick*."

"Nick—"

He was too late, though. At that moment, Kravayik and Claryce both appeared. I immediately forgot all about the late Emperor Diocletian when I saw their expressions. Kravayik looked aghast and Claryce . . . Claryce stared at me as if I were something akin to the beast that'd been feasting off of Fetch.

"Claryce! Kravayik! Why're the two of you here? She should be kept hidden—"

"Master Nicholas! Forgive me! I made a terrible assumption! I shouldn't have been so careless! I thought she knew! I thought she knew!"

I'd only seen Kravayik so upset once and that'd been when he'd lost the only person he'd ever loved—a rare emotion by Feirie standards—and learned that she'd been executed at the command of His Lord. What bothered me most, though, was that he continued to look as if he'd just betrayed me into Oberon's hands.

"You *are* him, aren't you?" she demanded. "It all makes sense with the story you told me! I didn't realize it! *You* are Saint George from the legends . . ."

My mind raced. I glared at Kravayik, who seemed to shrink into himself, then met Claryce's eyes. "It's true. I am. I thought you'd be safer if you didn't know—"

I stopped when her gaze burned stronger. Something I'd just said had only made matters worse.

"'Safer'?" Claryce seemed barely able to contain herself. "And is that what you thought when you failed to mention anything about *me?*"

I couldn't answer. Still facing Claryce, I asked Kravayik, "Just how much did you tell her?"

"She is the one who brought it up! Mentioned that she knew! Wanted me to explain more! Master Nicholas, with all she did know, I could not help but think you had opened up to her!"

With all she did know . . .

"Oberon . . ." I muttered. "Claryce! What he told you! He did it all to foment chaos! He knows—"

"I know what *he* wanted, *Nick.* I also know that after what Kravayik verified for me, what Oberon said was true enough. Kravayik told me about the *last* version of me. He told me just what Oberon told me about how she died."

I saw that death again, but with Claryce's distinct features on that incarnation, not the original ones. "I tried . . . I tried to save her, but I failed . . ."

"And you failed the time before that. Before *that,* too." Claryce had gone utterly white. Behind the anger and defiance, she'd been hiding tremendous fear. "And every time . . . every time before . . ."

She dropped onto one of the pews. Behind her, an even more dour

Diocles materialized. I understood now what he'd been trying to warn me about. He'd heard everything.

"I'm going to *die*, too, aren't I, Nick . . . Georgius . . . or whatever I should call you . . ." Claryce murmured. "I'm going to die . . ."

CHAPTER 17

"No! You won't die." Kneeling in front of her, I put a hand on hers. "This is different—"

"How? Exactly how?"

I didn't have any actual reason, only my utter determination. I know I'd felt something similar in past situations, but not to the extent I did now. Even if it meant sacrificing the dragon and myself, I'd not let Oberon hurt her. I *couldn't*.

"This is different," I began slowly. "because there're others after Oberon as well."

"'Others'?" blurted Kravayik. "Master Nicholas, are you referring to *her?*"

Claryce looked from me to Kravayik to me again. "You're talking about his queen, aren't you?"

"Her Lady, yes. She's got a hunter on his trail. A powerful one."

Kravayik steepled his long fingers. "You have seen this hunter? Can you describe it for me?"

I did, including at the end its possession of Moran's spy. By the time I finished, Kravayik looked even more pale than Claryce and even more pale than *he* generally was.

"A *Feir'hr Sein* . . ."

I knew more than a dozen languages, including the Celtic that had hints of its origins in Feirie, but still the word made no sense. "What's that mean?"

"'Tis from the older tongue, the one before that of the Court. There is no good meaning, but it is something akin to *hunger* in Court speech."

Hunger. That figured. From what I'd learned of Feirie over the centuries, *hunger* appeared to be a dominant trait of anything born there. Hunger for power, hunger for souls, hunger for all that others treasured.

Kravayik continued to look very troubled. "Master Nicholas, how is it such a hunter breached the Gate without notice? You are bound to the Gate; you know its cycles, its changes."

I knew them too well . . . and that was why I'd also been concerned by the same question Kravayik had just asked me. I thought I finally knew. "I never noticed because it's been here since the last time Oberon surfaced."

"Since the fire?"

"Since the fire."

Fifty-four years was nothing to most creatures of Feirie, their lives measured in centuries and millennia . . . if they managed to survive that long. I should've realized that Her Lady would leave nothing to chance; she'd known Oberon better than anyone. She hadn't taken his obvious death as that. It would've been nice if she'd clued me in to her thinking.

At some point back then, when the Gate had still been in slight motion and Oberon had kept it at least in part open so that his Wyld would have greater contact with the realm that gave them power, Her Lady had slipped this hunter through. Whether it'd hunted unsuccessfully for Oberon during that period or simply been set into waiting just in case he suddenly revealed himself, only she and it knew. I wondered whether it was the only one, too. If I somehow survived this, I vowed to scour the city, just in case.

Claryce had calmed somewhat. I wished I could do more to build her confidence, but my record continued look as bad as some of the recent Cubs seasons.

"Is this—this F-F-"

"Feir'hr Sein," Kravayik offered again. "Call it a 'hunter' and that will be good, Mistress Claryce. And to what you are trying to ask, yes, it is *very* efficient. It is a powerful ally you have, Master Nicholas."

"So long as Oberon lives, but we'll have to watch afterward."

"There is that, yes."

"A *princess*," Claryce abruptly whispered. She wore a rueful smile. "I never dreamed of being one when I was a child. I had a couple of friends who did. Now I find out I *was* one . . ."

"Claryce . . ."

She pushed back some loose hair. "Cleolinda, isn't it? That's who I am. Just a poor reproduction of a princess."

Before I could deny with all my heart that she was more, Kravayik interjected, "That is incorrect, Mistress Claryce! You are as unique as anyone! Yes, you have the spirit of the princess, but you are you! You are not the one I met, good though she was. You have distinct differences in personality and, if I may be so bold, those differences have given your beauty its own individual traits."

"Thank you, Kravayik."

"He's right," I finally added. "And I *won't* let anything happen to *you*, Claryce, because you're who you are. Not just because of a past life."

She reached a hand to my cheek, then, flushing, quickly drew it back. Out of the corner of my eye, I saw Kravayik backing away from us.

I appreciated his discretion, even though he needn't have bothered. Whatever I felt for Claryce, I didn't dare act on it.

"So much to think about," she went on. "Nick—Georgius—"

"Nick. Always Nick."

That made her smile for some reason, which made me smile before I could stop myself. "Nick. Kravayik told me how you chose that name. I was so shocked! The man wasn't just your emperor, he was your *friend*."

Diocles had stood silent all this time, but at mention of his name, the ghost let out a frustrated growl and vanished.

"He had his share of guilt," I replied, not willing to give him more than he deserved. "Worse, he listened to Galerius."

Claryce didn't hear the last. "I tried to defy him, but those *eyes* . . . Nick, I'd rather look into the dragon's eyes than his."

So Oberon had given her a slight hint of his true self. Another reason I wanted to separate his head from his body. "What else? Tell me everything."

"I told you about the statuette. He spent a lot of time on that. Most of the rest of the time, he talked about me and my—my previous self."

She was still leaving something out. "And what else?"

"He kept asking about some card. Like a playing card."

Just as I assumed. Still, while everything Claryce said made sense, including his desire for the card, I began to have a problem with the entire situation. This was Oberon I was dealing with. Nothing could ever be taken at face value, and I was beginning to wonder if Fetch had been as much responsible for her escape as Claryce and he thought he was.

"Never mind that," I finally answered. The less she knew about the card the better.

It turned out to be the *wrong* answer. Claryce's expression tightened again. "More things I just shouldn't *know*? Is it involved with some of my—some of my *deaths,* too?"

It *had* been. She must've seen that knowledge in my face. Suddenly, Claryce was on her feet, barging past me. I almost grabbed her, then thought better of it. As she rushed toward the front doors, I looked to Kravayik for help, but he'd taken the wiser course and vanished completely.

That left me with Diocles and his interminable advice.

"You should have told her the truth from the very beginning, Georgius. Only then could she be prepared for all this."

I gave him stare worthy of the dragon and hurried after Claryce. She'd already run outside. I just prayed that Fetch wouldn't let her out of his sight or get very far from the safety of the Cathedral grounds.

There was no hint of either of them as I exited. I swore and tried to decide which way to go.

From around the corner to my right, Fetch let out a bark.

When I got there, though, it was to find only *him*. Not what I wanted.

"Where is she, Fetch? Where?"

"Master Nicholas? Who do ye mean? Mistress Claryce? I thought she was inside with ye!"

"Damn! Come with me!"

I headed the opposite way, all the while hoping that she'd paused to think things over before running too far.

Fetch moved ahead of me. "Forgive me! I thought I saw somethin'! I went to go see! I was only gone for a moment, Master Nicholas!"

"Pipe down and just run on ahead!"

"Aye!"

He sped on, easily outpacing me. I watched Fetch vanish around the other corner and hoped that he already had her in view. It worried me that Fetch'd been distracted by something else; it could've been innocent, but I'd learned that very few things were so.

When I reached the corner, it was to see nothing. No Claryce. No Fetch.

Fortunately, at that moment, he let out a bark from across the street. I followed his path with my gaze and finally spotted Claryce sitting on a bench under a streetlamp.

Fetch paused in front of her. Claryce sat with her face in her hands, not looking up even when I joined them.

"Claryce . . ."

She finally raised her head, but wouldn't directly look at me. "Nick. I'm tired. I'd like to go back to my quarters."

"I understand." I offered a hand, not expecting her to take it. She surprised me by accepting it and surprised me further with just how cold she was. "We'd better get you back to Kravayik."

"Kravayik . . ." She shook her head. "No. I want to go back to your house."

"The house?" That was the last place I'd have expected her to want to go. "You're safer with Kravayik."

"Please, Nick." When she looked into my eyes this time, it was with begging I couldn't refuse.

"All right. Fetch, head to the auto. Make certain all's clear. We'll follow right behind."

"Oke!"

He darted off, while I tried one last time to convince Claryce that it would much better to remain at the Cathedral. "Holy Name is one of the safest, most untouchable places around the city. Unless they're a true convert like Kravayik, nothing from Feirie can enter."

"Kravayik. He *is* true to his new faith, isn't he?"

"Yes, and another reason why you'd be safer inside. Will you listen?"

She shook her head. "No. I'd like . . . I'd like the familiarity of the house. This place . . . I just don't feel comfortable around all of it. I *am* a woman."

It was a point we'd discussed earlier, and one I'd thought we'd settled, but if it was still bothering her, I could see that Holy Name wouldn't work out after all. I tried to convince myself that if Her Lady had had someone—probably her hunter—reconstruct the house, she'd done it so that we'd have a place even more secure from Oberon than the rooms above the old shop.

With Fetch in the back seat and his nose out the window, we left the cathedral. I vowed I'd call Kravayik when I got the chance; he deserved an explanation. Claryce remained silent most of the way, her eyes fixed more on the constantly changing view next to her. I'd no doubt that she was also thinking about what I'd held back from her all this time and was still angry at me for not trusting her.

As guilty as I felt about keeping those secrets, I knew I'd done so for good reasons. Every incarnation of her had shared a propensity for inquisitiveness and determination, both admirable qualities except when they meant walking into danger in the belief that it was the better course of action. Bad enough that Oberon had spotted her and made certain that she'd become an assistant to "William Delke" just so that he could use her as bait, but the more she refused to keep safe, the more likely that Oberon'd kill her. I couldn't let that happen.

We were just about to turn on the last street when I caught a glimpse of an auto just beyond the streetlight. I knew my neighbors well enough to know this wasn't one of theirs.

Let Eye reveal it . . .

"Go ahead," I muttered under my breath. I was beginning to appreciate this new understanding we had, although I tried to remain cautious. Through his emerald world, I got a much better view of the auto and its occupant.

I immediately parked the Packard. "Fetch, take Claryce around the back. Don't let the pair of you be seen by anyone."

To my relief, Claryce didn't ask any questions. She quietly followed him.

I had several notions as to what Detective Cortez was here for, but not why he should be waiting so late. If he had any reason to arrest me for the Alonso Perez murder, I'd guess he would've come with some help.

He does not see . . . strike . . .

I let out a small grunt, not only to quiet him and dismiss his eyes, but to let Cortez know I was near. He threw away the cigarette he'd been smoking and stepped out of the auto. I noticed that he kept his hand near his coat, right where his gun would've been.

"Nick Medea . . . been waiting awhile for you, you know?"

"In the dark? Is there a reason I should be concerned?"

"Maybe yes, maybe no. You ever get to Our Lady?"

I decided to be straight with him . . . to a point. "I went there. Everything was black."

"Yeah." While Cortez couldn't see my expression all that well, I could see his. He was more pensive than I'd ever seen him. "You talk with the man I spoke about?"

"Only the one time on the telephone." Before he could go farther with his questions, I asked, "If you're here, did something happen to him?"

He reached for yet another cigarette. "Dunno. No one's seen him."

By now, someone should've discovered the body. *Bodies*, since I'd left the one thug behind. Oberon had gotten someone to clean up after the situation.

I tried to keep control of the conversation. "This statuette. You know much about it?"

"Me? I take Maria and the little ones to church, ask the Lady to talk with God about my sins, and hope I do good, you know?"

While I understood what he meant by "the Lady," I'd had to fight with the knowledge that Her Lady kept watch on me behind my back for centuries. I couldn't help thinking about the reconstructed house, which Cortez appeared to know nothing about, either.

"Like I said," I continued. "The church was dark when I got there. Never got to talk with him."

"Yeah . . ." Although the cigarette hung in the corner of his mouth, he hadn't lit it yet. "Listen, Nick . . . I think you got the idea from me last time that there's something big brewing! Dunno what it is, but I think it's bigger than bootleggers! Scarface, Hymie, and Bugs might be part of it, but they ain't the ones in charge."

The good detective had it on the nose, but he didn't know the half of it. I chose the most logical route to keep him in the dark. "You think Papa Johnny's back on top?"

"Him? Nah, he's over." The cigarette shifted to the other side of his mouth. "Me? I think Mr. Business, Mr. William Delke, is something more than he says. I think he's got his fingers in a lot of pots, you know?"

"Delke?" For Cortez's sake, he needed to steer clear of Oberon. "That's probably stretching it."

"Maybe yes, maybe no—"

The cigarette dropped from his mouth. Cortez crossed himself twice in rapid succession as he stared past my shoulder.

I immediately looked where he was staring but saw nothing. That didn't mean he'd imagined whatever it was he thought he saw.

Cortez muttered something in Spanish. I didn't catch whether it was a prayer to Heaven or an admonishment to himself for having reacted so openly.

I gave him what I could. "Someone watching us?"

"Dunno." He regained his calm and pulled out another cigarette. This one he lit. "Just jittery nerves, you know? Trying to quit for Maria. Makes me imagine things, I guess."

Whatever he'd seen had been something nasty, and I had an idea just what it was. I needed Cortez to scram and scram quick. "Listen, detective, I've got a possible clue for you, but I need to check it out before I let you know if it's kosher or not. Let me get back to you tomorrow. It might have something to do with Delke. I'll find out."

He actually looked appreciative, which made me feel guiltier. Still, now I felt a chill growing in my soul, which meant that what watched us was drawing nearer.

Fortunately, Cortez took my promise to heart. He clapped my shoulder, then, with a grin, climbed into the auto.

From there, he leaned out. "You'll call me early tomorrow?"

"By noon, I think." I'd worry about what to do with the promise tomorrow. I kept silently urging Cortez to drive off.

"Oh, one thing more, sorry." He pulled a folded paper from the breast pocket of his coat. "Some things about the heist at the Art Institute. Thought you might be able to clue me in on them as well. Odd stuff, they took. Look it over, okay?"

More eager than ever to see the good detective leave, I immediately took the paper and stuffed it in my own coat. "I'll do that. I promise."

"Appreciate that, Nick Medea." He finally started the auto and left. I waited until he was out of sight, then, summoning the dragon's eyes once more, turned to face Her Lady's enforcer.

The grim reaper sprouted from the street, rising to his full well-over-my-head height. *Gatekeeper . . .*

"Where's your face?" I asked, speaking about the thug he'd possessed.

It waits . . . The sentinel explained no further, and I tried not to imagine what was left of the unfortunate spy.

"Why're you here?" I didn't like the thought of this creature too near Claryce. Her Lady wanted Oberon destroyed, and if she thought of some reason to use Claryce to achieve that goal, she'd act on that no matter the consequences.

She would have you know . . . there is a chance to strike soon and I will take it . . .

While that news initially cheered me, I immediately after had doubts that such a straightforward attack would work so easily. I knew that this sentinel had a variety of powers at his disposal—most of them as wicked as those wielded by his prey—but we were talking about Oberon here.

I also worried about possible innocents being involved. The sentinel wouldn't be bothered by additional victims; they'd only be humans, after all. "Just what do you plan?"

You will know soon, Gatekeeper . . . consider yourself warned . . .

He melted back into the street. I knew that somewhere within a few minutes' travel his stolen body waited. I remembered Oberon's shadow gunmen and thought how even they paled in comparison to the sentinel. He had a very good chance of succeeding in his task.

He also had a very good chance of creating even more chaos.

First Cortez and now Her Lady's creature. I was growing more and more wary again about keeping Claryce in the house as opposed to the quarters over the old hat shop. It'd been a mistake. I had to convince her to leave.

I entered through the back, just in case. Claryce was waiting for me in the kitchen. There was no sign of Fetch, but music rose from the room beyond. Either Claryce had gone into the other room and turned on the radio for Fetch, or he'd somehow used his paws or his muzzle to do it, something not out of the question.

Claryce rose as soon as I entered. She looked as if she'd just woken up. "What was it out there?"

"Who. Detective Cortez. He had a couple of questions."

"Oh." She accepted the answer easier than I'd expected. "That's all right, then. Detective Cortez."

I thought once more that she looked as if she'd been sleeping before my arrival. As much as I wanted to move her yet again, her exhaustion made me finally surrender. "Why don't you go upstairs and get some sleep?"

"What about you?"

"I've a few things to deal with."

Claryce gave me a sad smile. "How much do you sleep?"

"Enough."

"Nightmares?"

She startled me with that question. I thought for a moment, then nodded. "I've got nightmares. Nothing to concern you."

"I doubt that." Claryce leaned close, then suddenly kissed me on the cheek much too close to my lips.

Without thinking, I turned my head to better look at her . . . and this time it wasn't the cheek she kissed.

"Say, Master Nicholas—"

I couldn't say which was worse. Fetch's timing or my sudden pulling away from Claryce because of it. All I knew was that she gave me a look filled with both surprise and disappointment.

"Good night," she whispered, rushing past Fetch.

His ears flattened. "Did I do something wrong?"

I expected the dragon to laugh at my situation, but he remained quiet and subdued. I was grateful enough for this latest show of unexpected support to be calmer toward Fetch. "No. Nothing."

"It's just that I—"

"Was there something you wanted?"

"A side of beef, maybe?"

I didn't have anything on that scale, naturally, and suddenly wondered if there was any food at all. Like the safe house, this place had a sturdy Kelvinator . . . or at least it *had* before being burned to the ground. What looked like a Kelvinator stood in the right place. I rose and checked.

If I hadn't been certain that the house *had* burned down and been rebuilt by some servant of Her Lady, the contents inside the Kelvinator would've erased any doubt. Feiriefolk enjoyed their little jokes, and whoever had gone through all the trouble to recreate this place had stopped at the cold contents inside. I don't think I'd purchased a leg of mutton in maybe eighty years, nor kept a couple of tankards of what I assumed were ale in the back.

Not all the food was obviously to Feirie tastes, at least on the surface. I tried to assume that the eggs were from chickens and the milk from cows.

Fetch'd nosed his way by me and eyed the mutton with tremendous interest. Rather than have to mop up after his drooling tongue, I let him have the meat. I doubted that there was anything sinister about it, and he needed sustenance after all his troubles.

My own appetite remained untouched by the fare before me. I left Fetch by the Kelvinator gnawing away at the mutton leg. As I shut the door, though, the piece of paper Cortez had given me slipped free and dropped to the floor.

Mildly curious, I sat down and unfolded it. Instead of an official police report, I saw that everything'd been copied down by Cortez. He had a distinctive, sharp style of print, certainly better than I'd have done if I'd written all this down.

I read the first item on the list of things stolen, then the next . . .

At the third one, I nearly bolted out of the chair.

Fetch looked up from his meal. "Something not copacetic, Master Nicholas?"

I didn't answer him. I couldn't answer him. I was too busy running my gaze down the list just to verify my fears.

Bits of armor. A breastplate. A helmet. A shin guard. A broken spear.

Armor, according to the good detective's notes, said by experts to be roughly sixteen centuries old and of Roman issue. Armor discovered on an expedition in part of Italian northern Africa.

And unless it was just too tremendous a coincidence . . . *my* armor.

CHAPTER 18

When I'd been *buried*, after my execution, it'd been with my armor, of course. Even though I'd been condemned for refusing to denounce my faith and accept the gods of Rome, Diocles had granted me that much of an honor.

However, Galerius Armentarius—later called Gaius Galerius Valerius Maximianus Augustus when his dear father-in-law Diocletian had raised him up to be coemperor—had unfortunately had other ideas. He'd been the one to push for the Christian purge in the first place, so leaving any sort of honor to a dead tribune who happened to believe in the One God just wouldn't do. Galerius had been the one to order my tomb secretly ransacked and my armor and everything else taken. He'd commanded they leave my body be, though, probably savoring the fact that I'd lie abandoned and in two parts for the rest of eternity.

I could imagine the look on his broad, Thracian-descended face if I'd come to him four nights after the desecration and demanded my property back. I'd risen a week after my death, but not, of course, in the biblical manner, although Heaven'd no doubt played a big part in my revival. Whatever the truth, I'd been in no shape even then to go after what was mine and, by the time I was, my duties to the Gate had already been thrust upon me.

Where the armor and the spear—*that* spear—had gone was something I'd wondered for a while, then forgotten. The Gate didn't leave me that much time to concern myself about the past.

But now I was wondering if I'd made a terrible, terrible mistake in not pursuing the matter. Galerius might be long dead—from some suitably horrific disease maybe involving gangrene, too, I'd heard—

but someone had inherited his stolen treasures, and they'd obviously passed them along to someone else until the centuries had buried them for a time.

I crumpled up the paper. Fetch still eyed me, but I paid no attention. I wasn't being nostalgic about what had once been mine; I was growing more and more concerned. I'd guarded the Gate long enough to know that things that were bound to someone by former ownership could affect them as little else could. These antiques were as much a part of the "legend" as I was myself.

And not for a moment did I think that anyone other than Oberon had set their theft in motion.

I was stirred from my worries by a thump upstairs. Even Fetch couldn't move as fast as I managed. I wasn't sure if Claryce had just moved something, but I couldn't take the chance.

At the top of the stairs, I called her name. When she didn't answer, I drew Her Lady's gift and ran to her door.

I probably should've tried the knob, but I couldn't be sure that doing so would waste precious time. My kick sent the door flying open.

Claryce stood by the closet door. One hand rested on the knob. She looked at me as if I'd grown an extra eye, then focused on the weapon I wielded.

"Nick," she said quietly. "What are you doing . . . and why do you have that?"

Feeling very foolish, I lowered Her Lady's gift. "I heard a noise. A heavy thump. When I came up to investigate, I called to you. You didn't answer."

A slight smile crossed her face. "And you worried about me . . . How touching."

I felt even more foolish. With one swift movement, I returned the Feirie blade to its hidden place.

"I am so sorry," Claryce went on as she neared me. "I was still upset when I entered. I tried to keep from showing it, but I guess I shut the closet door harder than I intended." She exhaled, then added, "And I did hear you call. I just still felt too upset to answer. I guess I should have."

She reached up and caressed my cheek. Her hand was cooler than I expected, but very soft. It was more difficult than ever to pull away, but I did, this time with an appropriately apologetic look in turn.

With a giggle, Claryce indicated the door. "Will that still work, or do I need to find something to lean against it now?"

I took the hint, first testing the door to make certain that it did shut properly, then, after discovering that the power of Feirie had *already* repaired what I'd broken, stepped out into the hall. Claryce came to the door and, with another slight smile, shut it before me.

"All clear?" asked Fetch from the top of the stairs.

Instead of answering, I asked him a question of my own. "Have you almost finished with that mutton?"

"Aye. There's a bit more, but I'll be having that done soon, Master Nicholas."

"Finish it, then take up a place in the front room. You can use the couch, but leave the radio off."

"I can sleep outside and guard the perimeter—"

"No. Stay inside, this time. I might need your help."

He wagged his tail. "Thank ye. The couch'll be ritzy compared to my usual haunts . . ."

"You know you could stay here whenever you need, Fetch."

The lycanthrope looked as embarrassed as I'd felt upstairs. His tail drooped. "Ye've been good to me. I don't deserve it. Not after what I've—what I tried to do to ye back then."

I wanted to say more, but he scurried downstairs as best he could with the stiff back. Rather than make him feel worse, I headed for the other bedroom. Most times, I ended up sleeping on the couch myself, as much in the bedroom. It was generally safer that way. Tonight, though, I wanted to be near, just in case there actually *was* some threat to Claryce.

For the first time in a while, the dragon chuckled in my head. It wasn't the mocking chuckle to which I'd grown so accustomed over the centuries, but rather a softer one. He knew as well as I that I didn't just want to stay near to Claryce for her safety . . . I also just wanted to stay near.

I slept . . . and that meant I dreamed.

The nightmare.

I was charging the dragon . . . only I was also *riding* the dragon, and we were suddenly charging a giant. The giant became Oberon, with hands big enough to engulf both of us. One hand held Claryce, who tried to call to me but had a voice I could barely make out.

I raised the spear for throwing, but it transformed into Her Lady's gift. The Feirie blade stretched for miles, but it still couldn't quite reach Oberon.

The other hand stretched toward us, every finger a hulking Doolin. I cut off two Doolins at the waist, but they grew back in the blink of an eye. Each one pulled out an automatic and began firing.

From behind me, I heard Fetch's howl. Big as the dragon, he bounded past me. I wanted to warn him back, but he kept going.

But as he kept going, he started to dwindle. Halfway to the giant Oberon, Fetch'd shrunken to nearly his true size. A little farther, and he was even a bit smaller.

A few more paces, and Fetch just ceased to be.

There is only you and Eye, the dragon said in my head, even though I sat upon his back. He looked up at me with a wide reptilian grin. *Only you and Eye . . .*

And then his head rose up and twisted around like a snake and swallowed me whole—

At that point, I awoke with a gasp. I lay on top of the bed, fully clothed as usual. Instead of sweat, a chill coursed through me.

From outside the room, I heard a brief creak. Without a sound, I rose and headed to the door. There was another slight creak, this one farther away.

I opened the door just enough to give me a glimpse of the hall. When I saw nothing, I carefully opened the way farther.

The hall and the stairway were empty. I quietly walked to the steps, then descended.

Snores rose from the front room. Fetch lay on his side, his paws dangling and his tongue lolling. If not for the obvious stiffness in his back, he would have looked quite comfortable.

I started for the kitchen, then paused to look at the telephone. The receiver hung on the side as it should've, and there was nothing out of the ordinary that I could see, but for some reason I was drawn to it.

With some trepidation, I plucked up the receiver.

What sounded like the wind echoed from the other end of the line. I thought I heard a voice—

"I didn't hear ye come down, Master Nicholas!" Fetch bounded over to me, in his enthusiasm disturbing the table where the telephone stood. I grabbed for the candlestick base before the device could fall.

The wind—and the possible voice—faded. A moment later, an operator's voice asked me what number I wished to call. Rather than answer, I hung up and frowned at Fetch.

"Very sorry, very sorry . . ."

"Did you touch the telephone earlier, Fetch?" It was an odd question to ask him, but I needed to know.

Ears high and head cocked, Fetch answered, "Now who would I be calling?"

"Yeah, you've got a point." I looked at the ceiling toward where Claryce's room was. "Did she come down at all?"

"I was sleeping, but I don't think so."

While I could understand him not hearing me, I doubted that Claryce could've been so silent that his acute senses wouldn't have noticed her walking by.

Again, I had my doubts as to the good sense of having brought Claryce back here. More and more, I felt the presence of Feirie around me. This might look like the house I'd chosen, but it was now a thing of Her Lady's Court.

"All right. Go back to sleep."

With a wag, Fetch returned to the couch. If he smelled the presence of Feirie in the house, he said nothing about it.

I hesitated, then returned upstairs. As I reached the top, Claryce's door opened.

"Is there something wrong?" she asked in a sleepy voice.

"No. I just had to get something from downstairs." There was no sense telling her more. I didn't even know if anything *had* happened.

"All right." Claryce smiled. "Pleasant dreams."

I refrained from reminding her what my sleep was like. Better that at least she got rest.

My mind drifted to the Art Institute theft and the suspicion that not only were the items my ancient armor and spear, but that Oberon had some particular use for them. The logical conclusion was that he needed them to rid himself of me, but Oberon was never as straightforward as that. There was at least a second layer to this, one that I was still missing.

Somewhere along the way, I drifted off after all. Another variation of the dream took over, but thankfully I woke before it was over. To my surprise, a hint of light through the window indicated I'd slept until dawn.

I washed up quickly and stepped out of the bedroom. The house was silent, but with Claryce's door still shut, I had to assume that she at least was in bed. As quietly as I could, I descended.

Fetch was no longer on the couch, but I figured it was safe to assume he was in the kitchen gnawing on something he'd struggled out of the Kelvinator. I couldn't hear him in there, but if he'd done as I thought, he'd be trying to go as unnoticed as possible.

"Just relax, Fetch," I called as I entered. "You can eat whatever—"

The kitchen was empty. The back door was shut, but that didn't mean much. Even without proper hands, the lycanthrope could get most doors open.

I peered out the nearest window. I hadn't exactly left the Packard where it was by chance. I knew I could get a glimpse of it from here.

The only trouble was, the Packard was *gone*.

I shouted for Claryce. When she didn't answer, or even make some sound above, I ran from the kitchen up to her room. This time, I doubted she wasn't answering because she was still annoyed with me.

The room was empty, just as I'd feared. I thought about the telephone, and the odd sensation I'd felt about it. There was a connection there, but it eluded me as usual.

I suddenly thought of the paper Cortez had left me. There'd been some other info on it, but I'd been too caught up with the discovery about my lost armor to pay attention to the rest. Yet, something nagged at my mind.

I pulled the ragged sheet from my pocket and looked further down. Sure enough, there was something I'd seen and that I'd absorbed but hadn't really read. Information about the original donor, now dead some years. There was an address listed from the original donation papers, one that shouldn't have meant much after all this time.

Somehow, I knew that Oberon was using that address.

While I needed to get moving on the one clue I had, I couldn't rely on myself alone. I had no choice but to take a page from Oberon and Her Lady and use the one possible pawn I had.

Taking up the telephone, I told the operator the number to Cortez's home precinct.

The voice that answered wasn't the same one as last time. He was much more polite, even when I asked for Cortez. Unfortunately, his answer wasn't much help. The good detective had rushed out on some urgent call.

Silently cursing, I hung up. Without Cortez, I was now back to having only the old address as a possible clue to where Claryce and Fetch had vanished to.

I started for the front door . . . and stumbled back as it opened to admit *Claryce*.

"Nick! Hurry! I think I know which way they went, but we have follow quickly!"

She had her hand in mine before I could answer. Despite Claryce obviously having run back from wherever she'd been, she was still cool to the touch. That and her paler skin made me worry about her even as I followed her outside.

The Packard awaited us by the curb. I let Claryce guide me to the auto, then, as I took over in the driver's seat, asked, "What happened?"

"I came downstairs for some water and saw . . . saw a shadow drape over Fetch! It stole him away. One moment he was on the couch, the next he was outside, still asleep."

"How long ago?"

"Just before the first light of day!"

Not too long, but long enough. They could be far away. "But why take Fetch?"

"I don't know! Hurry!" She pointed south. "That way."

It was vaguely in the direction of the address I had. I took one more glance at the sheet, then stuffed it into my pocket.

"What was that?" she asked.

In answer, I pulled out the dagger and set the point at her throat.

Not at all to my surprise, Claryce only smiled at me, even though, despite what she really was, the dagger would've made her very dead if I chose to use it.

"Where is she?" I demanded, in my most even voice possible.

She put a hand to my cheek, a cool hand that I should've realized had stayed too cool to be human. "Claryce" gave me a pout worthy of Clara Bow as she cooed, "She has missed the Gatekeeper . . . it has been a long, long time since he came to her . . ."

I managed to repress a shudder. "Claryce" wasn't just talking about someone else. She was referring to *herself* in the third person . . . just as Her Lady always did.

Burn her! Burn her! my constant companion roared in my head. His reaction—so ardent after our last couple of days of relative peace with each other—surprised me even more than Her Lady sitting beside me.

No . . . my response was both to him and in regard to the thing wearing Claryce's form. This *wasn't* Her Lady; this was some puppet with mortal traces in it. Living, but not a thinking creature. In Feirie, they were called *changelings.*

At that moment, I didn't care whether it was a puppet or Her Lady herself. I batted her hand away. "*Where* is she? How long have you been plotting this?" My eyes narrowed as the answer to the second question immediately came to me. "You've always *known* . . . or at least suspected! Since that night! You expected Oberon to survive!"

Her Lady might've been viewing me from the Court in Feirie, but her changeling evinced a very real twitch of fear. Names were both power and fear in her realm and no name was still feared more than his.

She recovered quickly, though. The smile returned, the smile that was in no manner Claryce's. "Your little one sleeps, Gatekeeper . . . *She* only needed her semblance for a little while . . . to deal with *him.*"

It was even more frustrating trying to keep track of Her Lady's use of the third person while at the same time she spoke about another female, Claryce. I'd had enough of Feirie nuances and Feirie games. I kept the point close to her throat.

"This may not be able to kill you—though I'm pretty sure the same can't be said for your changeling here—but it *can* give you some pain. I want Claryce *now.*"

It was a bluff, and unfortunately, she knew it. "Dear Gatekeeper . . . we must be going . . . all is in place . . ." The changeling put her hand on the one holding the dagger. "She will sleep until we finish with *him*."

I had no choice. I got the Packard going. We raced toward the direction she'd indicated. It wasn't exactly toward the address I'd planned to head and that bothered me. Her Lady might've been a master plotter, but she'd learned at the feet of the most insidious.

At the next intersection, I turned left. A milk truck steered onto the sidewalk to avoid me, bottles spilling out the back.

The changeling's expression showed a distinct lack of amusement. "Gatekeeper . . ."

I didn't answer her. We were only a few blocks away from the address. I wasn't sure how Oberon was tied to the original donor, but if he was it fit his twisted humor. Maybe he'd had his human puppet donate the armor so it'd be in a safe place until the right time or maybe he'd left it there in plain sight wondering if I'd ever find out about it.

The Packard suddenly turned a different direction than I'd intended. Try as I might, I couldn't get it to steer where I wanted. I glared at her, but she only stared ahead.

There were oddly few autos on our path back to where *she* wanted us to go. Moreover, there were many odd, distinctive shadows about the vicinity. I didn't need the dragon's eyes to know that they were elements of Feirie. It spoke again how long and thoroughly Her Lady had worked to devise all this.

And yet, I still couldn't help thinking she'd assumed *too* much.

"Here."

No sooner had she spoken than the Packard stopped. The changeling slipped out of the car in one fluid and very surreal motion. I jumped out the other side, the dagger back in my coat and my hand now near where I kept Her Lady's gift.

That brought a side glance and a sly smile to the false Claryce's face. I pretended not to notice, instead reaching out to the dragon to let me see with his eyes.

He was hesitant, more so than I would've expected. I urged him again and he relented. The world shifted . . . and the Feirie shadows deepened. In their depths, I sensed hungers of varying kind, but all set in service to Her Lady.

For the first time, I began to wonder if maybe *Oberon'd* overplayed his hand. No one knew him better than Her Lady. No one.

The changeling gestured with her left hand . . . and the shadows began to converge. We were in a warehouse district, which shouldn't have surprised me, but still made me wonder.

"Gatekeeper . . ." She pointed at a long, iron door. I knew why. Even though Her Lady actually physically existed in Feirie, the power of iron was such to her that she'd still feel discomfort. It probably wasn't that much in this case, but I suspected that she wanted her entire concentration available.

I stepped in front of the door, than looked back. It didn't come as a shock that the changeling was nowhere to be seen, nor that the shadows were looming closer. Or that there was no one else in sight, for that matter. She'd considered everything, it seemed.

And since she hadn't given me any further commands, I assumed Her Lady wanted me to do as I thought.

Give me a hand, I demanded.

He didn't hesitate that much this time, probably because we were already caught between Oberon and Her Lady and he wanted to survive, even if only as a part of me. I felt the urge to let him take over completely, but fought that down. I only needed what I'd asked for.

And with that hand, I ripped open the door.

I let the hand revert to normal as I jumped in. By the time I was past the entrance, I already had Her Lady's gift drawn.

From the other side, the changeling walked *through* the brick wall. At the same time, shadows flowed in from all sides.

But, in a scene I found too familiar, there was nothing in sight except a single figure standing in the center of the room. He certainly wasn't Oberon, unless Oberon had switched forms. That the exiled lord of Feirie would choose a grimy hoodlum over the elegant guise of William Delke didn't make sense, though.

"Stand before me, my love," Her Lady uttered through the changeling, for one of the few times since I'd met her not speaking of herself in the third person. *"Come and feel my caress . . ."*

"No!" But my shout went unheeded. Her Lady still sensed Oberon's presence, just as he intended. I could see the darkness that represented her swelling power fill her side of the building, even as her servants, waiting for this moment for over fifty years, drew near from the other.

As they did, though, the figure raised its head, so that whoever stood before it could see the face clearly. By that time, I already knew that it'd be a face I vaguely knew.

I stared at the twisted face of the goon who'd been spying on the barrelhouse near the old millinery. His mouth gaped, and he didn't have eyes anymore. Just two hollows that went on and on if you looked into them too long.

Her Lady's sentinel had found Oberon . . . or Oberon had found him. It didn't matter which. There wasn't much left of the thing, nothing that could be said to be sane even by the standards of Feirie.

Too arrogant to listen to me, Her Lady acted through the changeling. Her power draped over the lone figure . . . and through it the changeling—and Her Lady—were snared by something inside the sentinel that held them tight.

And at that moment, other shadows moved. Shadows vaguely resembling men. Men with tommies.

Tommies aimed at both me and Her Lady's changeling.

CHAPTER 19

The same wicked sounds I'd heard the shadow guns make filled the room. Each time they struck one of Her Lady's servants, *that* shadow burned away. I ducked low as one aimed at me. I still remembered what those shots had done in the Delke house and wasn't keen on finding out what they'd do to my body.

A shrill scream that Claryce could never have uttered, even in her greatest agony, drowned out all other sounds. Out of the six gunners I counted, three were focused on the changeling. I couldn't imagine the extent of the pain Her Lady might be feeling, but her changeling already looked as if someone had literally punched holes in her. There was no blood, just holes. Black ones like what was left of the eyes of the sentinel.

My left arm suddenly stung. A glance showed me that I'd just barely been grazed. Even then, the pain continued to spread and it was all I could do to move the limb.

I rolled away as one shadow took aim again. None of the gunners were near enough for me to cut, and even then I wasn't sure if that'd accomplish what it had the last time. Oberon had set this trap for Her Lady and the sword'd been fashioned by her. Still, I had one hope, assuming that I could make it there.

The shadow gunners continued to fire away. They crept along the walls, distorting as they turned. We hadn't passed any autos in the vicinity, which meant that Oberon had managed to increase the distance of this particular spell.

I grunted as another shot seared my calf. The wound made me roll to the side and away from my target. The changeling's scream continued unabated.

I turned my roll into a squat and then a leap toward the center of the room. That brought me face-to-face again with the sentinel and his human shell. I brought Her Lady's gift up.

One stroke severed the top half of the long-dead thug.

There was no blood. I'd not expected any. He'd been dead the moment the sentinel'd taken him. Any life fluids had been used by the sentinel to keep him strong. The only problem was, they hadn't kept him strong enough. Oberon had probably known all along that he'd be sent by Her Lady to hunt her former husband and master down.

But I hadn't cut the corpse in half to save the sentinel any more suffering. There'd been almost as little of him left as there was the human he'd taken. Oberon'd no doubt tortured him very well. No, I'd cut the body in half for the simple reason that it was the only hope of also cutting the link to whatever kept Her Lady snared.

It worked. The changeling's scream immediately halted. Unfortunately, I had no time to see just how badly ruined it might be, for at that moment two more of the shadow gunners found interest in me. I raised Her Lady's gift and tried to decide which one was nearest—

That shadow vanished. The one next to it disappeared a second later.

The rest of the gunners vanished right after that.

I was left alone, the surviving shadow folk serving Her Lady also having retreated. I didn't even need to look to see that the changeling was gone, too. That stirred a combination of fury and fear in me. Her Lady had never actually given me a solid promise that she'd release Claryce from whatever slumber she'd put her in.

The only trace of the entire trap was the dried husk I'd cut in two. Since there was nothing to tie it to me, I left it where it was and headed back to the Packard. I had only one hope, and that hope relied on me finding a phone.

There was no pay phone nearby, but I found a jazz club about two miles south where the music was still going strong. The flappers and their daddies had danced away the night, unaware just how precarious life in Chicago really was right now.

The bleary-eyed bouncer wasn't keen on letting me in, "needing the telephone" likely an excuse he heard every evening. I gave him a brief glimpse of the dragon's gaze, just enough to make him probably wonder whether the dope he'd likely been smoking had been tainted.

I borrowed the telephone by the equally exhausted hat check girl and dialed the house. I expected nothing and so was pretty surprised when I heard her voice.

"Nick! Thank God! Where did you go to? I just woke up and found both you and Fetch missing!"

I didn't like what I needed to tell her, but I told her nevertheless. "Claryce . . . I need you to leave the house. I know you might not want to—"

"'Not want to'? Nick, I don't know why you brought me back here in the first place!"

She didn't remember demanding to go back. Now I understood just how long she'd been under Her Lady's influence. I suspected that the unlamented sentinel had had some part in that. I'd not cared for the thing before, and this made me even less sorry it'd died. I only wished it'd taken Oberon with it.

"Never mind," I said. I gave her a street address. "Find a cabbie there. You know the address of the safe house. Go."

"What about you?"

"I'll be there shortly." I hoped she'd believe the lie.

"All right . . . but hurry."

After she hung up, I decided to make one more call. Dialing Cortez's precinct, I tried for the good detective a second time.

"Cortez?" It was the first sergeant I'd spoken with. He chuckled, not caring if I might be a friend of the detective. I didn't care; the dragon's magic enabled me to use a little influence on him, make him answer what he might not always answer. "He's chasin' spooks down south. Some dago hooch place. Don't know when he's gettin' back."

Something bothered me. Pretending knowledge, I mentioned a particular address, adding, "I gave him the tip. He's down there this morning? Not tonight?"

"Got a call it was now or never. Is this Dog? Listen Dog, you know better—"

I hung up, not because I wanted him to think I was this snitch, but because he'd verified what I feared. Cortez was on his way to break up the barrelhouse right by where I'd sent Claryce. It *might've* been coincidence, but nothing thus far had been.

The Packard was too slow. I knew that Claryce would be there long before me. Cortez probably already was.

Let me give you wings . . .

I nearly took the offer, but it was one thing to do so in the dead of night, another to agree to it in daylight. I grimly climbed back into the Packard and sped off, hoping that the morning traffic wouldn't thicken before I got to the barrelhouse.

Oberon continued to control the game. He'd forced Her Lady to move during the light, when her power was weaker. She'd thought she'd been clever to bring her *own* shadows with her in order to strengthen her link with her changeling, but she'd only done as her former master had intended. After all, while Her Lady could make some adaptations to the light, Oberon had forced himself to dwell in it for more than fifty years.

I shuddered to think that perhaps part of his immunity came from the human skin he wore to disguise himself. There'd probably been an actual Delke somewhere down the family line, or maybe Oberon had let each generation procreate before he'd taken over the patriarch of that time. Either ghoulish way, Oberon had been thorough.

I still had no idea where Fetch was. The fact that he'd vanished only shortly before the changeling had come to me made me wonder if Her Lady had offered him a trip back home in return for serving her here. I wasn't sure if that boded well. Part of her offer might still be contingent on removing me once she was sure Oberon was *really* dead this time. We were supposed to have a truce after that last incident, but I now wondered if the truce had only come about because she'd realized I made a good pawn to move against him.

There was no point in finding another pay phone; Claryce wouldn't be near a telephone until—if and when—she reached the safe house. Someday, I hoped there'd be two-way radios able to be used in every auto, but for now I had to have patience. It was something I should've learned centuries ago, but I was still trying.

I neared the safe house with growing concern that had nothing to do with Claryce. If Cortez was chasing down the barrelhouse, he was doing it with very little assistance. I hadn't spotted a single cop or car, and from what I knew of such raids there should've been some by now.

It was so quiet, in fact, that I was able to get around to the back of the safe house and park the Packard without a problem. I had hopes that Claryce was already inside, but I didn't dare call out until I got upstairs.

Unfortunately, the quarters were empty. There was no note, which meant she probably hadn't even arrived here. She'd been nearer to the safe house than I'd been; she *should've* gotten here before me.

I heard an auto drive up. Keeping to the side, I peered out the front window in time to see two black roadsters. Even before he stepped out, I knew one of the passengers would be Doolin.

He kept his hands deep in the pockets of an oversized coat. I had what I thought was a perfect theory as to why Doolin kept those hands hidden until he pulled out one clutching a heavy heater. He waved the automatic at the four other hoods accompanying him, indicating that they should go around to the back of the distillery.

I had a bad feeling about Detective Cortez's tip. It wasn't the first time someone had tricked a cop into a place where he could be rubbed out. That Doolin was here told me that Oberon knew of Cortez's tenuous but real ties to me. Unlike what'd happened with Claryce, though, I didn't think that Doolin was here to question the good detective. Cortez was going to be another example to me of just how much Oberon controlled everything.

Part of me wanted to wait for Claryce and get her away from here, while the other knew I couldn't leave Cortez to Doolin and his friends. As Doolin's mob spread around the barrelhouse, I hurried down from the second story and out.

Hand near Her Lady's gift, I circled around to where I'd previously encountered the spy and Her Lady's sentinel. That gave me a view of the back door to the place, where Doolin and another man were already entering.

I didn't have any more choice. Each time I entered a building, it seemed to be to set off a trap by Oberon. Third time hadn't been the charm, but maybe fourth—or fifth, I'd lost count—would be. Maybe this time I'd turn things on him. Maybe.

Let me show you . . . he offered. I declined it for now, not wanting Cortez to see the dragon's eyes if I could help it.

There was no sign of his auto, but he'd probably parked it out of sight. I crept to the door Doolin had entered, then carefully opened it a crack.

A gunshot rang out.

It only took me a moment to realize that it hadn't been fired at me. Either someone had shot at Cortez or Cortez had fired first. Either way, I was left with no choice but to rush in.

The first thing I saw when the door swung wide was three stiffs sprawled on the floor near the distilling equipment. One of them I recognized as the guard who'd come across me on the initial visit. Drying blood pooled around them, while a pair of pistols showed they'd at least had a chance to try to shoot back.

I smelled Doolin's part in this. At Oberon's behest, he'd come here earlier, gunned down Capone's boys, and then arranged so that Cortez would come here. If they'd kept an eye on Cortez at all, they knew he often worked alone. That still didn't explain why he'd try to raid a barrelhouse himself, but this being Chicago probably at least two of his superiors were on the take to both gangs. It only took one command to make a supposed raid into the removal of a detective who was already undesired by most he worked with.

Even as I entered, more shots were fired. These came from nearer by. I saw Doolin and his hoods working to pin Cortez into the far corner of the room, away from any of the doors.

Doolin was too far away to reach with Her Lady's gift, but not the dagger. The smaller blade didn't have to be blessed to deal with an Irish gunman, just sharp. I switched to it and readied a throw.

Unfortunately, one of the other shooters took that moment to reload. As he did, he glanced back at the door and saw me.

"Watchit!" The half-loaded forty-five pistol came up at me.

There was no choice but to change targets. The dagger went flying at the thug. It caught him in the throat just before he could fire. His twitching finger pulled the trigger, but the two shots he managed before hitting the floor dead went wide.

I focused on Doolin again. He grinned, his position already shifted so as to keep me from trying anything from a distance. One of the other gunmen jumped around a barrel and began firing at me.

Despite Doolin's grin, I couldn't help thinking that this didn't look like a trap for me, after all. Unless Oberon had some even more devious plan in mind, Doolin had come here for Cortez and Cortez alone. Naturally, that didn't mean that he wasn't eager to take me on as well. He pumped off three quick shots my direction.

His aim was barely better than that of the dying hood. It was enough to force me to a kneeling position but no more. I could only assume that Oberon chose Doolin for talents other than shooting, such as torture.

Barely had Doolin fired than someone forced *him* to duck by sending a shot his direction. As Doolin vanished behind the barrels he'd chosen, Cortez followed up with another shot at one of the other gunmen. It missed, but it drew attention back to the detective and bought me a moment.

I drew Her Lady's gift. Although meant for Wyld, it was also good for easily slicing open a barrel full of hooch that I immediately turned toward the nearest thug. The bootleg whiskey spilled the direction I desired. I pretended to pull out a match, which was all the gunman I was toying with needed to scramble farther back.

It'd been my intention just to use his certainty I was going to set the whole place ablaze to keep him distracted for a critical moment. What I'd also done, though, was apparently put him right where Cortez could get a good shot. The goon sprawled forward as one well-placed bullet from the detective caught him squarely in the back.

Even with two of his boys already down, Doolin didn't seem the least upset. I found out a moment later why when two more gunmen broke in from the door to Cortez's left. One of them had a tommy gun and started spraying shots at Cortez the moment he saw him.

Fortunately, just like with O'Donnell, having a tommy didn't mean the gunner knew how to use it right. Most of the bullets hit well above and to the left of the detective and, when the thug tried once more, the weapon jammed.

Cortez tried to fire off another shot, this one at the hood with the tommy, but the gunner's companion opened fire with his pistol, forcing Cortez to shield himself again.

With everyone peering at what was happening with the tommy and Cortez, I charged toward Doolin. He now looked a bit concerned and fiddled behind the barrels. I wondered if his gun had also jammed.

I kicked aside the first barrel . . . and Doolin jumped at me, both hands now wearing the familiar gauntlets. The grin was back on his face, and I knew he'd only pretended concern to draw me to him.

I had no choice but to use the sword. I also had no choice but to stand there gaping as Doolin *caught* the sharp blade with one hand. What was more surprising was that he didn't lose that hand to Her Lady's gift. The gauntlet held the blade tight.

Only then did I see the intricate scrollwork and the twisted tree markings I knew represented the Feirie Court. I suddenly understood just where the gauntlets had come from. They were *Oberon's*.

My memories of the Night the Dragon Breathed didn't include Oberon wearing or not wearing the gauntlets. At the time, I'd been more concerned with the shifting Gate, the Wyld sent to rip me apart, the magic drawn from Feirie that was beginning to change the city, and, of course, the dragon. Still, I should've realized that any armor from the other realm would've had latent magic that could be utilized this close to the Gate. It surprised me that Doolin could wear them without becoming a twisted, inhuman thing . . . but then again, maybe inside he'd been like that even before Oberon found him.

All that flashed through my head as I tried to pull Her Lady's gift free while avoiding Doolin's fist. I managed the first part but failed miserably with the second. The mailed fist slammed into my side, and I distinctly heard a rib crack just before the immense pain left me shouting.

Doolin swung again, but I succeeded in swerving away enough to only let the knuckles graze me. Even then, the new agony proved nearly as intense as that from the initial blow.

I slashed with Her Lady's gift, but Doolin proved much more agile than I thought possible. He tried to snatch the sword away by the sharp edge, but failed.

One of Doolin's boys jumped up from my right and took aim. Caught between him and Doolin, my chances were slight.

With a snarl, Doolin grabbed a barrel with both hands and threw it at the aiming gunner. The man barely had time to jump before the barrel landed in front of him.

"The greaser!" Oberon's pet hood shouted at the frightened gunmen. "Keep on the greaser!"

The other hood wasted no time in evading Doolin's wrath. The giant Irishman grinned wider at me. "Guess I get to soften you up a little sooner than he thought!"

Other than he was speaking about Oberon, I had no idea what Doolin meant. I did know that the larger barrel he plucked up next probably should've been too much even for him, but Oberon's gauntlets obviously had several abilities.

The barrel came crashing down right where I'd stood. By then, I was back several feet. The whiskey I'd spilled now covered the floor beneath me, and if Doolin had decided to play the same game I had earlier—only in his case *actually* tossing a match—I'd have had to try to rely on the dragon more than ever.

But Doolin only lunged forward, bringing both fists at me. I twisted Her Lady's gift around and scored a hit on his unprotected arm. Oberon's henchman went white—and then recovered so quickly that he nearly managed to seize the tip of the sword.

He chuckled. "Gotta try better than that—"

From somewhere there came the sound of shattering glass. It was followed by a familiar howl. I couldn't say how he'd done it, but Fetch'd found me.

There was a shout and the rattle of the tommy. Bullets flew everywhere, probably as the gunner tried to get a fix on the lycanthrope.

Doolin was no longer smiling, but he also didn't look very concerned. I could see from his flexing fingers that he was imagining just how easy my throat would give if he got his hands around it.

Another shot rang out. This one creased Doolin's left cheek. He finally had the decency to look truly startled. I was startled, too, because not only had the bullet certainly not been a random shot from the tommy, but it also couldn't have come from Cortez, unless he'd managed a truly magical ricochet.

A second shot came within a hair of knocking Doolin's cap off. He muttered something in Gaelic, then pulled back.

"Nick! Over here!"

If Doolin had been startled, so was I. The last person I ever would've wanted in here was Claryce, yet not only had she found her way inside—and somehow I was certain Fetch was in part to blame—but *she* was the one who'd fire two very good shots at Doolin.

"Damned skirt!" He grabbed another barrel and threw it in her direction just as she fired for a third time. The bullet hit the flying barrel, spilling some of the whiskey inside as the barrel soared at her.

I didn't waste a thought, leaping hard and putting myself partially in the barrel's path. The lower end collided with my shoulder, the pain only tolerable because my ribs still throbbed worse from Doolin's punch. The barrel and I landed in an awkward heap just in front of Claryce.

A sharp whistle cut through the air and just enough into the fog of pain I was suffering. The gunshots tapered off into the distance.

"Nick!" Claryce's gentle hands touched my face, turning it to her. "Nick! Speak to me!"

Let me help . . .

I felt an abrupt surge of strength, an offering from the dragon. The agony subsided. I even felt the rib fix itself. Still, the aftereffect of his effort left me light-headed for a moment.

Another pair of shots echoed through the building. I heard a mournful whine.

"F-Fetch?" As best I could, I tried to rise.

"No, Nick! You can't push yourself so quickly!"

She had no idea what the dragon'd done for me. It was no simple gift, either. Each time he healed me, he drained himself for a while. There wasn't much left to him as it was, and when he did this, it meant that he couldn't do anything else immediately if we were threatened further. It would've been different if he'd been the dominant part, if he'd been here now instead of me. Then, his full power, his full strength, would've been available to him.

But that was something I couldn't do . . . even with the recent change in the relationship between us.

Despite Claryce's protests, I pushed myself up. There was still a bit of light-headedness, but it faded quickly. I used that time to snatch Her Lady's gift from the floor and return it to its hiding place.

Claryce stared at me with concern and confusion. She had both hands on me. The gun she'd stuffed in her belt. I looked from her to the gun and back again.

"I found it by that man—the dagger in him. I assume you did that."

"I did . . . and that's not the question I wanted to ask. Where'd you learn to shoot?"

She looked down. "I had a boyfriend. My first. He liked to hunt. He also wanted to be a policeman. I wanted to be with him, so I went with him when he took target practice." Claryce managed a slight smile. "I almost got as good as him before Wilson brought us into the war and Mike decided to join up with the American Expeditionary Force. He died in France."

"I'm sorry." There was something that nagged me about her story, but I forgot all about it as the gunshots and whining I'd heard before finally sunk in again. I grimaced and pushed past Claryce.

"Fetch brought you here, didn't he?" I asked, as I maneuvered around the barrels and the body. As I passed the man I'd killed I tugged free the dagger, wiped it on the hood's coat, and put it away. I still couldn't see any sign of Fetch or Cortez.

"No. I saw him across the street when I got to the safe house. He looked like he was judging how to get inside. I just followed after him—"

I didn't hear her after that, because I'd finally gotten a glimpse of Cortez. He was leaning against the far wall, gasping for breath but otherwise looking little worse for wear. The detective still had his service weapon out and was staring to his left.

And there, sprawled a few yards in front of him, three gaping wounds from that same gun expertly marking the furred chest, lay Fetch.

CHAPTER 20

Before I could stop her, Claryce ran over to Fetch. She cradled his head in her arms. Fetch's tongue lolled and from where I stood I couldn't see if he was breathing at all.

Cortez looked from her to me. "Nick Medea! Why—why am I not surprised to see you? Tell me that!"

I already had my story ready. "I had some of that info you wanted, but when I called the precinct, the sergeant said you'd left to break up this barrelhouse. I'd called to warn you that I found out someone'd set you up here . . ."

He grunted. "Well, it sure wasn't the dagos. They were already cold when I got here, you know?" Even though there wasn't any hint of danger left, Cortez kept his gun out. He also continued to eye Fetch. "And what's with el Lobo? I know I've seen that thing! It started to leap at me . . ."

Fetch'd probably done so to protect Cortez, and it'd cost him. I needed to separate the pair as quickly as I could.

"Never mind that, Cortez. You've got yourself a big story here. Shouldn't you be getting this reported?"

"Yeah, yeah . . . and maybe find out just where my backup's supposed to be, you know?" As he spoke, we heard a siren in the distance. The detective gave me a wink. "Ah! And here come my compadres now, Nick!"

"Maybe you better go out and meet them."

I wasn't fooling the detective on that point and didn't want to. Cortez cocked his head. "And it'll all be nice and empty here, won't it?" Before I could say anything more, he waved us off. "Go! We'll be talking, right?"

I gave him a noncommittal nod, which still was enough to satisfy him. Cortez pocketed his gun and stepped past Claryce and the prone Fetch without another glance. He was taking a big risk letting us go; if anyone spotted us leaving, it'd be on his head.

The moment Cortez retreated outside, I bent down to Claryce and Fetch. Claryce looked up to me with fright. "Nick . . . he's not breathing! I think he's—"

"Move to the side. Let me take him." I was glad she obeyed without a protest. She'd not dealt with Feirie; she didn't understand them.

This should've been handled differently, but with the cops fast approaching—*finally*, where Cortez was probably concerned—I had to stir things to action.

Fetch's body was cold and stiff, and the fur was caked with his blood. He was even stiffer than I'd thought, probably in part due to the strange wound Fetch had suffered during his capture by Oberon. I wondered if I'd guessed wrong, but there was nothing to do but keep going as I planned.

Drawing Her Lady's gift, I gingerly brought its sharp edge to Fetch's throat.

Claryce, of course, didn't like the look of things. "What are you going to do? You're not going to cut off his head . . . are you?"

Fetch's body convulsed. He let out a low moan that I smothered with my arm. The convulsions grew stronger, more rapid. I pulled away Her Lady's gift, the sword having done its work just by being very near. The powerful relic from Feirie had brought the lycanthrope's own abilities closer to what they'd been when he still lived in the other realm.

He let out a great heave, and the bullets Cortez'd pumped into him went popping out of his flesh. One clattered onto the floor just in front of a startled Claryce.

Fetch started breathing normally. His eyes opened. "Master Nicholas?"

"Try to be a little more careful next time, will you? I wouldn't put it past Cortez to carry silver, or at least blessed bullets . . ."

"But he's one of the buttons, one of the cops! I thought he'd see—"

He cut off as the sirens grew very loud. I saw that Fetch'd recovered enough to stand and prodded him. He moved quickly, even more eager not to cross the police than I was. Fetch'd never been caught by the police or even a dog catcher, but he'd heard enough stories about the pound to make him never want to take the risk.

Other than his stiff spine, he moved as stealthily as ever. He darted ahead of us as I took Claryce's arm and led her away from the carnage. I'd have expected the cops to crash in by now, but Cortez was probably stalling them. Our relationship had changed a lot since the start of this, and I wondered how much I could avoid him knowing. For his sake and that of his Maria and the kids, the detective was better off remaining ignorant . . . if that was at all possible anymore.

Once we were outside and well on our way to the safe house, Claryce finally asked, "What about Oberon's men? Will they catch them?"

"Since half of the Chicago Police are on the take with both sides, I doubt it. Even if Detective Cortez managed to pull Doolin in, he'd probably be out in the hour."

"They've got some of the best lips in the business working for them, Mistress Claryce," Fetch had to add.

"Their lawyers are good," I agreed. "No more talk out of you, Fetch. You're man's best friend, remember?"

He took the hint and returned to a more canine—and silent—persona. With everything going on nearby, we couldn't be certain that someone might not overhear us. Not until we were inside the safe house did any of us say another word.

Leaning against the table near the kitchen area, Claryce heaved a sigh. "I can barely even remember my life right before you," she told me. "It seems more of a dream . . ."

"And now you're in a nightmare," I added apologetically. "If I could've stopped Oberon from drawing you in here, I would've—"

"But there really wasn't any choice, anyway, was there? This has all happened before. You and I, I mean. Every time I—*she*—comes back, the two of you meet and something ends up killing me—us—" Eyes wide in growing consternation, Claryce shook her head. "I don't know *who* I am! I just know that I'll die and then some new version will eventually come along . . . if you aren't killed first, that is."

I took her by both arms and made her meet my gaze. "This ends here, Claryce! I won't lose you—"

"You mean *her*—Cleolinda—"

"*You.*" I leaned dangerously close, but I had to make her see the truth. "There's a part of her in you. I won't deny that. It's very likely the reason for the reincarnations happening. I don't know. Even Diocles can't explain it from his side—"

"Diocles? Who's he?"

I wanted to bite off my tongue for letting him slip into the conversation. Had he heard me now, he would've no doubt smiled victoriously at my lapse. "Someone who knows about the afterlife," I answered vaguely. "Not important otherwise. The point is, Cleolinda is part of my past; you've become part of my here and now."

She clearly wanted to believe me. I suppose I should've done like Valentino and swept her in my arms, but there was one very good reason I couldn't. I still hoped to break the curse between us, and the only way I could think of was to make certain that at some point Claryce and I parted ways forever. Unfortunately, Oberon—and it seemed Her Lady as well—wouldn't let that happen. I had to keep Claryce close to me until I could see to it that *neither* would toy with her ever again.

That was assuming that I didn't die first.

More and more of a clamor arose outside as the cops pretended to be what they were supposed to be and mopped up the mess inside the barrelhouse. I knew we were taking a risk staying so near to the activity, but I refused to bring Claryce back to the main house until I could be certain that whatever hints of Feirie surrounded it could be contained by me.

She continued to wait hopefully for more from me. When I did nothing but release her and step back, she looked openly disappointed. Nodding slowly, Claryce retired to the room I'd previously set aside for her, then shut the door behind her.

I noticed Fetch eyeing me. "What?"

He looked guilty. "Nothing, Master Nicholas . . . nothing."

Fetch didn't deserve my anger, but I was suddenly in too foul a mood to care. I had a sudden, growing concern on my mind that had much to do with Claryce's situation. Ignoring the shapeshifter, I abandoned the upstairs for the silence of the old hat shop. Down there, among the dust, I tried to clear my thoughts.

But no sooner had I tried to sit down in the back than I heard a voice out front. Moving cautiously to the crack on the front window, I peered out.

Claryce peered back at me from across the street.

I instantly knew I'd made a mistake and tried to pull back.

When I did, it was to find myself back in the *main* house.

I was upstairs in the bedroom I used. Everything was as it had been when last I'd been here except for the placement of the painting back on the wall. Leonardo's Cleolinda stood praying anxiously while St. George did battle with the dragon. It was a scene almost as fanciful as the actual event had been dangerous, but for the first time I noticed something he'd done in the course of creating it, something with Leonardo's typical cleverness.

I'd always seen myself eyeing my foe. The obvious thing. Now, though, standing exactly where I was, I saw that my gaze was elsewhere.

"St. George" was looking at the princess.

It was too much of a reminder of what I could be losing again. I started for the painting . . .

"A beautiful piece of art," she said from behind me.

Her voice might've sounded exactly like Claryce's, but I knew that she was the changeling. Her Lady had managed to heal the wounds of her puppet, and the false Claryce looked whole.

"I know you're not her. Stop pretending."

The changeling already stood too close. I couldn't be sure whether this was a dream or I'd been transported by the Feirie arts back to the actual house, but either way I didn't want her any closer.

"Poor dear Nick," she murmured, stretching forth a hand to me. "Won't you hold me?"

I took a step back . . . and yet suddenly her hand was on my cheek, and she herself was only inches away. She looked and even smelled like Claryce, yet I reminded myself again that not only was Claryce far from here, but she wouldn't have acted like this, especially considering how I'd treated her.

"I won't hold you, and I don't even want to touch you."

Her other hand reached behind me, and opened a door. I realized that I now stood in front of the closet in the room I'd given Claryce.

With the hand by my cheek, the changeling tried to push me into the closet. I grabbed the hand and spun us around, sending her inside instead.

It was a waste of effort. The room, the closet, the entire house vanished. I stood in a massive tangle of dark green oaks, with an underbrush so thick it would've been a battle just to take a step in any direction. Worse, I could feel that I wasn't alone. There were eyes everywhere, eyes from a number of different creatures who all shared one and one thing only.

They served as loyal followers of Her Lady's Court.

It was impossible that I should be in Feirie. That would require crossing the Gate. I'd have felt that passage in my bones and even if I hadn't, the dragon would've said something.

Of course, he wasn't saying *anything*, despite our surroundings, and *that* worried me, too.

The murky forest shimmered as if swayed by some unfelt wind. The Court could be seen in many ways. I'd known it in several forms but had seen it like this, too. I thought it generally matched Her Lady's moods and, if I was right, her mood was a bad one.

Her darling Gatekeeper . . .

Two of the trees became the tall backrest of an ebony throne. Its top was decorated by two black birds facing opposite directions, but each with one vile, red eye toward me. A third perch at the center of the backrest stirred my suspicions.

The other trees receded. Faint firefly lights gathered around the open grove, giving as much illumination as one could find in true Feirie.

Some of the half-seen shapes coalescing around me moved nearer as the trees retreated. I reached into my coat. The simple act made the shapes stop.

"That's better," I growled confidently.

Her darling Gatekeeper . . . she repeated, again using the third person, now that the changeling was not involved. Her voice wafted through my mind, its very essence seducing and frightening at the same time. These were her greatest tools—seduction and fear. I steeled myself against both, aware that, even together, the dragon and I had to be careful.

There was movement from my left. I glimpsed a stretched out figure with long, narrow features, who melted into the shadows almost as quickly as he appeared. Even though I didn't catch a good look at the face, I knew him for one of Kravayik's kind, the highest caste in Feirie, that from which Oberon and his queen had been spawned. That I'd seen him at all meant that I'd managed to keep him from doing whatever mischief he'd been commanded to do by Her Lady. That would earn him some slight punishment later, but I didn't care. I had no friend in the Feirie Court.

"Her darling Gatekeeper," the changeling murmured in my ear from the opposite side.

I pulled away, moving more quickly than I should've. I'd just marked my unease, a potential point of weakness to those of the Court.

"A pale imitation," I remarked, staring at the changeling. "Both you and this place."

Her eyes—no longer at all like Claryce's—burned black. I knew that mood, having seen it before. She suddenly flung her arms back, and, as she did, those arms became black wings. Her face twisted into an avian one and she shrank rapidly.

While there was no discernible difference between this black bird and the other two, I knew right away that this was the one that'd helped me for so long. Small wonder I'd never been able to figure out why it'd been exiled; it'd been a spy for Her Lady, even pretending to be shocked when her sentinel stirred. Her Lady must've laughed quite a lot.

The black bird fluttered up to the center perch, one ebony eye fixed on me. As it settled, Her Lady rose.

The shadowy figures of the Court receded farther, as the slim figure of their queen flowed toward me. She was tall, very tall, and her long, midnight hair shifted around her face, always partially obscuring it, but leaving enough visible to tantalize. Her Lady was beautiful, very beautiful, but her beauty was also that of a pale, drowned corpse. To love her was to love death, which was why the only one who could handle her had been Oberon.

Her darling Gatekeeper . . . you should have come to her long before this . . .

"I'd no plans to come to you at all. Oberon is my responsibility, one that would've been easier to handle if I'd been let in on all the little secrets!"

She raised her left hand, and, although she still wasn't near enough to touch me, I felt a caress across my chest. Inside, I sensed the dragon withdraw more.

She keeps no secrets from you, Gatekeeper . . . you only fail to see them . . .

Her Lady likely believed what she said, seeing things through black, Feirie orbs. She suddenly stood next to me, her blood-red lips near my own.

Let her show you things . . .

I could've and was *supposed to* take that in more than one way. When I didn't move, Her Lady stretched one impossibly long, tapering hand before us.

Here is your friend . . . Alejandro the Courageous . . . finding what the mongrel was supposed to lead him to . . .

"Mongrel" referred to Fetch, who had been given no name that I knew of when he'd served Her Lady in Feirie. I saw the chaos of the shootout in the barrelhouse. In the distance, I faced off against Doolin.

Then Fetch broke in nearer to the center of the image. He landed on top of one of Doolin's mob, sending the man crashing face-first to the floor. I watched in horrific expectation for Fetch to rip out the back of the hood's neck, but, instead, Fetch scared off another gunman, then began scratching at a long, covered bench atop which several barrels of hooch'd been set.

He scratched long enough that his work caught the attention of Cortez. The good detective started toward the covered bench.

That was when Fetch made the mistake of facing Cortez. Fetch in the midst of battle didn't look like any hound. He looked close to the monster he'd once been and, when he took a step toward the detective, that was all Cortez needed. Already wound up from the fight, Cortez fired with precision.

Before the bullets could strike, Her Lady caused the scene to change. There were cops everywhere, all of them trying to look earnest as they cleaned up. In the midst of it all, Cortez knelt by the covered area, searching.

He removed a false panel. I heard him murmur a prayer in Spanish. Cortez reached in . . . and, for the first time in some sixteen centuries, I beheld the very thing that'd started my curse.

It was long, made of good, strong iron, and very simple in its sleekness. Its point was long and sharp. It was a Roman spear, one that legends said had been broken into a thousand pieces. In fact, it'd only broken in two, but, even then, the front part had done its work. I'd used my sword for the mercy blow, though it hadn't turned out be that merciful, considering how both the dragon and I had ended up.

Cortez had found *my* spear, the one stolen alongside my armor from the Art Institute.

But something didn't ring true. "This was Capone's bunch," I muttered, not caring if Her Lady knew Scarface. "Oberon's been dealing with Moran and the North Siders."

I sensed rather than saw her amusement. *Her darling Gatekeeper knows so much about the other realm . . .*

It sounded like a compliment, but it wasn't. I understood immediately what she meant. I'd been naive enough to think that *Oberon* had been the one behind the theft of the relics, but he'd only pretended that. Her Lady's agents had been behind the theft, taking what Oberon had assumed safe in plain sight at the Institute. He hadn't counted on the one being as twisted in her way of thinking as him to figure out what he'd done.

I watched Cortez carefully oversee the removal of not only the spear but the bits of armor. Images of myself wearing those pieces flashed through my head. I refought battles and marched across a dozen landscapes. I knelt before my trusted lord Diocletian while the ambitious Galerius watched from behind him.

Beware . . . whispered a male voice.

The dragon's warning stirred me from the glamour Her Lady had been slowly and stealthily weaving about me. I was usually more on guard, but the vision of the spear had taken me unaware, which was all she'd needed. It didn't matter that I was her best hope against Oberon; she was mistress of Feirie, and her very nature demanded that she try to make me her slave.

I brought the point of the blessed dagger to her breast. It was the thing that she'd had one of her servants try to take. Her Lady didn't show any change of emotion at my threat, even offering her open décolletage to my blade. Still, I noticed that her attempt to play with my mind had stopped.

The image changed one last time. Under Cortez's guidance, three uniformed cops brought the spear and armor—now all wrapped in cloth—into the police station.

She protects her Darling Gatekeeper, Her Lady said, seeming to forget that she'd just tried to enslave me. *They are locked there . . .*

So although Cortez was an innocent, there were those in the precinct who willingly or unwillingly served Her Lady directly. And Chicago just thought it had a bootlegger war to deal with.

"Thanks, I guess." I purposely replaced the dagger in order to show her I had no fear here. I'd taken enough stock of my surroundings to better understand it. We were nowhere near the Gate, so I could never have crossed without realizing it. Instead, somehow, Her Lady had created a "bubble," a place outside of Feirie that offered a limited access to the mortal realm. It wasn't stable, which meant that she'd prepared for this particular confrontation before daring to open the bubble up. Oberon's reappearance had probably been the impetus.

I heard the flutter of wings and suddenly "Claryce" stood before me again. At the same time, Her Lady vanished.

"My darling Gatekeeper . . . this is more your preference? Would you serve me like this?"

I actually found the image of Claryce acting like Her Lady revolting, but I didn't come out and say it. Instead, I let my growing fury at her need to play games at this critical juncture take command. "No more games with *her* or anyone else. You understand that? You've already broken the sanctity of the Gate more than once, which puts you on *his* level. I might understand that considering what's at stake, but I won't forgive your manipulation of *her!*" For good measure, I tossed in Cortez. "And leave the detective be, too . . ."

The full, ebony eyes of Her Lady briefly shone through, as she revealed a hint of her own anger at being spoken to in such a manner. Then the changeling reverted to the black bird form and flew past me.

I admit it. I made the mistake of following instinct and turning back to watch it.

I stood in front of the closet again. The door was still open, but what greeted me inside was only the closet's interior. The bubble Her Lady'd created had either finally collapsed or, more likely, she'd sealed it off again to conserve whatever little stability remained of it.

Vertigo struck me. The room spun, then darkened.

I was back in the safe house . . . or rather, the millenary shop.

But I wasn't alone. I spun around, my hand already reaching for Her Lady's gift.

In the sinister light of its illumination, I made out the outline of Claryce. I didn't lower the blade.

"Nick . . . Nick, what are you doing? You were gone again! I couldn't . . . I came searching for you . . ." Her eyes glistened from moisture— *tears*. Tears with more than a touch of anger, though. "Damn you! All these comings and goings! All these secrets! You can't close me off. You have to let me know what you're doing and where you're going!"

I listened closely, but for more than one reason. I was certain that Her Lady couldn't have successfully imitated the concern I heard in that voice. Nor could she have had the changeling create such an intense expression as I beheld then. There was true fear . . . fear for me who didn't deserve such strong emotion.

Despite the deadly blade, Claryce reached for me. "Nick . . ."

I dropped Her Lady's gift on the floor as if were just one more dusty piece abandoned by the hat shop's former owners. Claryce melted into my arms and, despite all my misgivings about drawing her to me, I held her as tight as I could. We stood like that for probably more than minutes . . . and then she looked up and kissed me.

I knew I was probably condemning her, but I returned the kiss.

CHAPTER 21

Fetch stood at attention when I rejoined him. He looked wary, not a sign I liked.

"Master Nicholas . . ."

"You all yourself again?"

"Right as rain." His tone didn't match his remark, though. I had a suspicion about what bothered him, and he confirmed it immediately. "Master Nicholas . . . 'twas not by luck I found ye when I did. I was sent there, and only smellin' Mistress Claryce nearby did I suspect worse was afoot."

I signaled for him to lower his voice. Claryce was asleep. I wanted her to rest, to forget for a few hours the madness Oberon and I had dragged her into. My mind was already filled with regrets for my lapse. Now, I didn't know how I'd keep her from the thick of danger. "How long's she been controlling you again?"

He knew I wasn't referring to Claryce. Ears flattening and tail between his legs, the lycanthrope replied, "Not long. Days only. After the—the bird—told us about her sentinel in the area . . ."

"I know what the bird is, Fetch."

"Very sorry about that, too, Master Nicholas, but I didn't know the truth of that winged thing, either, until then. Imagine, *she* toying with me all those times . . ."

I could imagine it very well, considering how Her Lady'd played me. "So she ordered you to the barrelhouse?"

"Yes . . . yes. She . . . she said she'd tell you about the spear." He said the last word with a combination of awe and more guilt.

"She did. I saw you and Cortez. Sorry he got overexcited."

Somehow, Fetch managed to shrug. "I be better. 'Twas necessary for the flatfoot to find the stolen pieces, Master Nicholas. That's what she decided, anyway. Oberon was getting too close. His mugs had been standing over them without knowing it, but they were on their way back after Oberon found out about where the loot was stashed!"

So, I'd read matters differently than they'd been. Cortez had been sent on a false tip to the distillery at Her Lady's decision so that he could "find" the armor and take it somewhere more secure. Naturally, she didn't trust me with my own belongings.

I could fathom only one way Oberon had found the hiding place so suddenly. He'd no doubt found tortures even the sentinel couldn't withstand. It'd probably taken Oberon a little time to make sense of whatever information the creature had babbled, but he'd finally done so.

Oberon and Her Lady were making an awful lot of fuss over a bunch of relics that could only hurt me if I let the dragon take over completely. Since I'd never do that, even with our new relationship, the spear and armor were just so much more rusting metal.

At least, so I hoped. Fetch gave no sign of revealing any more pertinent knowledge where the spear and armor were concerned. He sat as if waiting for *me* to take command of the conversation.

"Why's she think Cortez'll bring the stuff somewhere safe, Fetch? The precinct's got to be rotten with corruption, and the Institute's already proven it can't protect things."

"I failed to ask her that question, if ye take my meaning."

True, for those of Feirie, questioning Her Lady could easily become a very fatal prospect. There had to be something or someone involved with the precinct that she believed could defend the relics from Oberon.

Of course, I'd already seen that Her Lady could be very mistaken as to the security of the places she hid things.

With Claryce asleep, I turned to the radio and listened for any news that might give me some hint of Oberon's activity. There was curiously no story about Cortez's raid, nor much about any continued violence in the ongoing liquor war. Both Capone and the North Siders had suddenly gotten very neighborly.

Claryce joined us. She smiled at me and, before I could help myself, I smiled back.

"Anything happen while I slept?"

"No. It's been quiet."

Her smile remained, but lost its warmth. "Don't they say that's what comes just before the storm?"

I couldn't argue with her there. The silence could only mean that Oberon's plan was coming to fruition.

That thought stirred me to a decision. "Let's take a drive."

Fetch immediately rose. "'Ride'?"

Claryce wasn't so eager. "Where to?"

"I need to speak with Detective Cortez about something that was stolen from me."

She raised an eyebrow. "From you? When?"

"When I was dead."

I'd never been to Cortez's precinct, but for some reason it didn't surprise me that it was almost exactly between the territories claimed by the two warring mobs. The vicinity itself looked fairly peaceful, but these days that peace could disappear in the blink of an eye, even around a police station.

I had Claryce and Fetch wait in the Packard while I walked a block to the station. I hoped not to be long, but I knew that I had to see the spear. It was almost as if it called to me . . .

There'd been no report of the relics' return to the Art Institute, so I assumed that Cortez had them secured somewhere near him. Why he'd do that made me very curious.

Two uniformed cops dragged a minor thug up the steps and into the three-story, brick structure. I hesitated a moment while they entered before crossing over to the building.

"Shine, suh?"

I started to shake my head when the voice caught my attention. Sure enough, I knew the elderly negro situated to the left of the station steps.

Michael grinned wide, showing white, white teeth. "Well! If it isn't the gentleman goin' to see the art! How are you, suh?"

"I'm fine, Michael—it *is* Michael, isn't it?"

"Yessuh! Michael as in the good archangel! Care for a shine?"

I'd nearly started at his mention of the other Michael. There was nothing about the man before me that bespoke of his Heavenly name-sake except what sounded like a good-natured honesty in his voice. Unfortunately, I couldn't even trust that honesty at the moment. "Pretty far from where I saw you last time. Why here?"

"Well, my boy—not the one I told you about but an older one— I've got seven young, though some aren't so young anymore—workin' not far from here. He wanted me to come for a visit for a while, so I thought, why not make a little business when he's at his job! Got a friend who had a spot here who was planning on being away for a short while anyhow, so things worked out just right . . ."

"Sounds like good sense." Nothing about Michael seemed different than what I could see on the surface, but running into him so soon in another part of a city as large as Chicago seemed like too great a coincidence. I hadn't changed my mind about coincidences in general, but Michael was at least making me question my choice in that regard.

"So . . . can I give you a shine?"

I was tempted to question him while he polished my shoes, but now was not a good time. "Maybe another day."

"Fine, fine, suh. They find what you lost?"

He had my attention again. "What makes you ask that?"

Michael ran a hand through the thinning white curls atop his head. "Well now, you seem a fine, upstanding citizen, suh, and you're walking calmly into the station, so I figure you must've lost somethin' and think they've found it. That's all, suh."

He smiled wider, then tried to get the attention of a well-dressed man coming up from the other direction. I stood there for a moment, then moved on. Until Michael stood before me with wings on his back and wielding a blazing sword, I'd just assume that he was what he appeared now.

I started toward the front desk, only to have Cortez walk out from one of the side hallways. He took one look at me and pursed his lips before heading my direction.

"Nick Medea," the detective muttered, in a tone that wasn't at all welcoming. "Ready to make that statement, huh?"

He steered me back to the hallway from which he'd come, then to an office that at first glance I'd thought was empty. Instead, behind the musty windows was a neat if spartan room in which the only personal items that marked it as Cortez's was the small figure of Our Lady of Guadalupe standing next to a photo of a dark, pretty Mexican woman and two small children, obviously hers.

I'd never seen his Maria before, but she more than fit the descriptions Cortez had given of her. "Nice family . . ."

"You've never seen them? Forgot that." Talk of his loved ones briefly cheered the detective, but then his dour mood returned. "Why're you here?"

"I heard you found the stuff stolen from the Art Institute. Wondered if I could see the items for a moment."

"Now what would make you think I still had them?"

I gave him a look. Cortez lit a cigarette and sat on the edge of his desk.

"How do you like this nice place?" he asked, with more than a hint of sarcasm. "My very own office! I tell Maria it's snazzy. She won't be coming down here, so it's safe to say. Imagine if she saw it, you know?"

"They just move you in here?"

"Yeah. Seven months ago. Been promised it'll be fixed up all this time, you know?"

I'd seen a lot of hatred over sixteen centuries, some of it warranted, most of it not. I'd seen many people in Cortez's position, too; picked out to work on a task no one else wanted to do and treated badly while trying to fulfill his orders.

But while I sympathized with him, I had a lot more troubles to deal with. "The relics?"

"Yeah, they're here, Nick Medea. Got 'em stashed nicely. Didn't know what to do with them at first, but at least I finally got some help there. Some captain out of headquarters popped down here right after we got the things into my office. Don't know how he heard so fast, but I tell you I really appreciated his taking over."

I wondered if Her Lady had a second changeling around or if it'd been the same one using a different shape. Either way, I hoped that nothing'd been done that would endanger those in the station. "What'd he do? Take it with?"

"Nah. We got it here. I thought we were supposed to bring it to the Institute, but they need it for evidence in some bigger heist. In the meantime, it's right in the room with us."

That surprised me. I hadn't sensed anything—not that I was sure I would—and I certainly hadn't seen anything. "Nicely hidden, if it is. Does that mean I can't see it?"

He pressed the tip of the cigarette into the ash tray on the corner of the desk. As usual, Cortez hadn't taken more than two or three puffs. If he was trying to quit, he was still building up an expensive habit in the meantime.

"Actually, I *want* you to see them." He walked around the back of the desk. The wooden floor creaked as he did, making me think at first they'd simply put the spear and armor under the boards. However, the detective instead continued on to a wooden file cabinet almost as tall as him and about as wide.

He didn't reach for one of the drawer handles, but instead reached back and pulled the cabinet forward.

"Wanna give me a hand?"

I joined him just as he turned the cabinet halfway around. Only then did I notice that it seemed deeper than it should've.

"Grab the edge, will you."

To my further surprise, he was referring to the wall behind, not the cabinet. I saw he had one hand on a barely discernible nail and that he was looking at another one near me. Taking hold of the second nail, I waited.

"Tug."

The nail was hard enough to grip, even harder to try to pull. I saw why. We started to pull out part of the wooden wall.

"Is this normal storage in a police station, or did the department save money and turn some speakeasy they raided into a precinct house?"

Cortez chuckled. "Seven months and I never knew this was here. The captain, he said he'd been assigned here right after it opened. Too many guys on the take even then. This's how they hid the pricey stashes back then, even before Prohibition passed. Somewhere along the way, folks forgot about it."

I'd be willing to bet that Her Lady's servants here had seen to the influencing of whoever had designed and built this place. While on the surface that seemed far-fetched, one didn't survive in Feirie for centuries without always setting aside hidey-holes and other safe places to not only store "pricey stashes" but themselves, too, if the balance of power shifted badly. With Her Lady assuming Oberon alive even after I thought he was dead, she'd no doubt set up dozens of these places, big and small, around Chicago.

And then I pushed aside all thought of the mad intricacies of Feirie minds as I saw set into the back of the hidden space the *spear*. So ancient, it should've been a couple of rusting fragments far too fragile to be hanging before me, but what I saw instead was a gleaming weapon looking freshly honed and ready for war.

The armor was in far worse order, more akin to what I'd expected to find. Why that was made no sense, until I thought of what I'd done the night before facing the dragon. While I'd not been aware of his endless task, I *had* been aware of his armored hide, his sharp claws, and his monstrous teeth. I also knew that he was rumored to breathe fire. Even for someone with a strong belief in God's work, it was a daunting confrontation.

I'd prayed for guidance, and guidance had come in the form of a grizzled hermit outside of Silene who'd heard my mumbled words to Heaven.

"If God is in your heart now, he will be in your hand tomorrow," the hermit had told me over the meager rations I'd offered him as a guest by my fire. "But if you set any stock in my humble life, I would be happy to ask that you receive Heaven's guidance when you face the wyrm."

"Can you ask Heaven to guide my spear?" I'd countered, taking up the weapon from beside me and holding it toward him.

In answer, he'd touched the tip with his gnarled fingers and smiled. For some reason, that'd been enough to comfort me. In fact, I'd grown so comforted that I'd fallen asleep shortly after . . . and when I'd awakened, it was to find him gone.

And only now, seeing how the fragments had, like myself, been put back together—made more than whole—did I suspect that the hermit had been other than mortal. I felt a tremendous urge to return outside and see if old Michael was who I thought he was. Still, I held back, suspecting that if I was meant to know I'd have been told.

"Doesn't even look real, does it?" Cortez remarked at that moment, drawing me back. "Been told it is, though. Me, I don't know what's so fantastic about an old sticker, but I got to admit there's something about it that makes me just want to see it's taken care of right."

"It's real all right." As I put my left hand near it, I felt a warmth grow through my body from my heart. It took much inner struggling to make me not just snatch it up and raise it to the sky. "Maybe . . . maybe we should seal this again."

"Yeah, maybe."

When we shut the hidey-hole, I felt like I was sealing up my own tomb. I wanted to tear the wall away again, reclaim what was mine. I knew, though, that it was better if I didn't hold the spear right now. I didn't know why, but I knew that.

"Who all knows about this, Cortez?"

"Just a couple . . . and you now."

I thought I detected some tone in his voice, but his expression was all innocence. I decided I'd better keep pressing the logical question, so that he'd not wonder why I took all this for granted. "This is still seeming like a heck of a lot of mystery and trouble to me. Secret passages in police stations hiding odd antiques? Doesn't make much sense . . ."

Cortez sought for his cigarettes, but only came up with an empty package. He went around to the back of the desk, while I maneuvered toward the door.

"I like you, Nick Medea," he responded, as he located another package of Luckies in the top drawer, "even if I don't always trust everything you do."

He had a right to the last thing, but I still pretended offense. "Listen, Cortez—"

The detective raised both hands in mock defense against my anger. "Easy, Bo! We all got our secrets, you know? Like you being a private dick on the side, though there's no license to be found . . ."

I'd laid the groundwork for such an assumption long ago, aware that someone might wonder why a ghost chaser would show up in some unlikely places. Cortez was the first person to get that far, even though in the end he was following a dead lead. Still, it was better than him knowing the truth. "It's there and all legal. You just have to know where to look."

"And you're not going to tell me . . ."

"Where's the fun in that, Cortez?"

"True." Drawing another cigarette, the detective joined me by the door. "Listen, Nick Medea . . . there's something big out there . . . maybe bigger than the Outfit. Something that a bigwig like Delke seems to be part of. Maybe the head."

"Why're you telling me all this?"

He shrugged. "Because a nice skirt we both know seems right in the middle of it. That's all."

I gripped the door knob. "Listen, Cortez, I appreciate your letting me see the relics. If I find out anything that might help, I promise I'll tell you."

The detective only nodded. I let myself out. The short walk through the station gave me just enough time to study the sergeant's desk again. The thin, scarred officer answering the telephone didn't have the voice I was most interested in, but I turned toward him nonetheless.

"Can I help you?" His polite, nasal tones didn't take away from the obvious fact that he'd faced some tough times on the beat before reaching this point in his career.

"I was looking for the sergeant who gave me some information earlier. Gruff voice. Colorful way of speaking about . . . some other people." I treaded a bit of a fine line with the last part of the description. There was a very good chance that this sergeant was good friends with the other one. If he thought I actually had a complaint against a fellow cop . . .

But all he did was shake his head. "Don't know who you mean. I'm generally here most of the day, each day."

"Every day?"

He chuckled, then swung the chair to the side so I could see his right leg . . . or where the upper half of it still was.

"Thought I'd make captain once the war was over," the sergeant explained good-naturedly. "Now, it's permanent desk. Every day. When'd you talked to this guy?"

I told him.

"Must have your precincts mixed up. I was definitely here at that time, then." He rolled back behind the desk. "Funny, I'd say it's O'Rourke you'd be looking for if not for one thing."

"What's that?"

Much of the sergeant's pleasantry disappeared as he answered, "Liam O'Rourke was gunned down six months ago when he was leaving the station. The bastard who did it was some dago trying to slip custody. Got poor Liam through the heart just by accident with one of his guards' gun . . ."

"I'm sorry. I won't bother you anymore . . ." Nodding gratefully, I carefully retreated from the sergeant, who was now dwelling on the loss of a comrade.

"Liam Michael O'Rourke," he went on, no longer paying attention to me. "A good man . . ."

Liam *Michael* O'Rourke. There it was again. I continued out, wondering if I'd see old Michael. Sure enough, he was gone, but there was nothing to prove that he hadn't just decided to pack it up after not finding another customer. The seating area was still there, naturally.

Part of me wanted to stick around to see if Michael'd return, but the more sensible part reminded the other that if Michael was gone for the day, I'd be waiting a long time.

Claryce eyed me anxiously when I returned. "Did you find out what you wanted to know?"

"Yeah . . . and I gained a lot more questions . . ." I stopped.

"What is it?" Claryce started to turn in the direction I glanced, but I waved her still. I then calmly left the Packard and headed across the street, where a restaurant with outdoor tables was situated. I didn't pay attention to what fare it offered; my only interest was in the elegantly dressed figure in spats seated at the front table by himself, sipping what appeared to be coffee—but probably was something far, far different if I knew him, despite mortal laws against such spirits.

"A good day to you, Gatekeeper." Oberon raised his drink as I approached. "A fine, *sunny* day, don't you think?"

CHAPTER 22

I looked around for Oberon's pet mountain. "Where's Doolin?"

"An amusing mortal creature, Doolin," Oberon remarked, gesturing to the one other chair at the table. "Reminiscent of a loyal hound I once had. How *is* Fetch, anyway?"

"Enjoying freedom." I didn't bother to sit. "What now, Oberon? Why're you here?"

"The ambience, naturally." His eyes flickered pitch black as he looked past me for a moment. "And the view, of course."

I didn't need to follow his gaze to know that he was looking at the station. Suddenly I wondered how wise I'd been to assume it a safe place to leave the spear, even though I still didn't know what use the thing would be for Oberon if I kept the dragon inside.

"Put an end to this, Oberon. Didn't you cause enough grief the last time?"

"William Delke" set his half-empty coffee cup down. At the same time, I noticed that the restaurant wasn't even open yet.

"There can never be an end to this until things are brought back into balance, Gatekeeper." The black eyes remained, though I doubted that anyone would've been able to see them besides me. "Please. Be seated. We should not be enemies. Not with my dear Titania controlling those vermin of the Court."

"I'll stand . . . and neither realm can survive your idea of balance. You remember what happened last time."

"That was without one of the cards, Gatekeeper." Oberon picked up the cup again. It was full. "That was without you." His smile was gone. "You remember your world before it changed for the worse, do you not?"

Suddenly we were renewing a discussion from over fifty years ago. "Unlike Feirie, the mortal world moves on, Oberon. Human ingenuity could only be held back for so long."

"How clearly I know that. I turned the Athenians' philosophies back to war, steered your Romans astray with their own excesses, and turned the Prophet's people against the very sciences with which they'd enriched the world . . . and yet, each time, some new voice would rise." His inhuman eyes narrowed dangerously. "Your friend Leonardo, for instance. A very troublesome, though admittedly intriguing character."

"He always spoke well of you."

Oberon leaned back. His smile had returned, but in a tight-lipped manner. "Humor. I find the mortal version still tricky to display. Fortunately, there are enough who see my way of thought that I do not have to hide all that I am."

I held back a shudder at how Oberon had displayed Feirie humor to his human underlings over the decades. In the Court, humor often meant how interesting one could make the torture of a victim before an applauding audience.

"I doubt that Bugs and Hymie would be happy to see Chicago and the rest of their world turned back to the Dark Ages." I noticed a movement out of the corner of my eye. *There* stood Doolin, looking quite eager to renew our acquaintance. He was a few yards down the street, near the corner. His hands were thrust deep in the pockets of his coat. I was pretty sure that if he pulled them out, they'd be wearing his master's gauntlets. "Tell him to heel, Oberon."

"Oh, he'll stay where he is. For a mortal, Doolin will make a fine addition to my new Court. He has a keen eye for what I desire." Oberon set aside the coffee, then reached into his jacket.

I doubted that he was going to pull out a gun or anything dangerous. I was right on the first count and wrong on the second.

He had one of the *cards*.

"Imagine the pristine forests that covered most of this particular land returned to their full glory," Oberon murmured, as he studied the Clothos card. He kept the back to me, preventing me from seeing which suit or number it was. "Imagine your precious humanity once more living peacefully, harmoniously. Imagine my Feirie rich again with its wondrous magic. Imagine the two realms melded together with such balance that the power of Feirie and the imagination of the mortal world create a paradise in which all prosper, in which all live peacefully . . ."

I knew Oberon believed every word he said, that he was certain that his notion of what should be was the perfect thing for both realms. The trouble was, his paradise meant crushing human spirit, not stirring its imagination except its fear of things that went bump in the night.

And for Feirie, it wouldn't be much better. There'd be a bloom of magic, one on which the Court would willingly feed, but that power would eventually become too wild for even the Court to control. Feirie would collapse into itself, returning to the primal energies from which it'd been spawned . . . and it would take my world with it.

Her Lady could see the danger. Many in her Court could, too. It wasn't that they didn't covet mastery of the mortal realm; they just knew better than to trust the path that Oberon had chosen.

"You know the cards never do exactly as you want," I pointed out, trying to decide if it was worth the attempt to lunge for the one he held. "And as for the world you want . . ."

He clearly understood my unfinished comment. Oberon frowned deeply and slipped the card back into his jacket. "The rigidity of the Court is nothing compared to your nature, Gatekeeper. You know why I took this more rash but necessary course. This "cold-meta" age of yours is already beginning to seep into my Feirie, poisoning it in so many ways apparently too subtle for my Titania to notice. First the magic will fade, then Feirie will fade. What will happen to the mortal world, then? No imagination, no soul. Everything will stagnate, then finally die here, too."

"So you say. The balance worked very well all these millennia, Oberon. You're the one that wants to upset it. Your idea of balance is this realm in thrall to Feirie and the people here frightened of every shadow."

"As they should be. As they need to be." He snapped his fingers, and from around the corner of the restaurant stepped another thug.

I took the Mick's measure and found him no danger. Oberon smiled at me as the sneering hood came up behind him. As Oberon stood, the thug pulled the chair back for his master.

"I will change our realms for the better, Gatekeeper. Whether with one card or two. You have the choice of having some voice in the matter. Think about it." He suddenly looked past me. "Ahh . . ."

I thought it was a ploy until I heard the footsteps. My silent pleas to Heaven went unanswered.

"William," Claryce said coldly as she neared.

"So good to see you again, my dear woman." Oberon snapped his fingers and the goon behind him retreated once more. "I'm sorry our last encounter was so short and ugly."

"Go back to the auto," I muttered to her, without taking my eyes off Oberon.

He chuckled. "She was always headstrong, was she not? I think this one is my favorite." Oberon bowed slightly to Claryce. "My belated condolences for your previous demise."

If he thought he was stoking her fears, he'd apparently thought wrong. Claryce smiled back, then replied, "You once complimented me for my attention for detail, do you remember, William?"

I noted not only her continued use of a name we all knew was false, but also that Oberon's smile seemed slightly less true.

"You served Delke Industries almost as well as the Delkes them-selves have, my dear. I truly did find you useful . . . and still could.

Your attention to detail was only one of your fine points. The Court could use your beauty . . ."

"I used to appreciate your flattery." Claryce wrapped her arm around mine. "But you can assume that I've quit for good. And as for my attention to detail, I saw that card you put away. Is it supposed to be significant, Nick?"

"Very."

She shook her head. "I don't know why. I remember William having it made. The artist did a very good job—hand-painted on both sides—but it can't be anything more than an expensive trinket, can it, *William?*"

Oberon glared. I'd been wondering why he hadn't tried to use his magic on us, but finally realized that I'd made assumptions about him based on his still having been linked to Feirie when last we'd met.

"It must take a lot of effort to stay out in the sun instead of the shadows," I remarked. "A lot of effort."

"No one else could have done it," he answered with typical pride. "No one."

"Tell that to Kravayik."

"Spare me one pathetic convert. He relinquished all that is Feirie to survive here. *Survive* surrounded forever by all this cold metal. A mighty fall for one who was my left arm . . ."

Oberon reached into his jacket. I knew better than to think he was pulling out a rod. He drew out the card he'd taunted me with, then tossed it on the table.

"Always a very clever female, in each incarnation," Oberon said, as he stepped back from the table. "Maybe that's why she's always died so quickly. Too clever for her own good."

Pulling away from Claryce, I started for the false William Delke.

As if from nowhere, the hood who'd held his chair for him reappeared with an automatic pointed directly at Claryce. I also noticed that Doolin now stood much closer to the restaurant. His hands were still stuck deep in his pockets, but I knew him for the worse of the two dangers . . . if one didn't count Oberon himself.

"Do these rats know the foul company they keep?" I asked. "You'd think even they had better taste."

The gunman just grinned. He evidently didn't care about anything as long as he was paid.

"The moon is full in three days," Oberon commented, as he casually stepped back. "It gives you time to think. Good day to you, my dear Claryce."

Oberon slowly walked around the corner, followed closely by the thug pointing the gun. I knew that Oberon preferred that there be no shooting now, but I couldn't be certain that his hireling wasn't too eager. I wasn't concerned about any danger to Claryce; I could easily leap in front of her. However, the wound I'd take would at least slow me down a little, and I couldn't risk that Doolin might do something to her while I was recovering.

But when I looked for him, Doolin'd also vanished. He moved very quickly for so big a body.

Claryce exhaled. "That was more unnerving than I'd thought it would be."

"You shouldn't have come . . . but thank you. If I'd kept assuming that card he had was real—" I stopped when I saw her expression. It was full of guilt.

"I couldn't stand not facing him again. I didn't want him to think I was afraid . . . even though I am." Her cheeks reddened. "I got out to watch. I saw him talking. I remembered how as William he dealt with business rivals and those whose companies he wanted to take over. That was why I had to finally join you."

I was only beginning to understand what she was leading up to. "You didn't really know that card was fake."

"I didn't . . . but I'd seen him act like that so many times and then discover that he'd completely bluffed the other side. I also suspected from the way you looked ready to pounce on him that the card was supposed to be something very magical. Is it?"

"Even only *one* of the Clothos cards is deadly."

"There's one somewhere in Holy Name Cathedral, isn't there? Kravayik knows about it, doesn't he?"

"Yes to both questions. Claryce—"

She was the one leading us back to the Packard. "It took everything to make Fetch promise to stay in the car. We don't want to keep him waiting any longer." As we headed back, Claryce continued, "I remember how he talked about the card when he had me. Never got too specific. I was distraught then, but when I saw him with the card now, I knew it couldn't be real. If it had been, he'd have used it already somehow as either William or Oberon. It's just inherent in him."

She was right. I should've thought of that, too. Every card could wreak havoc, which was why they'd all been dispersed separately. It was bad enough that I knew where the one was. Oberon, though, wouldn't have cared what chaos he created with his own card . . . which was why I should've seen what Claryce had.

"Thanks again."

"I worked closely with him for several years, Nick. I'm just glad he couldn't keep from showing his true self during that time."

Oberon'd had no reason to hide himself completely. The ruthlessness and complex dealings of the business world suited him.

Fetch wagged hard when we returned. "She made me promise to stay, Master Nicholas!"

"You did the right thing. Sit back."

As we drove off, I considered the spear and the station again. Oberon obviously knew where Her Lady had hidden the weapon and the armor. I knew she had protections around them, but I needed to verify for myself just why they should be safe.

Show me . . . I asked as I veered the Packard for a pass by the building.

Eye will . . .

His subdued response might've interested me more if he hadn't immediately obeyed. For that matter, nothing else concerned me more at that moment than why Her Lady might feel so confident.

She hadn't relied on the hidey-hole. I'd never expected that. I'd figured there'd be some Feirie magic near the vicinity of the artifacts.

What I hadn't figured on was that she'd manage to seal off the *entire* station from her former lord.

In the emerald world of the dragon, the station was now barely visible within a murky, constantly shifting shadow of Court power. I could see streaks of red lightning play along its surface and from past experience knew just how strong the defenses were if those were noticeable. I knew what the red streaks meant; not even Oberon's human servants could take the spear and armor from there. They could enter, but they couldn't leave if it meant carrying the items out.

All is well . . . you see?

I did. I doubted that my unseen companion was any more eager than I to have the spear rediscovered. He was probably very, very grateful to Her Lady, though I doubted he'd give any indication even to me.

I let my own eyes return.

"Is everything all right?" Claryce asked.

"As much as they can be."

"Where do we go now?"

I considered. "I have to make two telephone calls."

"Kravayik?"

I saw no reason to deny it. "Yes. Just to be on the safe side."

"Who's the other?"

"A man named Barnaby."

"Just a *man?*" Claryce asked with a frown.

I considered Barnaby. "More or less."

The answer didn't sit well with her, but it was the best I could give. I drove to a nearby pharmacy and parked. With Claryce and Fetch staying near, I went and immediately called Kravayik.

"I just had a visit with your former lord," I informed him.

"It would be too much to hope you slit his throat, may God forgive me for the suggestion."

"No." I gave him a quick summary of what happened, concluding, "And he mentioned the full moon in three days."

There was a pause. "Yes . . . that would make sense. The ties to Feirie will be strongest then."

That'd been my thought as well. "We need to be more on guard than ever."

"Even if it cost my life, Master Nicholas."

It was very possible that it would cost him just that. I thanked him—and he thanked *me* over and over—and then hung up so that I could ask the operator to make the second connection.

Barnaby answered. When he discovered it was me, he immediately reported on the rental auto. ". . . and then returned as you requested in your second call. All in order."

"Good. I'll have another auto for you to deal with soon. I hope. I'll let you know. This one I'm keeping." I'd found the Packard very useful, and I doubted that Moran's gang would be looking for it.

"Always glad to be of service . . . Oh, there's something else. It concerns your . . . your outside services."

He was talking about my ghost-hunting. I hesitated, then realized I'd feel great guilt if some innocent suffered because I left some renegade Wyld to grow its new lair unchecked. "Tell me."

"A friend of mine . . . he don't get out much more these days. Just to have a bite every now and then. I said I knew someone who'd check things out—"

"Details, Barnaby."

He gave me the information. It sounded pretty straightforward. Old house. Civil War era. Area untouched by the Fire. Lots of stories of ghosts from the War Between the States and after. The current owner, grandson of the original builder, kept thinking he heard voices from the cellar, a shut-off bedroom, and the attic.

"And you trust he's not just imagining this?" I'd already made my decision, but had to ask.

"He doesn't have much of an imagination, Master Nicholas. A good friend, but definitely not imaginative."

"All right. I'll see him tonight. You explained that part, right?"

"I said if you'd come, you'd want to do so close to midnight. He's fine. He thinks his gramp's haunting him. Guess the old Mick wasn't the best of men."

I wasn't worried about the ghost of an Irishman. "I'll take care of everything. Just make certain he's ready for me tonight."

"Of course. I appreciate this . . . and still appreciate what you did for . . ."

"Never mind." I uttered a quick goodbye and hung up before he could start repeating his immense gratitude for his son.

Returning to the auto, I told Claryce what I'd decided to do. I expected her to reasonably protest that we had a few more important matters with which to deal, but she kept her chin high in thought and nodded. "It could be something like what was stalking me in William's—Oberon's—house, couldn't it?"

"Wyld come in myriad forms," Fetch answered for me. "Some beautiful, many ugly."

"No talking back there," I reminded him. We were still in too public a place. To Claryce, I replied, "It could be like that. It could be a number of other things. When I was given the task of guarding the Gate, that included seeking out those who dared breach it."

"I understand. We should eat before we head over there."

"Claryce . . . you need to stay—"

Her eyes flared. "If you say one more thing about staying safe after what happened last time . . ."

I surrendered. "All right. Just be sure to do as I say."

"I will. I can promise you *that*."

She agreed so quickly, and with such confidence in me, that at first I was simply grateful. Then, I remembered that I'd said almost the exact words more than once before . . . and not to Claryce. I'd said them to *Clara*. I'd said them to *Cloette*. To others.

And each time, shortly after I'd said those words . . . I'd watched that incarnation *die*.

CHAPTER 23

I didn't want to return to the main house, but when Her Lady'd had it recreated, she'd even somehow managed to restore my collection of news articles and other gathered info. While Fetch slept—always stiffly, I thought—Claryce joined me in searching through a number of stories relating to full moons. There were a lot of them, but, while that daunted me, what caught Claryce's attention was something else.

"The *Chicago Herald*?" She picked up another yellowed piece. "The *Chicago Courier*?" Claryce studied the date on the last one. "This says *1875* . . ."

I didn't say a word. She studied me, then went back to reading the articles.

We didn't find anything that'd give me a hint as to what Oberon might be planning. It'd been a shot in the dark, but the disappointment still took its toll on both of us. Claryce finally retired to a place on the couch next to Fetch, while I tried a few more collections.

Only one caught my eye. I'd made it a habit to save *everything* that involved certain elements I could tie to Feirie. That meant even some of the odder stories, the small ones used to fill pages.

Odd, Arching Lights Claimed Over Lake Michigan, the article read. It was short, simply telling about the claims of several people who said they'd spotted lights high above the waters near where they'd finished Burnham's Municipal Pier just nine years ago. Police had investigated the rumors and found nothing. The claims had been written off as nothing.

But I had the suspicion that those witnesses *had* seen something. I knew the location well, having visited it many times long before Municipal Pier and its four unbuilt brothers had even been a thought. These witnesses had caught a glimpse of the *Gate*.

They'd only seen a hint of its majesty, but even that'd been enough to make them insist it was real in the face of public ridicule. Naturally no one else had noticed it afterward; only the pull of a full moon could blur the line between the two realms and thus also reveal for brief moments the passageway through from one to another.

A particularly *strong* full moon . . . like perhaps would rise in three days. Less now.

I was on the trail but couldn't follow it anymore until tomorrow. I was exhausted and not thinking entirely clearly. With the couch filled—mostly by Fetch—I decided to lean back and rest in the chair for a few minutes until I could focus better.

Naturally, I fell asleep, and naturally, I dreamed.

The nightmare erupted as before, with me atop my horse charging at the dragon. In the distance, Cleolinda prayed for me. This time, Diocles stood watching from a partial arena, his thumb already down. I wasn't sure which of us he meant, but I suspected it was me. Behind him stood a murky shadow I knew from other variations had to be Galerius.

But then, as had been happening too often of late, the nightmare took a new, twisted turn. Now, Oberon rode atop the dragon, spears identical to mine in each arm. Suddenly, he was the knight astride the noble steed while I was the foul wyrm. I tried to shout a protest at this change, only to have my words come out as a guttural roar.

Oberon lowered the spears. I reared but for some reason couldn't control my body. Instead of preparing for his attack, I wavered and left myself wide open to the spears.

They pierced my chest with precision. I felt a shudder run through me . . . and then the dragon and I fell apart. Yet, while I bled from the heart, the dragon simply laughed and fluttered off.

Soft hands reached for me. I looked up at Cleolinda, who became Claryce.

"I hope he gets on with dying soon, William."

William Delke stepped up beside Claryce. He drew her to his side. "He's been dead a long time, my dear. Just didn't know it."

I tried to reach Claryce, but my outstretched hand *crumbled*. My body began to decay everywhere. I managed to crawl a few feet, only to collapse in a heap at their feet.

Claryce laughed. William Delke laughed, his face reshaping to one resembling Kravayik's.

Claryce! I tried to shout. Unfortunately, my jaw lay on the ground, the bone already turning to ash.

Slim, bone-white hands thrust from the earth. They first caressed my rotting face, then seized me by the shoulders.

Her Lady's deathly beautiful visage rose from the dirt. She pursed her blood-red lips to kiss me, as her voice echoed in my head.

You're mine at last, Georgius . . .

And as she declared that, her eyes became the black pits that Oberon had left her sentinel. With impossible strength, Her Lady dragged me into the suffocating soil—

Whereupon I finally *woke*.

I straightened. Fetch still lay on the couch, albeit in a different pose, but Claryce was nowhere to be seen. Concerned, I leapt to my feet. The chair toppled over, the clatter startling Fetch awake.

Rapid footsteps pounded above. They continued to the stairs.

I met Claryce halfway. She eyed me with as much worry as I had for her. Her hair was fresh and she'd changed clothing, using the blouse and skirt we'd picked up for her on the way back here.

"You're awake!"

She said it with such relief and wonder I immediately looked toward the nearest window. It was dark outside.

"What time is it?" I asked.

"Nearly nine in the evening."

I'd slept an entire *day*. I knew I'd pushed myself hard, but this wasn't like me at all. "You should've woken me up."

Her expression turned peculiar. "I did. You told me it was better for you to continue sleeping, then you shut your eyes again and didn't move."

"She speaks the truth, Master Nicholas," Fetch added from near the couch.

Before I could ask her more, *his* voice whispered, *Eye decided it was better you slept. All our strength will be needed when the Frost Moon rises . . .*

"What do you mean?" I blurted out loud, confusing Claryce and Fetch. "What about the Frost Moon?"

It comes in the turning of the year from warmth to cold, when Feirie rises dominant. The better positioned the moon to the Gate, the stronger the pull to Feirie . . .

We'd not had many conversations past a few words over the course of the centuries. The dragon's explanation was one of the longest things I'd heard him utter. It was also one of the least promising things.

"You've never mentioned this Frost Moon before."

Eye would have, if danger had been present then . . . not all autumns bring forth a Frost Moon . . .

I refrained from remarking that with Oberon around we'd known there was danger present days ago. The dragon saw time and the world differently than humans or even Feiriefolk did. I'd lived with that fact for sixteen hundred years, but it still took getting used to.

Claryce joined me. "Nick, what is it?"

I told her, then glanced at Fetch.

"I knew not this Frost Moon, Master Nicholas, but mayhap only those highest in the Court did." His ears flickered. "I do admit I feel a bit more strength than usual."

"How bad is this, Nick?"

"I don't know. In the long run, it changes nothing. I still have to prevent Oberon from succeeding."

She nodded. "I wish we could've done something when he had the gall to confront us near the police station."

"If Oberon was willing to meet me in the open, he had everything planned to make me regret any attempt to take him there and then. I tried once in the past. They counted those people among the victims of the Great Fire, but they'd been dead hours before." I could still see the blank, staring faces, the awful agony that the searchers after the Chicago Fire had assumed were due to having been burned alive.

Their real fate had been much, much more terrifying.

Claryce's frustration grew. "I just don't understand this! If he's so powerful, why doesn't he just *kill* you? Why toy with you? Why toy with us?"

I put what I hoped was a comforting hand on hers. "Oberon's more limited than you think . . . and maybe than *he* even thinks. He wouldn't have found a use for Moran and Weiss. It's not that Oberon's got little power, it's that he needs to conserve it; he may've kept ahead of Her Lady's servants—even brutally slain them—but each time he uses his abilities, it drains him. I see why he's waiting for this Frost Moon . . . and why Her Lady probably is, too."

Small wonder Her Lady'd also been so reckless in her other attacks on Oberon. She knew as well as I did *now* that the stronger this particular moon, the more Oberon would be like his old self. His ruling self. Her Lady didn't want that any more than I did.

Thinking of Feirie's power growing with the moon made me remember something else. "I have to leave. I made a promise to Barnaby about his friend . . ."

She started to follow me. "Do you think this 'ghost' is so important right now? It hasn't harmed anyone so far, it seems."

All Feirie grows stronger with the Frost Moon . . . the dragon remarked, in what he no doubt thought was a helpful manner but wasn't.

"I swore not to risk others. Besides, I'm wondering if this particular Wyld just might have some connection to Oberon." It took tremendous effort for anything to cross the Gate without permission, even more to maintain itself and grow in the mortal realm. If they were sentient, they also knew they had to constantly hide themselves from my presence.

"We go now, then, Master Nicholas?"

"Now. Get in the auto, Fetch. I'll be there in a moment." I didn't bother to ask him if he needed me to open the door for him; knobs were a simple problem for the lycanthrope, even now condemned to his current shape.

I turned back to try to convince Claryce that she shouldn't come with us, but she was already following Fetch. When I took her by her arm, she shook her head.

I gave up and trailed behind.

There was no traffic on the street. I summoned the dragon's eyes, but the emerald world revealed nothing, either. Restoring my own eyes, I took the wheel and drove us on.

The neighborhood we sought was populated by Queen Anne houses almost identical to those around mine. It was also as quiet a neighborhood as the one I'd chosen. Few houses had any lights on and those nearest our destination were black as pitch. On the one hand, I was happy no one would observe our coming, but on the other I hoped that didn't mean that the possible Wyld inside had spread its influence beyond the single home.

I was surprised to see an old Whiting Runabout parked in front of the house. After fifteen years, they were already becoming rarities. I'd seen that particular squared-off cowl only a few times and always with the same driver.

"Wait here."

As I reached the door, it opened, and out stepped two elderly men who couldn't have looked more different from each other than if they'd been the recently broken up Vaudeville duo of Gallagher and Shean. The relatively tall figure with spectacles was my client, a Mister Desmond "Des" O'Reilly. He looked as if he'd stepped out of some farm house. His look was one of befuddlement at the moment.

The possible cause of his befuddlement was a short, round figure who would've been lucky if he managed five feet in height. A thick shock of white hair blossomed from his head in an unruly manner. He had a face that a bulldog would've admired, a face that hid as good a soul as his son's had been troubled.

Barnaby noticed me first. "Mas—Nick! I was just telling Bobbie it'd be better if he joined me for a pint—ur—cup of coffee at my house while you did your work."

"I don't know about leaving the house to a stranger," O'Reilly murmured almost sheepishly. "I know Barnaby vouches for you, but still—"

"But still there's no man more trustworthy than Nick here! I told you so, Des, and you can believe me!"

As he tried to cajole his old friend, I noticed Barnaby catch Mister O'Reilly's eyes. Barnaby didn't even realize what he was doing, but almost immediately, Des became more agreeable.

"Yes . . . yes, I suppose you're right. Will it take long?"

"Long enough for us to have a good, slow drink," Barnaby replied, glancing my way.

I nodded just enough for him to see. If he was getting his friend out of the house, then Barnaby believed that whatever "haunted" the place was more than just imagination after all.

"You climb into the Whiting, Des. I'll just have a word with Nick before we leave."

Still pliable, O'Reilly obeyed. After a glance at the Packard, Barnaby turned to me. "You always come alone or with the hound, but there's another with you. Is she like—is she like my son?"

"Never mind her."

"As you say. I meant to be here to keep Des occupied, but I suddenly had the creepiest sensation, as if Chaney's *Hunchback* stood behind me. I don't mind telling you I decided there and then to make certain we cleared out for you."

"Probably a wise move. Give me two hours."

"You'll have more than that. I brew a *strong* cup of coffee."

I didn't reprimand Barnaby for his stash of bootleg whiskey. In his case, a little whiskey, even illegal, was better than some of the memories he carried.

I waited until he had the runabout on its way, then returned to Claryce and Fetch. Claryce refused my final attempt to dissuade her from entering, but I did get her to promise she would stay in one of the open areas and not follow me into the actual room I had to investigate.

Desmond O'Reilly's home was cluttered but neat. Small knick-knacks from the Emerald Isle decorated the walls and shelves. Photographs of some pretty grim male and female figures revealed the two previous generations of O'Reillys. I could see why any of them would've made for some nasty ghosts.

But although ghosts certainly existed, I knew right away that what lurked inside was a Wyld. I could already feel it moving about, with a recklessness that almost surprised me. It either knew someone was coming for it, or it was so secure in its defenses it didn't believe any mortal creature could sense it.

"The cellar," I muttered.

Fetch immediately raced back outside. There'd been some outside entrance—either a door or a window—through which he could crash. He didn't carry any items with him this time; I needed him for distraction and to keep the Wyld from fleeing if it saw that things were turning against it.

I handed the dagger to Claryce.

"Don't you need this?" she asked pensively.

"Not as much as I need you."

I startled both of us with what I said. Before she could recover, I spun around and went to the cellar entrance. Even before I opened it, I knew that whatever lurked below was more deadly than what I'd found in Mrs. Hauptmann's attic.

Show me . . .

The dragon's world opened up to me, sending away the darkness and revealing every corner of the unlit cellar. I didn't bother with the house light, the better to take my quarry unaware. It'd assume the darkness would benefit it, which might prove a fatal mistake.

Not for a moment did I think I might confront some meek, frightened Feirie creature. Those tended to less ominous surroundings and never radiated a malevolence such as the thing in the attic and what I noted down here.

I reached the bottom unmolested, which surprised me considering how furiously the Wyld's energies radiated from the far left corner. I still couldn't make out what it was, but I knew the glamour it cast about itself wouldn't be able to last much longer against the dragon's magic.

I took another step and an outline began to form. Something spindly, almost like the creatures Oberon had sent to harass us in the alley. I doubted it was one of them, though.

Whatever it was remained behind its magic, confident of its ability to mask itself from the foolish human before it.

I saw no reason to prolong this. Its foulness was evident.

Drawing Her Lady's gift, I lunged.

The glamour faded, revealing for the dragon's eyes a thing with no evident eyes and a shape that was a parody of the sleek excellence of one of Oberon's or Kravayik's kind. The ruling caste of Feirie wasn't above mating with other things simply for the twisted sport of it, rarely acknowledging any of the monstrous offspring that their magic might help spawn.

I didn't care if this was Oberon's get or even one of Kravayik's. It couldn't have been on this side of the Gate for very long. I could sense its dark hunger and knew that Des O'Reilly had escaped from a terrible fate by the skin of his teeth.

Her Lady's gift cut a swath across the Wyld's torso . . . only the torso twisted back as if independent of the rest of the creature. As that happened, from the Wyld's sides emerged two more arms . . . both ending in hands wielding black silver blades as long as mine.

Gatekeeper . . . it greeted with mockery.

I ignored its attempt to taunt me, aware that words were as much weapons to Feiriefolk as swords. Her Lady's gift met one of the black silver blades. Instead of the clang of metal against metal, there was only a dull beat, as if from a dying heart.

The other weapon closed on me. I managed to deflect that, too, but this Wyld was a swift, skilled fighter. Whichever member of the Court had been one of his parents had evidently decided to take the mongrel under his or her wing and teach it some skills.

You will not take me back to Her . . .

I appreciated that it was kind enough to give me some glimpse as to its background. So, whatever its Court parent's status, it'd made the mistake of angering Her Lady.

Fetch had yet to make an appearance, even though I saw at least one window through which he could've crashed. Whatever the reason for his absence, I had to fight on.

Twice more, I struck with Her Lady's gift. On the last attack, the enchanted blade proved the superior of one of the black silver weapons. The heartbeat sound was this time followed by a wicked *cracking* noise.

The top third of the black silver blade went flying to the side. My foe reacted immediately by tossing the ruined sword at me.

The awkward projectile was easy to dodge, but it gave the Wyld the opportunity to charge me . . . which it *didn't*.

Suddenly I knew why, despite the glamour, this mongrel had been so glaringly evident.

I tried to turn as the *second* Wyld poured down from the ceiling and on top of me. It was akin to one of the things I'd fought days earlier, but that didn't help me at the moment. Its cold, cold body wrapped around mine, and I immediately felt a lethargy I'd only truly known once before. That'd been the moment of my death.

But even as I struggled against the second Wyld, I knew with certainty that the first was moving in to finish me.

Let Eye loose! Let Eye loose!

I didn't want to. I didn't dare to, even with our growing rapport. Still, a part of me began giving way to him as I felt the world fading away—

A shrill cry rose all around me. I vaguely realized that it came from the shadow creature devouring my life. It recoiled, once again revealing the cellar.

My strength flagged. My knees buckled. I had no idea what'd happened to the second Wyld, but sixteen hundred years of honed instinct warned me where the first had to be.

I turned Her Lady's gift behind me and thrust with all my remaining might. At the very last second, I felt the dragon add his own strength to my desperate jab.

This time, a hiss reached my ears, a dying hiss. Even aware that I'd managed to strike true, I continued to press Her Lady's gift hard into what I imagined had to be my opponent.

And then, when my legs couldn't hold me up any longer, I collapsed.

I never felt myself hit the floor. I did hear the voice in the distance, though. Claryce's voice. She called my name over and over, but I couldn't find a mouth with which to answer. I wanted to warn her to stay far away, in case one of the Wyld still lived.

Hearing nothing from me, she continued repeating my name. I heard her desperation. I wanted to answer.

Instead . . . the dragon spoke *for* me.

CHAPTER 24

"Take us from here," the dragon told her.

I saw the world through my eyes—his eyes now—and beheld Claryce as if from all the way across the cellar, even though she leaned down right in front of us.

"Nick?" she asked tentatively and rightly.

"We are," the dragon replied. "Help us up."

Claryce raised her left hand, revealing the blessed dagger. I knew now how the second Wyld had perished and was both grateful and worried for her. She should've stayed upstairs, now more than ever.

Claryce wisely pointed the dagger at us. "You're—you're the dragon."

"We are . . ." He stretched a hand—*my* hand—to her. "Help us up."

Keep away from her! I managed to warn him.

You are weak. Let Eye command the body for now! Remember, she is destined to be killed! Like all the rest of her . . . and perhaps imminently . . . Eye can help . . . take her where she will be safe . . .

The thought of him being her only hope somehow urged me to struggle harder. More and more I became a part of the world again . . . and at the same time, *he* lost his grip on my body.

Eye am stronger! Eye will protect her!

No . . . I will. I—thank you—for your concern . . . but I'll take care of her better . . .

There was a hesitation and then he acquiesced. *Yes . . . you will . . . you always will . . .*

I seized control of the hand, bringing it back down and using it to slowly push myself to my feet. Claryce kept back. She couldn't yet know just who was trying to stand.

"It's—it's me," I managed.

"Nick!" She let the dagger drop with a clatter as she rushed to take hold of me. "I saw your eyes switch back and forth! I saw them finally become normal . . . but I still couldn't be certain it was really you at that point."

I was grateful for many reasons for her arms around my waist. Foremost happened to be the fact that I could barely keep my balance. "Where—where's Fetch?"

"Here . . . Master Nicholas." Fetch emerged from behind Claryce. His hangdog expression made me forget most—not *all*—of my anger. "The only entrances I could find all had things piled in front of them! I finally deemed it better to come back through the front and down the steps if I was to aid ye in any manner . . . I am sorry . . ."

"Never—never mind." I looked for Her Lady's gift. It lay undisturbed to my right. Still wavering, I reached down for it.

That was when I saw the damaged edge.

I'd thought nothing could harm her creation, but I should've realized that black silver might be the one exception. I noticed that the weapon had now also lost much of its sheen. Worse, I couldn't feel the immense energies that always flowed through it.

Against Oberon, I knew I'd need the sword more than ever. I really had no other choice. I had to do the one thing I dreaded most.

"How long've I been here, Claryce?"

"You were unconscious maybe a half an hour . . . and then *he* started talking. I knew it was him, not you. He just couldn't sound . . . sound as if he had a soul."

"He . . . he meant well in this case," I offered.

"I suppose." Claryce's tone indicated she doubted it.

I suddenly noticed her shaking and recalled that, with everything else going on, I hadn't spoken to her about what *she'd* been forced to endure. "You were supposed to stay upstairs."

Her brow arched. "A good thing I don't listen all the time."

I decided not to respond to that fact. "Did that Wyld touch you in any way? Can you remember? Even a glancing touch?"

"No . . . nothing."

I took some relief from that, at least. Things of Feirie could live on by such simple acts as a light touch against another creature. I was beginning to think that somehow Oberon had accomplished that fact during the Fire. Maybe the original Delke.

A matter to worry about another time! The reprimand wasn't the dragon's, but my own. I was still trying to delay what I had to do.

"Get me to the Packard," I ordered Claryce.

"Are we done here?"

I looked around but saw no trace of either Wyld. Even the weapons of the first had already faded away. One aspect of my job at least had some benefits—the fact that shadow folk and their tools often melted away once the former was dead made cleaning up easier. "We are. Let's go."

Claryce plucked up the dagger. I gently took it from her, studied it for dangerous traces, then handed it back. "Keep this."

"I don't exactly go around with a sheath at my side like Douglas Fairbanks usually does." When I said nothing, she finally slid the dagger through her skirt belt. "Something bad's happening, isn't it?"

Instead of directly answering her, I looked at Fetch. "The sword's damaged."

He whined. "Nay, not the lake . . ."

"There's no choice."

Claryce looked caught between annoyance at my ignoring her to growing fear over what I'd just said about Her Lady's gift. "That sword is damaged? You know someone who can fix it fast?"

"I do . . . the one who created it."

"He means Her Lady," Fetch, of course, had to add.

"Her—Nick!" Claryce's eyes grew wider. "You're not letting her into this world . . ."

"No," I tried to look much stronger than I felt. "No . . . I'm going to hers."

I tried reaching Cortez before we left the O'Reilly house, but no one answered at the station. If I'd been in better mental shape at the time, I'd have probably been suspicious. As it was, I chalked it up to the late night only having a skeleton crew that now had to deal with breaking up some illicit party of half-drunken flappers and their sugar daddies. Wouldn't have been the first or the hundredth time that'd happened some Chicago night since the Eighteenth Amendment and the Volstead Act had first been enforced.

It was my intention to drive, but the first turn I made leaving my client's home nearly had us cross paths with a lamppost.

Seizing the wheel in time, Claryce helped me guide the Packard to a halt. "Nick, you can't do this! Even if you get to wherever you need to go by the lake, how can you possibly face her . . . there?"

In answer, I slid out of the driver's seat. "You'd better drive."

"I will not!" She folded her arms in defiance.

I started walking in the general direction of Lake Michigan. I wasn't quite sure at the time whether I was calling her bluff or actually thought I could make it there on foot, but fortunately Claryce surrendered to the fact that I intended to get there one way or another.

Pulling up beside me, she muttered, "I'll take us there . . ."

It was eerily quiet on the streets as we drove. I even took a look up at the night sky to verify that the full moon wasn't already upon us.

What *was* upon us was a strong wind that magnified as we neared an area just north of Municipal Pier. The rising wind had guaranteed that there was no longer anyone in the vicinity. I began to suspect that the wind hadn't originated on the lake but rather from somewhere just out of sight near it.

Claryce stared out at the darkened waters, then at me. We'd naturally had our coats on when we'd headed to Desmond O'Reilly's, but the cold, moist wind already had her clutching herself tight. "You're not going to take a boat out on those waters, are you?"

"No. I don't need a boat."

"Then how—"

Eye will not take us there! Eye will not!

You don't have to, I bitterly reminded him.

Stepping out, I walked to the shoreline. With the hungry waves just managing to lap at my feet, I drew Her Lady's gift and held it sideways high above my head.

Behind me, I heard Claryce gasp and Fetch growl low. Inside me, I felt the dragon withdraw to the deepest recesses of my mind.

And *ahead* of me, a portion of the turbulent lake seemed to first rise, then freeze. Any icy path formed, a path leading higher into the sky over Lake Michigan.

I took a step onto the path. My foot slid a little, but then held.

Open the way, I ordered.

The few faint stars visible in the sky suddenly fell from their usual spots. They gathered in a ragged arc far above me.

I tried to summon the dragon's eyes, but he refused me. Despite his defiance, I began walking the path.

The stars shimmered. They melded together, then stretched to form a more defined yet still ethereal arch.

It was not the Gate in its full glory, but I didn't need to see it so to enter. I took a few more steps over Lake Michigan . . . and then planted a foot in Feirie.

Where it'd been night, it was now dusk. It was almost always dusk in Feirie. I'd never actually seen the sun set or rise here and wasn't sure if it really did.

The twisted oaks greeted me everywhere. I felt like Hansel and Gretel . . . or maybe Papa Johnny when he'd taken a "vacation" down to Hot Springs, Arkansas, right after O'Banion's murder. The sensation that there might be something sinister lurking behind each tree wasn't mere fantasy, though. The shadow folk would sense my "outside" presence immediately.

The Feirie of Her Lady's "bubble" had been a cramped thing and in some ways so was the real Feirie. True, I could walk forever and ever without finding my way to the Court if she so decided, but I doubted that Her Lady would play that particular game. As a matter of fact, I was pretty certain even before the forest literally parted before me that she'd rush me to her.

Spectral lights floated around the clearing as the Court formed. Shadows that hadn't been there before suddenly clustered on each side of the clearing. I began to hear whispering in my head, whispering that might've snared my mind if I'd been a normal human being.

There was a flutter of wings, a shaking of cloth, and suddenly a figure that could've been Kravayik's twin—at least his twin if he'd never left Feirie—shaped before me. He stood tall and too thin, but radiated a deadliness that his dark, forest green armor and cloak only hinted at.

The sword is demanded by her . . .

I drew Her Lady's gift and without a word turned the hilt toward him. His narrow black eyes stretched in surprise at my willingness to disarm myself here. He and everything else could detect the lack of the blessed dagger on me. In the Court's eyes, I was now defenseless. It wasn't true, but they didn't know that.

And yet, no one tried to take me. They knew better. I walked beside Her Lady's seneschal—at least that's what I assumed he was—and kept pace despite his longer stride.

Small creatures barely seen ran from our path. They also served Her Lady, making certain that the Court was always immaculate.

Feirie always retained an image of elegance, even when executions were taking place.

Without warning, the seneschal again became a shaking of cloth followed by a flutter of wings. I was left alone. I didn't miss a step as I waited for Her Lady to make her presence known.

The oaks at the end of the clearing became even more gnarled. Some of them bent over. Their downturned crowns formed the base of what quickly became a towering throne atop a tall dais. Once again, there were three perches atop the throne, but on only one did a black bird alight this time.

A second black bird landed before the throne. It twisted and grew, becoming the seneschal. I saw no sign of the sword, though.

But what I did see was the slim yet curved shape that grew from the shadows over the throne. Her Lady sat primly yet somehow seductively as she first surveyed her Court, then her seneschal . . . and then, finally, me.

Her Darling Gatekeeper . . . she expected to see you before long . . . but not because of her ruined gift to you . . .

"Black silver must be of little value anymore," I responded. "Certainly seems enough of it going around to ship to the other side."

There was an unsettled rustling from the shadows that made up her Court. Out of the corner of my eye, I caught glimpses of faces showing dismay and fear. The fear was focused on Her Lady, who appeared to have lost her humor.

Her trust was broken by one with ambition who has been replaced . . . and the one replaced has been . . . educated . . .

The seneschal rose and faced me. He spread open one side of his cloak.

Mouth agape, the ravaged head of a male of the Court stared back at me from where it hung inside the cloak. The dark beauty inherent in all the members of Feirie's highest caste had been replaced by a monstrousness created by extreme torture. What made the sight even more hideous was that I could see that the traitor's spirit remained trapped in the head. Her Lady wasn't done "educating" him yet.

With the hint of a grin, the seneschal pulled his cloak tight around him again. I gathered that the traitor had been *his* predecessor.

"Did Oberon order him to do this?" I asked, ignoring the way the gathered Court tried their best to lean farther and farther away from me just in case their former Lord paid attention to my use of his true name.

Her Lady noted their reaction. The oaks rustled violently. Black birds cawed everywhere, though there was only the one to be seen.

The warning was effective. The Feirie Court once more resumed its false semblance of utter confidence in its mistress.

She will find the truth of that . . .

"I doubt we've time. You've probably known all along that he'd try to make use of the Frost Moon." I was greeted with silence. When it dragged on longer than I cared, I continued. "Fix the sword and I'll be on my way . . ."

The granting of this gift was not a simple one . . .

"Nor is facing Oberon with secrets being kept left and right by those I should have at least a *little* trust in. We might not've had to deal with this situation as it stands now."

I could tell that my defiance wasn't going over well with the assembled shadows. Most no doubt expected my head to be hanging next to the old seneschal before long.

Instead, Her Lady rose. Immediately, each of the shadows dropped to one knee.

Leave . . .

She only had to give the word and the entire clearing emptied save for Her Lady, myself, and the new seneschal. Head down, he continued to kneel.

Her Lady took a step down . . . and then stood before me. Having witnessed them so long and seen them for what they were, I'd long become unimpressed with Feirie tricks. If I'd wanted to, I could've had my hands around her throat the moment she'd materialized so close. Of course, she knew that, too.

What I couldn't get used to, but never gave a hint about, was her ghostly beauty. It wasn't that I wanted her; it was that she'd been born to make *all* men desire her. That'd worked fine until she'd become the mate of Oberon and discovered that her allure wasn't always to her benefit.

It is adjusted . . .

I wasn't sure what she meant until the seneschal rose and opened wide his long, long hands. In them lay Her Lady's gift, whole again.

"Well, that didn't seem like too much trouble after all," I quipped, as I reached for the hilt. My rudeness earned me a murderous glare from Her Lady's servant, and I guessed that he was not only serving her in his current role, but also in her bed. He looked willing to take the sword and give it to me point first.

I left him seething as I tested the blade and found it as well-balanced as ever. I made one false thrust at the seneschal, who, despite his best efforts, couldn't help leaping back a step. That earned me an even more murderous glare, not that I cared. I'd been mentally fighting off the influence of a dozen or more Feirie minds, including his. Everyone sought to influence the Gatekeeper, despite his lowly "human" status.

As I returned the sword to that hidden place in which I carried it, I caught a glimpse of something in her half-seen face that I'd never noticed before. A wistfulness. Almost as if my swordplay had resurrected some memory of a better time. It startled me the more because I knew somehow that she'd not meant it to be seen.

For the first time a little off-balance myself, I bowed my head. "Thanks. If your changeling still exists on the other side, I'll probably need whatever aid it can offer."

That will be yours . . .

"Good." But as I started to turn away, she surprised me again by raising a hesitant hand to stop me.

There is something else, Gatekeeper . . .

The seneschal drew dangerously near to her. No word passed between them that I could hear or sense, but he retreated just as quickly, his head bent low. He'd been reprimanded, though I couldn't say how.

Her Lady reached to her bosom and from a place dangerously hard to ignore she pulled up something hanging at the end of a silver chain. It was a teardrop-shaped gem nearly the size of a Peace Dollar and so black I knew it had to have some sinister curse or power attached to it.

She slid her hand until the gem lay in her palm. *Gifted to her at their wedding, it was a promise of a bond never to be broken . . .*

It took me a moment to realize the significance of what she'd said. "Ob—*he* gave this to you?"

The exchange of the deepest of gifts is part of what we are . . . Not once did her full lips move in conversation, but now they pursed even more as Her Lady obviously recalled a significant moment in her existence.

The silver chain turned into tiny eyeless sprites that darted into the surrounding forest. Her Lady extended her hand to me.

A single touch of his blood . . . an offering of his true devotion . . .

She hadn't said "love." I wondered about that . . . and then wondered about something else. "And what did you give him?"

Her Lady'd had millennia to practice her "human" expressions, but only now, only when pressed about her marriage to Oberon did I see something real among the ever-present shadows surrounding her. She grew more wistful, then solemn. Her dangerously fascinating eyes focused on me in a different manner.

Beware, her darling Gatekeeper . . . what she gives to you so many others would like . . . not merely the Court, not merely the Wyld, but even those exiles with whom you find better association . . .

By "better association," she meant those whom I considered close to *friends*, such as Kravayik. If Her Lady knew just how devout he'd become to his new life, she'd have been shocked.

While I was thinking of this, she gently—*gently*—set the gem in my grasp. I noticed for the first time that her palm had no lines on it like mine or Claryce's—or even Kravayik's—did.

Guard the drop until needed . . . and use only if necessary . . . it is power and it is poison . . .

"I don't—"

Use it if you must, her darling Gatekeeper . . . but use it rather than let him take it . . . you do not want it to be a part of him again . . .

I was stunned by the sadness I heard in her "voice." Sadness for *Oberon*. "What'll happen—"

Her Lady turned from me. As she did, the entire forest receded from me so swiftly that vertigo nearly overtook me. I watched her back shrink into the distance . . . and watched her seneschal continued to glare at me as he also faded into the background.

I felt myself flying backward to the Gate. I tried to slow my momentum, but only did so barely.

The strain began to tell. I didn't want to black out, but it was becoming harder to prevent it.

I reached the Feirie side of the Gate, which at the moment appeared like a mirror image of what I'd seen over Lake Michigan. Still fighting to stay conscious, I started to cross.

And at that moment, I was attacked. A heavy force crushed my mind, my soul, and my will, breaking through defenses I'd built up over centuries.

A wave of bitterness washed over me . . . only it wasn't *my* bitterness. It was his.

It slowly occurred to me that we lay on the shore of Lake Michigan again, but not near where I'd left Claryce and Fetch. Instead, we were even farther north of Grand Avenue and Municipal Pier.

Slowly, I rose . . . or rather, my body did. Once again, I felt like an onlooker. I could do nothing as my arms stretched and my legs slowly straightened.

What had been my eyes then peered down at the powerful thing Her Lady had given to me. The teardrop-shaped gem containing a single drop of Oberon's blood. All we supposedly needed to destroy him.

The dragon folded his fingers over the gem. "It is different this time," he remarked, in a voice that was and wasn't mine. "It is stronger . . . this stone . . . it must be why."

I realized that he was referring to why he so dominated my human form. It was one thing for him to seize command when fully unleashed in his natural shape, but another for him to so readily command our body as it was.

"Nick!"

Her voice was faint, but both of us recognized Claryce's call immediately. The dragon looked toward the cry, and through his emerald eyes we saw the distant figures of Claryce and Fetch running along the edge of the Lake toward us.

A dangerous hiss escaped our lips . . . and the dragon turned the body and fled from the lake, rushing with speed I couldn't and wouldn't have matched. I felt our muscles ache, our lungs strain, as he ran into the city and far from Claryce.

Gasping, the dragon looked back and forth across the first street we reached. He kept his thoughts shielded from me. Our heart pounded. I sensed both elation and fear. He'd never imagined achieving this point . . . and neither had I.

Once more, he eyed the gem.

"Yes . . . the bargain changes now . . ." The dragon held the teardrop high, setting it so that the moon shone just above it.

A moon, I saw with shock, that was already *full*.

CHAPTER 25

Time flowed differently in Feirie than it did in the human realm, but I'd hardly been gone long enough to make two days pass in Chicago. Yet there hung the evidence that the Frost Moon was imminent.

"To fly . . . to fly unhindered," the dragon muttered.

I expected us to sprout wings, but instead he lowered the hand with the gem and raised the other as a *cab* neared.

"Eye have watched," he said quietly, speaking with me. "Eye will play human . . ."

Stop this! Stop this now! I demanded uselessly.

The taxi veered toward us.

"Nick!" Claryce's voice rose loud. The dragon glanced over our shoulder. Panting, disheveled, she struggled to reach us. "Nick! We've watched for two days! Where were you? Where are you going?"

"Master Nicholas . . . are you—" Fetch clamped his jaws shut. I was caught between noticing that he could speak even so far away from me and understanding that he had suspicions the figure before the two of them wasn't exactly me.

"Go to the Packard," the dragon ordered in a much too reasonable imitation of me. I wondered how long he'd been silently practicing for just this moment. "Return to the safe house. Will meet you there."

"But—where are you going?"

"Have to meet someone. Will explain when I return. Go!"

Fetch leaned his heavy body against Claryce, preventing her from coming toward us. "We should do what he says, Mistress Claryce . . ."

"Nick . . ." She tried to maneuver around Fetch, but despite his still stiff back he kept in front of her.

The cab pulled up. Turning from Claryce, the dragon grinned at the driver. He hadn't been able to practice facial expressions much, and I knew without seeing it that the toothy smile only unnerved the heavy man at the wheel.

The dragon climbed inside. "State Street—"

"Nick!" Claryce managed to shove Fetch aside. "Come—"

The cabbie took off. The dragon sat back, the monstrous grin still across our face.

"Uh . . . where on State?" the cabbie asked with a thick Polish accent.

I didn't need to hear the number to already know where we were heading. There was only one place of importance to us on State.

He was heading for the cathedral.

"Eye do well . . ."

"You say somethin'?" the cabbie asked.

The dragon hissed low enough that the man didn't hear it. "Not to you. To State."

The cabbie shut his mouth and focused on the drive. He probably regretted picking up this fare and hoped he could get us to our destination before anything might happen.

This is wrong! I silently railed. *This is against your duty to the Gate . . .*

Again, there came a hiss. Our fingers squeezed the door handle and such was the strength of the dragon, even in my body, that I felt the handle twist and break.

"What's goin' on back there?" the cabbie demanded. "You ruinin' my cab—"

The dragon reached forward and seized the man by the back of the neck. It was all the cabbie could do to keep from swerving into another auto.

"To State . . . to the Cathedral . . ."

"Yes, sir, mister! I hear you!"

"Duty . . ." whispered the dragon angrily as he sat back. *"Ssslavery . . ."*

Slavery. I'd more than once considered my task in the same light but always in the end considered it duty first. I'd made the mistake of slaying the Gate's guardian and so, for as long as Heaven demanded it, I knew I had to serve as keeper.

But I'd never in sixteen hundred years actually considered how much he'd hated his burden. I'd only considered him a necessary evil, an unwilling ally. What had his existence been before he'd been condemned to serve the Gate?

The taxi came to a sudden halt. I thought the driver'd decided to flee his auto but through the dragon discovered that we were already at Holy Name.

Naturally, there wasn't any thought of paying the cabbie, who drove off anyway the moment the dragon stepped out. We studied the great cathedral, noticing that the door was opening and two men were stepping outside.

I recognized them as some of the staff. The dragon moved out of sight as the pair descended the steps. When the area was empty again, the dragon took us up to the huge doors.

He seized one door and tugged. I felt the strain of our muscles as he pulled open the door.

There was no one in sight. The dragon strode through the hallowed chamber with a contempt worthy of Galerius at the height of his monstrous crusade. I expected the dragon to topple statues and shove aside pews just for the sake of chaos, but he surprised me by remaining focused on one thing and one thing only.

"Georgius?"

I would've actually welcomed the appearance of Diocles if I thought he could've done anything, but he was a ghost without any ability to haunt anyone but me.

The dragon naturally ignored him, instead heading to where the

Clothos card lay hidden. He grabbed at the hiding place . . . and failed to open it.

"Georgius," Diocles called again. He materialized next to us. "Just what is—"

The dragon glared at him. I'd not thought about the fact that he might be able to see Diocles.

My former master recoiled. He, in turn, obviously saw that there was something amiss with "me."

Diocles crossed himself. "The beast walks among us! Where is Georgius?"

"Leave us, dead one . . ." the dragon snarled.

"Who is out there?" asked the voice of the last person I wanted here now. "Who is it?"

"The beast has Georgius!" Diocles cried out. "Beware!"

But unlike the dragon, Kravayik couldn't see or hear the former emperor. Instead, all the exile saw was me.

"Master Nicholas! What brings you here? Is something amiss?"

The dragon smiled again. I guess he'd noticed the cabbie's response, because this smile was more subdued and *almost* human. "The card! We must see to the card . . ."

Kravayik could no more hear my warning than he had Diocles's. The exile blinked, then nodded vigorously. "If you say it must be so, then it must be, Master Nicholas!"

"It must be."

"Open your damned eyes, sprite!" the ghost shouted. "That's not Georgius! 'Tis the beast!"

But Kravayik eagerly joined the dragon. I wasn't surprised when the dragon proved versed in what was needed to open the card's hiding place; he'd probably watched closely each time I'd done it.

I had to give Diocles credit for once; understanding that it was futile to keep yelling at Kravayik, he materialized in front of me and swung a fist. It went through us, but made the dragon hesitate, which meant he and Kravayik had to start over.

"Are you all right, Master Nicholas?" the exile asked.

"Begin again!"

His tone made Kravayik pause, but before my hopes could rise more, the cathedral's caretaker nodded and resumed his part in the ritual.

Diocles shouted, then swung once more. This time, though, the dragon remembered that the ghost was only a distraction. As Diocles and I both watched in mounting concern, the dragon and Kravayik opened the way to the card. I wanted to shake Kravayik, make him see that it wasn't me, but of course that option wasn't there. Even though, I had no mouth, I still tried to scream a warning.

All to no avail. No one heard, of course. The false me wasted no time in drawing out the card.

He did so with such impatience that Kravayik grew disturbed. "Master Nicholas! With all due respect, that aberration should not be handled so! Even that could cause some sort of change—"

"—not the blessed saint, but the foul wyrm using his body, damn you! Listen to me, Kravayik!" Diocles shouted.

And to the surprise of all *four* of us . . . Kravayik *did*.

"Who *are* you?" the caretaker demanded of Diocles, Kravayik having heard of the emperor's ghost but obviously never having seen him.

"Never mind me! That is not Georg—Nick! That is the dragon in his—"

Kravayik didn't wait for Diocles to finish. The exile'd lost none of his swiftness, despite his change of heart. Faster than any killer Capone, Moran, Weis, or the others could hire, he had a short blade out that was already well on its way to my throat.

But even though I'd have welcomed death in order to avoid catastrophe, the dragon proved even faster. He caught Kravayik's wrist with his free hand, then twisted the hand up. I heard bone crack as the dragon forced the blade from his adversary's hand.

Kravayik was hardly daunted, though. His other hand was halfway to my chest, right at the point where the proper use of force could completely shove the air from my—and the dragon's—lungs.

The dragon pressed the card against Kravayik's hand.

The former enforcer for Feirie let out a scream that had to have been heard even beyond the walls of Holy Name. He fell back, and, as he did, his body shriveled.

"No!" Despite no longer having a body, Diocles leapt at the dragon. I think all three of us were equally surprised again when the late emperor not only collided hard, but sent the dragon and himself sprawling to the floor.

With a long hiss, the dragon swatted at Diocles. Unfortunately, the price of being able to attack meant that my former master could also be hit in turn. Diocles went crashing into the first pews.

The dragon leapt to his—my—our—feet. He looked around for the card.

I spotted it first . . . near Diocles. Diocles noticed it, too, and despite having experienced the first real pain since he'd died, managed to crawl over to it. It was clear that Diocles expected his hand to go through the card, but his fingers managed to grasp it. Such was the power of the card, even when not used as it'd been meant to be, that it gave ghosts solid form just by being near.

I couldn't see what'd happened to Kravayik, which left only Diocles to stand before the dragon. Diocles struggled to his feet and held the card's face toward us.

"Stand back, beast, or I'll—"

"Will you execute me again, Diocles?" the dragon asked in the softest tones I'd heard him use yet.

I couldn't give the late emperor any warning. He acted exactly as both I and the dragon expected. Expression shaken, Diocles lowered the card slightly and muttered, "Georgius . . . I can't say—"

The dragon lunged forward, snatching the card with one hand and striking the solidified phantom hard on the side of the head. Diocles fell, whether stunned or worse, I couldn't say. His guilt over my ancient execution had let him be tricked at the most vital moment.

The dragon glared at the transparent body, then spun toward the door. I heard sounds from elsewhere in the cathedral, but the dragon didn't wait to see what might happen. He raced to the door and out into the night.

There were no taxis about, but for where he needed to go simply crossing the street was enough. Staunchly religious despite their depravities, the North Side Gang had its headquarters right across from the cathedral. I'd known that each time I'd visited Holy Name, but I'd also known that one thing Moran's gang wouldn't do was desecrate the religious edifice. And even once I'd discovered Oberon's connection with the North Siders, I'd been aware that not only did even Doolin not dare cross Moran and the others and break into the cathedral, but Oberon'd also understood that only I could actually remove the card.

Only I—and the dragon, apparently.

I could sense him calculating his possibilities as he reached the curb. He had control of my body, but I'd been surprised so far at his lack of willingness to transform. I began to wonder if he dared do that.

A black roadster suddenly veered around the nearest corner, pulling up short in front of us.

Doolin leaned out of the front passenger seat. "He said you'd want to come with us . . ."

The dragon hesitated, then nodded. Doolin reached back to the door behind him and swung it open.

At that point, I saw that Oberon's pet mountain wore both gauntlets. A wise measure, considering their new passenger.

We entered. In addition to Doolin and the driver up front, another hood sat in the back. This one carried a tommy across his lap and I knew when he eyed the dragon he only saw me. His cockiness would vanish in an instant—along with his life—if the dragon decided he didn't like his expression.

"Get a move on," Doolin growled to the driver.

As the roadster drove off, the dragon finally pocketed the card and took one last glance at Holy Name. At that point, I noticed something I understood and he didn't. A slight if double-edged hope. Above the doorway, a lone black bird perched. Her Lady's changeling, although there was something different about it I couldn't put my finger on and unfortunately didn't have time to study more. I could only pray that through it she knew what she had to do . . .

It was already evident that we weren't just driving across the street. The dragon didn't seem to think anything of this, even though he'd also be aware of the location of the North Siders' headquarters.

But what bothered me, if not him, was that the roadster was taking a route sending it *back* to Lake Michigan. We turned from State onto East Chicago St., only to take a left a moment later onto Michigan. An archaic, shadowed structure rose on one side, a peculiar sight that caught the dragon's attention more than anything had thus far.

The old water tower still stood, a monument to that fiery night. The dragon eyed the small castle-like edifice until it was out of view, then settled down again.

The roadster took another turn, this one odder than the previous. I wondered why until I heard first one siren, then another.

Snickering, Doolin leaned back to look at the dragon. "You like fires?"

The dragon said nothing, but his eyes narrowed. Doolin grinned. "Bet you do. You're missing a good one right now. The boss had it set just in your honor, so to speak."

When the dragon still didn't answer, Doolin shrugged and turned back. The driver took another turn . . . and started on a route I knew would take us much too near to where the dragon and I had only just left the Gate.

As we neared the lake, both the dragon and I noticed that the wind picked up. Thanks to his glance as we drove, I also saw that the moon was fuller than before . . . in fact, too full for a normal moon and much too pale in a different way.

More like frost . . .

The roadster veered again and we left the main streets for a smaller one leading out to the shoreline. The auto shook as the driver brought us off the paved areas and onto one of the twenty-plus miles of beaches along the Chicago shoreline.

I knew our general location and that was enough to surprise me that we'd stop here. We were still a distance from the Gate.

As we arrived, a second roadster, hidden by the dark, turned on its lights. I kept expecting the dragon to adjust his gaze, but he continued to keep his influence on our body to a minimum.

The dragon started to open the door, but the gunner next to him suddenly tapped us on the shoulder with the end of his tommy.

"Not until the boss says so, boob—urk!"

The dragon wrested the weapon from the thug with one smooth swipe, crushing the tip in the process. He threw the ruined submachine gun out the window, then opened the door and stepped out.

Doolin faced him, the man-mountain chuckling. "Pay no mind; he's just a dumb mug who should know better. That'll come outta your pay, Crank!"

Crank groused, but from the relative safety of his seat. The dragon didn't care about the gunman nor even Doolin. He only had eyes for the shape outlined by the blinding car lights.

"Have the others arrived yet, Doolin?" asked Oberon.

"Not yet. They'll be here."

Oberon strode close enough that we could see his face—or rather, William Delke's. He smiled at the dragon—or me, I couldn't tell.

"Fifty-odd years really is not that long a time for us, is it?" he asked cheerfully. "Yet if there is one human trait I can appreciate . . . well, other than their capacity for destruction . . . it is their impatience. I understand it now, having had to wait for this moment . . . just as you've had to wait for sixteen centuries for your freedom . . ."

"Longer . . ." hissed the dragon bitterly.

"Ah, yes . . . forgive me. I should have counted your servitude to the Gate, as well. All that is soon to be a thing of the past, too, as per our agreement."

I struggled hard within when I heard the last. Some things were making sense. That odd encounter in the Art Institute, when I'd been helpless for some time and yet left untouched by Oberon. He hadn't wanted me dead just then; he needed to reach into my mind and make contact with the dragon.

He'd not only made contact, it seemed, but he'd offered a deal that even my ageless companion couldn't resist. It could only be freedom . . . which meant utter mastery over our shared body.

And yet . . . I knew that Oberon didn't dare let the dragon succeed. Not only was there a slight chance I might survive and take command again, but the dragon was too great a power to coexist in Oberon's imagined world.

Oberon suddenly turned his attention back to Doolin. "You found him by the cathedral?"

"Just like you said, boss. Comin' out almost perfect timing."

The former lord of Feirie eyed the dragon and I closely. "The card?"

To my surprise, the dragon shook our head. I knew the card was in a pocket, but evidently not even Doolin had noticed that.

"Small matter. That situation finally has a remedy, too. I assume you have the teardrop, though . . ."

In answer, the dragon opened up his hand.

"Jeez, lookit the bauble," one of the nearby hoods muttered.

It wasn't *hard* to see it, but not because of the car lights. A deep, green glow emanated from the gem, a glow that intensified when Oberon took a step toward it.

"Blood calls to blood, they say on both sides of the Gate," Oberon murmured almost wistfully. "She kept it safe all this time, then decided to betray me with it at just the moment I predicted."

Oberon reached for it, but the dragon closed our fingers over it.

I felt a surge of uneasiness from my eternal companion. He had as little trust in Oberon as I did, but Oberon had something he wanted. Fortunately—or unfortunately for me—the dragon had the teardrop. From what Oberon'd hinted, after tantalizing the dragon with the thought of freedom, the former lord of Feirie had explained just how that could come about. Play up to me . . . show me a humanity I should've known the dragon couldn't actually have. Then, wait for when I'd *have* to cross and speak in person to Her Lady.

I couldn't say whether the Wyld whose black silver blade had damaged Her Lady's gift had been part of the plan, though that was very possible. With fifty years to watch and wait, it wouldn't surprise me that Oberon'd pegged Barnaby long ago as part of my loose network of "associates" and planned for Desmond O'Reilly's sudden haunting.

But whether that incident was part of the plan or not, Oberon knew I'd very likely *have* to see Her Lady before things came to a head. She, in turn, would've *had* to give up the most precious if dangerous item she had in order to keep her former mate from succeeding.

And with me properly beaten and weakened, the dragon had been able to seize mastery of our body at the right moment. I also didn't doubt that Oberon'd even been watching for our return through the Gate and made certain it was a harsher arrival back than it'd needed to be.

"You know I need that to achieve our goal, my friend," Oberon remarked, the smile still on his face but lacking the humor it'd worn a moment before.

Doolin shifted his stance. The three visible guns nearby did the same. Moreover, I noticed something through the dragon I hadn't before; there were *other* underlings around, but not human ones. Wyld.

The dragon continued to hesitate. "The spear. You promised about the spear."

At that moment, a sleek Packard drove up. The fact that no one seemed surprised didn't surprise me either.

I'd not tried again to regain control, aware that I'd have one chance and one chance only. The dragon's distrust was growing by the second, only his desperation to be free keeping him here. I'd understood his hatred for our situation—I carried my own share—but'd never seen him in this light.

I was worried that they'd captured Claryce, but the occupants of the Packard only turned out to be more hoods. Two of them were carrying something long, wrapped in a silvery cloth that I knew had not been woven in this world.

"Ah!" Oberon, his humor restored, clapped his hands as they joined the gathering. "Now, we can forego any more questioning. I've made a promise and a promise I'll keep."

He snapped his fingers and Doolin stepped over and removed the silver cloth from the top. As he did this, I felt our heart beat faster and faster and realized that the dragon was *afraid*. He was afraid, not of Oberon . . . but the contents of the cloth.

It shone in the moonlight, shone with a brilliance almost exactly opposite the kind of glow the teardrop'd radiated.

Oberon gestured from the dragon to the cloth. "There. The bane . . . and now the *salvation* . . . of your existence."

The dragon and I stared at the spear.

CHAPTER 26

"The fire at the police station went well, boys?" Oberon asked the new arrivals.

"Clubhouse burned real nicely," answered the lead one. "That stuff you gave us made it go up real quick."

"Delke Industries makes nothing but the best." Oberon winked at the dragon . . . or so I mistakenly thought. "I know you're in there, Gatekeeper. You should see what supplying both sides in the war can do for profits, not to mention entertainment. We did very well with mustard gas, for instance, though we never officially put that on the list of our products." He chuckled. "You know, I have really become quite fond of this persona. It will be a shame to have to part with it. I suppose the finest actors feel the same . . ."

"Enough babble . . ." growled the dragon. "Enough talk!" He held the teardrop for Oberon to see again. "Enough of everything . . ."

Doolin leaned in. Whether he wanted to snatch the gem or simply readied himself for whatever command Oberon gave him, I didn't know. However, Oberon waved him back, probably a wise move considering that our heart was beating rapidly. I doubted even the former lord of Feirie knew just how on edge the dragon was.

"Oh, we have a moment more to wait. You know that. The Frost Moon is not quite high enough . . . and we *are* missing one of the players in this game, you know. We can't proceed without *her*, naturally. I'm sure she would like to be here to witness this, too."

Claryce. I tried to control myself, but Oberon'd mentioned the one thing I couldn't simply ignore. I couldn't think of any reason that Oberon'd truly need her. I could only see one reason, simply to taunt me with her death.

I stopped biding my time. I fought for control with all the will I could muster.

The dragon's own wariness left him off guard. He belatedly tried to fight back, but my impulse had been so strong, so abrupt, that he was forced back into the recesses of *my* mind.

And none of this was noticed, even by Oberon.

But what he couldn't fail to notice was that I thrust the teardrop into another pocket and then reached for Her Lady's gift.

Oberon backed away. "Doolin!"

I'd been expecting Doolin to go for me the moment Oberon warned him. Drawing Her Lady's gift had been a feint; instead, I seized Doolin by his grasping hand and threw him past me as hard as I could. That was a lot harder than normal people could. Doolin went flying across the beach and into the nearby water.

The thugs holding the spear used the moment to follow Oberon. I expected Oberon's boys to start firing, but instead each and every one of them beat a hasty retreat into the darkness beyond.

I didn't wait for whatever was going to happen. Now actually drawing Her Lady's gift, I charged after Oberon.

The sand and dirt beneath my feet exploded upward, followed by a leafy tentacle outlined by the car lights. I didn't waste any time on this Wyld, slicing not at the nearest part of the tentacle but at the very base. I knew from experience that the lower I cut, the more I damaged it.

Her Lady's gift severed the tentacle with ease, but another came up right behind me. At the same time, the lights from the rest of the autos suddenly flared bright.

The lights bothered the tentacles more than me. I knew there had to be some sinister reason for them, but I took advantage of their illumination to cut the second tentacle as I'd done the first.

But as I turned toward the autos, I caught a glimpse of one of the gunmen's shadows . . . with no body to cast it.

Worse, the dragon chose that moment to fight back. I abruptly stood frozen in place as the silhouettes of tommies focused on me.

"Do you want to live or die?" I growled to my unseen companion.

He relented just in time. I dove for the ground as the now-familiar *phut-phut* sound of shadow bullets preceded a bizarre but deadly barrage around me.

I was frustrated by the fact that none of the threats I was facing actually meant anything other than danger to me. I needed to face Oberon—

The firing halted. I barely had time to wonder why before a pair of hands took hold of me and threw me toward the auto in which we'd arrived. I crashed against it, leaving a huge dent in the hood and making every bone in my body quiver.

"See how you like gettin' tossed about!" a soggy Doolin roared. The water hadn't done anything to ruin Oberon's gauntlets. They retained every bit of foul magic they'd always had and Doolin looked more than happy to use all that magic against me.

The collision had knocked Her Lady's gift from my grasp, but fortunately it hadn't fallen far. I rolled over to the driver's side and dropped to my knees next to the weapon.

As I rose, I discovered the motionless bodies of Crank and the driver inside the auto. I reached for the driver as Crank suddenly stirred. Unfortunately for him, while his shadow tommy worked, the real one remained broken. Before he managed to remember that, I'd brought my elbow into his jaw.

The driver also started moving again, but that only earned him a head slammed into the steering wheel. Even though I had Her Lady's gift, I seized the driver's tommy and fired at wherever I could see headlights.

Half of the lights shattered, dimming the area. The tommy jammed after that, but it'd served its purpose well enough for me. I wasn't much for guns, even if I'd trained with them for at least three hundred years. All I cared about was reducing the illumination and, thus, reducing the reliability of the hoods' enhanced shadows. I knew they needed *some* light to be able to function and, while the moon was getting brighter by the moment, it'd be a few minutes more before it was good enough to serve the gunmen's purpose.

But, as I threw the tommy away, the dragon struggled against me a second time. My legs became lead. My grip on Her Lady's gift faltered again.

And from behind me—always behind me—Doolin hit me hard on the back with a mailed fist.

Together, the dragon and I made for a being far tougher and more resilient, but Oberon's gauntlets enabled Doolin to hit me so hard I fell completely stunned. He might've tried to finish me off then, but instead he began grabbing at my coat.

Let Eye out! Let Eye out!

Even though half of me knew the dragon could salvage this situation better than I could, his betrayal had been too recent for me to dare let him do anything. I knew why he wanted to stop Doolin; it was for the same reason I did. Neither the teardrop nor the card could fall into Oberon's hands.

Ignoring my immense desire to just lay there and let the world fade away, I swung my free hand around and managed to catch Doolin too occupied by his search to pay me any mind. I didn't doubt that he'd rightly assumed that no normal person could survive a blow like that.

My own swing might've lacked Oberon's gauntlets, but it was hard enough to send him sprawling. I succeeded in dragging myself forward before he could recover, only to find myself facing a toadlike face that hadn't been born on this side of the Gate.

Legends called them kobolds, and in Feirie they had another name that better fit their hideous nature. "Ugly" was sufficient for me, especially this close.

He snatched Her Lady's gift in his thick, four-fingered hands, his wide, wide grin indicating he had every intention of seeing how the sword worked on *me*.

He was still grinning when Her Lady's gift sucked his life essence out of him faster than I could blink. Her Lady had assumed from the beginning that there'd be many from her Court and from Oberon's Wyld that'd be eager to get their hands, or whatever they used, on the blade. Her magic had made it possible for those with no animosity toward her to be able to hold it, though expertly wielding it was another matter. The two possible exceptions were the dragon—a thing unto himself—and Oberon, who was the only denizen of Feirie who might still be more powerful than her. Of course, for him, she'd put in other safeguards, which was probably why he hadn't bothered trying to take the sword when he'd had the chance.

I seized Her Lady's gift from the kobold even as a violent wind swiftly added his crumbling ashes to the beach. As I rose, though, I saw two of Oberon's hoods taking aim. There wasn't much in the way of protection between myself and them, and I knew that I was very likely going to have to rely on the dragon's power to keep me alive. I'd been able to sympathize with the pain endured by Fetch when he'd made his body reject the bullets because I'd gone through the same sort of ordeal several times. Of course, that'd been before the advent of the tommy gun, which could fire a dozen shots into me in a single breath.

But instead of firing, Oberon's boys just kept their weapons trained on me. The reason became clear when Doolin raced past me, heading in the direction I'd last seen Oberon go.

My free hand immediately went into the pocket where the teardrop should've been.

It was still there. I breathed a sigh of relief . . . and then remembered I'd also need to check the *other* pocket.

The *card* was missing.

The dragon's dismay mirrored mine, but I couldn't help briefly reminding him that he was the reason the card had been brought here in the first place. He'd believed that he could control the situation and manipulate the master manipulator. It didn't matter how ageless the dragon was; this was *Oberon* he'd been trying to outwit.

Thunder rattled the area, even though at first there wasn't a cloud in the sky. Then, just as suddenly, the thick clouds *were* there . . . only they covered every bit of sky except where the Frost Moon hovered.

As Doolin vanished into the darkness, I dove back to the auto in which we'd arrived. No longer needing to keep from shooting Doolin, the other hoods opened fire. Bullets perforated the auto. I heard a painful moan and knew that either Crank, the driver, or both, had been hit. Oberon had no use for those who failed him.

I planted myself behind the auto as it continued to suffer a hail of gunfire. I still didn't trust the dragon even so much as to demand his eyes, which kept me at a greater disadvantage than usual. The wind had grown so wild that now great waves smashed onto the shore. It also stirred up a lot of sand, which I'd been waiting for. I couldn't do anything to stop whatever Oberon was doing at the moment, but I'd been prepared to at least make what use I could of his actions.

The auto suddenly flew high in the air. I flung myself away as the largest tentacle yet burst from the sandy beach and sought for me. Gunmen scattered as the ruined vehicle came crashing down near them.

Near the shoreline, I caught a faint glimpse of Oberon illuminated by the Frost Moon. Doolin stood close by. Oberon had the card raised above his head.

And something was stirring in the water, something living.

I couldn't pay them any more mind; the tentacle was dropping down to crush me. I had no time to escape. Instead, I braced myself, held Her Lady's gift upward, and muttered to the dragon, "This's both our hides, remember that . . ."

The sword pierced the heavy tentacle, sinking halfway to the hilt as it did.

The tentacle struck us hard.

I should've been crushed, but the dragon did his part, if reluctantly. His primal power protected us enough so that I only had a resounding headache that fortunately lasted just a few seconds.

Weary . . .

He wasn't simply making a comment. I could feel his presence receding. He'd strained himself with his betrayal, and now defending us this way had put him at his limit for the time being.

So deep inside the tentacle, Her Lady's gift could now work its full, dark power. The size of its victim didn't matter. The sword did as much to the tentacle's owner as it had to the unfortunate kobold. The slick skin grayed, then started to crumble.

I struggled free . . . just in time to get a solid knock on the jaw that would've broken it if not for the dragon's fading power still protecting me for the moment. Even then, I couldn't keep my grip on Her Lady's gift. It spiraled into the air and landed on the other side of the swiftly decaying tentacle.

I looked up to see Doolin looming over me, not only with the gauntlets covering his hands, but also with a short hand ax in his right hand. Its black silver head gleamed wickedly in the Frost Moon and almost as wickedly as Doolin's gaze.

"Don't know why the boss thinks you're so special," the man mountain rumbled. "Just another chump ready for a long swim to the bottom of the lake . . ."

He punctuated the statement by taking a swing at me with the ax. I realized Doolin had hit me with a fist just so he could have me look at him when he chopped me in two.

It was his mistake. He wasn't at a good angle to kick at, but he *was* close enough to be rewarded with a face full of sand. Doolin let out a snarl as he tried to quickly wipe the sand from his eyes.

It wasn't quick enough to prevent me from leaping up and crashing into him with enough force to even knock Doolin down. Unfortunately, keeping him there proved to be no easy task. I'd fought few men as physically strong as Doolin and he also had the gauntlets to magnify that strength. I'd seen Eugen Sandow at the World's Columbian Exhibition in '93 and suspected that Doolin could've held his own against Ziegfield's famous strongman.

Thunder shook the beach. The wind became a gale. I didn't know what was going on beyond my fight with Doolin, but I worried about Her Lady's gift . . . and even more about how far along Oberon was with his plan.

Doolin got one hand on my throat, erasing any thought other than survival. I tried to call on the dragon, but it was as if he was no longer a part of me.

I was certain that I could eventually take Doolin, but I didn't have the time to find out if I was right. The next rattle of thunder felt like an earthquake.

The tremor bounced us around, to my regret ending with Doolin at the advantage. He continued to try to crush my throat as he managed to get up on one knee.

A growling form landed atop Doolin, its momentum carrying both of them from me.

I didn't recognize at first what fought with Doolin. It had a somewhat manlike shape, but also one more like that of a four-legged beast. Its snout was too long for the creatures it most resembled and its body too thin and wiry even for a greyhound.

Only when he shouted my name did I understand that I was staring at *Fetch*.

"Protect her, Master Nicholas!" he roared, as he tried to rake Doolin's face with one paw. "And forgive me . . ."

I didn't know what I was supposed to forgive Fetch for and would've dearly liked to know, but his first words had warned me that he'd not come alone. Claryce also had to be here . . . in a place where the odds of her being killed were almost a certainty.

Yet what I saw initially wasn't Claryce, but rather the black bird. It soared high in the sky, visible only because the Frost Moon continued to shine through a menacing hole in the otherwise turbulent heavens. The black bird looked unhindered by the wind as it disappeared over the lake, for what purpose, only Her Lady knew.

A painful whine rose from Fetch's direction, but I'd already turned and found Claryce. I hadn't known what I'd expected, but it hadn't been to find her standing against a blurry piece of shadow with Her Lady's gift in her hand.

Not only in her hand but wielded very naturally.

She slashed with the blade, cutting the shadow in half. As it dissipated, Claryce took a few steps toward the lake.

I knew without a doubt what she hoped to do . . . and also knew without a doubt I couldn't let her try. She wanted Oberon's head. I couldn't blame her, but, even with Her Lady's gift, Claryce wouldn't get very far . . . especially now that another shadow was forming right by her, this one wielding the silhouette of a tommy gun. The Frost Moon had grown bright enough that Oberon's goons could use their special toys once more.

"Claryce!" I shouted.

She looked my direction, smiled—and then immediately ducked at my direction. The *phut-phut-phut* of the shadow gun was barely audible in the growing storm. The sand around Claryce exploded in several places, fortunately none of the spots too near her.

I started toward her, but she pushed herself up enough to look back at me. "No! Oberon! You have to stop Oberon . . . and watch out for Fetch!"

I was more confused than ever, but I knew she was right. None of us had a chance if Oberon succeeded in bringing this world and Feirie together. Even if it meant losing Claryce . . . I did have to do as she said. There would be *nothing* if he was not stopped here now.

Before I could have second thoughts, Claryce rolled away from me and toward the firing shadow. She swung and *again* seemed to handle the sword as if born to it.

I saw Her Lady's cunning in this. She'd planned for the eventuality that the one person close to me might need the sword. Her Lady could yet prove more adaptable than her former mate . . . if we all survived this night.

I ran after Oberon.

To my amazement, he still stood at the edge of the lake, the card raised toward it. In the midst of the storm, Lake Michigan *foamed*. Even worse, the sense that something huge moved in those waters also grew harder and harder to deny.

"Gatekeeper!" Oberon shouted, even though he still faced the water. "You took longer than I imagined . . ."

"Sorry for the delay!"

He peered over his shoulder, still wearing the mask of William Delke despite the critical moment. "I tried to keep you from your foolishness! I tried to scare you away using the female who keeps returning! I thought if you worried about her, you would do the sensible thing and take her far from here . . ."

I edged closer. I didn't have Her Lady's gift, but I still had the teardrop in my pocket. I knew the potency of such a talisman, the potency and the danger. I'd have to use it only when there was no other choice . . . something that was likely to happen much too soon.

"You know there's nowhere I could take her that'd be far enough away from what you're doing, Oberon!"

"But it would have given you time to understand that I am doing what is best for both realms!" He finally turned around to face me, a frown much too wide for a human now across his face. "Time to understand the only true course is to remove forever the taint of cold-iron . . ."

I sensed someone behind me, probably Doolin. This time, I wasn't going to fall prey to one of Oberon's tricks.

Spinning, I struck out with stiffened fingers for where I knew Doolin's throat had to be. The hit wouldn't kill him, but it'd leave him choking and no more use for Oberon.

"Master—"

It *wasn't* Doolin, though. Instead it was *Fetch.* I managed to steer my attack to the side at the last moment, but it was still enough to bowl the lycanthrope over.

He lay sprawled on the ground, eyes wide with fear at what I'd nearly done. More than ever, he looked like some monstrous matching of man, wolf, and greyhound.

"Get back to Claryce!" I ordered him, as I turned back to Oberon. "I'll take care of—"

With a mournful growl, he bit my forearm.

I pulled away in shock. Fetch could've taken the entire lower half of the limb at that point, but instead he immediately released his hold. He stared at me with a combination of anxiety and shame. I noticed then that his back was straighter, as if whatever great stiffness had affected it had finally gone away.

"I am so sorry, Master Nicholas . . . I . . . wish I could make you understand . . ."

"Under—" I didn't get any farther. A coldness that burned at the same time coursed through my veins. I knew its origins too well. Somehow, Fetch's bite had been tinged with black silver just like a cobra's was with venom.

His shortened ears completely flattened. He dropped down on all fours and slunk back as Doolin stepped up from behind him. The gigantic thug grinned, no doubt at what he intended to do to me now that I was no danger.

"I did give you every chance . . ." I heard Oberon shout over the storm. "If not for you and the female, then for you and the salamander, at least! You forced this on yourself . . ."

I keeled over. The beach rose up and slapped me hard in the face.

Through the rumble of the unnatural storm, I heard only two other things now. Doolin's nearing laugh . . . and a sudden cry I knew could only be from *Claryce*.

CHAPTER 27

My body shivered. My condition wasn't helped by a sudden kick in my ribs, courtesy of Doolin.

Deep, deep within, I could sense the dragon trying to make himself small, unnoticeable. He was suffering the effects of the black silver, too, but that wasn't why he was doing what he did. He was still trying to somehow keep himself separate from me, as if my death wouldn't mean his own as well. Sixteen hundred years together and we were still two creatures in utter opposition, even now.

I felt hands tugging at my coat. Doolin's curse filled my ears. He was looking for something. I tried to think what it was, then remembered the teardrop. Oberon still needed it. It wouldn't be enough for him to bring Feirie and Chicago together if he couldn't maintain mastery over it. The teardrop was also the deadliest weapon against him.

Despite the poison simultaneously burning and freezing my soul, I did my best to keep Doolin from his goal. When he pulled at the coat again, I let the momentum turn me over and sent my fist at him.

"Still kickin'?" he growled. "Good! Lets me have a little more fun with you!"

I tried to grab at Doolin, but the effort was too much. My failure was made worse by the fact that he only wore one gauntlet at the moment, the other off so that he could better check my coat for the gem.

Somewhere in the distance, I heard Fetch's mournful howl again. I must've reacted more than I knew because my expression made Doolin laugh harder. "Your mongrel's taking care of the tomato, dope . . . pity . . . boss wouldn't let me have her. He's too much of a gent there, I guess, though I seen him do things . . ."

He grabbed my throat with the gauntleted hand, apparently a preferred target for him. What little air I'd been able to draw in was cut off.

Get your damned self here! I silently shouted at the dragon.

But he still wouldn't listen. So caught up in his failed dream of being free from me, the dragon was more frozen than me. He was going to die and couldn't seem to understand that—

Doolin screamed.

I didn't understand why until a warm fluid spilled over my face, and most of Doolin's forearm, including the covered hand, tumbled next to me.

A spate of harsh, Celtic curses escaped him as he stumbled away from me. I lost sight of him as another shape hovered over me.

"Nick! Can you hear me?"

Claryce leaned close. I was grateful for her presence this near to death. I only wished that somehow I could keep her from following me.

"Nick . . . listen . . . the other bird . . . he said to take hold of the blade!"

Barely conscious, I wasn't sure what she was talking about, especially when what she held over me wasn't Her Lady's gift but rather the blessed dagger.

"You've got to touch the tip to the bite yourself! It has to be you who—"

Claryce dropped the blade atop me and pulled out of sight. A moment later, I heard Doolin's rumbling voice. I couldn't understand what he was saying, but he was certainly furious.

Afraid for Claryce, I fumbled for the dagger. My first thought was to try to throw it at wherever he stood, but then recalled what she'd said. The black bird wanted me to touch the poisoned bite with the point. I knew Her Lady must've had a good reason for that, though what it was evaded me.

Managing to grip the short blade, I slid it over to the bite. A shiver almost made me lose my hold, but I gritted my teeth and planted the tip of the dagger where it was supposed to go. At the same time, I suddenly wondered why Claryce had referred to the black bird as a *he*—

I shoved aside that question and others as an intense heat swept over me. It was quickly replaced by a soothing warmth that then rapidly ate away at the numbing cold. I gasped with relief as my strength returned in a burst.

My recovery was so swift that I was already able to push myself up to my elbows. That, though, gave me a view I didn't like. A few yards away, Claryce stood with her back to me, Her Lady's gift held ready with both hands. Doolin faced her, his one arm missing halfway down, but not bleeding at all. The sleeve was bound tight, but I could only imagine it was Oberon's magic that kept him from bleeding to death.

His remaining hand was once more clad in the other gauntlet. I knew that even the one glove gave Doolin the strength to rip the sword from Claryce. The murderous glare in the man-mountain's eyes made me fight to my feet even as Claryce tried a lunge that was more designed to keep Doolin back than kill him.

I shifted my grip on the dagger, then shouted, "Doolin!"

He looked my way.

I threw the dagger.

Doolin gasped as the blade sank halfway into his chest. He staggered, started to slump . . . and then, his breathing ragged, started tugging at the dagger. Once more, even the lone gauntlet gave him the strength to survive a mortal blow.

But what he couldn't survive was Her Lady's gift through his stomach. Blood spilled from the belly wound and then from Doolin's mouth. Claryce pulled the sword free, the edge utterly clean of the hood's life fluids.

Doolin made a fist. The gauntlet flared. Blood staining his mouth and chin, he took a step toward Claryce just as I lunged for him.

Doolin collapsed into the sand. Unlike me, he wouldn't be

getting back up. Her Lady's gift'd proven more powerful than Oberon's gauntlet.

Claryce exhaled. I wished I could've done the same, but we were
hardly safe. The raging storm had Oberon's thugs momentarily pinned
down by their autos, and the amplifying magic drawn together by the
card evidently had most of his Wyld equally at bay.

But in the end, all that mattered was that Oberon was in command
of the situation.

I looked around for Fetch, but he was nowhere to be seen. If he
knew what was good for him, he'd taken it on the lam to somewhere
far, far from me. Feirie would be safer for him, assuming I survived.

"Nick! Here!" Claryce tried to give me Her Lady's gift.

"No! You hold onto it!" It was her best bet for survival, especially
against a certain traitorous shapeshifter, if nothing else.

Before she could argue, a tornadic wind tossed us both into the air.
As we both struggled in the unnaturally violent surge, I saw Doolin's
body and one of the autos fly past.

I desperately grabbed for Claryce as she flew past me. She tumbled
to the ground a short distance from the surf, Her Lady's gift fortunately only slipping a few inches away. I, meanwhile, fell hard too near
Oberon for my location to be chance.

"Can you feel the change in the air, Gatekeeper?" Oberon roared
with pleasure. "Can you feel the melding of the worlds?"

I managed to get to my feet, but that was about it. The card had
already put everything around the Gate in flux.

"Give me the teardrop, Gatekeeper," he said in a quieter voice
that, thanks to the magic he controlled, easily carried through the
storm. "I have, through fortunate circumstance and the naive expec-
tations of your scaled companion, obtained the card. I'd expected
to retrieve it after dealing with you, but, as the human saying goes,
apparently good things do come to those who wait!"

He wanted the teardrop. I was perfectly willing to give it to him, but not the way he thought. I reached into my pocket . . . and found *nothing*.

Oberon laughed. "So, in the end, you do not even have that! What a champion my dear Titania chose! Better she would have kept that fool Kravayik at her side . . ."

I lunged—and the wind threw me back. I tried again, with the same result.

Oberon grew serious. "You would one day see the necessity of what I do, Gatekeeper . . . A pity I cannot permit you to live to see that day . . . but at least this time you will not die alone . . ."

He turned the card toward me. The water churned, then reached for Claryce.

This is for both of us, damn you! I berated the dragon. *Both of us!*

He finally stirred, if only hesitantly. It was not enough, but it had to be.

I let out a roar that in no manner sounded human. I drew from the dragon as much as I could and felt my body alter, even as I again threw myself at Oberon.

If I thought he'd be shocked by the change, I was sorely mistaken. He smiled and suddenly the gale threw my still-transforming body toward Claryce.

"As I said, I can at least grant you the chance to die together for once . . ."

But I caught the wind with wings that spread wider by the moment, long, arched, and webbed wings, with which I was already very comfortable. I soared up into the storm as my arms and legs turned and bent at angles they shouldn't have. Long, curved claws stretched from my changing fingers. My chest swelled to mammoth proportions as my lungs corrected to take in the air I needed for flight in this chaos.

And slowly, very slowly, I felt the dragon begin to join with me, to become a part of me.

Shaking our crested head, we roared again—this time through a long sharp muzzle filled with teeth nearly a yard in length—and even the thunder of Oberon's storm couldn't completely drown out our cry. Our long, long tail whipped back and forth. The Frost Moon added a sheen to our glittering, golden-scaled body, now easily several times the length and girth of one of the elephants in Lincoln Park Zoo. For the first time since Chicago burned, we flew in our full glory over the city.

We didn't fly high for long. We dropped down and seized Claryce and Her Lady's gift, taking both inland to a place far enough from the confused gangsters to keep her safe. We then dove low over the beach, intently seeking the teardrop, even as thugs foolishly wasted their bullets on our thick, scaled hide.

But even with the acute eyes of the dragon turning the darkness into a brighter emerald, there wasn't a sign of the gem. Either it was buried somewhere in the sand or Oberon already had it. I had to hope the former, even if it meant that I only had the dragon's power against that of the card.

Ignoring the damage to his fine suit, Oberon continued to step back deeper and deeper into the lake. The rough tide ripped fragments of the suit from his body . . . and then ripped what I realized was *not* fabric but part of William Delke. The skin sloughed away, revealing underneath it a longer, thinner form that immediately clad itself in a forest green and onyx black suit of armor more flexible than cloth.

And as the water reached his chest, Oberon's human mask split in the middle and folded away, revealing the much longer, thinner, pale face of Feirie's former lord.

Oberon resembled Kravayik, just as all of the Court's high caste resembled one another. Yet Oberon was an even more handsome version, although there was a bitter cast to his features I didn't remember from fifty years earlier.

If he'd thought to hide beneath the waves—which he could do—he'd forgotten that the dragon's gaze could see him under the churning surface. I suspected he really hoped to delay us so that the card could complete its monstrous work, but in that case he'd finally made a fatal error.

Keeping Oberon in focus, we dove.

It nearly proved to be *our* fatal error instead.

The water rose to meet us. It didn't do so because Oberon's magic made it do it, it did so because it *wanted* to.

The almost equine face opened its watery maw wide and exhaled. A column of water struck us dead center. We might as well have been a novice flyweight going ten rounds with heavyweight champ Jack Dempsey. The wind knocked out of us, we crashed into the beach.

Lake Michigan continued to roil, but now the water gathered together and grew into a shape larger and wider than the dragon. I'd never seen a kelpie before, but I knew what it was. Of course, the kelpies I'd been told about by Kravayik and a few others had only been as big as elephants, not so gargantuan that they could dwarf the dragon.

Even as the lake continued to seethe, the water that made up the kelpie's body also churned within. The creature shook its long, weedlike mane and let out a roar that sounded more like that of a dragon than the stallion its top half resembled. The kelpie lowered its head to eye us, its natural adversary, and in doing so revealed that it had a rider.

Oberon's smile was a grim yet satisfied one. He wore a helmet with a crest akin to the kelpie's wild mane and a nose guard that ended in a sharp point. Oberon's left arm guided a weapon I knew very well, since I'd wielded it myself.

Staring at the spear, I suddenly understood that, once more, not only had I been played all along, but so had the dragon. I only had to gaze at what was taking shape behind Oberon and the kelpie to know just what the former lord of Feirie's intent had been for us all along.

Whether by accident or—more likely with Oberon—design, the Gate now framed him and his savage mount. Moreover, it was no longer the fainter collection of stars I'd seen just before crossing into Feirie. Now . . . now the Gate was as I'd witnessed its rising the moment I'd discovered I was now and forever its keeper.

The arch rose high above the Tribune Tower and probably anything else men had ever built. I'd never understood its grand nature, only that it was a power unto itself even more than the dragon. I'd never discovered just who or what had created it; Heaven, maybe, or even the Clothos Deck's mad designer. I only knew that sometimes I thought it seemed alive, even a thinking creature.

Before, it'd looked as if a few stars lined its edges. Now, it was as if every celestial body in all the universe had gathered to give it definition. The colors of the finest rainbow paled in comparison. The Gate shimmered with a glory I could only imagine existed nowhere else.

And through its stormy arch, I spotted what at first looked just like Chicago illuminated by a strange emerald glow. Only when I took into account the dragon's gaze did I realize that there was something transposed over the city. A mountainous, forest land.

Feirie.

The kelpie plunged forward, dragging the lake waters with it as it came to shore in pursuit of us. Oberon kept his head low, but I could see his satisfied smile thanks to the dragon's eyes.

You still think he ever planned to separate us other than in death? I demanded.

My constant companion didn't reply, but I finally felt some of his fear lessen. Oh, he wanted nothing of the spear, nothing of the weapon that'd proven just how vulnerable he'd been despite what he was, but he couldn't bring himself to remain as helpless as a hatchling before the kelpie.

Eye will fight beside you, Saint George . . .

He startled me with using that title. In all these centuries, he'd never referred to me so. He also gave *me* free rein over our shared body, even though it was in his form at the moment.

When Eye must, Eye will command . . .

It was a fair enough trade, considering we both still stood a good chance of being slaughtered. Not only did we have Oberon, the spear, and the kelpie to deal with, but the storm itself was growing more and more surreal. Blue flashes of lightning now played everywhere above, too much of it concentrating near us.

No sooner had I thought that than twin bolts fried the beach where we lay . . . or *had* lain a heartbeat before. Whether his instinct, mine, or both, we'd taken to the air just in time to prevent being seared.

Of course, that was exactly the way Oberon'd planned it.

Guided by Oberon, the kelpie veered to meet us. Oberon tightened his grip on the spear. I wasn't surprised by the almost fanatic eagerness I could read in his body as he neared. He'd lied again, this time about trying to give me a chance to run away with Claryce. I wondered if Oberon even knew what truth was, anymore. Lying was a far more natural trait in Feirie.

He needed us dead, but not just because of the threat we presented. The card could manipulate Feirie and the mortal realm, but there was one thing I finally understood that neither it nor the entire deck could probably touch. The Gate.

But the dragon and I . . . we were tied to the Gate as nothing else was. Oberon believed, rightly or wrongly, that our deaths would impair the Gate and allow his reshaping of the realms with the permanency he desired. So long as the Gate remained, there would *always* be a chance, however remote, that Feirie and the mortal world would separate again.

We dropped in an effort to avoid the spear.

Lightning struck us once, twice, three times.

We spun about, barely able to keep conscious. Neither the dragon nor I could regain enough control to take our mutual body from the midst of battle.

An agonizing pain tore through our left wing. Somehow, we succeeded in pulling away, though merely flying now demanded more effort than we really could offer. A savage tear now crossed a good portion of the wing's membrane where the spear had not only pierced the skin but had created a long rip when we'd been forced to retreat.

The kelpie's long head darted in. I managed to maneuver the dragon's claw forward in time to catch the kelpie at the snout. The powerful claws ripped through the equine muzzle.

But the damage vanished instantly, the kelpie as much water as the lake itself. The gouges filled in even before the claws finished passing.

The kelpie exhaled. Another barrage of water assailed us.

We had no choice but to retreat, flying low over the beach and momentarily away from the lake's edge. The dragon wanted us to head into the city, but I was more interested in what I saw below.

Fetch squatted on all fours, his nose close to the sand. He sniffed twice, then thrust his muzzle into the loose ground.

Even before we passed him, I saw him pull the teardrop out with his teeth. Worse, I saw Claryce, Her Lady's gift still clutched in her hands, moving to confront the lycanthrope.

A dragon's hearing is very acute and can focus on particular sounds. I heard Claryce shout Fetch's name and I heard him snarl back in warning. I didn't have to hear the words that followed to guess what was going on. Fetch had once been a highly favored servant of Her Lady, sent to track down those who'd disobeyed her. He could bring them back alive or in pieces. When Her Lady'd believed it better for me to die than live, she'd sent her unfailing hunter after me. I'd not only stopped him, but saved his life and earned his debt of gratitude.

But what he'd earned in turn from Her Lady had been a life scrounging on the streets. I knew that part of the reason Fetch'd refused my aid had been because it only reminded him what he'd lost.

Now . . . now, with the teardrop his, he had the chance to win all of that back.

The kelpie flowed deeper onto the beach, its huge forelegs kicking at the sky in challenge to us. I could feel the dragon falling more and more prey to his base desire to meet his enemy head on. His fear had faded away as primal instincts had taken over. I had to make sure I kept him in check until the most critical moment.

If we lived that long.

I caught one more desperate glimpse of Claryce and Fetch. I saw a Fetch I hadn't seen since that fateful night we'd fought, a savage two-legged beast half again as tall as me. He clutched the teardrop in one hand and glared at Claryce . . . Claryce, who bravely held the point of Her Lady's gift underneath Fetch's chin in a manner that showed she had no qualms about thrusting it the last inch.

Then, all I could see or hear was the kelpie.

I knew that Oberon had to be using his magic to enhance it. He couldn't continuously use the single card to both change worlds and feed power into his mount. He needed us dead and soon, for many reasons.

Instead of giving him his wish, we gave him a bathing in flames. For this, I let the dragon have full mastery. He breathed as he hadn't since that last battle more than fifty years ago.

But the fire never touched Oberon. It surrounded him, but probably did nothing more than warm him slightly. The kelpie's watery nature enabled it to douse the flames without even slowing its pursuit of us.

Something dove down in front of Oberon and began clawing at his face. He slapped at the feathered form, but missed. Her Lady's changeling flew in again and again to harass the former lord of Feirie, managing just to evade his grasp each time.

This was our chance and we both knew it. Together, the dragon and I surged forward.

The kelpie kicked at us with huge translucent hooves. We maneuvered around the attack, then exhaled.

This time, the flames struck Oberon . . . with just as much a lack of results. He'd known better than to rely just on the kelpie's power.

But even Oberon had to have his limits. I knew him almost as well as Her Lady did. I knew what he could do. I knew what the card could do . . .

And I realized at that moment that our only hope lay in not facing Oberon after all. At least, not yet.

Veering away, we darted toward where last we'd seen Claryce and Fetch, only to find no sign of them. We rushed over the area, scattering hoods and even sending a spiderlike shape hurriedly burrowing into the sand. We scorched the ground where it went under, just in case, and ignored the pathetic hail of bullets one foolhardy thug fired at us with his tommy.

We listened. We smelled. There were traces of both Claryce and the lycanthrope, but not strong enough for us to locate . . . which meant that we also couldn't locate the teardrop.

The kelpie let out a roar that hardly fit its equine semblance. Despite misgivings, we arced around to face Oberon and his steed again.

Only . . . we weren't alone. There was a huge, winged shape confronting the kelpie, a shape it took us a moment to recognize despite the obviousness of it.

The changeling, still in the form of a black bird, had swollen to proportions nearly matching the dragon. It took me a moment to understand how Her Lady could've unleashed such power in the mortal realm. It was because this *wasn't* exactly the mortal realm any longer. I'd underestimated the swiftness of the card's influence. In fact, I only had to glance at the city to see just how little time there actually was remaining.

The Gate still stood, but the boundaries had blurred almost completely . . . and what lay beyond the Gate now was neither Feirie *nor* Chicago . . .

CHAPTER 28

The nightmarish gallimaufry created by the two stunned me so much that I failed to notice the dragon seize control of our body. My gaze was torn from the melding realms back to the battle between the black bird and the kelpie, a battle the dragon sought to join.

He refused my warnings, refused to even acknowledge me. On the one hand, my guidance thus far hadn't been all that successful, but on the other, I knew him to have only two basic parts to his nature. Either he crushed what he could crush or, since "dying" at my hand, flew from that which he knew might send him to oblivion again. He still feared the spear and the fact that Oberon wielded it, but Her Lady's interference meant to him that the edge in this battle was now against the former lord of Feirie.

I wasn't so certain of that . . . but the choice was no longer mine.

The giant avian and the kelpie fought with more than beak and teeth, claws and hooves. A torrent of water continued to assail Her Lady's changeling, while a fearsome wind sought to tear the watery beast into countless useless drops. Neither seemed to be gaining ground but the fact that Oberon looked not at all concerned in itself concerned me.

But still my warnings went unheeded by the dragon. What also went unheeded was a shout that only I might've cared about. It was *Claryce's* voice, either warning us or trying to tell us something of the utmost importance.

What tore at me more was that it was punctuated by another sinister growl that I knew had to come from Fetch.

We stopped in midair. It wasn't the dragon's choice. It was mine, and it surprised us both with its absolute abruptness. He strained

351

to keep going, but I wouldn't let that happen. Instead, I made us turn back and, despite his protests, flew to where I thought I'd heard Claryce. Nothing mattered more than her at the moment, not even the Gate.

Our inner struggle for control was cut short by an ear piercing shriek from above. We paused in our duel in time to see the unthinkable. Her Lady's black bird was caught in the viselike grip of the kelpie's mouth . . . *mouths*. The water spirit sported *two* heads, something I'd never heard the few Feiriefolk who'd spoken of the creatures ever mention. I gathered that Her Lady hadn't known that particular bit of information either, which meant that this was another trick of Oberon's he'd been saving for just such a moment.

The kelpie shook both its heads hard . . . and the black bird ripped into pieces that scattered in the storm. There was no blood, no bones. Just countless bits of what looked like feathers flying everywhere.

I figured out right away that Oberon'd planned to use this trick on us but couldn't pass up his impetuous former mate's attack. I suspected that Her Lady had suffered as well. That meant we couldn't expect any other aid from her, not that she'd done this to help us in the first place. If she had, she'd have let us in on it.

The kelpie turned its twin gaze at us. The dragon started to rise to meet it . . . only to have *me* turn us back to the beach.

He fought me tooth and nail. I kept him at bay, my control fueled by my fear for Claryce, always Claryce. I swept over the beach one more time, noting that it, of all places, hadn't been affected by Feirie's melding. I assumed that had something to do with the Gate and that gave me some hope. It also reminded me that I'd been right; despite his words, Oberon *needed* us dead to weaken the Gate enough to let the single card complete its dire work.

It was Fetch I spotted first, Fetch the lupine monster, the assassin from Feirie, the supposed friend. He bounded across the sand and only paused when he sensed my nearing.

I could sense the dragon ceasing his battle against me for the moment, as he felt my antipathy toward Fetch. Had it been up to the dragon, the shapeshifter would've been left burnt ash that night he'd tried to kill me—us. The thought of finally getting to do that tantalized my ever-present companion.

Yet, before I could see that done, Fetch pointed behind him. I couldn't help looking back . . . and saw Claryce racing in the opposite direction. She gripped Her Lady's gift in one hand, while the other she kept tightly shut.

Something made Claryce look behind her. She stopped dead in her tracks. "Nick!" she shouted at my huge, scaly form above her, somehow finding me in there despite everything. "Nick! I've got it! Fetch showed me how we can use it—"

She got no farther. We all heard the kelpie's double roar. I peered over one wing and saw that Oberon continued to reveal just how long and thoroughly he'd been planning his vengeance, vengeance further amplified by the dragon's foolish belief that he could use the card as a bargaining chip.

The kelpie *split*. The second head tore away from the first, bringing one of the forelegs with it. A third foreleg formed between the pair and then itself tore in two. For a moment, I was reminded of the Hilton sisters, vaudeville's current favorite conjoined twins . . . but Oberon's mount didn't stop there. The two upper halves tugged away from one another and suddenly there were two complete, gargantuan creatures, the second of which bore Oberon and immediately surged toward Claryce.

The dragon wanted no part of an Oberon armed with the spear, the card, and very likely the teardrop, but my will continued to overrule his. I *would not* let Claryce die . . . Claryce, not Cleolinda or any of the previous ones.

But the other kelpie came between us. I forced the dragon's body above the water monster and hoped that without Oberon to add his protections it would be more susceptible to our magic.

And then a small black, avian form, only visible to us thanks to the dragon's eyes, fluttered up behind the riderless kelpie.

I couldn't figure out how Her Lady's changeling had managed to pull off an escape. It shouldn't have been possible. Then, I remembered my glimpse of the avian on the way here and realized I felt the same odd difference. This *wasn't* the changeling . . . but neither was it some simple bird accidentally caught up in the struggle.

That last fact, at least, was verified when it displayed its talons, one set of which gripped none other than Oberon's wedding gift to Her Lady.

The kelpie must've sensed something. It twisted its head around at an unnatural angle and tried to snap up this second black bird. Fortunately for us, the bird was able to fly above its maw, though it was clear by its careful movements that the teardrop was no simple object to carry. The smooth surface of the gem threatened to slip free. If it fell into Lake Michigan, there'd be no finding it in time.

Against the dragon's better judgement—and mine, too—I forced us forward as fast as our wings could beat. We straightened as much as possible, becoming like a torpedo or an arrow.

Still intent on the black bird, the kelpie didn't turn back in time. We barreled through it, sending great globs of water spilling all over the raging lake. The kelpie simply fell apart, its body merging with the churning water below.

I didn't know if we'd managed to destroy this one or if it'd reconstruct itself in a few moments. I only knew that Claryce had sacrificed herself to see to it that the teardrop got to us and, despite my wanting with all my heart to protect her, I had to make certain we controlled the gem.

The black bird dived to meet us. As it neared, I noticed a subtle difference in its shape. Either the changeling had decided to alter this form for some reason, or this wasn't the same avian.

The answer came the moment it—*he*—stared into our eyes. I *knew* his, even if they were shaped to suit the black bird's head. I knew exactly . . . and realized I should've known all along.

I've damned you enough for not helping, I thought to the black bird, not caring whether he actually heard me or not. *I never even knew if you were listening . . . assuming that you even* are *Michael . . .*

The avian cawed and stretched the talon holding the teardrop toward me. We were tantalizingly close.

But so was Oberon.

He'd most likely noticed something was wrong the moment we'd crashed through his kelpie. We should've been chasing after him in the hopes of saving Claryce—or at least the gem, by his Feirie thinking— and when we'd instead focused solely on the other beast, he'd realized his mistake. Unfortunately for us, he'd realized it too quickly.

The spear came as if out of nowhere, its sharp point impaling the black bird from behind as Oberon and his mount rose up. The kelpie was fast. Too fast. His master not only had time to skewer the avian but also to flip the wriggling body up. When the trembling talons released the teardrop, the gem fell straight into Oberon's waiting palm.

And without missing a breath, he then dropped the spear down just in time to drive it into our chest.

But his catching the teardrop, while spelling disaster for everything else, at least for now bought us life. As swift as the kelpie was, we managed to be just a little swifter. Instead of the heart, the point jammed closer to the shoulder. We were in renewed agony, but at least we were still breathing . . . for the moment.

Pain sent us fluttering back. The spear, deeply imbedded, came with us. The kelpie tried to pursue in order to finish us. We exhaled, and while the flames did nothing to actually harm Oberon and the kelpie, they did momentarily blind them. That bought us a few moments more of badly needed respite.

"Birds of a feather flock together, they say," the exiled lord of

Feirie shouted cheerfully, as he held up the teardrop to examine. "A clever trick on both Claryce's part and that of my dear Titania to have this second little puppet aloft! I would not have imagined she'd have the strength left after our first encounter . . . It should be entertaining to revive our passion once I have set these worlds to right!"

It didn't matter that he was wrong about the second black bird being her servant. I knew enough about Her Lady's fear of Oberon to understand that only he would find their reunion "entertaining." If there was anyone Oberon intended to test the full fury of his dark arts upon, it'd be his treacherous spouse.

I'd my own misgivings about Her Lady, especially at this moment. She'd given me the teardrop as if it would be the perfect weapon by which to rid us of Oberon. Yet I'd already witnessed it survive the dragon's breath, which few things could . . . among them now Oberon, apparently. If I couldn't do anything to the gem, how was I supposed to use it to stop Oberon's madness?

"The card, the Gate, you, and now my blood returned to me! Can you not see that the stars have aligned for me? Can you not see that mine is obviously the only true path of survival for my beloved Feirie . . . and your realm as well? I must slay you to finish this, Gatekeeper, but I would have you understand . . ."

I wasn't sure whether it was the dragon, me, or both of us who growled out our response. I only knew for certain that we were in utter agreement. "We understand . . . that you are mad . . ."

Oberon shook his head. He already had the card out—and experience'd already shown we couldn't do any damage to it, either—and now he held the teardrop over it.

We tried desperately to remove the spear, only find out that something else was wrong. The claw that should've easily torn the lance free instead shook so uncontrollably that we couldn't get a grip. Worse, it became a greater strain to try to keep our wings flapping hard enough to prevent us from plummeting into Lake Michigan.

"It will be over for you soon," Oberon called, as he touched the teardrop to the Clothos card, "and over for this realm . . . did you think I'd leave matters just to the simple strength of the spear?"

Whatever poison he laced the tip with worked fast. My thoughts grew sluggish and I could feel the dragon falling prey to the same. I couldn't think of any way out of this situation, but even more important than my life—and even the city's survival—was protecting Claryce. She was going to die again . . .

"Poor dear Titania," Oberon blithely went on, as the teardrop began to take on a strange, softer appearance. "I wonder exactly when she first tried to unseal the blood I'd given her, only to find that she could not break the barrier I'd placed around it! She would have needed more of my blood to open it, not that I ever permitted her the opportunity!" He smiled wider, that too-wide elven smile that generally meant foul things. "Of course, for the moment, the card will work much faster . . ."

Even though our gaze had begun to grow blurry, it was still powerful enough to pierce the night and even see the transformation the Clothos card had wrought on the teardrop. I was surprised to see that the crystalline structure itself was transparent; what was blacker than pitch was Oberon's *blood*. It was so black—all the better to match his thoughts—that it'd made its prison seem the same.

And then, even through the poison and pain, I saw the one chance of stopping him.

It took all the will I had left, plus stirring the dragon up as much as I could, to enable us to summon enough breath to exhale one last time. Matters weren't made any easier by the fact that I needed the blast as focused as possible.

The stream of flame shot out, barely missing the kelpie's wild crest. Oberon noticed what we were doing and began to laugh . . . until he understood what I had in mind.

He'd worked more than five decades to protect himself from the dragon's breath. I had the feeling that we hadn't seen him for fifty years in part because the first few had been spent recuperating from what should've been his death. Oberon'd wanted to make certain that this time nothing could truly harm him.

Of course, he'd never had a chance to do the same for the drop of blood his bride had kept to herself all these centuries. Encased in its prison, it'd been safe enough.

But now . . . nothing protected it.

The flames washed over Oberon and the tiny drop of blood he'd freed. Had this been some human—even one as monstrous as Doolin—it wouldn't have mattered if the drop'd been burned away. Oberon, though, was of Feirie—*was* Feirie—and so the blood he'd given his bride was linked to his own vulnerability.

The drop of blood boiled away, turning to mist in scarcely the blink of an eye.

Oberon took longer to burn. Not much, but longer.

He shrieked as his body erupted in fire. There was as much anger as horror in his cry. Even in the end, he couldn't accept that he wasn't going to have things as he desired. The imperiousness that'd once ruled the Feirie Court meant nothing now, though. Oberon burned as quickly, as completely, as a dry piece of wood might've.

The flames had not only engulfed him, they also meant the end of the protections he'd cast on the kelpie. Oberon's own fading cry was swallowed up by that of the gargantuan beast as it sizzled and turned to vapor. The kelpie writhed and shook itself in what was clearly an effort to throw off the flames, but being of the dragon's magic, the fire just grew stronger, hungrier.

What remained of the kelpie collapsed into Lake Michigan. As it did, I spotted the ash, bone, and twisted armor fragments that were all that remained of Oberon dropping toward the murky waters. With them fell the only thing untouched by the magical fire . . . the Clothos card. The card and Oberon's plummeting remains were outlined not only by the Gate but by the horrific changes already over-taking Chicago. I knew that the Gate would survive, but the card had more effect on the two realms than I'd hoped. Chicago was a mass of forest-enshrouded hills mixed with a multitude of buildings. I didn't know what the inhabitants of both places were suffering, but I knew that they'd only be the first victims if I didn't stop things now.

We were already racing after the card, despite the spear and the poison taking a constantly greater and greater toll on us. Once, our vision grew so unfocused that I feared we'd lost the card. I couldn't trust that the bottom of the lake would be sufficient to keep it from hands willing to use it.

Barely a couple of yards above the surface, we managed to seize hold of it. That didn't stop *us* from hitting the water, which felt like concrete. The collision finally proved enough to dislodge the spear, which dropped into the lake. That didn't lessen the pain, though, and now that the wound was open it bled faster.

Somehow, we managed to keep from sinking under the water, even though death was looking more attractive. Sheer stubbornness enabled us to get our wings to flap twice more . . . at which point we crashed onto the beach.

Despite the dragon's protests, I forced us back up into the air. The poison was well into its work, but I didn't care.

The Gate's illumination vied with that of the Frost Moon's. In their combined light, we saw Chicago and Feirie melded together as I suspected even Oberon hadn't intended. The tall buildings had become twisted in the manner of the dark oaks, while the oaks them-selves were several stories taller than they'd been during my recent sojourn there. Shadowy things flew above the city, things that could never be mistaken for planes, zeppelins, or even one of the new auto-gyros I'd heard about.

Howls arose in parts of the ever-shifting tableau. Other noises I didn't want to guess at. There was gunfire nearby, but I ignored it as

I held up the Clothos card and concentrated as best I could. As I did, I noticed the Gate flare brighter. On a hunch, I stretched the empty claw out to it. Some of the poison's lethargy faded, along with a bit of the pain left over from the wound caused by the spear.

I wasn't thinking well. I'd never wielded one of the cards myself, only sealed this one away as soon as I could. With no idea what to do, I simply focused on the card and demanded that it separate the two realms again. I repeated the command over and over . . .

The Gate burned brighter, but this time I didn't feel any better. In fact, I was near to passing out, the dragon with me. Just before we couldn't keep our wings beating any longer, I thought I saw Chicago and Feirie start to separate . . . and then we were spiraling earthward.

Even through the storm, I heard a female scream and a growl that seemed to take place right in my ear. Just before we struck, I realized that our wings had shrunken to little more than nubs, and we were only a fraction of the size we'd been. Our body was turning human . . . at probably the worst moment.

But what we struck didn't feel like the beach. In fact, it *cradled* us as best it could. I heard something crack and this time the howl *was* in my ear.

After that, both the dragon and I blacked out. I wasn't entirely gone, though whether that meant I was halfway to Heaven or Hell, I couldn't say at the time. Instead of the howl, I heard what sounded like sobbing, then sirens.

Then I felt the cold of the grave wash over our—my—body . . . and knew that Her Lady'd come to claim her victory and *me*.

CHAPTER 29

I continued to hear gunshots, including what sounded like tommies, but the noises seemed to come from far away. What *did* come from nearby were two female voices, the first that of Her Lady, the second . . . Claryce.

Aware of the danger to Claryce, I tried to rise. It was as if I didn't have a body, anymore. Now both the dragon and I floated in some limbo, unable to act.

I couldn't understand what they were saying, only that Claryce kept treading more and more dangerous water with her sharp tone.

Then, just like that, Her Lady's chilling presence vanished. With her departure, I felt some hint of the world around me return, especially in the form of Claryce's fingers touching my cheek.

"Nick . . ." she whispered. "Nick . . . say something . . ."

But as quickly as Her Lady'd vanished, she returned, this time *inside* with me.

Her darling Gatekeeper, a spot of darkness on my soul murmured to me. Without warning, I stood in a mockery of the Court, a tiny circle of oaks barely taller than me.

I forgot about the oaks as Her Lady materialized in front of me. Her gown was only hints of shadow that shifted constantly, ever teasing of the glory that she was and what I could have if I desired.

Her darling Gatekeeper . . . Georgius . . .

It was the first time she'd ever called me by my ancient name. It was also the most gently she'd ever spoken. What made it more shocking was that I knew none of it was part of her usual masquerade.

I sense him nowhere.

Her use of "I" intrigued me almost as much as her information did. Her Lady couldn't sense any hint of Oberon. That meant that this time I'd finally gotten that part of the job done right . . . I hoped.

They sing of you in all Feirie . . .

"Because you order them to?" I was startled to find I had a voice in this . . . whatever it was.

They sing because you are the one to vanquish . . . Oberon . . .

I could see where that might actually have earned me praises in Feirie, at least outwardly. Despite Her Lady's word, I doubted that so many of her subjects were that happy their former lord was dead . . .

Speaking of dead . . . "And have you come to take my soul?"

I expected her to laugh, but instead, she answered in a surprisingly reflective tone, *Only if you gave it freely . . .*

Her Lady leaned close—very close—and the scent of lilacs bathed my nostrils. I knew what she wanted me to do, but I held back.

Showing no disappointment, she pulled back. *The Court is always open to you, Gatekeeper . . . and a seat beside me as well . . .*

Her Lady started to fade.

"Wait!"

She solidified again, her smile more enticing.

I doused her spirits immediately. "Oberon . . . he *is* dead, right? He's nothing but ash, isn't he?"

Let us assume that he is more dead than he was last time, Her Lady replied cryptically. A slight smile returning to her perfect features, she added, *Until then, I shall keep a special eye on my champion . . . for his own safety . . .*

With that, she was gone.

"Nick!"

The false Court vanished. I felt a sense of displacement, then figured out that I now lay on my back in the sand. I also managed to figure out that something had happened to heal me of not only the fall but the poisoned spear, too.

"You said she'd cured him!" Claryce shouted. "You promised!"

"You had the sword pointed at her, Mistress Claryce! She swore by it and swore that she'd drawn the poison out! She wouldn't pull a double-cross then! It was the least she could do, she said . . ."

I was surprised to hear Fetch. Surprised and still bitter. I knew that he'd betrayed me. That, more than even Claryce, forced me completely conscious. I snatched at where I heard Fetch's voice and was rewarded by his startled yelp as he managed to pull his leg free of my still-weak grip.

"You can—can run," I rasped, "but I'll find you . . ."

Claryce seized me by the arms, in the process blocking my view of the lycanthrope. The sword lay nearby, and she had the dagger thrust in her belt. I didn't want to think what she'd had to do to retrieve the latter. "Nick! Listen! He helped save you! I know—I know what he did before, but he came back to his senses in the end!"

There was shouting going on somewhere in the dark, but I didn't care about it for the moment. Fetch's half-seen lupine form shifted behind Claryce. I forced her aside enough to get a better look—

If I'd not known better, I'd have sworn that he'd died after those gunshots Cortez'd pumped into him. Fetch was back to his mongrel self, but a soaking wet, emaciated, ragged, and even *burnt* variation. "What happened to you?"

"Everything," he muttered. "Master Nicholas . . . ye knew Oberon . . . but ye didn't know Oberon . . . ye never knew the full seductive powers at his command, the way he can twist one's desires and make one agree to what they regret . . . only too late."

He turned to the side. I saw that his entire spine was scorched black. "What's that from?"

"The thing he set in me to poison ye. I'd no sooner agreed to doing his bidding to bring Feirie to safety and be returned to my station than he used my bound word to seal that beast within!" His ears flattened. "I could feel it squirming in there! Like a flapper gone giddy! It drove me mad!"

"So what happened to it?"

He grinned in a manner not possible for normal animals. "Mistress Claryce did some carving with that big shiv! Sliced it right outta me . . ."

"It was disgusting," she interjected. "Like some kind of giant slug . . . I ran it through for good measure and the sword just *absorbed* it!"

"'Twas a *myurka*," the shapeshifter added. "The Court often used their poison . . ."

That made me wince for him. "Couldn't have been pleasant."

The grin vanished. "Better'n I deserve . . . and not near as painful as when ye landed atop me—"

"I did what?"

"He helped save you," Claryce explained, assisting me to a sitting position. Whatever Her Lady'd done had healed me pretty good. I wasn't about to feel beholden to her, though, not after all her subterfuge.

"He *caught* you," Claryce continued, pleading Fetch's case. "Nick, he *broke* his back catching you! He was still—still—"

"I was still my original self . . . the one ye remember, Master Nicholas. I was already changing again, but I thought I had time . . ."

Even if I didn't trust Fetch, I did trust Claryce. "He did that."

"Yes . . . if it wasn't for . . . for *her* . . . he'd probably be dead from the injuries."

I believed her. I was grateful to Fetch, but looking at him, I knew there was something I still wasn't being told. I had a suspicion I knew what it was. "What did she offer *you*?"

He had the decency to look guiltier. "A place at her feet. Her loyal servant once more . . ."

"A high honor . . . and you said . . ."

Fetch nervously cleared his throat. "Said I'd have to stay here and keep watch on a so-called saint who'd be dead a dozen times over without my guidance . . ."

I rewarded him with a grunt. He took that as a sign I wasn't going to use Her Lady's gift to slice him in two and wagged his tail. Matters weren't right between us, but I couldn't deny I'd needed Fetch in the past and probably would need him in the future.

Fetch shifted and I saw behind him the *spear*. I understood now why he was also soaking wet. He'd gone and retrieved the spear, though how he'd survived underwater long enough with all his other injuries I couldn't say.

"Thanks for that, too," I finally muttered.

He wagged his tail.

The distant shouts rose to the point where I couldn't ignore them anymore. I tried to see what was going on, but without the dragon's eyes only caught glimpses of light. "What's that? Oberon's goons still after us?" I forced myself up. "You should've warned—"

"No, Nick!" Claryce kept me from taking a step toward Her Lady's gift. "Listen first! It's the police! Detective Cortez has them rounding up what's left of Oberon's gangsters!"

"Cortez?" My thoughts tried to gather. Cortez should've been dead or at least injured, a victim of the attack on the station. "He's all right?"

Before either of them could answer, the shouting died down. I tried to see what was happening.

Let Eye help . . .

I got over my surprise at the dragon's sudden emergence as his emerald world ate away the darkness. I saw several squad cars and a paddy wagon surrounding the crooks' autos. There were at least two bodies that I could see, both of them obviously from Oberon's gang. I didn't see or sense any of the Wyld and assumed that they'd either fled or been taken by Her Lady.

Thinking of Her Lady again, I quickly retrieved the sword . . . and the card. I was surprised that Her Lady'd left the card. There was no mistaking that it was the real thing. I could feel its odd power even now. I stuffed the card into my pocket and put the blade back in its special hiding place.

I also glanced toward the Gate. It was barely visible even to the dragon and growing more faded yet. Her Lady'd been able to reach more strongly into the mortal realm while Oberon'd had everything in flux, but now the Gate was all but sealed again . . . thankfully.

The right thing should've been to wait and speak with Cortez. Instead, I took Claryce by the arm and started leading her away. "The Packard near?"

She pointed ahead of us. "It's up this way."

"Good." I eyed Fetch and pointed at the spear. He was clever enough to immediately snap it up in his jaws like any dog would a stick and trot ahead of us.

"Nick, shouldn't we—"

"No." There were too many questions. I needed time to think. I also needed time to deal with the Clothos card . . . and while I was at it, Claryce.

Claryce sat in the back row of the cathedral while I saw to the card. I was pleased to see that Kravayik was all right, if a bit bruised.

"I have not had the occasion to fight since I left the Court," he muttered, as we finished sealing the card inside again. The exile winced as he tried to bend his wrist. "I suppose I should attend to the body as well as the soul from here on . . . just in case. I was not much help, I am sorry to say."

"You're fine. You didn't want to hurt me."

"There is that, I suppose." The exile peered at the card's hiding place. "Will this be enough?"

"It has to be. At the very least, *he* won't be able to pretend he's me

to gain access again. It'll recognize who exactly is wearing this flesh."
I stepped back. "As always, thank you, Kravayik."

He shook his head. "No, Master Nicholas. Thank *you*." Kravayik
bowed slightly. "I will lock up after you and the lady are gone. . . ."

"Try to get some rest."

"You need it more than I, Saint George." He turned and melted
back into the shadows before I could reprimand him for using that
name and title.

Shrugging, I headed toward Claryce, only to have Diocles materi-
alize next to me. "Is it true? Did you see him?"

I kept walking in the hopes he'd get the hint. "St. Michael? I
don't know. I've seen and heard about a lot of Michaels. Don't know if
any of them were him or simply someone he used . . . if he even used
them at all."

"It was no coincidence, Georgius. You and I are proof that such
things can be."

"Maybe." I couldn't shake the feeling that if St. Michael did exist
and was finding excuses to lend me a hand even when he wasn't supposed to be, it was because something very, very bad was happening
that went beyond Oberon.

I would've liked to have questioned my fellow "saint"—questioned him about a lot of things, actually—but thus far I hadn't seen
any hint of any version of him. I still remembered the second black
bird and how painful it'd looked when it'd been skewered. If that'd
been St. Michael, he'd felt far more pain than Her Lady had. Maybe
that'd been the price he'd had to pay for doing what he did for me.
Maybe.

I suspected that this wasn't the end of this situation.

"I've given some thought to the spear," the late emperor commented, turning to what he likely thought a safer subject. "There is a
place. You know it. The perfect place to bury it in hallowed ground,
where it belongs . . ."

He didn't have to go farther. I knew where he meant. It was actually a good idea, but I kept quiet.

Diocles sighed. "Just be careful, Georgius."

He faded away. I suppose I should've replied before he vanished completely, should've thanked him for his part in trying to stop the dragon . . . but I didn't. The only thing I did was nod. He deserved better . . . but he didn't get it.

Claryce rose as I neared. As we headed out the door, she asked, "Now what?"

I didn't get a chance to answer, because a much-too-familiar auto chose that moment to pull up. An overly cheerful Cortez stepped out.

"Nick Medea!" he greeted. "And Miss Claryce!"

I glanced over at the Packard, where I caught a glimpse of Fetch crouching out of sight. Now that the Gate was sealed again and the moon was normal, he looked exactly like the mongrel hound Cortez'd seen before, but I was still happy that Fetch had chosen to hide himself. The less questions the detective had, the better.

"Hello, Detective Cortez," Claryce interjected when I said nothing. "How are you?"

He offered both of us a Lucky. We declined. Shrugging, Cortez stuck one in the corner of his mouth, but didn't light it. "Quite a night! I tell you, it didn't start out too well, what with some goon we brought in turning arsonist on us! We'd have been in worse shape if some old shoe-shine guy hadn't spotted it right after it started. Made a lot of smoke—a *lot* of smoke—for some reason, but that was it."

"What about the armor and the spear?" I asked, curious how that loss had played out with his superiors.

Cortez frowned. "Don't understand, Bo . . . you mean the Art Institute robbery? We're still trying to find that loot, though I think it's sitting pretty in some swell's swanky estate, you know?"

I could imagine Claryce's surprise on hearing this, but to her credit, she kept quiet. Cortez's mention of an "old shoe-shine guy" left me with no doubt as to who'd manipulated events—and memories—as best as he was permitted after Oberon's men had circumvented Her Lady's protections. My fellow saint'd been busy.

As for Cortez, I just nodded, then replied, "You're probably right. Lost forever, then. Sorry for you."

"Ah, that's okay! Night got a lot better after the smoke! You should know something about that, Nick! Had a big haul tonight! Buncha Micks that appear to be working for a so-called honest bigwig you and me talked about." He rubbed his chin. "Say, didn't know you knew the captain I mentioned at the station, but it figures you did. Michael said you and he go way back."

"Michael . . ." I muttered. "Yeah, way back. Farther than I thought."

"Yeah, well, Michael—don't remember his last name, but you know it already—he said he got this tip from you about these hoods meeting down here and that there'd be fireworks. Said I should get down here fast. He wanted to join us but said his chief was already on his case for crossing the line too often. Said you'd understand, you know?"

I did. And didn't. I'd been going to St. Michael's Church for years, both to pray for and curse my existence. Apparently, I'd been heard. Also apparently, he who'd heard me wasn't supposed to help me in any way, but'd done what he could. I appreciated that, even if I could've used a lot more help against Oberon.

I made a note to make a special prayer at St. Michael's the next time I was there . . . assuming he was still able to hear it.

"So all went well, then," I finally replied. Then, "And how'd you know to find me here?"

"That? Just happy coincidence, you know? I saw you come out of the cathedral and decided to stop." He pulled out the unlit cigarette. "As to why I'm here, we're just givin' Bugs and Hymie a little drive-by, just to keep them on their toes! Pretty sure they had some tie to this, even if we probably won't be able to prove it." Cortez tipped his hat at Claryce. "Speaking of which, you understand we're speaking of Mr. William Delke, don't you, Miss Claryce?"

"Yes . . ."

"Now, Nick and I, we know you've nothing to do with him, but if I could ask you to come to the station and make a statement, that'd be helpful."

Claryce nodded. "Of course. First thing in the morning all right?"

"That'd be nifty."

"Maybe you'd better take her with you now, Cortez," I suddenly interjected. "I wouldn't wait too long to get all the info you can about Delke Industries. Someone's bound to be trying to burn papers soon."

"There is that," Cortez agreed, though he didn't look happy. He no doubt wanted to get back to his Maria and the kids, but I'd brought up a point he couldn't ignore. "Miss? Can you come now?"

Claryce wasn't any happier than the detective. "Nick, couldn't I—"

I stared deep into her eyes. "It'd be best if you went now."

She frowned. Without looking at Cortez, she asked, "Can I have a moment, detective?"

"Sure thing." He nodded at both of us, then trotted back down to his auto, where he toyed with his cigarette.

"What's this about, Nick?" Claryce whispered. "Why do I need to go with him right now?"

I decided to be blunt. "It's time to end this. I gave it plenty of thought, Claryce. I don't want to do this, but I need to do it. You're safest far away from me. You need to finish up with the police about Delke Industries and then leave Chicago. Go somewhere on one of the coasts. It's your best hope—"

Her gaze burned with a fury worthy of the dragon. She fought to keep her voice down. "You can't be serious about this! After what we've been through! I can't leave you—"

"You have to! I don't want you to die . . ."

"Remember that William—Oberon—found me first. I didn't even know who you were. To me, that says I'm safer *with* you than away from you."

I'd been afraid she wouldn't agree. I turned to the one other I thought might give me support. *You know what I need. Help me . . .*

Eye will not. It is her choice whether she lives or dies, you know that. Eye will miss her strong will, either way . . .

He ended with a low, mocking chuckle, but I had no time to argue with him. Claryce was already stepping back.

"I'm ready to come with you now, Detective Cortez," she called out. To me, she added, "And I'll see *you* when I'm done . . ."

Cortez held the door open for her. She thanked him, then entered. The good detective grinned at me and went around to the driver's side.

I watched them drive off, considering one chance I hadn't thought of before. Claryce'd been a client; therefore, now that the case was over, she was prey to the shunning spell. Even if I'd wanted her to remember, there was a good chance she'd still forget.

I waited for the dragon to contradict me. I waited for him to tell me that Claryce was immune, that she'd remember everything.

But he said nothing.

I had one final act to take care of that night. I had to wait until later, when no one would possibly be around. There was some risk to what I needed to do because it took me very near Cortez's home. I didn't know how long he'd need to keep Claryce at the station but hopefully long enough for me to finish my task here.

My plan had originally included Fetch, who was expert at digging, of course. Unfortunately, he'd not been in the Packard when I finally returned to it. He'd seen the argument between Claryce and me and no doubt hadn't wanted to risk being on the receiving end of my bitterness. That'd probably been a wise choice.

I could've asked for the dragon's aid, but I didn't. I grabbed a shovel left by a worker and dug deep into the ground where they were just beginning to outline the foundation. When I thought I'd dug deep enough, I grabbed the long, wrapped parcel in the auto and brought it to the hole.

Ten minutes later, I had the spear securely buried.

"It will be a fine church," Diocles declared.

I didn't flinch. "Hasn't even been built yet and you're already haunting it?"

"It has been chosen to be a holy site and has been made more so by what you have placed here."

"Hmmph." I put the shovel back where it belonged.

"You sent her away, did you not?"

I wanted to ignore him, but his bringing Claryce up was too much. "I did the right thing. You know that. You know how all the others died . . . I can't lose Claryce!"

His brow furrowed. "'Claryce'? Not Cleolinda? A bit different this time, I think."

I started back to the auto.

"Georgius! You know what I mean! This is—"

His voice cut off just as I knew it would. The moment I'd left the grounds set aside for the church, his link to it had vanished. He was now back in St. Michael's, which I intended to avoid for at least a day or so until I got my bearings. This was twice in the space of hours I'd rejected Diocles's attempts to build on his efforts to protect me and the card, and while I felt guilty I wasn't yet ready to let our ancient past die.

Climbing into the Packard, I peered at the dark area where soon the new version of Our Lady of Guadalupe Church would soon rise. I said a silent prayer to her and asked that she might find a way to watch over Claryce. Whether or not the shunning erased her memories of me, I swore I'd make sure that I'd never let us meet again . . . even if she hoped otherwise. For me there was only my eternal duty to the Gate. Nothing more.

The dragon *chortled*.

I tried not let his abrupt reaction disturb me as I drove off. I tried very hard.

However, if I'd known that the moment Claryce finished speaking with the police that she'd hailed a taxi and given the cabbie the address to the house recreated by Her Lady, I'd have not bothered trying at all. I'd have just continued to be very worried about her future, especially the likely brevity of it.

And if I'd also known then that Detective Alejandro Cortez *hadn't* gone home to his Maria but instead *followed* Claryce without her being aware of it . . . I'd have been worried about much, much more . . .

But I didn't know any of that just then. The only significant thing I knew that bore watching at this point was whether there'd be any reaction by anyone other than Claryce come morning when daylight shone over Chicago. Before coming here, I'd made a detour to the Delke offices just in case there *was* something that needed to be removed from mortal eyes. I'd found very little to worry about inside, but there'd been one major surprise confronting me even before I'd parked.

The Tribune Tower'd changed. Saarinen's smooth, simple design was gone. What loomed over the skyline was a neo-Gothic giant replete with buttresses, crown, and even gargoyles. It reminded me of what I'd heard about the second-place winner in the contest.

I wondered what else had been altered just by that one card. I suspected I'd find out before too long.

And I suspected that at least *something* caused by that alteration would come back to haunt me and maybe offer the dragon another chance to free himself again . . . even if more than a city burned next time . . .

ACKNOWLEDGMENTS

Thanks to the people at Pyr Books for bringing this novel to publication. I would specifically like to thank my editorial director Rene Sears, Editor-in-Chief Steven Mitchell, cover designer Jacqueline Nasso Cooke, and the publicity team!

I'd like to also thank all those who have had my back for so long. You know who you are!

ABOUT THE AUTHOR

Richard A. Knaak is the *New York Times* and *USA Today* bestselling author of *The Legend of Huma*, *WoW: Dawn of the Aspects*, and nearly fifty other novels and numerous short stories, including works in such series as Warcraft, Diablo, Dragonlance, Age of Conan, and his own long-running Dragonrealm saga. He has scripted a number of Warcraft manga with Tokyopop, such as the top-selling Sunwell trilogy, and has also written background material for games. His works have been published worldwide in many languages.

In addition to *Black City Saint*, his most recent releases include *The Horned Blade*—the final volume in his Turning War Trilogy for the Dragonrealm—and *Wyrmbane*, his first entry into the Iron Kingdoms world from Privateer Press. This year will also see a collection of his earlier works through Permuted Press. He is presently at work on several other projects, among them, *Knights of the Frost* for the Dragonrealm and a new Pathfinder novel. Future plans also include an intended sequel to *Black City Saint*.

Currently splitting his time between Chicago and Arkansas, he can be reached through his website, http://www.richardaknaak.com. While he is unable to respond to every e-mail, he does read them. Join his mailing list for e-announcements of upcoming releases and appearances. Please also join him on Facebook and Twitter.